# The Dreadnought of the Air

*by*
Percy F. Westerman

# The Dreadnought of the Air
## by Percy F. Westerman

Copyright © 2024

All Rights reserved.

No part of this publication may be reproduced, stored in a retrieval system, or transmitted in any form or by any means, electronic, mechanical, photocopying or Otherwise, without the written permission of the publisher.
The author/editor asserts the moral right to be identified as the author/editor of this work.

ISBN: 978-93-68096-75-7

Published by

# DOUBLE 9 BOOKS
2/13-B, Ansari Road
Daryaganj, New Delhi – 110002
info@double9books.com
www.double9books.com
Tel. 011-40042856

This book is under public domain

# ABOUT THE AUTHOR

Percy F. Westerman (1876–1959) was a British author renowned for his adventure novels, many of which focused on themes of heroism, military service, and technological innovation. His books, popular among young readers, often centered around daring heroes navigating thrilling challenges in maritime, military, and aviation contexts. Westerman's works reflected the spirit of early 20th-century British imperialism and the emerging technologies of war. His novels, including The Sea Scouts of the "Petrel", 'Gainst the Might of Spain, and The Dreadnought of the Air, captured both historical events and contemporary military advancements, such as the Spanish Armada and early airship warfare. Westerman also wrote about British colonial ventures in Building the Empire, which focused on the North-West Frontier. His writing was characterized by action-packed plots, technical detail, and a strong sense of duty and bravery. Westerman's legacy endures in his contributions to boys' adventure fiction and his exploration of military and technological themes.

# CONTENTS

**CHAPTER I**
CONCERNING SUB-LIEUTENANT DACRES ..................................... 9

**CHAPTER II**
THE FRENCH INSTRUCTOR ................................................... 13

**CHAPTER III**
REMOVED FROM THE NAVY LIST ............................................ 18

**CHAPTER IV**
THE MYSTERIOUS AIRSHIP ................................................... 24

**CHAPTER V**
A MOMENTOUS TRAIN JOURNEY ............................................ 29

**CHAPTER VI**
CHALLENGED ..................................................................... 36

**CHAPTER VII**
THE RETURN OF THE AIRSHIP ............................................... 43

**CHAPTER VIII**
WHITTINGHAME'S NARRATIVE .............................................. 51

**CHAPTER IX**
THE FLIGHT TO LONDON ..................................................... 56

**CHAPTER X**
THE STOLEN PLANS ............................................................ 63

**CHAPTER XI**
THE "METEOR" .................................................................. 69

**CHAPTER XII**
THE "METEOR'S" DEBUT ..................................................... 74

**CHAPTER XIII**
AN OFFICIAL AND AN UNOFFICIAL INSPECTION ....................... 80

**CHAPTER XIV**
ACROSS GREENLAND .......................................................... 85

CHAPTER XV
   THE NORTH POLE .................................................................... 91
CHAPTER XVI
   IN THE NICK OF TIME ............................................................ 98
CHAPTER XVII
   ZAYPURU'S BOLD STROKE ................................................. 103
CHAPTER XVIII
   THE DISASTER TO THE "LIBERTAD" ................................. 109
CHAPTER XIX
   INVESTIGATING THE WRECK ............................................ 115
CHAPTER XX
   A HAZARDOUS PROPOSAL ................................................ 121
CHAPTER XXI
   WITHIN THE CAVARALE PRISON ..................................... 130
CHAPTER XXII
   DACRES REMINDS THE ADMIRAL ................................... 138
CHAPTER XXIII
   LOCOMOTIVE VERSUS AEROPLANE ............................... 145
CHAPTER XXIV
   A BRUSH WITH THE INDIANS ........................................... 152
CHAPTER XXV
   THE CAPTURE OF THE CAVARALE ................................... 159
CHAPTER XXVI
   UNABLE TO RISE .................................................................. 169
CHAPTER XXVII
   PREPARING FOR THE PRESIDENT'S VISIT ...................... 173
CHAPTER XXVIII
   A PRISONER OF WAR .......................................................... 179
CHAPTER XXIX
   WORK FOR THE SEAPLANES ............................................. 186
CHAPTER XXX
   THE FALL OF NAOCUANHA .............................................. 191
CHAPTER XXXI
   A SURPRISE FOR DACRES ................................................... 199
CHAPTER XXXII
   A SUBMARINE ENCOUNTER ............................................. 205

**CHAPTER XXXIII**
NEWS OF DURANGO ............................................................................ 211

**CHAPTER XXXIV**
THE CHASE ......................................................................................... 218

**CHAPTER XXXV**
THE THUNDERSTORM ........................................................................ 225

**CHAPTER XXXVI**
THE ABANDONED FLYING-BOAT ....................................................... 233

**CHAPTER XXXVII**
THE GALAPAGOS FISHERMEN .......................................................... 240

**CHAPTER XXXVIII**
CORNERED .......................................................................................... 247

**CHAPTER XXXIX**
DACRES' PROMOTION ....................................................................... 253

# CHAPTER I
# CONCERNING SUB-LIEUTENANT DACRES

IT was Thursday afternoon—Make and Mend Clothes Day as it is known in the Royal Navy. H.M.S. "Royal Oak," a Super-Dreadnought now relegated to the second class, lay at moorings off Singapore. Two cables' length ahead of her swung her sister ship the "Repulse," flying the flag of Admiral Maynebrace commanding the Special Squadron, now on a cruise round the world in order to display the White Ensign in foreign waters as a gentle reminder to petty potentates that the British Lion's tail could not be twisted with impunity.

The heat was terrific. The sun's scorching rays beat down with relentless violence upon the white awnings that shrouded the warships from bow to stern. The glare, reflected from the oily sea, seemed to penetrate everywhere on board in spite of electric fans and the latest type of ventilators. Officers and men, used though they were to the heat of the Tropics, were reduced to a state of perspiring listlessness. Alacrity seemed for the time being no longer the characteristic of the British seamen. One and all they barely existed in Nature's stew-pan and waited for the sun to set.

To add to the discomfort the crew of the "Royal Oak" were rankling under a grievance. Hitherto first in the list for prize-firing, they had been ousted from their proud position by the flagship: and the flagship didn't forget to crow over her success. Had the contest been carried out under equal conditions and the "Royal Oak" had "gone under" the disappointment would not have been so great; but the "Repulse" had gained the position of "top-dog" more by a fluke than anything else.

"Makes one feel jolly rotten," remarked Eccles, the "Royal Oak's" gunnery jack. "The Service papers at home will publish the results and add a lot about the superb efficiency of the flagship and the lamentable falling-off of the 'Royal Oak's' gun-layers. All that sort of twaddle, you know: penny-a-line stuff from a fellow who does not know a fifteen-inch from a seven-pounder."

"You'll bet your bottom dollar, Eccles, there won't be a word said about the flagship making her record with the Beaufort Scale logged as O (a flat calm), while our packet was shoving her nose into it with the fo'c'sle awash and everything battened down. Ugh! It makes me wild," rejoined Commander Bourne. "Healthy rivalry is all very well, but——"

"I don't know whether you heard the yarn," said Eccles, "but indirectly an outstanding row between the Admiral and the skipper has something to do with it: a little misunderstanding they had when they were at Osborne, I believe. And the fact that Maynebrace is now an admiral and Staggers only a captain doesn't improve matters. The owner forgets sometimes that the Admiral's grandfather was an earl and his only a post-captain."

"I did hear something of the sort," replied Bourne. "It's a pity that personal matters are taken into consideration in the Service. Anyway, Captain Staggers would be glad of a chance to pull the Admiral's leg."

"Hear that?" asked little Dick Alderney, the midshipman of the watch.

"Rather," agreed Sub-lieutenant Basil Dacres emphatically. "It almost gives one a cue."

Basil Dacres was a tall, alert-looking young officer of nineteen. His features were clean cut, his complexion tanned to a deep brown by reason of exposure to the sun and the salt breezes of three of the five oceans. His athletic frame betokened a zest for sport, for in spite of the heat he paced the deck with an elasticity of tread that denoted exceptional physical energy. It did not take long for an observer to come to the right conclusion that Basil Dacres' solemnity of manner when on duty was an acquired one. Those dancing clear blue eyes betrayed the inborn love of a high-spirited nature. Even the rigid rules and regulations of the Service could not break his fondness of practical joking.

Yet, somehow, he contrived to wriggle out of the dire consequences without dishonour, and upon calming down he would enter into the preparatory stages of perpetrating another joke. Upon the eve of his departure from home on the present commission this trait asserted itself. Dacres' little pranks were invariably intended to be of a harmless nature, but sometimes the result surpassed his expectations.

Dacres' father was a retired colonel who, possessed of ample private means, kept a large establishment in the West End. The colonel was absolutely military to the backbone, a martinet even in home life, although "his bark was worse than his bite." One thing is certain, Basil Dacres never inherited the lighter vein from his father, for the latter was never known to have spoken a funny sentence except by a sheer accident; and then, when the rest of the mess laughed, he was completely puzzled to know why.

It happened that the Thursday on which the sub was to leave to join his ship was his mother's at-home day, and Mrs. Dacres' at-homes were always well-attended. On this occasion there were present a colonial bishop and his wife in addition to the usual "smart-set" in which the hostess moved.

Now Mrs. Dacres' Georgian silver tea service was the envy and admiration of her guests, and Mrs. Colonial Bishop had been previously told to pay particular attention to the magnificent teapot. In came the head footman, resplendent in his fine livery and powdered hair, and placed the tray in front of the hostess. The far-famed teapot, enveloped in a huge cosy, was for the time being hidden from admiring and covetous eyes.

"Pouring-out" was one of the great events of Mrs. Dacres' at-homes: it was a sort of sacrifice at the altar of conventionality.

The hostess, after having asked whether the guests took cream and sugar, made a preliminary flourish ere removing the covering that hid the gorgeous silver teapot. The act was a silent appeal for attention, and all eyes were fixed in anticipation upon the piece of plate that held the fragrant beverage.

With the dexterity of a practised conjuror Mrs. Dacres lifted the cosy....

In the place of the teapot was a huge tortoise that blinked solemnly at the sudden transit from darkness into light, and proceeded to slowly waddle across the slippery silver tray.

The next instant, amidst a chorus of shrieks, tortoise and tea-things, including the choicest Crown Derby, clattered on the floor.

The sub's departure took place under a cloud. His mother's farewell was somewhat chilly, while the colonel spoke his mind in a very blunt manner.

"Mark my words, you confounded young fool!" he said, "unless you stop this sort of thing there'll be trouble. It will end with your being court-martialled and kicked out of the Service. And, by Jove! if you are, don't look to me for any sympathy."

But the funny part about the whole business was that Basil knew nothing about the tortoise episode until after the tea cosy was removed. His part of the joke was to take the blame upon his broad shoulders and to chuckle at the idea that he had been accused of what he had not done. He was not asked for an explanation, nor did he give one. He had no wish that punishment should fall upon the real culprit—his ten-year-old brother,

Clarence; for the fond parents never for one moment suspected that guile could be found in their cherub-faced youngest-born child.

"Give you a cue—what about?" asked the midshipman.

The sub brought himself up with a round turn. He realized that perhaps it was not altogether wise to confide in his subordinate over the plan that had readily resolved itself in his brain.

"H'm!" he ejaculated. "Eccles seems rather up the pole about the prize-firing result. I suppose it's natural."

"Well, aren't you, sir?" asked Alderney. "I know I am, and so are the rest of the gun-room. Just fancy! the midshipmen of the flagship, whom we licked hollow at cricket, actually had the cheek to row round the ship with a cock perched on a jack-staff in the bows, and the whole crowd crowing like anything. Beastly bad form, I call it. After all, gunnery isn't everything, as the Admiral ought to know he had with the 'Aphrodite.'"

"The submarine? Yes, I remember. She's 'M. I.' now. That business has given us a good lead in submarines and pretty well knocked the Flying Branch into a cocked hat, worse luck."

And Dacres shook his shoulders deprecatingly. He had volunteered for the Service with the Naval Wing of the Royal Flying Corps, but owing to an unexpected decision on the part of the First Lord to cut down that part of the Service his offer had been declined.

Just then Sinclair, the duty-sub for the First Dog Watch, came on deck, and Dacres, freed from his responsible duty of doing nothing in particular, made his way below to the gun-room.

There the conversation was mainly upon the bumptiousness of the flagship. Dacres said little, but thought the more. After a while he went to the half-deck and knocked at the Gunnery Lieutenant's cabin door. He was there for nearly an hour, at the end of which time he applied for leave till eight bells (noon) on the following day. This he obtained without difficulty, then changing into mufti he went ashore.

# CHAPTER II
# THE FRENCH INSTRUCTOR

SINGAPORE in the year 1919 was a very important naval station. During the last six or seven years it had undergone great changes. The practical abandonment of a powerful war-squadron on the China Station, owing to the understanding with Japan, had led to a decline in the greatness of Hong-Kong as a base. And what Hong-Kong had lost Singapore had gained—with compound interest. Henceforth that little island at the extreme south of the Malay Peninsula was to be the greatest British naval station on the portals of the Pacific.

Additional docks, capable of taking the largest battleships afloat, had been constructed, with smaller basins for submarines, of which twelve of the "C" class and six of the "D" type were stationed there. Bomb-proof sheds for seaplanes had been built, and the whole defended by modern forts armed with the most up-to-date and powerful guns.

At half-past eight on the morning following the event recorded in the first chapter a signal was made from the dockyard to the flagship of Rear-Admiral Maynebrace. It read: "Commander-in-Chief to 'Repulse': French instructor will proceed on board at four bells. Please send boat to meet him at Kelang Steps."

The receipt of this message was duly acknowledged and then communicated through the manifold yet proper channels to the gun-room, where the midshipmen received it with ill-concealed disgust.

They had planned a picnic along the well-kept country road that, fringed on either side by unbroken avenues of fruit-trees and luxuriant palms, led to the lofty Who Hen Kang. There they had hoped to revel in the gorgeous glades, eating pine-apples and coco-nuts till the services of the sick-bay staff might have to be called into requisition. The prospect, ignoring the consequences of their injudicious appetites, was most alluring; till almost on the eve of the anticipated picnic came this disconcerting message that the French instructor was about to come off to the ship.

French lessons with the temperature at ninety-eight in the shade! This ordeal was sufficient to crush even the resistance of a punch-ball, let alone a dozen irresponsible midshipmen.

Such terrors did not exist for Rear-Admiral Maynebrace. He had forgotten all the foreign languages that had been dinned into his head forty years ago, and since the King's Regulations say nothing about flag officers polishing up their French, Maynebrace felt no qualms. As it happened he had an invitation to meet the Governor.

With due ceremony the Admiral was piped over the side and his motor-pinnace landed him at the Kelang Steps. Somehow there was no conveyance in waiting, not even a rickshaw, so Maynebrace and his flag-lieutenant had to walk.

On his way through the dockyard the Admiral's attention was directed towards an individual who, even amidst the quaintly-costumed inhabitants of Singapore, looked singularly bizarre.

The person who attracted the notice of the mighty Maynebrace was tall, inclined to corpulence, and bowed in the shoulders. His sun-dried face was partly concealed by a bristling black moustache and an imperial. His hair, or at least what was visible outside a top hat of wondrous style, was grey.

A white waistcoat, buttoned almost to bursting strain over his *embonpoint* and fitting where it touched elsewhere, was cut deeply at the throat, revealing a wide, turned-down collar and an enormous red silk tie. His frock coat was of a late nineteenth century pattern; while his trousers, baggy fore and aft, were at one time "white ducks": now they were saffron colour. Sky-blue socks and brown canvas shoes completed the extraordinary "get-up."

As this remarkable personage passed the Admiral he hesitated a moment, then removing his "stove-pipe" made a most elaborate bow, a compliment that Maynebrace returned by stiffly bringing his right hand up to the edge of his white-covered peaked cap.

"Rummy codger," remarked the Admiral.

"It's the French instructor, I believe, sir," said the flag-lieutenant.

"H'm! fancy that on board my ship!"

"Regulations, sir; paragraph 574d says: Whenever practicable instruction in French is to be given to midshipmen by French instructors domiciled in British ports."

"Well, well. Thank goodness I'm not a midshipman," ejaculated Maynebrace, as he frantically signalled to a passing rickshaw-man.

Whatever opinion the Frenchman had of Rear-Admiral Maynebrace he wisely kept it to himself, and trotting along with short jerky steps he reached the place where the gig from H.M.S. "Repulse" awaited him.

The coxswain could scarce suppress a grin as the instructor stepped into the stern sheets. His surprise was still greater when the latter took the yoke-lines and gave the order to "Pull you to ze ship!"

Bending their backs to the supple ash oars the boats crew made the gig dart rapidly through the water. Some of them, possibly, wondered what order the grotesque object in the stern-sheets would give as the boat ran alongside the flagship. As a matter of fact he gave none, but pulling at the wrong yoke-line he made the light gig collide bows on with the accommodation ladder, jerking the rowers backwards off their thwarts, and causing himself to sit ungracefully upon the gratings.

Considering his corpulence the instructor picked himself up with agility and, not waiting for the boat to be brought properly alongside, made his way from thwart to thwart, gaining the foot of the accommodation-ladder by way of the bows of the gig.

At the head of the ladder he was met by the Officer of the watch. Greatly to the latter's disgust the instructor committed a most heinous offence: he spat upon the sacred precincts of the quarter-deck and coolly threw his cigarette end upon the snowy planks!

So flabbergasted was the duty-lieutenant that he said not a word, and before he could recover his composure he was anticipated by First-lieutenant Garboard.

Garboard was an officer who owed his position to influence rather than to merit. He shone in the reflected light of his parent, Sir Peter Garboard, till lately Commander-in-Chief at Portsmouth.

He was one of those officers, luckily becoming rarer, who believe in cast-iron discipline amounting almost to tyranny. He would bully and brow-beat at the ship's-police when there were not enough defaulters to do the odd jobs requisitioned by the commander. When the childish punishment known as 10*a* (which consisted of compelling blacklist men to stand on the lee side of the quarter-deck from 8 to 10 p.m., to have their meals under the sentry's charge and to be deprived of grog and tobacco) was abolished, Garboard, then a junior lieutenant, asserted that the Service was going, to the dogs. He was never happier than when bully-ragging the men of his watch, under the plea of efficiency.

Wishing to air his French the first lieutenant remarked: "*Il fait très chaud, monsieur.*"

The instructor whisked off his stove-pipe hat and bowed ceremoniously.

"Show?" he repeated. "*Oui*, ver' fine show," and looked about him as if he expected to see a floating Agricultural Hall.

"Blockhead!" muttered the discomfited Garboard as he beat a retreat, signing to a quarter-master to take the Frenchman below to the midshipmen's study.

The dozen disconsolate youngsters were already mustered, and awaited with no great zest the arrival of their instructor; but their apathy changed when the Frenchman appeared. They seemed to scent a lark.

But they were sadly mistaken if they hoped to rag that oddly-garbed individual.

"Sit you down," he said sternly. "Sit you down. You tink I haf not imparted ze instruction to ze midsheepmens before, eh? You make great mistake. Ze first zat acts ze light-headed goat he go in ze capitan's report: zen, no leave for a whole veek."

Taking up a piece of chalk the instructor wrote in a firm hand:—

"*Mon frère a raison, mais ma soeur a tort.*"

"Now, zen," he continued, "zat young zhentleman with ze red hair. How you translate zat, eh?"

Mr. Midshipman Moxitter's particular weakness was French translation. It had caused him hours of uneasiness at Osborne and Dartmouth. By a succession of lucky shots he had foiled the examiners and had managed to scrape through in that particular subject.

Upon being asked to translate the sentence, Moxitter stood up, squared his shoulders, and said solemnly:—

"'My brother has reasons that my sister's a tart,' sir."

A roar of laughter, audible even in the captain's cabin, greeted this information. The rest of the midshipmen nearly succumbed to apoplexy, while even the Frenchman was obliged to pull out his pink silk handkerchief and press it tightly to his face.

"We vill not dispute ze point, monsieur," he said after an awkward pause. "Ze affairs of your family are of no concern to ze rest of ze class, mais you are a good-for-nothing rascal, I say. If you no better are at ze rest of ze work on ze sheep zen I say you are a young rotter."

For the full three-quarters of an hour the instructor bullied and badgered the midshipmen in a manner that outvied Lieutenant Garboard's treatment of the men. They had to submit: the alternative of having their leave stopped by the captain put all idea of resistance out of their heads. Finally he made each midshipman write in bold characters, "*Mais, que je suis sot,*" and sign this humiliating confession.

Gathering up the papers the instructor went on deck.

"Will you take any refreshment before you leave?" asked the officer of the watch.

"No, sare, with many tanks. Permit me: my card."

The lieutenant took the proffered piece of pasteboard, and watched the Frenchman go over the side. The coxswain of the gig had been previously cautioned not to allow the instructor to handle the yoke-lines again.

As the boat headed for Kelang Steps the officer of the watch glanced at the instructor's card. It was written in a flowing hand:—

"*Jean le Plaisant, professeur de litérature et des langues, Singapore.*"

The second time the officer of the watch looked at the piece of pasteboard more intently. He even tilted his cap on one side and scratched his closely-cut hair.

"Fetch me the French dictionary from the wardroom," he ordered, and the quarter-deck messenger hastened to carry out his instructions.

Seizing the book the lieutenant hurriedly turned over the pages, then looked dubiously at the retreating gig, now out of hailing distance.

"H'm," he muttered. "I'll speak to the commander. By Jove! I will."

# CHAPTER III
# REMOVED FROM THE NAVY LIST

"WELL?" asked Eccles, as Sub-lieutenant Basil Dacres came off to the ship at the expiration of his leave.

"Ripping time, by Jove! I'll tell you about it when you've done your trick. Is the commander below?"

Receiving an affirmative reply the sub made his way to Commander Bourne's cabin, bubbling over with suppressed excitement.

"I've done it, sir," he announced. "Spoofed the whole jolly lot of them, Admiral included."

"Hope you've covered up your tracks?" asked his superior anxiously.

"Rather! I snubbed Garboard, twitted Oxley and played the very dickens with the flagship's midshipmen. It was hot work, though. Fancy spending a couple of hours on a day like this with a pillow stuffed under your waistcoat, and false moustaches tickling like billy-ho."

Bourne laughed heartily as Dacres related the details of the joke he had played, but his face grew serious as he remarked:—

"'Pon my word, Dacres, I'm rather sorry I let you carry out this mad prank, after all. It's bound to leak out."

"It may, sir. If it does the flagship's people won't say much. The less they say the better, for they will be the laughing-stock of the squadron."

"I don't know so much about that," rejoined the commander. "You see, we must do our best to keep it to ourselves. The culprit must be screened. If there is a row, of course I must own up to my share."

"You must do nothing of the sort, sir," said the sub firmly. "This is my pigeon, you know. Anyway, they haven't tumbled to it yet, and when they do they'll have to go a long way to spot me."

During the First Dog Watch the commander told the captain, who laughed till the tears rolled down his mahogany-coloured cheeks. The chaplain had it third hand from the skipper, and passed the news on to the ward-room. As for the gun-room they heard it directly from Dacres.

So far so good. Loyalty to a brother officer joke a sure bond that the joke against the unpopular flagship would be kept a secret. But Jones, the captain's valet, heard his master and the padre laughing immoderately—was human enough to put his ear to the keyhole of the captain's cabin. In less than an hour the whole of the lower deck heard the yarn, and Mr. Dacres was unanimously acclaimed a "thunderin' brick."

Everything passed off quietly until the following afternoon. It was the calm before the storm.

Basil Dacres had just completed his trick as "Duty Sub," and was enjoying a cooling glass of lime juice in the gun-room when a signalman knocked at the door.

"Chit for Mr. Dacres, sir," he announced.

The sub held out his hand for the folded slip of paper. His intuition told him that something was amiss: it was.

"Flag to officer commanding H.M.S. 'Royal Oak.' Mr. Basil Dacres, sub-lieutenant, is to report himself on board the flagship as soon as possible."

Dacres said not a word to his messmates, but the deep flush that swept over his bronzed features told its own tale.

Without waiting to give explanations or to receive condolences or advice the sub hurried off to his cabin and changed into No. Eight Rig. In the midst of the operation Commander Bourne entered. He had, in the course of his duty, initialled the message and guessed its purport.

"Look here, Dacres," he exclaimed impulsively, "I'm going with you. There's bound to be a most unholy bust-up, I'm afraid; but I mean to stand by you."

For a moment the sub hesitated. He quite realized the need of a friend to back him up during the coming ordeal, but his independence quickly reasserted itself.

"I don't think you need, sir," he replied. "You see, it may be something else. In any case, I'd much rather I went through by myself."

"You would?"

"Yes, sir."

"But, look here, Dacres——"

"It's no use, sir. I'll stick to it somehow. What's the good of getting other men mixed up in this affair when one can bear the brunt. Sharing the blame will not make things any easier for me, I'm afraid. After all, I had a rattling good time."

There was a ring of determination in the sub's voice that compelled his superior officer to give way.

"Very well, then," said Bourne reluctantly. "You go alone. But, mark you, if there's to be any serious bother I, as your commander and a fellow conspirator, will stand by you."

"All right, then, sir," replied Dacres, "that's agreed. If I am in danger of going under I'll look to my superior officer for assistance."

Just then Eccles and Plumbly, the assistant paymaster, entered the cabin and expressed their intention of "standing in."

"Standing in—what about?" demanded Dacres.

"About hoaxing the flagship, of course," replied Eccles.

"You've done your part of the business," retorted the sub, "now let me carry on with mine. For one thing I'm not sure that the Admiral wants me in connexion with that affair. How on earth could he find out? Now sheer off, there's good fellows, and let me finish dressing."

Young Alderney was midshipman of the duty boats, and on the run to the "Repulse" he added his condolences till Dacres peremptorily cut him short. The sub hated outward expressions of sympathy almost as much as he detested formal praise. He vastly preferred in matters of this sort to be self-reliant.

Gaining the quarter-deck of the flagship he saluted with the utmost coolness, and turned to follow the lieutenant who was to escort him to the Admiral's cabin. Three or four youngsters, whom he recognized as being members of the French instructor's class, were on deck, evidently anticipating his discomfiture. Something about his bearing impelled them to return to the shelter of the after barbette, feeling rather sorry for the man who had so recently "pulled their legs."

Vice-Admiral Maynebrace was alone. He had sent his secretary away on some convenient duty, and well-nigh bursting with indignation he stood prepared for the fray.

"Well, sir," he began, as soon as the door was closed. "Do you recognize this?"

And he held up the pseudo Jean le Plaisant's card.

"Yes, sir," answered the sub calmly.

"Then, perhaps, sir, next time you have an opportunity to impersonate a French professor you might have the sense to remember that *littérateur* is spelt with a double 't.' Had it not been for the perspicuity of the officer of the watch your senseless joke might have passed off undetected—at least for a time. Now, sir, you, on your own confession, have been guilty of the heinous offence of bringing his Majesty's uniform into contempt. A senseless joke, sir! There are no extenuating circumstances."

Admiral Maynebrace paused to recover his breath. He had completely forgotten his early days, when, a ringleader of a little mob of midshipmen from the guardship, he had gone ashore at Southampton in the small hours of the morning and had artistically decorated the two lions guarding the historic Bargate. Dacres had heard of the episode and how young Maynebrace was jockeyed out of what promised to be a serious scrape; and he was half tempted to remind his superior of that little delinquency, but the sub had steadfastly made up his mind not to say a word save to reply directly to questions put to him.

The Admiral had fully expected that the culprit would metaphorically go down on his knees and beg for pardon, but he had mistaken Dacres' character. The sub's silence and coolness goaded him to a further outburst.

"Confound you, sir!" he roared. "You're a discredit to the Service, sir. You have two alternatives: either to stand your trial by court-martial for unbecoming conduct, or to send in your papers. You understand?"

"Yes, sir," replied Dacres.

The pros and cons of the two alternatives flashed through his mind in a brief instant. He was fully convinced that the old martinet meant to have him kicked out of the Service. A court-martial could but bring in a verdict of guilty and with no extenuating circumstances. The publicity and disgrace were most undesirable. By resigning he might be able to make a fresh start in another sphere, without the taint of ignominy. His father's words, "Unless you stop this sort of thing there'll be trouble. It will end in your being court-martialled and kicked out of the Service. And, by Jove! if you are, don't look to me for sympathy," came home with redoubled force.

"I'll send in my papers, sir," he said steadily.

The Admiral looked searchingly at him as if to detect any signs of remorse in his words. There were none.

"Very good," he replied with an air of finality. "You may go, sir."

Vice-Admiral Maynebrace spent a restless night. Possibly it was the tropical heat, but more than once he thought of the young officer whose career was in jeopardy.

"If only the young fool had said he was sorry," he soliloquized, "I would have let him down lightly. Hang it! I'll send for him again in the morning and see if he's amenable to reason."

But when morning came, before the Admiral could carry out his good intention, Sub-lieutenant Basil Dacres' papers, duly annotated by his captain, were sent to the flagship accompanied by a written application for the young officer to be allowed to withdraw from his Majesty's Service.

The receipt of this document was received by both ships with feelings of regret. The officers of the flagship, in spite of the fact that they were indignant at the prank that had been played upon them, were good-natured fellows. They fully expected that the culprit would "climb down" and apologize for his delinquency; but they were mistaken. They had misjudged Dacres' peculiar temperament, for the sub, regarding himself as being with his back to the wall, was as obstinate as the proverbial mule. Now that the sub had taken the desperate plunge, they felt genuinely sorry.

As for the ship's company of the "Royal Oak" they were all completely taken aback. Dacres was a favourite with his brother-officers and well-liked by the Lower Deck. It seemed incomprehensible that the Admiral should take such a strong step; but it was not the first time that drastic measures were the result of comparatively slight offences against discipline.

At the eleventh hour Admiral Maynebrace sent a message to the "Royal Oak" to ask whether Sub-lieutenant Dacres had reconsidered the matter. In vain Captain Staggers tried to reason with his subordinate.

"Look here, Dacres," he said kindly. "Think over this affair. Remember your career is at stake. It was a silly thing to do to attempt to hoax the flagship, in spite of the circumstances. Of course you realize that we were in sympathy with you, but that was a mistake. If you think you are going to come out 'top-dog' in your difference with the Admiral the sooner you put that idea out of your head the better. I don't believe in the whole of naval history that a junior officer has done so with any degree of success. You see, it's against all principles of discipline."

"Thank you, sir," replied Dacres, "but I'm afraid you cannot understand my motives, and I cannot very well explain. All the same, I don't wish to withdraw my resignation; and as to scoring over the Admiral, well, the idea never entered into my head until you mentioned it. But I may, even yet," he added.

Nettled by the sub's refusal, the Admiral used the power entrusted to him under the revised King's Regulations. He accepted Dacres' resignation, without having to wait for Admiralty authority; and before noon on the same day Dacres ceased to be an officer of his Majesty's navy.

"Look here, Dacres," exclaimed Commander Bourne impetuously, "you're a young rotter. You remember what I said: 'If there's any serious bother I, your commander and fellow conspirator, will stand by you.' To that you agreed; so I'm off to the flagship to bear my share of the brunt."

Dacres looked at the commander for a few moments, then, doing what he would not have dared to do but an hour previously, he tapped him familiarly on the shoulder.

"Look here, Bourne," he said, "you are no longer my superior officer, so the deal's off. If you attempt to put your finger in my pie I'll give you the biggest hiding you've ever had in your life. So don't make matters worse, and I'll be thankful to one of the best pals I've ever had in the Service."

Bourne agreed reluctantly. He had fully intended to interview the Admiral, but now he was somewhat relieved to find that Dacres had vetoed the proposal. The commander's prospects were no longer in danger; and since Bourne's chances of promotion depended solely upon merit—for he had no outside influence—he was genuinely grateful for the principal culprit's magnanimity.

That same afternoon the squadron, with the exception of the "Royal Oak," weighed and proceeded to sea. The "Royal Oak" had developed slight engine-room defects and was left behind in order to effect necessary repairs.

Thus an opportunity occurred of giving a demonstration that otherwise could not have taken place; for as Dacres went over the side of the battleship for the last time the officers turned out on the quarter-deck to bid him good luck, while by a purely spontaneous impulse the men gave three rousing cheers for the youngster whom they could no longer regard as one of the ship's company of H.M.S. "Royal Oak."

# CHAPTER IV
## THE MYSTERIOUS AIRSHIP

ON his homeward voyage Basil Dacres had plenty of opportunities for pondering over his future plans. Having once taken the plunge he was not a fellow to repine. His thoughts were of the future and not of the past.

"In any case," he thought, "I'll be as independent as I can. I don't want to come to loggerheads with the pater, but goodness only knows how he'll take it. If I can have a quiet chat with him before he learns the official version of the row, I may be able to explain matters with a certain degree of satisfaction. After that I'll go abroad, and get an appointment under one of the South American governments. There will be plenty of scope in that direction."

At Suez the liner received a batch of English mails, and, as usual, there was a great demand for newspapers to supplement the meagre details of the world's doings as received by wireless.

Dacres hurriedly scanned the columns of four successive weeks of the journal, but to his relief he saw no mention of his resignation being reported. That gave him hopes of being able to be first in the field as far as his parent was concerned.

Having assured himself on this point he proceeded systematically to wade through the news with the zest that only those who have been cut off from home ties know how to appreciate.

Presently his eye caught sight of a heading, "The mysterious airship again."

"H'm, this sounds interesting," he soliloquized, for anything in connexion with aviation appealed to him. When his services for the Naval Flying Wing were declined the refusal hit him far harder than his being asked to withdraw from his Majesty's Service.

"They say 'again,' I notice. I wonder for how long this airship has been claiming the attention of the great British public? It's a pity I've been unable to see the first account of its appearance. Seems like starting a book at the sixth chapter."

Settling himself in a comfortable deck-chair Dacres was soon lost to his surroundings in the account of the remarkable exploits of an airship of entirely new design. It was seen within a few hours at places as far apart as Newcastle and Plymouth, and Holyhead and Canterbury. Although the eye-witnesses' accounts varied considerably in detail the general description was sufficiently unanimous to prove conclusively that the airship was not a creation of an excited imagination.

It was agreed that the airship was of immense length and of exceptional speed. She invariably flew at a great altitude. Her appearance resembled that of a lead pencil pointed at one end, but the observers were unable to state whether there were planes, cars, and other appendages. There was none of that gently see-sawing motion of the British military and naval dirigibles: she flew as steadily as a seaplane on a calm day, and created a far greater impression of speed.

Near Newcastle she was spotted by a pair of belated motorists who were travelling over a road that follows the old Roman wall between Chollerford and Heddon. It was a moonlight night, although the sky was frequently obscured by drifting clouds. While brought up to make good a slight defect one of the motorists noticed a dark object overhead and called his companion's attention to it. Both simultaneously expressed their opinion that it was an airship, while one of the men found by extending his arm that the extremities of the craft coincided with the length between his outstretched little finger and thumb, while its breadth was roughly half the thickness of the nail joint of the same finger. Taking the breadth to be forty feet it was reasonable to suppose that the length of the airship was nearly thirty times that dimension, or one thousand two hundred feet. The airship was then travelling rapidly in a westerly direction, the time being 1.30 a.m.

So impressed were the travellers by this unusual sight that they proceeded to the offices of the "Newcastle Daily Record" and stated the facts to the sub-editor who happened to be on night duty.

Just before four on the same morning the coastguard on watch at Yealm Head, near Plymouth, "spotted" the airship still flying at a great height, but in an easterly direction. He followed it through his telescope until it was lost to sight, but owing to the airship being against the growing dawn he was unable to give any details as to its construction. His description, however, tallied with that of the Newcastle motorists, whose report was published in a special edition of the principal London papers.

Since Newcastle and Plymouth are roughly 360 miles apart the speed of the airship could not be less than 150 miles per hour, and that not taking into consideration the fact that on each occasion the craft was shaping a course at right angles to the direct line between these two places.

Two days later came an even more startling report, this time from Canterbury.

It appears that a shepherd employed at Wether Farm, Petham—a small village five miles from the Kentish cathedral city—had occasion to visit a fold at some distance from the farm-buildings. This was at three o'clock, an hour before sunrise, but it was just light enough to distinguish surrounding objects.

Suddenly he saw a huge object falling through the air. All he could liken it to was a haystack. It struck the ground quite gently and about two hundred yards from the place where he stood. At first he was afraid to move, until, thinking it might be a balloon that had met with an accident, he ran towards the spot. As he did so he heard voices, evidently discussing the situation; but before he could get close to the "haystack," the object gave a bound and shot skywards.

He stood stock still watching the balloon growing smaller and smaller till it approached an object that had hitherto escaped his notice—an airship resembling a "wooden meat-skewer," according to his description. Of what happened to the smaller balloon he had no idea, but as he watched he saw the airship soar still higher till lost to sight.

Curiosity prompted him to examine the spot where the balloon had alighted. The marks on the dew-sodden grass gave him an opportunity of measuring its base, which was twelve paces square, or, roughly, thirty feet. There were footprints showing that two men had alighted, but had not moved far from the spot. Although he made a careful search he found that nothing had been left behind that might give a clue to the occupants of the balloon.

This story the shepherd told to his master, who, knowing that a mysterious aircraft had been sighted at Newcastle and Plymouth, took the first opportunity of reporting the matter to the military authorities at Canterbury. Asked if he could vouch for his informant's trustworthiness the farmer replied that the man had been in his employment for thirty years, and as far as shepherds went, was intelligent, honest, and not given to immoderate drinking.

When this was reported in the Press the interest in the mysterious airship redoubled. Various theories were advanced as to the presence of the balloon, or airship dinghy as a facetious correspondent suggested. Crediting the airship with a mean speed of 150 miles per hour, it was still doubted whether it would be possible to tow a balloon with it, while, on the other hand, it was equally impossible to deflate and stow the gas-bag within the airship during the short interval that had elapsed according to the shepherd's statement.

Then, of course, there was the alarmist section; People who wrote demanding that the Royal Flying Corps should be brought to book for neglecting their duty. It was pointed out that in the course of her nocturnal voyages the airship had passed the prohibited areas without being challenged by any of the air patrols. It seemed incredible that the mysterious giant of the clouds could be here, there, everywhere, from the north of England to the south, without being seen except by chance by a few individuals. Where, also, could a huge aircraft, measuring at least a thousand feet over-all, be housed in complete secrecy?

Then from the wilds of North Wales came an astounding report. This time the narrator was a signalman on the North Western Railway, who witnessed a remarkable sight from his box near Llanfaelog in the Isle of Anglesey. It was at midnight. The moon had just risen in a cloudless sky, and there was hardly any wind.

The man had just cleared a goods train over his section and was about to set the signals, when he was aware of a huge object rushing with a rapidity greater by far than that of the most powerful express train. It passed almost overhead and, according to his estimate, at about a hundred feet from the ground. After it passed the leaves of the trees close to the signal box were violently agitated and a sudden blast of air swept the papers off his desk, but in spite of the commotion in the air there was hardly any sound from the mysterious airship, save a subdued buzzing.

Recovering his presence of mind the signalman promptly telegraphed the news along the line, but the terrific rush of this gigantic aircraft was unnoticed by any of the other railway employés on duty.

At six o'clock, however, two fishermen put into Dulas Bay, on the north coast of Anglesey, and reported that at dawn they had seen a large airship break in two at a distance of about two miles N. N. of where they were fishing. Both men were unshaken in this statement, that a complete severance had taken place, and that both portions, instead of falling into the sea, headed off at great speed in a westerly direction.

It was pointed out to the Government, in a strongly-worded leader in "The Times," that something must be radically wrong with our system of policing the air, since it was conclusively proved that an unknown aircraft, possessing superior power of propulsion and radius of action to any yet known, had cruised over the length and breadth of England and Wales—and perhaps further afield—without being officially reported.

Although there were no evidences that the mysterious aircraft was flying under the auspices of a foreign power, it was quite possible that she hailed from a country other than our own. If not, and she was built and controlled by a British subject, the Government ought to take steps to secure a right to build others of her pattern; otherwise the bare margin of safety set up by the Aerial Defence Committee was in danger.

Awaking out of its customary lethargy the British Government accepted the advice of "The Times," and steps were taken to locate the base from which the airship operated, and also, if possible, to trace her complete course during one of her nocturnal flights.

Searchlights were temporarily installed on almost every important hill-top from Berwick to Land's End, and from the South Foreland to Holyhead; airmen, both military and civilian, were encouraged to make night flights with the idea of being able to sight and perhaps keep in touch with the giant dirigible; while destroyers and seaplanes patrolled the coast, ready on the first intimation by wireless to concentrate at any rendezvous on the line of flight that the sought-for airship was likely to adopt.

"H'm!" ejaculated Dacres, as he carefully folded the latest newspaper that it was possible to obtain. "This looks lively. Things are getting exciting in the Old Country. Perhaps, after all, I may get a chance of a berth with one of the private flying schools, even if I can't manage to join the Flying Corps. I'll have a shot at it, by Jove!"

# CHAPTER V
# A MOMENTOUS TRAIN JOURNEY

UPON the arrival of the liner in the Thames, Basil Dacres took the opportunity of leaving the vessel at Tilbury, thus avoiding the tedious passage up to the docks.

Still uncertain as to what his reception by his father would be he booked his scanty belongings at the London terminus, and proceeded west.

Although outwardly calm his heart was thumping violently as he knocked at the door of Colonel Dacres' house. A strange footman answered him, and in reply to an inquiry said that Colonel Dacres had let the house for the season.

This was astonishing news, for in his last letter the colonel had made no mention of his intention, and to let his house was quite a departure from his usual plans.

"Can you give me Colonel Dacres' present address?"

"Yes, sir," replied the man; "it is Cranbury House, near Holmsley, Hants."

"I wonder what possessed the governor to rusticate," thought Dacres as he turned away. "Well, the sooner we come to an understanding the better, I suppose. I'll get some lunch and then take the first train to this out-of-the-way show. I can't say that I've heard of the place before."

Whilst having lunch Dacres asked for a time-table, and by dint of a considerable tax upon his brain-power he discovered that Holmsley was a small station in the New Forest. An express train, leaving Waterloo at five, would take him as far as Brockenhurst in an hour and fifty minutes. Then, as is usual with railway companies' arrangements, he found that he had three-quarters of an hour to wait until a slow train took him on to Holmsley.

The daily papers gave no further definite information about the unknown airship. It appeared to have escaped notice for nearly three weeks, although during that interval there were several unauthenticated accounts that it had been "spotted." Many reports turned out to be deliberate hoaxes, while in one instance a company of Royal Engineers at Portsmouth turned out with a searchlight, only to find that the "airship" reported by a belated and slightly inebriated clubman was a large telephone cable spanning the narrow roadway between two lofty blocks of buildings.

Finding he had plenty of time on his hands Dacres decided to walk to Waterloo. After an absence from Town he had a strong desire to see some of the familiar haunts, so after walking along Piccadilly and thence to Trafalgar Square, he turned down Northumberland Avenue. Under existing circumstances he gave the Admiralty buildings a wide berth, for he had no inclination to come in contact with any of his former brother-officers.

Just as he was passing the Metropole, Dacres nearly collided with a powerfully-built, athletic-looking man who looked anything between twenty and thirty years of age.

In the midst of mutual apologies the stranger suddenly exclaimed:—

"Why, bless my soul, what are you doing here, Dacres?"

"Hythe, by Jove!" ejaculated Dacres.

"Right you are, old man. You haven't altered much since I saw you last. Let me see, that was when we paid off in the old 'Cornwall' in 1914. But we needn't stand here; come to my club—it's only a few minutes' walk."

Arnold Hythe was in more respects than one a fortunate individual. In recognition of his services in connexion with the submarine "Aphrodite"—now the prototype of the British "M" class—he had been promoted to the rank of Inspecting Commander of Submarines after less than a year's service as lieutenant. This was creating a precedent, but circumstances warranted it, and when the unusual appointment was announced, the shoals of congratulatory telegrams that poured in from his brother-officers showed that in this case there was little or no grumbling at Hythe's well-deserved promotion.

"Dacres, old man, I am awfully sorry," remarked Hythe with genuine concern when Dacres had told his story. "I cannot imagine what possessed old Maynebrace to take such drastic measures. Of course I had a lot to do with him when he was Admiral Superintendent at Portsmouth, and, personally, I found him quite a genial old fellow. Possibly his being sent to sea from a dockyard commission without being promoted to Vice-Admiral may have soured his temper a bit. By the by, what are your plans?"

"Nothing definite at present. Ultimately I hope to do something in the way of flying. Always had an inclination in that direction."

"Yes, I remember you had. A little affair with that aviator at Dartmouth, for instance. Thank goodness, it isn't in my line. Give me six fathoms of water any day of the week."

"I suppose so," rejoined Dacres, "but I'm not keen on submarine work. It lacks the sense of freedom that you get when rushing through the air."

"H'm!" ejaculated Hythe. "My experience does not lead me to agree with you, at least, as far as aeroplanes are concerned. I had a nasty tumble at Zanzibar."

"Yes, I recollect: it was while you were doing your unlawful commission in the 'Aphrodite.' By the by, what's your opinion about this mysterious aircraft? It's making as much commotion as when Captain Restronguet shook us up a couple of years ago."

"Cannot say," replied Hythe laconically.

"But in the event of her proving to be in the employ of a foreign power, how would you propose to collar her?"

"I wouldn't give much for her chances if she came within range of one of our aerial torpedoes."

"An airship moving at over 150 miles an hour wants some hitting," remarked Dacres. "Besides, supposing she keeps clear of the sea?"

"That's out of my bearings," said Hythe. "It's a case for the military authorities. Anyhow, there's been nothing heard of her for days past, so no doubt she has transferred her activities elsewhere. Personally I have but little faith in the command of the air. So long as we keep command of the sea there's not much to trouble about. But to get back to more personal matters, Dacres, where are you bound for?"

"Going to pay the governor a visit."

"But you were shaping a course in the opposite direction when I crossed your bows."

"The pater has let his house and gone to live somewhere in the New Forest—near Holmsley. It's a matter of three hours' journey, even by express."

"Why not hire a 'plane? All you've to do is to tube to Richmond and get one from the Metropolitan and Suburban Volo Company. You'd be at Holmsley in three-quarters of an hour."

Dacres shook his head.

"Can't run to it, old man," he said gravely. "I haven't any too much shot in the locker at present."

Hythe's hand was in his pocket in an instant.

"Don't be offended, Dacres," he said hurriedly, "but if I can let you have——"

Dacres shook his head.

"Thanks, old chap," he replied, "I'd rather not."

"As a loan, then?"

"No, thanks all the same. It hasn't come to that yet, and I hope it never will. It's awfully good of you, Hythe."

"Sorry you won't let me show my sympathy in a tangible manner, Dacres. Still, you know my address. If there's anything I can do, don't hesitate to write."

"I won't, forget," said Dacres. "There are not many old shipmates I would care to look to for a favour, but you are the exception, Hythe. Well, I must be getting under way once more. It's close on quarter to five."

By a few seconds Dacres caught his train. He travelled first class, for in spite of his dwindling purse he resolved to maintain the dignity of the family. It was one of the few concessions he made to appearances.

As the train was moving out of the station he bought an evening paper, and settling himself in a corner seat, scanned the pages. In the "stop press column" appeared a report to the effect that the elusive airship had been sighted by the S.S "Micronome" in Lat. 51 degrees 4 minutes N. Long. 30 degrees 25 minutes W., or roughly midway between Liverpool and New York. The tramp was plugging at half speed against a furious easterly gale. The sky was obscured with dark clouds, and although it was noon the light was very dim. The airship, travelling at an estimated speed of one hundred miles an hour, passed at a height of eight hundred feet above the vessel, and was seen by the captain and second mate, who were on the bridge, and also by four of the dockhands. The force of the wind was registered at fifty miles per hour, yet the airship flew steadily and without the slightest inclination to pitch.

The information was received by wireless at Valencia at 2.15 p.m. and immediately transmitted to the Admiralty. Presuming that the speed and direction of the airship were uniformly maintained she ought to be sighted by the coast-guards on the Kerry coast by 6 p.m.

Dacres finished reading the paper without discovering any news bearing directly upon the actual doings of the gigantic aircraft; then, having devoured the advertisement columns for the simple reason that there was nothing else to read, he threw the paper on to the seat and began to take a slight interest in his fellow-passengers.

They were two in number, One, a short, redfaced man whose chief characteristics were a white waistcoat, a massive gold chain, and a large diamond tie pin, was evidently a well-to-do City man. Dacres' surmise was strengthened by the fact that the man was deep in the pages of the "Financial Times."

The second passenger was a man of a very different type. He was about five feet nine inches in height, and heavily-built. He was clean-shaven, revealing an exceedingly sallow complexion. This, together with the fact that the "whites" of his eyes were far from being white and were of an aggressively bilious colour, seemed to suggest that this man had been born under a tropical sun. His hair was dark and inclined to curl, while Dacres noticed that the "half-moons" of his finger-nails were of a purple hue. His lips were heavy and of a pale pink tint.

"Touch of the tar-brush there," soliloquized Dacres. "Finger-nails of that colour invariably betray a dash of black blood. He doesn't look any too well dressed, either."

The stranger was attired in a shabby brown suit; his dirty collar and frayed red tie were in keeping with his sombre appearance. Altogether he looked as unlike a man who habitually travels first class as anyone could possibly imagine.

Dacres made his examination with assumed and well-guarded indifference, but his scrutiny was none the less minute. He had the knack of being able to read a person's character by observation, and was rarely at fault.

"A truculent bounder," was his summing-up. Twenty years back he would have made a fairly tough customer in the ring. "Unless I'm much mistaken he is too fond of bending his elbow. I'd like to hear him talk: ten to one he has a South American accent."

As the train tore past the Brooklands Flying Ground two large biplanes were in the act of ascending. They rose awkwardly, bobbing in the stiff breeze, then, gradually overhauling the express, passed beyond the limits of Dacres' observation.

"Untameable beasts," remarked an evenly-modulated voice, and turning from the window Dacres found that the sallow-faced passenger was addressing him. The City man, deep in his paper, had paid no heed to the aeroplanes in flight.

"Think so?" asked Dacres. "They seem to be making good headway, especially as they are plugging right in the eye of the wind."

"While they are under control they are—well—safe," rejoined the man. "But one never knows when they take it into their heads to side slip or bank too steeply. To my mind accidents are bound to happen till a means is found of counteracting the force of gravity."

"Which is only obtainable by means of hydrogen gas-bags," added Dacres.

"Up to the present," agreed the stranger. "Still, one never knows. A compromise between an airship and an aeroplane, for example?"

"The speed would suffer in consequence," objected Dacres.

"Oh? Take the case of this mysterious airship which has been seen in various parts of the country. Her speed exceeds that of the swiftest monoplane that the country possesses."

In spite of his adverse opinion of the man Dacres felt interested. He felt inclined to admit that he had made a mistake in putting him down as a South American. His accent was almost perfect; in fact, almost too faultless for an average Englishman, yet there was not the slightest trace of a foreign pronunciation in his sentences.

"That is where submarines score," continued the man. "So long as they retain their reserve of buoyancy they are practically safe. They can return to the surface and remain motionless. Of course I am alluding to peace conditions. A helpless submarine lying awash would stand a very poor chance in action if exposed to the fire of a hostile vessel. I presume, sir, that you are a naval officer?"

"Your surmise is at fault," replied Dacres. "I have no connexion with the——" he was about to say "service," but checking himself in time substituted "navy."

A shade of disappointment flitted across the stranger's face.

"Thought perhaps you were," he said apologetically. "The subject of the navy interests me. By the by, does this train stop at Southampton Docks?"

"No," replied Dacres. "Only at Southampton West. It's quite a short distance thence to the Docks."

"Ah, that is good. You see, I am a cold storage contractor, and this is my first visit to Southampton. My duties hitherto have been confined to Liverpool and Manchester. Thanks for the information, sir."

Then, drawing a notebook from his breast-pocket, the stranger broke off the conversation as abruptly as he had started.

"That's strange," thought Dacres. "He seemed very much inclined to yarn till I told him I had no connexion with the service—worse luck. He shut up like a hedgehog after that. Cold storage contractor, eh? With a red-hot temper, I'll be bound. Pity the poor bounders under him."

Shortly afterwards Dacres happened to glance in the direction of the livery-looking individual. He was still deep in his notebook. On the cover, partially concealed by the man's flabby hands, was the title in gilt letters. Enough was left uncovered for Dacres to read the words "Telegrafos y — —"

"H'm! My yellow-skinned fellow-traveller understands Spanish after all," he soliloquized. "Perhaps my original summing-up is not so much at fault after all."

The man made no further attempt to enter into conversation, but just as the train was rushing through Winchester station he stood up, took his handbag from the rack, and went out into the corridor.

The express pulled up at Eastleigh for a few minutes; then, just as it was on the move, Dacres happened to catch a glimpse of his late fellow-passenger seated in a Portsmouth train by the furthermost platform.

"H'm! Decidedly funny way to get to Southampton Docks by that train," he muttered. "That fellow was trying to pull my leg over the cold storage business, I'll be bound. Bless me, if I like the cut of your jib. I am not generally given to presupposition, but something seems to tell me that you and I will fall foul of each other before very long."

# CHAPTER VI
## CHALLENGED

REFERRING to the back of an envelope on which he had jotted down the times of the trains, Dacres found upon alighting at Brockenhurst junction that he had three-quarters of an hour to wait. Since he did not feel inclined to cool his heels on the station platform he made up his mind to take a stroll through the village, have tea, and thus turn the interval of waiting to good account.

The air was cool, the dense foliage afforded a pleasant shelter from the slanting though powerful rays of the sun, and Dacres began to feel quite easy in his mind.

"By George!" he ejaculated. "That airship seems to interest me far more than my forthcoming interview with the governor. I wonder if she has been sighted again. I'll get an evening paper at the bookstall when I return to the station. How jolly fine the forest scenery is. Now I am not surprised that the pater came down to this part of the country if the scenery around Cranbury House is anything like this."

A plain but substantial tea filled Dacres' cup of contentment to the brim. English bread, fresh country butter, and watercress, after the fare obtainable on board the "Royal Oak" in the Tropics, combined to make the most appetizing meal he had tasted for months past. It reminded him of the saying of an old chief boatswain on returning to England after a two years' arduous commission mostly in the Persian Gulf.

"Bless you, sir," said the warrant officer emphatically. "Directly I set foot ashore at Portsmouth I'll order a prime beefsteak and a tankard—not a glass, mind you—of ale."

Two months later the chief bo's'un retired with the rank of lieutenant, and forthwith settled down in the country. One of his first acts was to hire a man to stand outside his bedroom window every evening from ten to eleven, his duty being to throw buckets of water against the panes.

"Couldn't get to sleep unless I heard the sea breaking against the scuttles," he explained.

Dacres wondered whether the call of the sea would come back to him with such vividness. Perhaps; but up to the present he felt no such overwhelming desire. It was just possible that he had not yet had time to realize his position.

In the midst of his meditation the traveller remembered that he had to catch a train.

Pulling out his watch he found that he had fifteen minutes to get to the station and, since he did the outward journey in ten minutes, it was an easy jaunt back to the junction.

"Where are you for?" asked a porter as Dacres arrived on the practically deserted platform.

"Holmsley."

"Your train's just gone, sir," announced the railway employee with the air of a man who has imparted a joyful surprise.

"But——" Dacres pulled out the envelope. "I thought it went at seven-four."

"Did till this month, sir," was the unconcerned reply. "Now it leaves here at six-fifty-six. Next train at eight-two."

"They must have had an old time-table in that restaurant," muttered Dacres disgustedly. "I was a bit of an ass not to make sure, and a doubly confounded idiot not to have asked when I arrived here. However, can't be helped. 'What's done can't be undone,' as the landlubber remarked when he tied a slippery hitch in his hammock lashing and found himself sprawling on the mess-deck ten seconds later. This time I keep watch here, I don't mean to be let down a second time."

When a fast train bringing the evening papers from London stopped at the station Dacres hurried to buy a copy. The news as far as the airship was concerned was woefully disappointing. She had not been sighted anywhere in Great Britain or Ireland.

There was one item of news that interested him, however. It was a wireless message from Cape Columbia, announcing that Lieutenant Cardyke and four men of the British Arctic Expedition had started on their dash for the North Pole.

"Plucky chap!" ejaculated Dacres. "I hope he'll pull it off all right. It's a jolly risky business, though. Never fancied that kind of job myself, but Cardyke was always keen on Polar work. I remember how he used to devour Scott's and Shackleton's works when he was at Osborne. All the same, I wonder they don't make a dash for the Pole in an up-to-date dirigible, instead of tramping all those hundreds of miles. I'd volunteer for a Polar airship expedition like a shot."

The loud ringing of an electric bell warned Dacres that his train was signalled. Folding the paper and placing it in his pocket he rose from his seat and waited for the train to run into the station.

The last stage of his journey was a short one and he chided himself for not having walked. The sun had just dipped behind the heather-clad hills as Dacres alighted, while already the evening mists were rising from the shallow valleys.

A typical country porter took the tickets of the three passengers who left the train, and in response to Dacres' inquiry as to the direction of Cranbury House, scratched his head in obvious perplexity.

"Garge, du 'ee knaw whur be Cranbury 'Ouse?" he sung out to a shock-headed youth who was struggling with a truck on the opposite platform.

"Yes," was the reply. "A matter of a couple o' mile t'other side o' Wilverley Post."

After a lengthy and complex explanation of how to reach Wilverley Post, Dacres found himself almost as much enlightened as before.

"Can I get a motor or a cab?" he asked.

"Naw, zur; not onless you'm ordered 'em. There be a bus, only it doänt meet this train."

Dacres was not a man to be daunted by difficulties. Emerging from the station he swung along the road, breathing in the pure moorland air, determined by hook or by crook to reach his destination with the least possible delay.

The road was quite deserted. Not even a motorist passed, otherwise he would have boldly asked the favour of a lift. Overhead a deep buzzing caused him to look upwards. Two aviators, making towards Bournemouth, glided swiftly through the gathering gloom. In this part of the country, Dacres reflected, there were more men in the air than on the highway.

Presently he reached a signpost at the junction of four cross roads. By this time there was just sufficient light for him to decipher the directions. Lyndhurst—he did not want to go there; Ringwood—equally undesirable, as were the other places mentioned.

"I suppose this is Wilverley Post," he thought. "Here I must bring up and wait till some one comes along. That ought to be fairly soon. What a deserted-looking spot, though. However," he added optimistically, "it might be a jolly sight worse. For instance, it might be raining hard and blowing half a gale. Ha! Here's a cart coming along."

In response to a hail the driver pulled up, but he was quite at a loss to give the desired information. He had lived at Ringwood all his life, and had never heard of Cranbury House.

Ten minutes later a large motor-car came swinging along. The chauffeur obligingly stopped, but was likewise unable to state the locality of Colonel Dacres' property.

"If it were this way, sir, I would give you a lift with pleasure," added the man, "but ten chances to one it would only be taking you farther out of your way. If you like, though, I'll run you down to Christchurch and you can put up there for the night, sir."

"Thanks all the same, I want particularly to get to Cranbury House tonight," said Dacres.

With a civil good-night the chauffeur sped on his way, while Dacres prepared to resume his vigil by the gaunt signpost.

Presently his ready ear detected the sounds of footsteps plodding methodically along the hard tarred road. Out of the darkness loomed the shape of a powerfully-built man, bending under a load of faggots.

"Cranbury House, zur? Sure I knaws 'ut well. If 'tweer light enow oi could show you the chimbleys, over yonder. Du 'ee taäk this path an' 'twill bring ee right agin the gates of t'ouse. It'll be a matter of a couple o' miles. If ye like, zur, I'll come along wi' ee," said the man, setting his load down by the roadside.

"I won't trouble you, thanks," replied Dacres, bestowing a shilling upon the man. "It's a fairly easy path, I hope?"

"Yes, zur, 's long as you keep to un. There be some bad bogs close on hand. Why, only t'other evenin' old Bill Jarvis as lives down Goatspen Plain wur a-comin'——"

But Dacres was not at all anxious to hear of the nocturnal adventures of the said Bill Jarvis.

"I'll keep to the path all right," he said. "About two miles, eh? Thank you and good night."

The path, showing grey in the misty starlight, was barely wide enough for two persons to walk abreast. On either hand were clumps of furze and heather, that at places encroached to such an extent that the sharp spikes tingled the pedestrian's calves. Here and there the footway, worn by the action of rain and the passing of cattle, was several feet below the surface of the surrounding ground. It was far from level, for all around the country seemed composed of a series of hillocks, all divided by wreaths of mist.

For ten minutes Dacres walked on at a rapid rate till he was suddenly brought up by the bifurcation of the path. So acute was the angle between the two ways and so alike in width that he stood stock still in deep perplexity. His informant had made no mention of the forked paths.

"Perhaps they reunite farther on," muttered Dacres. "It looks like a case of pay your money and take your choice. Why not toss for it? Heads the right hand, tails the left."

He spun the coin. He missed it and it fell dully upon the sandy ground. Three matches he struck before he discovered it standing upright in the soft earth.

"Ah! That bears out my theory. The ways meet again. Anyway, I'll take the right hand one."

He had not gone very far when, with a rush and a swish amidst the heather, four black objects darted across his path, within an ace of capsizing him altogether.

"Pigs," he exclaimed. "Fancy those beasts roaming about in this deserted spot. I wonder if there's a cottage handy?"

A hundred yards further on the path was joined on the left hand by another, which apparently confirmed his suggestion that it was the reunion of the two forked routes. With this reassuring discovery he redoubled his efforts until he found that the path was growing narrower and eventually broke off in three fairly diverging directions.

Taking his bearings by means of the Pole Star Dacres chose the path that followed the direction he had hitherto pursued. Down and down into a wide yet shallow valley it plunged, till once more it split into two ways. To add to the perplexity of the situation both of them bore away to the right and in quite a different direction from that which he supposed to be the proper one.

Dacres brought "all standing." Not a sound disturbed the stillness of the night. He could easily imagine himself to be "bushed" in the Australian wilds as far as the presence of human beings was concerned.

Again he glanced upwards to ascertain his bearings, but in the hollow the mists were considerably denser and rose high above the ground. The stars were completely blotted out.

"I'll take the left hand path this time," he muttered impatiently, for his peace of mind was now considerably ruffled by the vexatious delays that he had experienced. "It's bound to lead somewhere, so here goes."

But before he had covered a hundred paces he found that his progress was impeded by a brook that trickled over the now ill-defined track. On either hand the ground was marshy and, bearing in mind the incompleted narrative of Bill Jarvis's experience, he acted warily.

"It won't be the first time that I've entered the paternal dwelling with muddy boots," he reflected as he waded through the shallow stream, prodding the bed of the brook with his stick at each step.

When, at length, he negotiated the twenty feet of water he found to his intense disgust that there were no signs of the path being resumed. Evidently that track was made by cattle for the purpose of going to the stream to drink.

Away on the left rose a rounded hill crowned with a gaunt tree, the outlines of which were curiously distorted by the layers of mist.

"Here goes!" he exclaimed desperately. "I'll make for that hill. Perhaps it will be clearer up there, and I may be able to strike a fresh path."

Forcing his way through the heather, dodging aggressive clumps of gorse, and slipping on the loose sandy soil, Dacres reached the summit of the knoll. Here he was no better off, for the sky was still overcast, while as far as he could see in the dim light the surrounding country was enshrouded in mist. In vain he attempted to retrace his steps, till sinking ankle deep in marshy ground warned him that he was not only lost but in danger of being trapped in a bog.

"Ahoy!" he shouted in stentorian tones.

His hail was quickly answered by another "ahoy."

"That's good," he exclaimed. "There's a sailor somewhere about. I've heard that pensioners frequently settle down in these out of the way wilds."

"Ahoy! Where are you?" he hailed again.

"Where are you?" came the voice.

"Hang it all," said Dacres dejectedly. "It's only an echo. I am merely wasting precious breath. If only there were a breeze I could keep a fairly straight course. Luck's quite out this trip."

Striking a match and glancing at his watch Dacres discovered that it was a quarter to ten.

"No use stopping here," he decided. "I'll plug away and trust to find another path. Wish I'd accepted that fellow's offer and got him to pilot me through this wilderness. That's the result of being so beastly independent."

On and on he went, dodging between the thick masses of furze. An hour later he had a shrewd suspicion that he was describing a large circle, for one peculiar-shaped tree struck him as being familiar; yet no longed-for path rewarded his perseverance.

"Hurrah!" he exclaimed as a tiny speck of light leapt up at some distance ahead of him. "Now there's a chance of finding out where I am."

Recklessly he plunged through the undergrowth, his eyes fixed upon the friendly gleam that came from the midst of a deep shadow. Suddenly the light vanished, but the shadow resolved itself into a dense clump of trees extending right and left like a huge wall till lost in the night mist.

Now he could hear voices: men talking rapidly and earnestly, while the clatter of a metal object falling upon hard ground raised a sharp reproof.

"Midnight motor repairs," thought Dacres. "A broken-down car, perhaps. Then, these trees are by the side of the high road. Ha!"

Further progress was impeded by a barbed wire fence upon which he blundered with disastrous results to his trousers and coat sleeves. The pain caused by one of the spikes cutting his wrist made him utter an exclamation of annoyance.

Simultaneously a bell began to tinkle faintly. The men's voices ceased.

Dacres paid scant heed to these ominous warnings. His one desire was to get into touch with human beings once more. Standing upon the lowermost wire and holding upon the one above, he wriggled adroitly through the fence, then hurried through the wood, half expecting to find himself upon the road.

But no highway rewarded his efforts. Pine trunk after pine trunk he passed until it began to occur to him that he was in danger of being lost in a wood, which was as undesirable as being adrift in the midst of a foggy moorland.

He paused. All was quiet.

"I'll give a shout," he thought, but before he could raise his voice there was a sudden scuffling to the right and left of him and a deep voice exclaimed:—

"Collar him, lads. He's one of them."

# CHAPTER VII
# THE RETURN OF THE AIRSHIP

IT was no time for explanation. Dacres could just discern the outlines of two men in the act of springing upon him. At this uncalled-for outrage is blood was up. He would resist first and explain afterwards.

Stepping agilely aside Dacres thrust out his foot and sent one of his assailants sprawling on his hands and knees. His comrade, within an ace of tripping over the other's prostrate body, thought discretion the better part of valour, and slipped back until he could obtain assistance.

"What's the meaning of this?" demanded Dacres angrily. "I'm not a poacher. I've lost my way."

"A likely story," exclaimed the man who had given the order for the attack. "All the same, you've got to come with us."

"Got to?" repeated Dacres, standing on his guard. "There are two sides to that question."

A minute before he would have gone anywhere with anyone, and with the utmost willingness. Now, the aggressive nature of the reception completely destroyed any such desire.

As he stood with his arms in a professional boxing attitude he heard other footsteps, crunching on the dry pine-needles.

"Look here," continued the speaker. "It's no use resisting. We are five to one. You've jolly well got to be brought before the governor. It may be all right for you or it may not. We've got our orders and we mean to carry them out. Now, then, are you coming quietly?"

"Evidently they take me for a poacher," thought Dacres. "Perhaps I am on the pater's preserves. It will be rather a joke if I am, and they run me in before my own governor."

"Very well, then," he said aloud, "I'll come quietly; only keep your hands off me."

"We will if you promise to give no trouble," replied the leader of the party in a mollified tone, "but orders are orders, you know."

"And this is an illegal arrest," added Dacres.

"Maybe," retorted the man coolly. "Anyway, it isn't our pigeon. You can argue that out with the governor. Quick march, you men."

Two of Dacres' captors faced about with military precision; two more formed up behind him, while the spokesman kept in the rear. In this order, and like an escort marching a deserter through the streets, the men set off through the wood.

Presently they emerged into a circular clearing, measuring roughly two hundred yards in diameter. The ground was covered with grass mown as short and as evenly as a cricket pitch, while at equal distances were five lofty wooden sheds, their fronts level with the surrounding forest and extending backwards into the dense masses of trees. In front of each of these buildings a red lamp was burning brightly.

"Can we get him across to the house before——?" whispered one of Dacres' captors.

"Yes, if we hurry. No, we can't, by Jupiter! There she is."

Overhead, its extremities hidden by the lofty tree tops, was a huge cylindrical object. In a moment the truth flashed across Dacres' mind. The mysterious airship was returning to its place of concealment, and he was the first outsider to stumble upon its secret hiding-place.

"Remember your promise," hissed the leader of the men. "This is a mess. I'll have something to answer for. Come on, you chaps."

Followed by three of his companions the man bounded across the open space. Dacres' remaining captor touched him on the shoulder.

"Get back," he ordered.

"I think not," replied Dacres coolly, although inwardly consumed with excitement. "I mean to stay where I am."

"You jolly well must," said the man threateningly.

"Thank you, but I'm not used to being ordered about," rejoined Dacres with a sternness that commanded respect. "I will take the risk. I am perfectly aware that this is the secret hiding-place of the airship that has been causing such a stir, and I mean to see my part of the business through."

"You'll be sorry for it, then," muttered the man. "We guessed as much. I won't give much for your chances when——"

"My friend, you were not asked to," retorted Dacres. "Remember, I'm giving no trouble, as I promised. Any trouble which arises depends solely upon yourself."

The man, powerful though he was, realized that single-handed he was no match for his athletic prisoner. The rest of his companions had to hasten to assist in the berthing of the airship. To appeal to them would be useless. Fortunately, however, the detained intruder made no attempt to escape.

Fascinated, Dacres watched the strange scene. The airship was almost touching the tree-tops. It was too dark to distinguish any details of her construction. She showed no lights, nor was there a suspended platform visible. He could hear men's voices conversing in subdued tones, although he was unable to distinguish what was being said.

Presently coils of ropes were thrown down and secured by the men who had recently been Dacres' assailants. There came a faint hissing sound like that of escaping air, and, as he watched, Dacres saw the midship section of the huge envelope drop slowly out of line. Held by the ropes it sank gently to the ground, and from it emerged two of the crew, who, assisted by one of the men in waiting guided it into one of the sheds that Dacres had previously noticed.

Another section followed, and then a third, both of which were placed under cover. Only the bow and stern portion now remained, till, smoothly as if they were gliding on a pair of rails, they came together without the faintest suspicion of a jar.

Even with the removal of the major portion of its bulk, the remaining sections of the airship were of considerable dimensions. The extremities almost touched the surrounding trees as the massive fabric was brought to earth.

Dacres could distinguish no signs of any propellers. The remaining remaining sections were very much like those already housed, except for the pointed bow and a long cylindrical projection on either side and parallel to the major axis of the main body.

Nor were there any elevating planes or rudders to be seen. The whole fabric seemed to be remarkably simple and business-like in design.

By this time the fore and aft sections of the airship had shed their crew, and nearly thirty men were holding on to the guide ropes. Again came the faint hissing sound and once more the giant envelope swung apart.

Within ten minutes from the lowering of the first rope the huge leviathan of the air was securely housed in the sheds erected for its reception. The red lights were switched off and darkness brooded over the open space.

"Now for it," thought Dacres, as several of the men crossed the green and approached the spot where he was standing.

"Here is the man, sir," announced the fellow who had directed the capture.

Without saying a word the person addressed flashed an electric torch full in the captive's face. It struck Dacres that this was taking rather a mean advantage, for no man can be at ease with a powerful glare temporarily blinding him.

"You have made a mistake, Callaghan," said the stranger at length, as he switched off the light. "This gentleman is not one of our undesirable friends. You ought to have exercised more discretion."

"I thought, sir——" began Callaghan.

"Never mind what you thought," interrupted the stranger peremptorily. "What is done is, unfortunately, hardly remediable at present. Excuse me," he continued addressing himself to Dacres, "but the zeal of my man rather outran his discretion. I think I am right in assuming that I am speaking to an Englishman and a gentleman?"

Dacres bowed stiffly. He was still unable to see what his questioner was like, but judging by his voice he was a comparatively young man.

"I think I can claim to be both," he replied. He was now in no hurry to furnish explanations. The situation appealed to him, and the more he could prolong his stay on the forbidden ground the better, he decided. Cranbury House was for the time being far remote from his mind.

"Allow me to show you the way to my modest dwelling," continued the unknown. "There is no need for you to hurry away."

Whether there was any significance in the latter sentence Dacres could not quite determine. He cared still less, for here, apparently, was a chance of learning more about the owner of this mysterious airship.

After giving various directions to his men, the stranger took hold of Dacres' arm in an easy yet dignified manner.

"Now," he said, "this way. It is rather a rough path."

"It couldn't be rougher than the path I traversed this evening," said Dacres, but the remark drew no response from his self-constituted companion.

The track seemed a perfect labyrinth. It wound in sharp curves between the thickly-clustered trees; sometimes ascending and sometimes dipping steeply into hollows crowded with dense undergrowth. The darkness under the foliage was intense, and without his companions guiding arm Dacres must have collided with the tree trunks more than once; but the stranger seemed to possess the instincts of a cat, for unhaltingly he pursued his way with the certainty of a man familiar with his haunts.

Presently the two men came upon a road that cut its way boldly through the wood. This the stranger followed for about a hundred yards, till he stopped in front of a gateway in a tall brick wall.

Had Dacres wished to escape there seemed no reason why he should not take to his heels, for the roadway was evidently a carriage-drive, and must lead somewhere. But without hesitation he complied with the unknown's unspoken request as, with a wave of the hand, he indicated that his guest should enter.

"Here we are," said the stranger apologetically as they reached the door of a long rambling house. "We have not the convenience of electric light here, so I must strike a match and light the lamp."

These words were spoken in such a matter-of-fact way that Dacres could hardly realize that the speaker was one and the same as the daring airman who had stirred not only the United Kingdom but the whole of the civilized world.

Unhesitatingly Dacres followed his host into a plain but substantially furnished room, and when the lamp was turned up the former was able to discern the features of his companion.

The owner of the aircraft was the shorter by two inches. He was sparely built, yet his breadth and depth of chest betokened more than average strength. His limbs were long in comparison to his body, while the long, tapering fingers indicated an artistic temperament. His face was oval, and of a deep tanned colour, his eyes were grey and evenly set beneath a pair of heavy brows. His hair was brown in hue and neatly parted in the centre, giving him at first sight a slightly effeminate appearance. Dacres guessed his age to be about twenty-five.

His dress consisted of a brown Norfolk suit and riding breeches, box gaiters and brown boots. Round his neck was a dark green muffler. His golf-cap and doeskin gloves he tossed upon the table.

"Now we can discuss this little matter, Mr.——?" He raised his eyebrows interrogatively.

"Dacres is my name—Basil Dacres."

"Ah! Any relation of Colonel Dacres, my nearest neighbour?" he asked. "His son? That's quite a coincidence. I owe the Colonel a duty call, but I have been so excessively busy of late that I really haven't had time. By the by, my name's Whittinghame—Vaughan Whittinghame. I don't suppose for one moment that you've heard of me before."

"I have reason to dispute that," said Dacres.

"Well, then, as an individual you might, but as far as the name is concerned——"

"I happened to meet a Gerald Whittinghame in town about five years ago," said Dacres.

"Oh—how?"

"During the College summer vacation. I met him at General Shaldon's house, when I was staying with my friend Dick Shaldon. Whittinghame was then a man of about twenty-two. He had just come home from somewhere in South America. He was a rattling good left-hand bowler, I remember."

"That's my brother," said Vaughan Whittinghame quietly. "By the by, are you a 'Varsity man?"

Dacres shook his head. He did not at present feel inclined to lay his cards upon the table.

"To get straight to the point," continued Whittinghame, looking his guest full in the face, "how came you in my grounds this evening?"

"That's easily explained," replied Dacres. "I was on my way to Cranbury House—I've never been there yet—and I lost my way. Nearly got stuck in a bog more than once. Eventually I saw a light, and crawling through a fence"—here he looked regretfully at his torn clothing "—I found myself confronted by some of your men."

"It is as well you thought better of resisting," said Whittinghame quietly. "They are tough customers and they know their orders. I may as well tell you, Mr. Dacres, that I am compelled to detain you here for a few days."

"Very well," replied Dacres with perfect sangfroid.

It was Whittinghame's turn to look astonished.

"There's nothing like making the best of a bad job," he remarked as soon as he had mastered his feelings. "'Pon my soul you are a cool customer. I fully expected that you would have made a dash for it, when we reached the drive."

"There was nothing to prevent me from so doing," rejoined Dacres.

His host smiled.

"There you're wrong You gave your word you'd come quietly, and I wanted to test you. If you had attempted to escape you would have been laid by the heels in a brace of shakes. You honestly assert that you had no idea that my little airship had her head-quarters here when you broke through the fence?"

"No, I did not; but honestly I'm glad I found out."

"I am afraid your knowledge will be of no service to anyone save yourself until there is no further need for concealment, Mr. Dacres. I trust that your enforced detention will in no wise inconvenience you?"

"Not in the least," declared Dacres fervently. "I have no immediate plans."

"But Colonel Dacres?"

"Does not expect me."

"Excuse me, but would you mind telling me what you are?" asked Whittinghame. "If you do not feel inclined I will not press the point; but I am interested to know."

"What I am and what I was a few weeks ago are two very different conditions," said Dacres without hesitation. "I was once a British naval officer. Now I am a—well, one of the unemployed, I suppose."

"Sorry, 'pon my word," said the other sympathetically. "Let's hear your story—but wait: you must be famished. I'll get something to eat and drink."

With that Whittinghame left the room, ostensibly to order refreshment. He also took the opportunity of consulting the latest quarterly copy of the official Navy List.

"By Jove! I'm in luck," soliloquized Dacres. "Whittinghame's quite a decent sort. I may even be able to get him to let me have a trip with him. Anyway, it's something to occupy my mind, and since the governor doesn't know I'm in England our somewhat delicate interview can wait."

He looked round the room. There was nothing to denote the aerial propensities of his host. Over the mantelpiece was a pair of huge horns covered with a metallic substance resembling silver. On the walls were oil-paintings of country scenes which looked suspiciously like Constable's work. In one corner was a gun rack containing several twelve bores and rook-rifles; a few fishing-rods and a pair of waders occupied another. A smoker's cabinet stood on the massive oak table. The room might well be the den of an ordinary country gentleman.

Presently Whittinghame returned followed by a serving-man bearing a loaded tray.

"That will be all to-night, Williamson," said his master. "You can lock up and go to bed."

"Very good, sir."

"H'm!" thought Dacres, looking at the black-garbed man. "You're a bit of a quick-change artist, I know." For he recognized the fellow by his voice: he was the one who had been left to keep an eye on the captive when the airship returned.

"Now, set to," continued Whittinghame genially. "Then, if you're not too tired, we can yarn over a pipe."

Until Dacres commenced eating he had no idea how hungry he really was. The food was plain but appetizing, the cold ham especially, and he did hearty justice to the repast.

"Fill your pipe—or do you prefer a cigar?" asked his host pointing to the cabinet. "Try that chair; you'll find it fairly comfortable. By Jove! your boots are wet. Let me offer you some slippers."

"Yes, I feel sorry for your carpet," said Dacres apologetically as he stooped to unfasten his bootlaces.

For a few moments both men smoked in silence. Dacres felt that his host was watching him narrowly, yet he imperturbably puffed at his pipe.

"Look here, Dacres, old man," Whittinghame suddenly exclaimed, "what do you say? Will you ship along with me?"

# CHAPTER VIII
# WHITTINGHAME'S NARRATIVE

VAUGHAN WHITTINGHAME had not made the proposal on the spur of the moment. He already knew the circumstances under which Dacres had left the Service; he was aware that the young man was "down on his luck;" he also had found out that he had volunteered for the Royal Flying Corps.

Dacres was a man who could be useful to him in more ways than one. He was used to command; he had a thorough knowledge of armaments, and what was more essential he was used to navigating a ship and could determine his position by either solar or stellar observation. The coolness with which he had followed Whittinghame into what might have proved to be a dangerous trap convinced the latter that the ex-naval officer was a man on whom he could entirely depend.

"Conditionally—yes," replied Dacres, whereat his companion was even better pleased. He was not a hot-headed man, he reflected.

"What stipulations do you lay down?" he asked.

"One only," answered Dacres. "That I am not called upon to assist in committing any acts prejudicial to the interests of King and country."

"That I can safely agree to. But before I give you any details as to the nature of my masterpiece I ought to explain the reasons why I have undertaken a definite mission."

"Quite so," assented Dacres.

"You are not too tired? Would you rather turn in?"

"Not in the least. Fire away; I am all attention."

"You've heard, of course, of Valderia?" began Whittinghame abruptly.

"Yes, that rotten tin-pot South American republic that owes its very existence to the jealousy between Chili and Peru."

"That's the average Englishman's idea of Valderia. You can take it from me that that republic is greatly under-rated. The inhabitants, of course, are of the usual South American type: the better class are Creoles and the lower class are a mixture of Spanish, Negro, and Indian blood. You may remember President Santobar? He was assassinated about two years ago—in March, 1917, to be correct. He was a most able ruler as far as order and progress went. Under his presidency Valderia became prosperous. Gold was found there, and also, although not generally known, platinum. That pair of horns, for example, is overlaid with thin platinum from the San Bonetta mines. At current London prices that metal is worth at least eight thousand pounds.

"My brother Gerald had a mining concession at San Bonetta, which is less than thirty miles from the capital, Naocuanha. He was held in great esteem by President Santobar, who often asked his advice on matters concerning internal transport.

"After a while prosperity turned the Valderians heads. They hankered after military and naval supremacy amongst the South American republics; and since Santobar was of a peace-loving disposition, there was a revolution and he was deposed. Four days after the revolution the president was murdered, and an octroon named Diego Zaypuru became dictator.

"A glance at the map will convince anyone who studies the situation of the favourable physical conditions of Valderia. It has a fair extent of coast-line, possessing several deep and land-locked harbours, while a semicircle of lofty snow-capped mountains, breaking off abruptly at the coast on the northern and southern frontiers, form a well-nigh impossible barrier between it and the neighbouring states.

"Although the climate on the littoral is unhealthy it is quite the reverse on the three great terraces that lie between the sea and the Sierras. Not only is there abundant mineral wealth, but two of these plateaux are extremely suitable for raising corn and rearing cattle.

"Had the Valderians contented themselves with their commercial advantages they might easily, within a few years, have become the most prosperous state of South America, but their aptitude for commerce was outweighed by their desire for the hollow glory of feats of arms.

"One of President Zaypuru's first acts was to purchase a Super-Dreadnought that had been constructed at Elswick to the order of another South American republic; four ocean-going destroyers were bought from the Vulkan Yard at Stettin, and six semi-obsolete submarines were obtained from the French government. These formed the nucleus of the Valderian navy, while docks were constructed at Zandovar, the port of Naocuanha.

"At the same time an army of fifteen thousand men was raised, armed with modern rifles, and drilled by ex-non-commissioned officers of the

German army. Of course, President Zaypuru must have an aerial fleet, and with this object in view he sent for my brother.

"Gerald and I had always been very keen on all matters appertaining to aviation and aeronautics. Before he left England for Valderia we prepared plans in duplicate of a veritable Dreadnought of the Air—in fact, they were the plans from which my airship was constructed.

"It was agreed that as soon as Gerald made sufficient money he was to return home, and both of us were to carry our long-cherished plan into effect.

"Somehow, Don Diego Zaypuru came to know of the existence of these plans, and sending for my brother offered him immense sums if he would superintend the construction of an aerial Dreadnought on the lines indicated in the design.

"Gerald had sufficient foresight to be prepared for a rupture. He had already sent home an amount more than enough to defray the cost of building and maintaining the projected airship. He was actually about to leave the country when the President's arbitrary summons was presented to him.

"There was no love lost between my brother and the murderer of ex-President Santobar. Gerald point-blank refused to have any truck with Zaypuru; and because of this refusal my brother was arrested and thrown into prison, where he still remains.

"It is with the primary object of rescuing my brother from the clutches of President Zaypuru that my Dreadnought of the Air—the 'Meteor,' as I have named her—has now become an airship in being."

"But surely," remarked Dacres, taking advantage of a pause in the narrative, "surely the British government would take up the matter, since the life and liberty of one of its subjects is at stake?"

"You have not yet heard all of the business, Dacres. In the first place, the lethargy of the British government is proverbial. The time has passed when England would strike and explain afterwards. Now a long-winded and generally futile course of diplomatic relations is the order of things. My own opinion is that sooner than release my brother President Zaypuru would put him out of the way, disclaim knowledge of the act, and if pressed offer apologies and a monetary indemnity.

"But there is another phase in the story of Valderia. You remember, of course, a renegade called von Harburg?"

"The fellow Captain Restronguet tracked and eventually discovered dead somewhere in Portuguese East Africa. Yes, and curiously enough I met Hythe in town this afternoon."

"In all probability you'll meet again ere long; but to carry on. Von Harburg's base was in the Dutch East Indies, and, when the 'Vorwartz' was captured, the renegade's Sumatran retreat was occupied by Dutch troops and the remainder of his gang dispersed.

"The fellow whom von Harburg had left in charge of his repairing-base was a Mexican named Reno Durango. He is a clever rascal, from all accounts, for on being pushed out of Sumatra—he managed, by the by, to get clear with a tidy sum of money—he volunteered his services to President Zaypuru as adviser to the submarine branch of the infant Valderian navy.

"The semi-obsolete French submarines were equipped with many of von Harburg's really dangerous means of offence; while Durango managed to build a large airship from the plans which had been found in Gerald's house. Of course that airship does not embody all my inventions, still it is not to be despised. I would class it as superior to any dirigible now owned by the Great Powers.

"But to get back to the submarine part of my narrative. Reno Durango's ambition was to acquire the secrets of the British 'M' class of submarines—those built to the same type as the renowned 'Aphrodite.' And with this object in view, I hear from a very trustworthy source—from one of my brother's native assistants and a real loyal man to his employer's interests—that Durango is on his way to England to attempt to steal the specifications from the British Admiralty."

Dacres smiled.

"Surely," he said incredulously, "the fellow doesn't know the utter impracticability of his scheme. His appearance, his accent, would betray him. Besides, see how jealously those secrets are guarded."

"Perhaps you do not know that this rascal was educated in England—at a public school near London. He speaks English perfectly. He is as wily as a fox, and since he has ample funds—well, there have been instances of high officials being known to sell state secrets for a considerable bribe, you know."

"The Admiralty ought to be warned."

"I agree with you. I mean to do so; but there is plenty of time. Durango is still on the high seas. Now you can follow my plan of operation. The 'Meteor' has now passed her final trials. In a few days I mean to offer my services to the Admiralty and to ask for a letter of marque to destroy the airship that the Valderian government has taken under its protection. In the course of this operation I hope to rescue my brother."

"But Valderia is a friendly state. The republic has been recognized by the Powers," objected Dacres.

"Admitted; but the airship is still the private property of Reno Durango, and since that rogue is branded as an outlaw—for the declaration by the Great Powers against Karl von Harburg and his gang has never been withdrawn—he is still the lawful prey to anyone who can lay him by the heels."

"When taking refuge in a neutral country?"

"We'll see about that later on," rejoined Whittinghame grimly. "Suppose we knock off now; you've quite enough to dream about to-night."

"One moment," said Dacres, a thought flashing across his mind. "What is this fellow Durango like?"

"I'll describe him—no, I won't. I've a photograph of him somewhere. I'll fetch it."

"Don't trouble."

"No trouble at all. Have another cigar."

Whittinghame hurried out of the room, soon to return with a cabinet photograph in his hand.

"Here you are," he announced. Dacres took the photograph. One glance was sufficient.

"It strikes me rather forcibly that you are mistaken about Reno Durango," he remarked. "He is not on the high seas: he's in England. I travelled from Waterloo in the same carriage with him this afternoon."

# CHAPTER IX
# THE FLIGHT TO LONDON

WHITTINGHAME sprang to his feet, the muscles of his face working with excitement.

"That's serious—decidedly serious," he exclaimed. "We can't afford to underrate that fellow. Look here, Dacres, there's a job for you the first thing to-morrow. Your formal introduction to the 'Meteor' can wait."

"Very good; what is it?"

"You told me you knew Commander Hythe; go up to town to-morrow morning and warn him. Don't give him the name of your informant, merely say that Reno Durango is in England, and was seen in a Portsmouth train. That will be enough—he knows the character of the rogue. If we can nab the fellow on English soil that will save a lot of complications, for otherwise it won't end only in a rupture between Great Britain and Valderia. Valderia is only a pawn in the game as far as Durango is concerned. If he succeeds in obtaining the secret specifications and getting back to Zandovar he will, of course, apply his knowledge to the improvement of the Valderian submarines."

Whittinghame paused to wipe his face. The perspiration was slowly trickling down his forehead. He was labouring under intense mental strain. Dacres made no remark. He allowed his companion to take his time. Presently Whittinghame resumed.

"No, Valderia hardly counts in Durango's estimation. He is playing for higher stakes. Once he has succeeded in working the specifications what is there to prevent him from negotiating with some of the Great Powers? Should the secret pass into the hands of our avowed rivals, in a very short space of time they would possess a fleet of submarines of the 'Aphrodite' type, and our present unquestionable superiority would become a thing of the past."

"I see the drift of your argument," said Dacres. "In a way, Durango indirectly gains you the sympathy of the government, and your plans to rescue your brother will be facilitated."

"You've hit the right nail on the head, Dacres," observed Whittinghame. "Now let's see about turning in. It is half-past one."

Dacres was shown into a small but well-furnished bedroom. He noticed, with considerable surprise, that his small handbag for immediate use was placed on a chair by the side of his bed.

"Hang it!" he exclaimed, as soon as he was left alone. "I clean forgot all about that bag. I must have dropped it when Callaghan and Co. tracked me in the wood. Well, I'm in luck—by Jove, I am! Here I am signed on for service in the mysterious airship—and already entrusted with an important mission. By the by, I wonder what that fellow Callaghan meant by saying, 'He's one of them!' I'll ask Whittinghame in the morning."

Even the momentous events of the day did not keep Dacres from sleeping. In less than ten minutes he was lost to the world in a sound, dreamless slumber.

At seven o'clock Dacres was awakened by a knock on the door, and in reply to his "All right" the man Williamson, who had acted as butler on the preceding evening, entered.

"Your bath is ready, sir," he announced, "and Mr. Whittinghame presents his compliments and would you care to make use of this suit of clothes until you can get your luggage?"

Half an hour later Dacres, rigged out in a suit of his host's—which fitted him fairly well considering the slight difference in height—entered the diningroom, where breakfast was already served.

"Hope it's not too early for you," remarked Whittinghame after the customary morning greetings, "but the matter is urgent. One of my monoplanes will be ready for you at half-past eight. With luck you ought to be at the Admiralty soon after ten—that, I believe, is the usual hour at which the officials arrive preparatory to duty. All being well you should be back by noon. If, for any unforeseen cause, you are detained you might communicate with me."

"How?" asked Dacres; "by telegraph?"

Whittinghame shook his head.

"Too risky, in spite of the vaunted 'official reticence' of the Postmaster-General. No, there is another way—by wireless."

"By wireless?" echoed Dacres.

"Why not? The monoplane is fitted with an installation of the latest type, and Callaghan, who is to pilot you, is a skilled operator. You give him any message and he will transmit it in code."

"There was one thing I meant to ask you," said Dacres, in the course of the meal. "Have any persons attempted to trespass upon your property?"

"Yes, several," was the reply. "At first I had a lot of trouble with poachers, until I effectually scared them off. After that I had to deal with one or two members of Durango's gang."

"Then, Durango knows of the existence of the 'Meteor' and of her place of concealment?"

"Oh, no. He knows through his spies that I have taken a house in the New Forest, but I do not for one moment think he suspects that the 'Meteor' is hidden here. To conceal an airship of over a thousand feet in length in a comparatively small plantation seems illogical. That is the beauty of the whole scheme. He knows right enough who the owner of the 'Meteor' is—he has good reasons for so doing—but it is to his own interests to keep that a secret."

"Why do his agents prowl about here?"

"Under his orders. I don't believe that they even know who or what he is, but money will work wonders. If these fellows had the opportunity I don't suppose they would hesitate to kidnap or even murder me; but I don't give them the chance. You may recollect that when you made your way through the fence a bell rang?"

"Now you mention it, I do."

"That is for the purpose of raising an alarm. Also two of the wires of that fence are electrically charged. By a thousand to one chances you missed them. Had you touched them you would have been held powerless till my men released you. Again, had you made a dash for liberty last night, you would have found the drive barred by a gate. Naturally you would either open it, or vault over the top. In either case you would have been stopped by the live wire and become as helpless as a fly stuck to a fly paper."

"Then, perhaps it's as well I didn't attempt it," remarked Dacres with a smile. "I'm jolly glad I didn't for other reasons. But what happens when tradesmen and *bona fide* visitors call?"

"They are few and far between," replied Whittinghame. "We make due allowance for them. Fifty yards beyond the electrically-charged gate is another gate. The lodge-keeper has to open that, and if he is certain that the callers are above suspicion, he switches off the current and telephones up to the house."

"Then, where is the generating station?"

"Underground. In fact, all the gas-producing plant and workshops are underground. I'll show them to you when you return. By a rare slice of luck the house is built on the site of an old royal hunting-lodge, and the extensive cellars still remain, although long forgotten until we discovered them by pure accident. Otherwise, had the workshops to be above ground, the risk of detection would be infinitely great. But it's close on the half-hour. Are you ready for your journey?"

On a lawn in front of the house was a two-seated monoplane, one of the standard "Velox" design that had recently become popular in Great Britain. Aviation as a means of making a journey had become quite common, and an aeroplane in flight attracted no more attention than a taxi in the Strand.

Callaghan, a burly, good-natured Irishman, was already in the pilot's seat. On his left was the wireless installation which, since the monoplane was automatically steered when once in the air, could be worked without detriment to Callaghan's other duties. The passenger's seat, in the rear and slightly higher than the pilot's, was protected from the wind and rain by an enclosed structure resembling the body of the now defunct hansom-cab. To view the country beneath him the passenger could make use of the two sponson-like windows on either side, through which the traveller, leaning sideways, could see immediately below.

There was no necessity for half a dozen men to hang on to the monoplane's tail. As soon as Dacres had taken his seat, Callaghan thrust forward a short lever and the propeller began to revolve. The passenger was made aware that the flight had begun by reason of his head coming into contact with the padded back of the cab, and by a sinking sensation in the region of his waist like the experience when being suddenly jerked up in a lift.

Beyond that there was nothing to give an impression of flight. The glass protected him from the wind and silenced the buzz of the powerful rotary motor, and it was not until Dacres looked over the side and saw the moorland and forest slipping away beneath him that he realized that he was being borne through the air at one hundred and twenty miles an hour.

Even at that terrific speed the light westerly wind caused an appreciable drift. In eight minutes the monoplane was over and slightly to the west of Southampton. Here Callaghan altered the course to counteract the cross air-current, and three minutes later Winchester, nestling between the downs, glided underneath like a panoramic effect. Then Alton and Aldershot were left behind in quick succession, and forty minutes after leaving the ground Dacres discerned the Thames looking like a silvery thread amidst the meadows and woods of Middlesex and Surrey.

With the rapid progress and popularity of aviation many of the restrictions that had been placed upon the pioneers of this branch of aeronautics had been abolished. It was no longer forbidden to fly over towns, and the metropolis was no exception. In fact, a portion of Hyde Park had, with part of other open spaces, been allotted to the use of airmen.

It was to the Hyde Park alighting station that Callaghan steered. Had he been a stranger to London he could easily have found his way by reason of hundreds of aeroplanes making for or returning from the most central aviation ground in the metropolis.

Speed was reduced to a safe forty miles an hour, which, after the rapid rush, seemed to Dacres more like a painful crawl in a motor-bus through Cheapside.

Almost immediately beneath them was Hyde Park. The monoplane was circling now in company with ten more, spread out at regular intervals like a flock of wood-pigeons in flight.

Presently Callaghan's practised eye caught sight of the signal he was waiting for: a huge red and white disk rotated till its face was visible from above. It was to signify that the ground was clear to receive the next batch of waiting 'planes. Fascinated, Dacres watched the sward apparently rising to meet him. The volplane was so steep that it seemed that nothing could prevent the monoplane from being dashed to bits upon the earth. So acute was the angle that he had to plant his feet firmly against the front of the cab to prevent himself from slipping from his seat.

Suddenly the whole fabric tilted upwards, then with a barely perceptible jar and a strange sensation in the back of his neck, Dacres found himself on terra firma in the heart of the metropolis.

"We would have done it in forty-eight minutes, sir, if it hadn't been for that block," remarked Callaghan apologetically, as he opened the door. "You'll find me over by that pylon, sir. We are not allowed to wait here."

"Very good," replied Dacres, and feeling rather stiff in his lower limbs, hurried to the exit, called a taxi, and was soon bowling along towards Whitehall.

"I wish to see Commander Hythe," he announced to the petty-officer messenger on duty at the Admiralty.

The man consulted a register.

"I'm sorry, sir," he replied, "but Commander Hythe is not in the building. Mr. Wells is doing duty for him. Would you wish to see Mr. Wells sir?"

"I don't know the man," thought Dacres, "and I don't suppose he'll know me. In any case, he can tell me where Hythe is with more certainty than the messenger. Very well," he said. "I'll see Mr. Wells."

Much to his disgust Dacres had to cool his heels in a waiting-room for full twenty minutes until the official was at liberty to receive him.

Commander Hythe was on duty at Portsmouth, Dacres was informed. It was quite uncertain when he would return: it might be a matter of a few hours or it might be a couple of days.

"We've got to run down to Portsmouth, Callaghan," announced Dacres as he rejoined the monoplane. "Send a message to Mr. Whittinghame and explain that Commander Hythe is away on duty and that I am going to get in touch with him."

"Very good, sir. I'll send off a wireless when we are clear of this place. I'll land you on the Officers' Recreation Ground."

"That will do nicely," agreed Dacres as he took his seat.

Thirty-nine minutes after leaving Hyde Park the monoplane shaved past the tower of Portsmouth Town Hall and alighted at the spot the Irishman had suggested.

From a police inspector at the Dockyard gate Dacres elicited the information that Commander Hythe was engaged with the Commander-in-Chief, and that it was very doubtful whether he could be seen.

"But I must see him," declared Dacres peremptorily, "the Commander-in-Chief notwithstanding. This is official and not private business. Would you mind letting me have paper and envelope? I'll write a note and one of your men can take it to Commander Hythe."

Five minutes later a telephone message was received at the gate to the effect that Commander Hythe would receive Mr. Dacres at once.

"Hulloa, old man!" exclaimed the youthful commander as Dacres was shown into the office.

"You've come at a very busy time. I can give you five minutes only. What can I do for you?"

Hythe's usually cheerful face looked drawn and haggard. It seemed as if he had aged ten years since yesterday, when Dacres met him in Northumberland Avenue.

"I've been sent to warn you that the plans of the 'M' class of submarines are in danger."

"To warn me," echoed Hythe grimly. "My dear fellow, you're too late. The plans and specifications were stolen from the manager's confidential record room between six last evening and this morning. That's why I'm here."

# CHAPTER X
# THE STOLEN PLANS

"RENO DURANGO is the culprit," said Dacres. "If you lay him by the heels the secret will be safe."

"But the fellow isn't in England," objected Hythe.

"Perhaps not," agreed Dacres. "But he was last night. I saw him in the train."

"Then why on earth didn't you report the matter?"

"Simply because I had then no idea who or what he was. I know now."

"Come and see the Admiral," said the Commander, taking his friend by the arm.

"One minute. Look here, old man, I'm in a bit of a fix. I'm not a free agent in the matter. Besides——"

"Can't be helped. This is a matter of national importance."

"Very well, then; only don't give the show away that I once held his Majesty's commission."

Dacres found himself in the company of the Commander-in-Chief, the Admiral Superintendent of the Dockyard, two naval secretaries, the Superintendent of Police, and two high officials from Scotland Yard.

To these he related the circumstances under which he had met the Mexican in the train, and that he had come purposely to warn his friend, Commander Hythe, that the plans of the submarines were in danger.

"Did you come here on your own initiative, sir?" asked one of the Scotland Yard men.

"No," replied Dacres. "I was acting under instructions."

"Whose, might I ask?"

This was an awkward question. Dacres hesitated.

"One who has good reason to wish to see Durango arrested," he replied guardedly. "I'm not at liberty at present to divulge his name."

"But suppose we insist?" asked the Commander-in-Chief bluntly.

"No useful purpose would result, sir," said Dacres boldly. "In fact, the chances of recovering the papers would be considerably retarded. I will return at once to my principal and inform him of the loss of the documents. No doubt he will act promptly and unreservedly in conjunction with you. Meanwhile, I would suggest that you ascertain what ships left Southampton between six o'clock yesterday and the present time. By giving a description of this Señor Durango you will possibly be able to find out whether he has left the country."

"That we propose to do," said one of the Scotland Yard officials with owl-like wisdom. As a matter of fact, such an idea had not previously entered his head.

"Very well, gentlemen," said Dacres firmly, "I will now take my leave. I can assure you that at present I can be of no further use to you. No doubt my principal will communicate with you in due course."

Dacres certainly held the whip hand. He was no longer a naval officer subject to the King's Regulations; there was not the faintest excuse for arresting him, while his vague hint as to what might happen if he were detained could not be ignored.

Hythe followed him into the ante-room.

"I say, old man," he exclaimed, "what sort of enterprise have you embarked upon?"

"Something that will never cause me to regret leaving the Service," replied Dacres. "You'll be surprised when you are told, but I cannot say any more about it at present. Cheer up, old fellow! We'll get those plans before there's any serious damage done."

"Stop at Southampton, Callaghan," ordered Dacres, as calmly as if he were giving directions to a taxi-driver. "Somewhere as close to the shipping offices as you can."

The pilot was "all out" to break records, and within eight minutes of the time of rising from the ground he alighted at Southampton—a distance of sixteen miles as the crow flies.

Dacre's instincts prompted him first to visit the offices of a Brazilian steamship company. Fortune favoured him, for he made the discovery that a man answering to his description of Señor Durango had booked a passage on board the S.S "Maranhao." The ship had cleared Southampton Docks at 10 a.m.

"She's well down Channel by this time," soliloquised Dacres. "The rogue is safe for the time being, for the authorities dare not arrest him on a vessel flying Brazilian colours."

"What is the speed of the 'Maranhao'?" he asked of the English clerk in the firm's office.

"She's a fairly slow boat, sir," replied the man apologetically. "You see, she's running a relief trip, because the 'Alagoas' has broken her mainshaft. Twelve knots would be her average."

Dacres thanked him for the information and inquired when the "Maranhao" was likely to arrive at her destination—Pernambuco.

The man was unable to hazard an opinion, but in answer to further inquiries said that the distance from Southampton to Pernambuco was 3920 seamiles.

Allowing for a stop at Cape Verde Islands, Dacres came to the conclusion that the "Maranhao" would take at least thirteen and a half days to reach Pernambuco. This was reassuring, and having thanked the clerk for the trouble he had taken, he rejoined Callaghan and gave instructions to be whirled back to Whittinghame's retreat.

"We're too late," he announced as Vaughan Whittinghame came from the house to meet him. "Durango has contrived to get hold of the plans."

"Knowing the man I am not surprised," replied the owner of the "Meteor" calmly. "Have they collared him?"

"No; he's on the high seas. In another thirteen or fourteen days he'll land at Pernambuco—if he doesn't double on his tracks and disembark at Las Palmas or Cape Verde."

"He won't," said Whittinghame. "He'll get across to Naocuanha as sharp as he can possibly manage it. We'll try to nab him when he enters Valderian territory. It would be too risky to do so before."

As briefly as he could Dacres related the incidents of his aerial journey and his interview with the authorities at Portsmouth.

"I told them that in the interests of the Empire you would doubtless communicate with them direct," he added.

"I will," assented Whittinghame.

"When?" asked Dacres eagerly.

"Plenty of time. Let them have a chance to indulge in a mild panic. We will pay them an official visit at the end of the week—say on Saturday."

"We?" repeated Dacres.

"Yes—in the 'Meteor' There are times when dramatic moments are desirable, and this is one of them. I'll write to the Commander-in-Chief and inform him that the airship that has caused so much stir in official circles will appear at Portsmouth at 10 a.m. on the 9th instant, and that her commander will, in support of his deputy's assurances, communicate an important announcement to the representatives of My Lords Commissioners of the Admiralty—sounds imposing, eh? Well, let's have lunch, and then I'll introduce you to the 'Meteor.'"

During the meal Whittinghame studiously avoided talking "shop." He discussed topics of ordinary interest with consummate ease, his knowledge of all branches of sport being especially profound. He had all the noteworthy records of athletics at his fingers' ends, and had the happy knack of imparting his knowledge without conveying the idea that he was trying to be pedantic.

"Before we go outside," he said, after lunch was over, "suppose we have a look at the workshops?"

"I should be delighted," assented his guest.

"This is my private entrance," announced Whittinghame, touching an almost invisible projection on the wall and causing a secret panel to open. "At one time it was a boast that an Englishman's house was his castle, but that is no longer true. Since I cannot prevent the minions of the Government from entering my house and taking an immense amount of data for some useless purpose, I must protect my own interests by this means. I discovered the secret panel after the under-ground cellars had been opened up from outside. Evidently it was a 'Priest's hole,' or refuge in troublous times. This is a seventeenth century house built over cellars of a much older date. Mind the steps; they are a lot worn in places."

At the lowermost step Whittinghame stopped and unlocked a baize-covered door. A faint buzz greeted Dacre's ears.

"The doors are almost sound-proof," continued his guide. "Wait while I switch on a light."

The brilliant glow from an electric lamp revealed the fact that they were standing in a long narrow passage, with a door at the far end similar to the one that had just been opened.

"You wonder why I use lamps in a house when there is electric lighting in the cellars?" asked Whittinghame, noting the look of surprise on his companion's face. "It's easy to explain. If I had electric fittings installed in the house they would cause comment. By retaining the old-fashioned system of lighting it helps to keep up the deception that this is a remote country house and the home of a simple country gentleman of limited means. This is the retort room," he added, opening the second sound-proof door.

The place reeked of gas. Dacres felt somewhat apprehensive, for there were no visible means of ventilation.

"Quite harmless," said Whittinghame reassuringly. "We use electricity for producing the gas ultra-hydrogen we term it. I had the secret from a German scientist who was unable to sell his priceless formula in his own country. He was regarded as a lunatic, poor fellow. This ultra-hydrogen has, under equal conditions of density and capacity, three times the lifting-power of ordinary hydrogen. Nor is that all: it is absolutely non-inflammable."

"By Jove!" ejaculated Dacres, too surprised to say anything else.

"Yes," continued his companion. "You may well express astonishment. Just think: nine-tenths of the dangers to which an airship is exposed are by this stupendous discovery. Thanks to the practical non-porosity of the ballonettes of the 'Meteor' we have not yet found it necessary to recharge them. We are, however, laying in a reserve supply of ultra-hydrogen and storing it under pressure in cast-steel cylinders."

"Then, what happens when you want to descend?" asked Dacres. "Has not the gas to be released?"

"No, otherwise we should have to continually rely upon our reserve of ultra-hydrogen. It is six weeks since the 'Meteor' made her first flight, by the by."

"Then, how do you manage to husband the supply of gas in the ballonettes?"

"There are no less than a hundred of these sub-divisions. Each consists of two skins, the outer one of rigid aluminium, the inner of flexible non-porous fabric. When we wish to descend—apart from the action of the horizontal planes—the ultra-hydrogen is exhausted from the required number of ballonettes and forced under great pressure into steel cylinders similar to those you see here. Air at the normal atmospheric pressure is then introduced into the ballonettes until the weight of the airship is slightly heavier than air.

"These men you see working here also form part of the crew of the 'Meteor.' In due course I shall muster them and give them proper notice of your appointment as navigating officer to the vessel. I might mention, however, that every one of them has seen service in the Royal Navy. They are all trained men, who, under the rotten short service system, have been cast aside by the Admiralty when they might be of the best possible use."

"Aren't you afraid that some of them might betray your secret?"

Whittinghame laughed.

"No," he replied emphatically, "I am not. Many people imagine that nowadays there is not such a thing as honour. Government officials wonder why important secrets leak out. They threaten their employees with dire pains and penalties, instead of paying them decent wages and appealing to their sense of honour. I know that for a fact. My experience teaches me that so long as you pick your men carefully in the first instance, pay them adequately, and treat them considerately, they'll stick to you through thick and thin with unswerving loyalty. Now let us visit the workshops. There is not much to be seen, for all the constructive work is now completed, but you will be able to form some idea of how an airship of over one thousand feet in length was constructed in secret."

The next cellar was about fifty feet in length and twenty-five in breadth, and practically bare.

"This is our mould loft," explained Whittinghame. "Through dire necessity we were compelled to make the work in comparatively small sections. Each subdivision was assembled here before taken into the open air. I might add that the whole work of finally assembling the parts was done without the use of a hammer. Over thirty thousand bolts and nuts were used in setting up the completed craft. In the next room are the lathes and fitters' benches; beyond that are the electric rolls for making the aluminium sheets, and the hydraulic presses for moulding them into shape. But I do not think we need waste time there; suppose we devote our attention to an inspection of the 'Meteor'?"

# CHAPTER XI
# THE "METEOR"

WHITTINGHAME conducted his companion to the open air by a different route from that by which they had gained the subterranean workshops. It was a fairly broad way, of quite recent construction, and sloping gently for quite eighty yards and finishing, up by a steep incline.

Dacres found himself in the midst of a thick wood, an avenue the width of the passage terminating at the rear of a large shed. But instead of entering the building, Whittinghame broke away to the left by a narrow footpath, which by a circuitous route gained the open space where Dacres had obtained his first glimpse of the returning airship.

At first he was puzzled. There was the circular clearing with its closely-mown grass, but no signs of the five airship-sheds.

Pulling out a whistle Whittinghame gave two sharp blasts. This signal was almost immediately followed by the appearance of three men clad in dungaree suits.

"Open up No I. shed, Parsons," ordered the "Meteor's" owner, then turning to his companion he observed: "That's my chief engineer. He is absolutely part and parcel of the 'Meteor's' machinery. What he doesn't know about motors is hardly worth troubling about. Now watch."

The engineer and his two assistants disappeared behind a clump of trees. Then, even as Dacres looked, a number of lofty pines moved bodily sideways with regimental precision, disclosing the end of one of the sheds that he had seen overnight.

"We have to disguise our sheds as much as possible," said Whittinghame. "Those trees are dummies set in a base that travels on wheels on a pair of rails. They would defy detection unless anyone were warned as to their nature. The roof too, is covered with artificial tree-tops. An airman passing overhead would have no idea that there were five sheds each two hundred and forty feet in length, forty-five feet in height and forty in breadth hidden in this comparatively small wood. Now, this is the bow section of the 'Meteor.' A noble craft, I think you'll admit."

As soon as his eyes grew accustomed to the semi-gloom Dacres saw that the pointed bow was facing him, while on either side of the main fabric was a smaller cylinder open at each end.

"Those contain the propellers," explained his guide. "The airship has four cylinders with two propellers in each. The foremost propeller works at 1,200 revolutions per minute, and the backdraught is taken up by the rear propeller, which runs at twice that speed. The cylinders form a partial silencer, so that, except through an arc of about eleven degrees, its centre parallel to the major axis of the airship, the whirr of the blades is practically inaudible when at a height of two hundred or more feet above the ground. Do you notice those plates of metal lying against the outer envelope?"

"One above and one underneath the propeller covering?"

"Yes, those are the elevating planes and rudders, 'housed' for the time being to allow the craft to enter her shed. The motors are in the centre of the body, the propeller shafting being chain-driven." "What do you use—petrol?" asked Dacres.

Whittinghame shook his head.

"Too dangerous," he replied. "We use cordite."

"Eh?" ejaculated Dacres incredulously.

"Yes, cordite: the ideal fuel for internal combustion engines. You must be perfectly aware of the properties of cordite. In the open air and not under pressure it burns slowly; but under pressure its explosive capabilities are enormous. Our motors are actuated by introducing small charges of cordite into the cylinders and exploding them by electricity. The principle is similar to that of a maxim gun, only of course we don't use cartridges on a belt. The cylinder chamber itself acts as a cartridge case. Suppose we go aboard?"

Whittinghame indicated a wire rope-ladder running from a doorway about twenty feet from the ground.

"The whole of the underbody of the outer envelope is watertight," he remarked. "The 'Meteor' can float on the sea if necessary. Of course there are observation scuttles and bomb-dropping ports, but these can be hermetically sealed."

Agilely Dacres swarmed up the swinging ladder and passed through the doorway. He found himself in a room twenty feet square, and ten in height, with circular ports on one side and doors on the transverse bulkheads. In the floor were two rectangular openings furnished with plate-glass, but for the time being shuttered on the outside by closely-fitting slides.

"This is our forward bomb-dropping compartment," continued Whittinghame as he regained his companion. "The devices for that purpose are behind that partition. All the ammunition is stored in the 'midship or No. 3 section and transported along these rails as required. We also keep stores here, the idea being that should the various sections of the airship have to part company each will be self-supporting in a double sense.

"The next compartment for'ard contains the mechanism for actuating the vertical rudders. Above that are the motor-rooms, while right for'ard are the twin navigation-rooms. We'll have a look at the motor-rooms first of all. By the by, those are the cylinders for storing the ultra-hydrogen under pressure. At the present moment the dead weight of this section is less than fifty pounds."

"But we weigh more than that," observed Dacres.

"Quite so; but the buoyancy is automatically maintained. As you crossed the threshold of the doorway you stepped upon a plate resembling the floor of aweigh-bridge. At once a sufficient quantity of ultra-hydrogen is introduced into the ballonettes to counteract your weight, and, in fact, the weight of any person or article brought on board."

"I'm afraid I'm curious," said Dacres, "but what will happen when we go 'ashore'? Will the volume of the gas in the ballonettes be correspondingly reduced?"

"Yes, but not wholly automatically. You will have to record your weight on an indicator, and the adjustment then takes place. That dial you see on the bulkhead gives the total lifting power of the whole of the ballonettes. That instrument to the left makes the necessary compensating adjustments to the airship according to the temperature, altitude, and amount of moisture in the air."

In the starboard engine-room Dacres noticed that each of the two motors had four cylinders of comparatively small bore considering the horsepower developed.

"These are not air-cooled?" he asked pointing to the motors.

"No, water-cooled. This system serves a dual purpose, for the water circulates throughout all the cabins of the section, and if necessary through Nos. 2 and 3 section as well, thus affording a warmth that is appreciated when we are flying at a great altitude. Ten to twelve thousand feet is our favourite height, for then we can command a field of vision—provided the atmosphere is clear—of anything up to one hundred and twenty miles. Now for the upper navigation-room—your future post."

This compartment was situated under the commencement of the tapering portion of the envelope, its roof and walls being formed by the rounded surface of the outer skin. Here there were several observation panes, so that a fairly extensive view could be obtained. It was impossible, however, to see immediately below, and on this account the necessity of a second navigation-room was apparent.

It reminded Dacres strongly of the conning-tower of a battleship, except that the scuttles were much larger than the slits in the armoured walls of the latter. A standard compass, chart-table, gauges, indicator, voice-tubes, and telephones left very little space unoccupied.

Professional habit prompted Dacres to unfasten a sextant case and critically examine the instrument. "Can't say I altogether like this chap," he observed bluntly. "If you don't mind I'll use my own sextant. It's with the rest of my luggage at Fenchurch Street Station."

"We'll send for it, by all means," said Whittinghame. "I frankly admit that I'm not much use at fixing positions, and one sextant is very much like another to me. The difficulty of getting hold of a competent navigator worried me considerably until you trespassed upon my property. I'm jolly glad you did."

"And so am I," said Dacres cordially.

"Now you've seen practically everything of importance in the foremost section," continued his companion. "The rest of the available space is taken up with ballonettes. No. 2 section is devoted to crew space, stores, and of course more ballonettes. No. 3 contains the wireless-room, the ammunition and reserve of cordite for propelling purposes, in No. 4 the officers are berthed, while the aftermost, or No. 5, is practically identical with No. 1."

"But how are the various divisions kept in position?" asked Dacres.

"By means of double-cam action bolts. The 'Meteor' is of a semi-rigid type. Her great length would be a positive danger if she were otherwise, while she would be most awkward to manoeuvre. As it is we can turn her in a radius equal to twice her length. In violent air-currents she 'whips' considerably; it's a weird experience until you get accustomed to it, but therein lies another proof of safety. It is analogous to the case of a tall chimney that sways in a gale. If it didn't it would snap like a carrot.

"The upper surface of the envelope is flattened, and we have a promenade deck exactly one thousand feet in length. Of course it is only available when we are running at a greatly reduced speed or are brought up. At a very high rate of speed you would be unable to keep your feet and run a great risk of having the air forced out of your lungs."

"A most marvellous craft!" exclaimed Dacres enthusiastically. "How I shall enjoy a cruise in her!"

"I hope you will," added Whittinghame gravely.

"Are you making another trip before you take her to Portsmouth?"

"I think not. I do not believe in purposeless flights. Her final trials have been successfully passed, and now nothing remains to be done until she is required to perform some task for the well-being of the British nation."

As the two men prepared to descend the ladder Whittinghame suddenly remarked:—

"You'll meet the rest of the officers to-night, Dacres. Hambrough, our doctor, turns up at five. You'll like him, I think. He's a real good sort, and as keen as anything on the voyage. I don't suppose he'll have much to do, for these high altitudes are so beastly healthy; but there's no telling. He hasn't seen the 'Meteor' yet; in fact, he's only just resigned his post as medical officer to a North of England hospital. Setchell, who will be next in seniority to you, is at present on leave. We dropped him near his home at Plymouth about three weeks ago. He had urgent domestic affairs to demand his attention, and our wireless man here got in touch with us as we were passing over the Pennines. We made a rattling good run down to Plymouth—rattling good—but cut it rather fine in getting back here. I was almost afraid that we should be spotted, but luckily we descended without being detected. Setchell will also be here at about the same time. Callaghan will pick the pair of them up at Holmsley Station. By Jove! It's close on five already. How time flies when you're busy. We had better get back to the house."

# CHAPTER XII
# THE "METEOR'S" DEBUT

SETCHELL and Dr. Hambrough arrived before Whittinghame and his companion had completed their preparations for dinner, and as soon as the formal introductions were gone through, the thin ice of reserve quickly vanished.

Dacres instinctively felt that he would have true comrades on his first commission in the Dreadnought of the Air.

The two new arrivals were quite different in temperament. Setchell was vivacious—even boisterous at times; while the doctor was grave and dignified—at first one might have thought he was taciturn.

They were both fairly young men—under thirty—and as keen on their work as Whittinghame could possibly desire.

"We're now practically ready to put the 'Meteor' into full commission," observed Whittinghame. "All her stores are on board. Dacres has to have his kit brought from London, and there is about another half-day's work to complete the charging of the reserve cylinders. So we'll have 'divisions' to-morrow, and put the men into their proper watches. You brought those rifles along with you all right, Setchell?"

"Rather. There are two cases of them at Holmsley Station, and four boxes of ammunition. With the eight thousand rounds we already have—I suppose you haven't expended any yet, sir—that ought to be ample."

"Very good," assented the skipper. "We'll send a trolley for them early to-morrow morning. By the by, how did you get on after we dropped you at Yealmpton?"

Setchell laughed.

"You might have been more discriminating, sir, but I suppose we must make allowances for the fact that it was pitch-dark and we could show no light. As a matter of fact I found myself in a piggery. When I managed to struggle out of that and over a very aggressive fence I struck a fowl-run. Did you hear the noise those creatures made?"

"No, we were too far off by that time," replied Whittinghame.

"At any rate," continued the third officer, "the farmer turned out with a gun. I had to pitch up some sort of yarn, so I told him I was a tourist who had lost his way. The old chap promptly harnessed a pony and drove me to the outskirts of Plymouth."

"Talking of that," remarked Dacres, "the shepherd of Canterbury said the section of the airship that dropped to the ground was about the size of a haystack."

"So it was," replied Whittinghame. "When we wish to make hurried descents we can detach a subdivision of No. 3 section. It is also handy for landing in fairly confined spaces, where the length of a complete section might be too great for safety. I'll show you that arrangement to-morrow; but what do you say to a game of billiards, gentlemen? It may be our last opportunity for a considerable time, for, with all her wonderful mechanism, I cannot guarantee a level bed on board the 'Meteor.'"

This proposal was received with acclamation, and the four men adjourned to the billiard-room, where they amused themselves till the clock struck eleven and warned them that it was time to retire to rest.

At ten on the following morning all hands formed up on the open space between the sheds. There were thirty-two men, exclusive of the four officers, and a fine athletic set they made, rigged out in neat yet serviceable uniforms.

Whittinghame, as captain, headed the starboard watch, with the doctor as his assistant for executive duties in the after-part of the ship; for Hambrough was not content to act simply as surgeon to the ship's company. Williamson was chosen as first quartermaster of the watch, the rest of the division consisting of ten "deck hands" and five mechanics for engine-room duties.

Dacres had charge of the port watch, Setchell being responsible for the after-guard during the "watch on deck". The stalwart Irishman, Callaghan, was appointed quartermaster, and the rest of the crew consisted of an equal number of hands to that of the captain's watch.

The men were then served out with small-arms, the rifles being up-to-date automatic weapons firing twenty-two cartridges and having a range and velocity equal to the latest service rifles. Bayonets were also issued, and since the crew had had a thorough training whilst they were serving in the Royal Navy they were now able to pick up their drill without much difficulty.

Under Dacres' orders they were exercised for nearly an hour. The ex-sub-lieutenant had reason to be very well satisfied with them, and expressed his opinion to Whittinghame that if necessary they could give a very good account of themselves. As for the men, they recognized that they had an officer over them who knew his work, and they respected him accordingly.

At length the eventful Saturday came round, and just after eight o'clock the fore-section of the airship was taken out of its shed and, to use Dacres' expression, "sent aloft."

The bow portion, with its complement of nine men, was the first to leave the ground, anchoring at a height of seventy-four feet from the surface—the "ground-tackle" consisting of a bridle with a single loop running through a huge pulley fixed in the earth, and back to the bow division of the "Meteor."

No. 2 section was sent up, and by means of a wire hawser hauled into position, so that the cam-action could come into play. Only three and a half minutes elapsed between the time of its leaving the ground and of its being united to the bow-section.

Divisions 3 and 4 were "launched" and joined up in a similar fashion, "and then there was one," as the nursery rhyme goes.

Dacres found himself with six men to man the aftermost section of the airship. He had already "got the hang of it," although he could not quite see how any of the crew could be left behind to guide the huge fabric on its ascent to unite to the still greater bulk that floated serenely above the tree-tops, her propellers churning slowly ahead to counteract the faint breeze that blew from the south-west.

"Give the word for the men to get aboard, sir," said Callaghan, who, being an ex-gunner's mate, knew how to prompt judiciously young officers who were not quite up to their work.

Dacres complied. He was glad of his quarter-master's assistance, although fully determined to master his part of the routine as soon as possible.

When the last man swarmed up the rope-ladder Dacres followed, and took up his station at the open doorway in the for'ard bulkhead.

"All ready, sir?" asked Callaghan.

"All ready," echoed the newly appointed officer.

"Here's the lever for charging the ballonettes, sir," continued the quartermaster. "Turn the indicator to eighty, sir. That will be enough to raise us."

Gently and almost imperceptibly the after-section rose clear of the ground, guided by a light wire rope joining it to the already coupled-up portions of the airship. With a rhythmic purr the windlass, worked by a supplementary belt from one of the motors, hauled in the slack till the "Meteor" was complete and ready for flight.

So nice was the adjustment of the various sections that connexion with the telephones and electric telegraphs was made automatically by the contact of insulated bushes in corresponding position to the exterior bulkheads.

From the navigation-room for'ard Whittinghame asked if all were ready, and received a confirmative reply from the after-end of the ship. As far as Dacres was concerned he was now at liberty to "stand easy," for it was his watch below, and Setchell had come aft to take charge.

"Captain says he would like to see you for'ard," announced the third officer. "Hold on till she gathers way, old man."

Warning bells tinkled in various parts of the giant airship. Instantly every man grasped some object to prevent himself from being thrown across the floor. Simultaneously the eight propellers began to revolve.

For quite half a minute Dacres felt as if he were seized by an invisible arm round his waist and was being forced backwards. Then the tension ceased as the inertia was overcome, he was part and parcel of a mass flying through the air at more than twice the speed of an express train.

Dacres glanced at his watch—it was twenty-five minutes past nine—then, lurching along the alley-way, for the "Meteor" was trembling and swaying as she cleft the air, he made his way for'ard.

He found Whittinghame standing in front of one of the observation scuttles in the lower navigation room. Williamson was at the wheel controlling the vertical rudders, while another man had his eye upon the indicators of the horizontal planes.

"Look!" exclaimed the captain, pointing downwards.

Dacres did so. Nine thousand feet beneath him stretched a ribbon-like expanse of water like a silver-streak between dense woodland on one hand and green fields on the other. Away on the starboard bow this streak merged into a wide stretch of sea, backed by hills that were dwarfed to the size of a mere series of mounds.

"By Jove! We're passing Southampton Water," ejaculated Dacres. He again glanced at his watch. It had taken him three and a half minutes to traverse the length of the "Meteor," and in that space of time the airship had travelled eleven miles.

"Top speed now," announced Whittinghame. "We're doing one hundred and ninety. We'll have to slacken down now; we're nearly there."

As he spoke the Captain rang down for half speed. The order being simultaneously received by both engine-rooms, resulted in a gradual slowing down till the mud-flats of Portsmouth Harbour hove in sight. Even then the "Meteor" overhauled a naval seaplane as quickly as an express runs past a "suburban" crawling into Clapham Junction.

"Still sou'west," remarked Whittinghame pointing to the smoke that was pouring out of a tall chimney between Fareham and Gosport. "We'll bring her head to wind in any case."

Down swooped the "Meteor" till she was less than three hundred feet from the ground. She was now following the main road to Gosport. On her left could be discerned the battleships and cruisers in the harbour, their decks and riggings black with men, while hundreds of craft of various sizes, crowded with spectators, literally swarmed on the tidal waters between the Dockyard and the western shore.

Swooping past the new semaphore tower, and skimming above the lofty chimneys of the electric light station, the "Meteor" shaped a course towards the Town Hall clock tower. So quickly did she turn that it seemed as if a straight line between the bow and stern would cut the masonry of the tower. Looking aft the appearance of the twelve hundred feet of airship reminded Dacres of a train taking a curve. Her starboard planes were within twenty feet of the cupola of the tower.

But the helmsman knew his business. He was well to leeward of the improvised "pylon," and before the thousand of spectators gathered in the Town Hall square could recover from their astonishment the "Meteor" was heading back to the dockyard.

Slowly, with her propellers revolving enough to keep her up against the breeze, the Dreadnought of the Air hovered over the Government establishment, seeking a place where she could come to rest. The swarm of vessels in the harbour made it impossible for her to descend without great risk to the spectators.

"There's the semaphore working," announced Dacres, pointing to the two arms that were set at the "preparatory" sign.

In response to an order, one of the "Meteor's" crew, armed with two hand flags, made his way up to the platform of the promenade deck. As soon as he replied, the semaphore began to spell out the message:—

"Berth ready for airship in Fountain Lake," said Dacres, translating the signal for his chief's information. "That's on the north side of the Dockyard and between it and Whale Island."

"Easy ahead," ordered Whittinghame; then, "Stop her."

A series of hisses, similar to the sounds that Dacres had heard when he first beheld the "Meteor," announced that the contents of several of the ballonettes were being pumped out and forced into the metal cylinders. Slowly and on an even keel the giant bulk sank lower and lower till a gentle roll announced that the airship was riding head to wind upon the sheltered waters of Portsmouth Harbour. The "Meteor" had made her debut.

# CHAPTER XIII
# AN OFFICIAL AND AN UNOFFICIAL INSPECTION

PROMPTLY the naval picket-boats had taken the bow-hawsers of the airship and had passed them to two mooring buoys. Other wire ropes were run out astern, till like a fettered Cyclops the "Meteor" was securely moored.

"Commander-in-Chief coming off, sir," announced Dacres, as a green motor-boat flying the St. George's Cross in the bows, tore towards the airship.

"So the reception is to be held on board the 'Meteor,' eh?" remarked Whittinghame. "I'm sorry I didn't provide an accommodation-ladder. The Admiral may find it rather awkward to swarm up a swaying rope-ladder. Will you see that the after entry-port is opened?"

The officers of the "Meteor" assembled ready to receive the Commander-in-Chief and his staff, while a "guard of honour" stood at attention, to do honour to the distinguished visitor.

Admiral Sir Hardy Staplers—"Old Courteous," as he was nick-named in the Service—was one of the most popular officers of Flag rank. His nickname was an apt one, for he was invariably polite to every one he came in contact with. Nothing seemed to ruffle his composure. He was a strict disciplinarian, and woe betide the subordinate—be he officer or man—who deliberately shirked his duty. On the other hand, he was keenly observant to reward zeal on the part of those under him, but whether admonishing or praising he was uniformly urbane.

Considering his age—for Sir Hardy was bordering on fifty-five—he climbed up the swaying rope-ladder with marvellous agility, and, greeted by the pipe of the bos'n's whistle, he advanced to meet the Captain and owner of the Dreadnought of the Air.

Accompanying the Admiral were his secretary, several officers of the executive and engineering branch, and—to Dacres' satisfaction—Commander Arnold Hythe.

"You have a wonderful craft here," observed Sir Hardy, after the usual courtesies had been exchanged.

"I think we have, sir," replied Whittinghame modestly. "Would you care to look round, or would you rather discuss the business that brought us here?"

The Commander-in-Chief expressed his desire to make an inspection of the "Meteor," and, escorted by his host and followed by their respective officers, Sir Hardy and Whittinghame proceeded on their tour of the airship.

"You are a lucky dog, Dacres," said Hythe, for the two old friends had contrived to "tail off" at the rear of the procession. "So this was the business which you so mysteriously hinted at? Mind you, I'm not envious. The submarine service suits me entirely, but I am glad for your sake. Do you know how Whittinghame proposes to put a stopper on that rascal Durango?"

Dacres shook his head.

"I do not know exactly," he replied. "At any rate, we are waiting till he lands in South America."

"The Scotland Yard men are at a loss to know on what ship he took passage," remarked Hythe. "They made inquiries at the offices of all the steam-ship companies running boats through the Panama Canal, but without success."

"I'm not surprised, old man. Durango was too artful to book by any of those lines. His plan was to make for Pernambuco, and cross to the Pacific coast by the new trans-continental railway. I know that for a fact."

"You do?" asked the Commander surprisedly. "How?"

"Simply by making enquiries at the Brazilian Steamship Company's office. We'll get your plans back again, Hythe, or I'm sadly mistaken in my estimate of the 'Meteor' and her skipper."

The inspection finished, Admiral Sir Hardy Staplers and Whittinghame retired to the latter's private cabin to discuss the proposals for the "Meteor's" future. They were alone for the best part of an hour, and when they rejoined the others both their faces simply beamed with satisfaction.

"President Zaypuru has foolishly played into our hands, Dacres," said Whittinghame, when the Commander-in-Chief and his staff had taken their departure. "An incident has occurred of which, strangely enough, I have hitherto been in ignorance, although I am generally well posted in events taking place in Valderia. Sir Hardy has just informed me that two men belonging to a British trader have been arrested on a trumped-up charge at the port of Zandovar. In spite of the protests of the British Consul the men were taken to Naocuanha and thrown into prison, while His Majesty's representative was most grossly insulted by the President.

"Evidently the Valderians have a poor opinion of British prestige, for their Government refused to apologize. Knowing the pig-headed obstinacy of Don Diego Zaypuru I am not surprised, but it will end in a declaration of war between Great Britain and Valderia. Of course, although it would hardly admit it, the British Government is glad of the opportunity to strike a blow at that elusive and daring outlaw, Durango."

"How do you think your brother will fare?" asked Dacres.

"That is what is troubling me considerably," replied Whittinghame. "If there is a rupture and a fleet is sent to chastise the Republic, Zaypuru may, and probably will, make reprisals. It may be taken for granted, however, that the President will go gently until Durango is back at Naocuanha. Our plan will be to act promptly at the very first intimation of hostilities, liberate my brother Gerald and capture Durango before the Valderians are aware of the presence of the 'Meteor' on the west side of the Sierras. Sir Hardy approves of my plan, and has promised to get official concurrence from the Admiralty; so everything will be square and above board."

"Are we remaining here long, sir?" asked Setchell, who, being the officer of the watch, had all his work cut out to refuse repeated requests for the occupants of the swarm of small craft to be shown over the airship. Whittinghame's orders were adamant. No one was to be allowed on board on any pretext whatsoever. Nevertheless, in spite of the heroic efforts of the water-police, the crowd of boats lay thickly round the "Meteor," their crews patiently waiting for the huge airship to resume its voyage, or else clamouring to be allowed on board.

"For why?" asked the skipper.

"Well, sir, the crowd is getting a bit out of hand. There are some fellows hammering away at the side. They'll be chopping bits off as souvenirs, I'm thinking, or else painting advertisements on the hull. And what is more, sir, there's a reporter sitting on the after horizontal plane on the port side. He cannot climb up, and he declines to budge until he's had an interview with you."

"Oh, I'll see about that," said Whittinghame grimly. "Come aft, Dacres, and let us see what this enterprising member of the Press is like."

The fellow was evidently not lacking in pluck and determination, for he had coolly passed a length of rope round the plane with the deliberate intention of "sitting tight."

"Hulloa, sir!" he sung out as Whittinghame made his way out upon the platform above the propeller-guard. "I represent the 'Weekly Lyre.' I've asked half a dozen times to be allowed on board to interview you."

"You are as much on board as you can reasonably expect to be," replied Whittinghame genially. "You are trespassing, you know. I shall be greatly obliged if you will go back to your boat, as we are about to move. I haven't time for an interview." "Then I'll wait," replied the man, to the great delight of the crowd of spectators afloat. "I'll have the distinction of being the first man, apart from your crew, to experience a flight in your airship, sir. Here I stick."

"You'll be blown away if you remain there."

"I risk that," replied the reporter imperturbably. "I'll lash myself on."

"Have the goodness to go," said Whittinghame with a faint show of annoyance.

The man shook his head. He had the appearance of being a resolute sort of individual.

Without another word Whittinghame walked to the after motor-room and gave orders for the propellers to be started easy ahead. Then he went outside, fully expecting to find the man gone.

At the first sign of movement the dense pack of boats had given back, but the pressman still stuck to his precarious post.

"There's pluck for you," commented the skipper. "That's the sort of man we could very well do with. But I'm not going to be balked. Just wait here for a few minutes, Dacres, and watch developments. Telephone to me when he's gone, and then take care to get inside and close the sliding panel as sharp as you can."

"He's lashed himself on, by Jove!" said Dacres.

"It will be a case of suicide if he's there when we gather speed," rejoined Whittinghame. "The sharp edge of the plane will cut through that lashing as if it were a piece of worsted."

With that the Captain went aft, leaving Dacres on the platform to report the course of events.

In response to an order the after hawsers were cast off, while the crew stood by ready to let go the for'ard springs that alone held the "Meteor" head to wind.

Suddenly Dacres saw the horizontal plane dip into an almost vertical position. The unfortunate reporter slid until brought up by the rope. For a few moments he hung there, struggling frantically to gain a foothold upon the smooth surface. His efforts only caused the rope to chafe through on the sharp edge of the plane and with a splash he fell into the sea.

Quickly rising to the surface he struck out for the nearest boat, amid the laughter of the onlookers, while Dacres, mindful of his warning, returned to the shelter of the outer envelope.

Whittinghame was about to give the order to let go for'ard when Callaghan entered the navigation-room.

"Wireless just come through, sir," he announced.

"Important?"

"Yes, sir," said the man gravely.

Half dreading that it was bad news from Naocuanha the Captain took the proffered paper.

The message was not from Valderia, but from the Admiralty. Its wording was indeed serious:—

"To Captain Whittinghame, airship 'Meteor.' Advises from British Polar Expedition state that communication with Lieutenant Cardyke has been interrupted for forty-eight hours. Feared disaster has overtaken party. Is 'Meteor' capable of rescue?"

Whittinghame turned to the operator.

"Reply, 'Yes; will proceed at once,'" he said.

# CHAPTER XIV
# ACROSS GREENLAND

VAUGHAN WHITTINGHAME was one of those men who make up their minds almost on the spur of the moment, yet possessing the rare capability of weighing the pros and cons of the issue with lightning speed.

Admiral Sir Hardy Staplers must have communicated with the Admiralty with the least possible delay, for one of Whittinghame's conditions was that he and his crew should receive official recognition. By giving him the title of Captain the authorities had tacitly expressed their consent.

Apart from that the appeal for aid was such that no man with humane principles could refuse.

The undertaking—navigating a huge airship through the intensely cold atmosphere of the Arctic—was a hazardous one, but Whittinghame was ready and willing to attempt the task.

In obedience to a general order all hands were mustered in the large compartment of No. 4 section. Officers, deck-hands and mechanics all wondering what had happened to cause the Captain to suspend suddenly the operation of unmooring, eagerly waited for Whittinghame to address them.

"My lads," said he, "I have been asked to make a voyage of three thousand four hundred miles and back. Not to Valderia but to a region where the climate is quite different. To be brief, the Admiralty have informed me that Lieutenant Cardyke and four men who made a dash for the North Pole some weeks ago are in pressing danger. Their Lordships appeal to me to proceed to his assistance, and I have signified my intention of so doing.

"It will be a hazardous task, for there are conditions to be met with that were not taken into consideration when the 'Meteor' was projected. Since you, my men, were not engaged to undertake a Polar Relief Expedition, I must ask for volunteers. All those who are willing to take part in this work will step two paces to the front."

Without the faintest hesitation every man stepped forward. A flush of pleasure swept across the face of their young Captain.

"Thank you," he said simply. "This is just what I expected. Now, dismiss. There will be half an hour's 'stand easy.' If any man wish to take advantage of that interval to write to his relatives or friends, opportunity will be found to send the letters ashore."

While the ship's company were thus employed, Whittinghame stood by the entry-port, pondering over his plans for the voyage.

As he did so, he became aware that the flotilla of boats still hovered around, and prominently in the foreground was the pressman, who seemed none the worse for his involuntary bath.

"May as well do the chap a good turn," soliloquised Whittinghame, and beckoning him to approach waited till the boat was alongside the rope-ladder.

"Sorry I had to drop you overboard, but you asked for it, my friend," said the Captain blandly. "I hope you bear no ill will."

"Not in the least," replied the reporter with a laugh. "It's not the first time I've been 'chucked out.' Besides, as you say, I asked for it. Are you going to invite me for a trip, sir?"

"No," replied Whittinghame, "but here's some information for you: it's perfectly genuine."

The man caught a folded slip of paper on which Whittinghame had written a few words. He opened it, then gave a searching glance at the Captain's face. He had been hoaxed before and was consequently cautious.

But that glance was sufficient. He was convinced. With a few words of thanks to Whittinghame he bade the boatman row like greased lightning for the shore. Twenty minutes later the "Weekly Lyre" issued a special with the exclusive information that the airship "Meteor" was to proceed to the relief of the British Arctic Expedition.

Meanwhile, Sir Hardy Staplers came on board to bid the departing aircraft God-speed, while, acting upon an "immediate demand note," suits of Arctic clothing were sent aboard from the clothing department of Royal Clarence Yard.

By twenty minutes past four all preparations were complete, and for the first time in her brief yet exciting career the "Meteor" hoisted the Blue Ensign; an Admiralty warrant having been hurriedly granted for that purpose.

Amid the deafening cheers of the thousands of spectators the "Meteor" rose majestically to a height of four hundred feet, then gathering way, darted forward in a northerly direction towards the desolate regions of the Far North.

Whittinghame, knowing that every moment was precious, gave orders for every possible knot to be screwed out of the motors, and nobly the engineers responded to the call. Within ten minutes of the start the speed indicators hovered around the two hundred miles an hour mark.

"Seventeen hours ought to do it," remarked the doctor.

"Hardly," corrected Whittinghame. "In the rarefied air we shall have to slow down a trifle. There will be less resistance to the vessel and correspondingly less resistance to the propeller blades. With luck we ought to reckon on twenty hours."

The navigation of the "Meteor" was entirely in Dacres' hands. There could be no rest for him until the voyage ended, for he alone of all on board could shape a course in these high latitudes, when the compass is useless to any but men skilled in the art of applying complicated magnetic variation adjustments.

Already the needle was pointing thirty degrees west of north, while hourly the angle was increasing.

Just before eleven Dacres pointed to the setting sun.

"That's the last sunset we'll see for some days, I fancy, doctor," he remarked. "We are nearing the Arctic Circle."

"Of course, I didn't think of that," replied Hambrough. "I was imagining us ploughing along in the pitch dark night with our searchlight on."

"It would be looking for a needle in a haystack were it not for the midnight sun," said Dacres. "By Jove, it is getting cold in spite of the hot water pipes. Would you mind bringing my coat from the cabin?"

By the time the doctor returned Dacres was able to report that the coast of Iceland was in sight.

"Where are you making for?" asked Hambrough. "The west coast of Greenland?"

"No," replied Dacres. "Here's the chart. We're making almost a bee-line for Cape Columbia. That will take us across Greenland from Scoresby's Land to the Humboldt Glacier and over the icy-clad plateau which the eye of man has never yet seen. Excuse me a minute while I look up this variation chart."

"You must be tired," observed Hambrough.

"Can't afford to be," said his companion. "It's a thirty-hour watch for me. All the same, doctor, if you can give me something to overcome this sleepy feeling I shall be glad. I suppose it is being unaccustomed to the altitude."

"I'll fix you up all right," declared Hambrough. "It won't do for you to be knocked up, or we'll be in a bit of a hole."

"It's not that. The 'Meteor' is quite capable of finding her way back to temperate regions. It was young Cardyke I was thinking of."

"You know him, then?"

"Rather. Lucky youngster obtained his promotion over the 'Independencia' affair."

Before Dacres could relate the incident Whittinghame entered the navigation room.

"How goes it?" he asked.

"Right as rain," replied Dacres cheerfully.

"Good! Now you take a spell and have some food. I'll stand by the helm and you can sing out the compass-course as you re eating. I'm sorry I didn't apply to the Commander-in-Chief for a navigator to take turns with you. Honestly, flying to a course in these regions is beyond me."

Already—it was twenty minutes past twelve by Greenwich time—the sun was rising—a pale, watery-looking disc. Six thousand feet beneath the airship could be seen the sea dotted with masses of floating ice, dwarfed into insignificance when viewed from above.

"We've struck the drift-ice rather far south, I think," remarked Dacres. "It's rather a bad sign, although, of course, there may be a higher temperature in the corresponding latitude in Baffin Bay."

"Let us hope so, in any case," rejoined the captain. "But isn't Parsons doing well? I don't think our speed has dropped to 190 since we started. I mustn't boast, though."

Hour after hour Whittinghame remained with the navigator. He scorned to sleep when such a luxury was denied his comrade.

On nearing the Greenland coast the "Meteor's" speed was reduced in order that Dacres could go on deck and take an observation. The cold cut him like a knife. His fingers could scarcely feel the vernier-screw of the sextant.

"I'm not cut out for an Arctic explorer," he muttered as he hastened below to work out his position. "If it's like this on the coast what will it be like over there, I wonder?"

"Well?" asked Whittinghame anxiously, as his companion straightened himself after bending over the set of figures.

"Here we are," announced Dacres, pricking off the portion on the chart. "Twenty miles farther north than I expected. We must have underestimated the strength of the wind. I'll take good care to make allowance for that in the future."

"What a waste of desolation!" ejaculated the Captain, looking down upon the snow-clad land. They were far above the northern limit of trees. The ground rose steeply in places, black granite precipices loomed menacingly against the white mantle which covered the gentle slopes.

Lower and lower fell the temperature. The crew, muffled in their fur garments, were already feeling numbed in spite of the hot-water apparatus. Higher and higher rose the airship, until a height of twelve thousand feet above the sea level was recorded. Yet less than nine hundred feet below was the summit of that ice-bound plateau—the portals of death.

Presently Parsons, the chief engineer, entered the navigation room.

"We'll have to shut off the heating pipes in the cabins, sir," he announced, "or the water will freeze and burst them. The heat of the motors is not enough to warm the jacket of the cylinders. I've even had to melt the oil before I could fill up the lubricators."

"Very well; carry on," replied Whittinghame. "We must endure the cold as best we may. Are the engines all right otherwise?"

"Running splendidly, sir."

"What temperature have you in the motor-rooms?"

"Minus ten for'ard and a point above zero aft, sir."

The Captain glanced at the thermometer on the navigation room bulkhead. The mercury stood at minus twenty-five degrees or fifty-seven below freezing point.

"I almost wish we had taken the east coast route and gone through Davis Strait," remarked Whittinghame. "It wouldn't have been anything like so cold."

"She'll do it all right, sir," declared Parsons. "Besides, we shan't find it any colder at the Pole itself."

"And it will save us at least six hours," added Dacres.

Acting under his suggestion two quarter-masters took ten minute spells at the wheel, for beyond that period a man's outstretched arms would be numbed.

Mile after mile was reeled off with the utmost rapidity. There was nothing to be seen but the dreary expanse of cliffs, snow and ice—cliffs that outvied the canons of Colorado for height, and snow and ice that had covered what at one time might have been a fertile land for perhaps millions of years. It was a vision of the earth during the Glacial Age.

At seven o'clock, or twenty-two hours after the "Meteor" had left Portsmouth, Dacres pointed to a huge winding track of ice that, according to the most modest estimate, was at least fifty miles wide.

"We're nearly there, sir," he said. "We've struck the head of the Humboldt Glacier. With luck we ought to sight the open sea in another hour. We are covering one degree of longitude every three minutes now."

Whittinghame nodded. It was almost too cold to talk. Speaking was accompanied by a volume of white vapour that, rapidly congealing, fell upon the floor in showers of fine ice. To touch a piece of metal with bare hands caused painful blisters, as many of the crew learnt to their cost. The airship was little more than a floating icebox.

Presently Dacres touched his comrade on the shoulder.

"The sea!" he exclaimed.

It was the sea. Right ahead was an expanse of open water, though greatly encumbered with huge bergs, for the "Meteor" was now passing over the birth-place of those enormous mountains of floating ice that find their way down into the Atlantic as far south as the fortieth parallel.

Even as he spoke there was a terrific crash, like that of a peal of thunder. The voyagers were just in time to see a mass of ice, nearly three miles in width, topple over the end of the glacier and fall into the sea. Almost instantaneously the placid surface changed to that of a tempestuous sea, as the iceberg rolled and plunged ere it gained a position of stability.

Ten seconds later the "Meteor" struck the first of the air-waves caused by the sudden disturbance of the atmosphere.

Well it was that she was of the non-rigid type, for otherwise the shock would have broken her back. As it was she writhed like a tortured animal. The crew, holding on like grim death, looked at each other in amazement akin to terror. At one moment her bow was pointing upwards at an angle of forty-five degrees; at the next the airship was banking steeply downwards.

It was a nasty two minutes while it lasted, but by the time the "Meteor" settled on an even keel she was tearing over the open sea.

# CHAPTER XV
# THE NORTH POLE

AT the twenty-third hour after leaving Portsmouth the "Meteor" came to rest on the ice under the lee of Cape Columbia and within three hundred yards of the "New Resolute," the ship of the British Arctic Expedition.

News of the airship's approach had already been communicated by wireless, and as she gracefully settled upon the ice she was greeted by three tremendous cheers from the crew of the ship.

But Dacres knew nothing of this. As soon as Cape Columbia had been sighted he went to his cabin to snatch a few hours' well-earned and needed sleep. For the time being his responsibility was not in request.

Compared with the severity of the climate above the Greenland plateau the temperature at Cape Columbia was milder. The "New Resolute," although moored to the ice, was still afloat, and sheltered from all gales by the land-locked harbour.

From the captain the "Meteor's" people soon had a fairly definite idea of the state of affairs.

Lieutenant Cardyke, with four men, had pushed on towards the pole, the party being accompanied by thirty-two Esquimo dogs. A portable wireless installation had been taken, so that the progress and welfare of the expedition could be communicated to the base.

Favoured by fine weather Cardyke and his companions made rapid progress compared with the distance covered by previous Arctic explorers. They reported that the hummocks gave considerable trouble, but there was no sign of open water.

Then with startling suddenness all wireless communication was broken off. A rescue party immediately set off, only to find that at a point 150 miles north of Cape Columbia their progress was checked by an expanse of open, agitated sea that had been formed by the separation of the ice-fields since Cardyke had traversed them. Reluctantly the second party had to turn back, and were almost hourly expected by the "New Resolute."

The "Meteor" did not wait long at Cape Columbia. Having secured the services of two junior lieutenants to assist in the navigation of the airship, Whittinghame started on the 500 mile journey to the North Pole.

Greatly to the relief of all on board, the motors began to work without the faintest hitch. The cordite fired at once. Had petrol been the fuel it was quite possible that the low temperature would have greatly diminished its efficacy. Parsons was most enthusiastic over the matter. Although at first dubious about substituting cordite for petrol he was now firmly convinced that a perfect ignition charge had been found.

Within half an hour after leaving Cape Columbia the "Meteor" passed over the relief party, who were dejectedly making their way back to the ship. A greater contrast would be difficult to find: the airship cutting rapidly and evenly through the air at three miles a minute; and half a dozen men, looking more like bundles of fur, plodding painfully along, glad to be able to cover two miles an hour. Even the dogs seemed to share their masters' dejection. Yet failure of the rescue party did not prevent them from waving their arms to the fleeting airship, a compliment that the "Meteor," by reason of her speed, was unable to return.

When at length Dacres awoke he knew by the motion of the airship that the "Meteor" was again under way. Quickly he made his way for'ard, to find two strangers in charge of the navigation room.

"It's all right," said Whittinghame genially. "There's no slur upon your prowess as a navigation officer, Dacres. We've obtained reliefs for you. Allow me to introduce Mr. Quinton and Mr. Baskett to you."

Armed with powerful binoculars Whittinghame and his assistants swept the snow-field. According to the opinion of the "New Resolute's" officers the airship was now fairly close to the spot where Cardyke was last heard of. There was nothing to indicate the tracks of the sledges; a recent fall of snow had accounted for that. All they could hope to do was to pick out some outstanding object, such as a tent or a snow hut, where the young officer and his four men might be sheltering.

Speed had been reduced to fifty miles an hour, while frequently the "Meteor" made a deviation in order to give the look-out an opportunity to examine a dark patch upon the white waste. Invariably the patch turned out to be the shadow of a hammock cast by the slanting rays of the ever-present sun, till Dr. Hambrough called his companions' attention to a dark speck away on the starboard bow.

Round swung the "Meteor," the eyes of the watchers riveted on a fluttering object that rapidly resolved itself into a flag. More, the flag was a

Union Jack. Close to it, and hitherto invisible, was a rounded hut made of blocks of ice, and half-buried in the snow.

"There they are!" exclaimed Setchell excitedly.

"I'm afraid not," said Lieutenant Baskett. "I can see no signs of their skis or of the sledges. But we're on their track, that's one blessing."

Again the "Meteor" descended. Whittinghame would not run the risk of detaching one of the compartments, especially as there was abundant room for the whole length of the airship to settle evenly. Her anchors held admirably in the rough ice, and with hardly a tremor she brought up on terra firma.

Quickly the entry port was opened and the rope-ladder dropped. Whittinghame was the first to land, quickly followed by Dacres and the two naval lieutenants.

With beating hearts they made their way over the ice and snow till they gained the hut, the four men gravely saluting the national flag as they passed by.

The doorway of the ice-hut had been blocked up—not by drifting snow but by human hands. Whether this had been done from the inside or from without could not at present be determined. The ice was as hard as iron.

In response to a signal to the "Meteor," three of the crew came up with ice-axes and shovels, and began a fierce attack upon the door. When the obstruction was removed the Captain entered.

His fears were realized. The hut was empty.

"Here's a tin containing some documents," he announced. "By Jove! Cardyke claims that this is the North Pole."

"He can't be so very far out," said Lieutenant Quinton. "Does he say anything about the route?"

"No, only that he is returning after verifying his position, and asks that the finder of the document should transmit it, if possible, to the Admiralty."

"Run and fetch my sextant, Williamson," said Dacres.

"And mine," added Baskett.

Before the men could return Whittinghame pointed to a staff projecting a few inches from the ground. Attached to it were the fragments of a flag, and by dint of removing a couple of feet of snow the nationality of the flag became obvious. It had been the Stars and Stripes.

"Peary's flag, by Jove!" ejaculated Whittinghame. "All honour, gentlemen, to that intrepid American. Even if an Englishman were not the first to plant his country's flag at the North Pole there is no little consolation to be derived from the fact that an Anglo-Saxon established the priority."

When Williamson returned with the instruments the two officers made careful separate observations, afterwards checking each other's figures. There was no mistake. The rescue party was standing on the northern extremity of the Earth's axis.

"Well, this won't find Cardyke, gentlemen," said Whittinghame sharply, breaking in upon the reveries of his companions. "What do you propose to do? Return by a slightly different route?"

"Supposing Cardyke and his party are incapable of finding their way. They might be partially exhausted by their exertions and have blundered in a totally different direction," suggested Baskett.

"Such an instance is not unknown," added Quinton.

"Then I propose to make several ever-widening circles. We ought to command a field extending twenty-five miles from the Pole. Let us return to the 'Meteor.'"

Rising to a height of five hundred feet the airship began to circle. In five minutes she had passed through every one of the three hundred and sixty degrees of longitude.

Miles of dreary waste lay beneath them. There was nothing to mark the position of the North Pole save the almost invisible hut and two flags, and nothing to break the horizon where the white plain merged into the pale blue of the Arctic sky.

Presently Dacres discovered signs of open water. A broad sea, its coastline extending through a hundred and eighty degrees of longitude, proved conclusively that Cardyke could not have blundered far in that direction. It was fairly evident the five men had retraced their steps. The question that puzzled Whittinghame was, how could the "Meteor" have missed the party on its flight to the Pole?

"We'll make our way back," he announced. "By keeping a zig-zag course we ought to come across some traces of them. Fifteen miles to the right and left of their supposed route ought to be ample."

To this the two naval officers agreed; but as the vertical rudders were being put hard over, Dacres called the Captain's attention to a dark object in a hollow at less than two miles off.

"It's far too large for a tent, Dacres," said Whittinghame. "But we may as well investigate. To me it looks like a——yes, by George, it is! It's a derelict balloon."

"André!" exclaimed Baskett.

"I think you are right," said Whittinghame.

"Yes, it has been a balloon. There is the car, half-buried in snow. Evidently in strong winds the snow-drifts are uncovered, or otherwise in twenty years the remains would be buried fathoms deep."

"Are you going to investigate, sir?" asked Dr. Hambrough.

"Much as I should like to," replied Whittinghame gravely, "I must decline. The claims of those who may yet be living are more pressing than those of the gallant dead. Perhaps, another time——"

He broke off abruptly to conceal his emotion, then having steadied the "Meteor" on her course, he relinquished the navigation into the hands of his able assistants.

For a long time no word was spoken. The memories of that mournful wreck deeply affected the spirits of the intrepid rescuers. They felt the irony of the situation, for had the gallant Frenchman delayed his ill-fated aerial voyage but a few years he might have been able to have made good use of a dirigible instead of drifting helplessly to his doom amid the awful solitudes of the Arctic.

Zig-zagging against the wind after the manner of a sailing-ship tacking, the "Meteor" resumed her quest. Two hours passed without result. The airship was now almost within sight of the newly-opened sea caused by the breaking up of the ice-floes.

The crew were almost despairing of success, for twice the supposed route of Cardyke's party had been examined. The Lieutenant and his men had left the Pole: they could not cross the barrier formed by the open sea. Where had they gone? Had they been buried beneath an almost irresistible blizzard? To add to the difficulties of the look-out, the sun was shining almost into the men's eyes, while an enormous tract of snow was covered by the reflected glare.

"We'll carry on till we are above the end of the pack-ice," said Whittinghame. "Then, if we haven't sighted them, we'll turn again and go back to the Pole. It is just possible——"

"What's that, sir?" interrupted Hambrough, his usually quiet manner giving place to intense excitability. "See! almost beneath us!"

In another fifteen seconds the "Meteor" would have overshot the mark. Signalling full speed astern, Whittinghame kept the spot indicated by the doctor under observation.

Five hundred feet below was a small black patch. It seemed so insignificant that it resembled a fur cap accidently dropped upon that trackless waste.

Under the retarding influence of the propellors the airship trembled so violently that it was almost an impossibility to bring glasses to bear upon the desired object, but when the "Meteor" lost way and orders had been given to the engineers to stop the motors, the occupants of the navigation-room were able to examine the solitary relic.

"By Jove!" ejaculated Dacres. "It's a tent. Look. There are the skis sticking up in the snow. Seven, eight, nine, ten of them. Then, the five men are there."

"Hurrah!" shouted Baskett. "Are you going to let off a rocket, or hail them, sir?"

"Neither," replied Whittinghame shortly. He was tremendously excited, only he knew that there was a chance that even now they might be too late.

Quickly the powerful pumps were set to work, and as the required number of ballonettes were exhausted the "Meteor" sank gently to the snow-clad ground. Thanks to the almost total absence of wind her anchors held without difficulty, although she had grounded nearly eight hundred yards to leeward of the tent.

Leaving Setchell in charge, the rest of the officers lost no time in descending the rope-ladder and making for the resting-place of the explorers. Somehow the rescuing party felt strained. They could hardly understand why, in almost perfect weather as far as the Polar climate went, the five men were not resuming their homeward march. The utter solitude of the black fur tent seemed ominous.

Although presenting the appearance of a level plain when viewed from above, the ground was rough, and encumbered with hummocks, while here and there deep but narrow fissures required care and skill on the part of the rescue party. Occasionally a deep groaning sound betokened the appalling fact that the ground was one vast ice-floe in momentary danger of breaking up.

If the five men were still alive, how could they be indifferent to the danger that now threatened them?

Whittinghame was the first to gain the tent. With numbed fingers he cut the lashings that secured the flaps of the outer and inner coverings and peered within.

Five fur-clad forms lay upon a pile of skins, their heads buried in their arms. Whether they were sleeping the long last sleep that knows no awakening in this world, Whittinghame could not tell. Nervelessly he backed out and signed to Dacres to enter.

"Dead?" asked Dacres laconically.

# CHAPTER XVI
# IN THE NICK OF TIME

"CAN'T say," replied the Captain. "It is more——See what you make of it, Dacres."

For a moment, like a swimmer contemplating a "header" into icy cold water, Dacres hesitated; then with a swift determined movement he disappeared within the tent.

Grasping the nearmost man he turned him over on his back. His face was as black as that of a seaman engaged in a coaling ship; but to Dacres' great relief he opened his eyes and stared wonderingly at his rescuer.

"So you've come, old mate?" he muttered, like one in a dream. "Thought you would, somehow. We got there all right—no kidding, we did."

"Get up and turn out," said Dacres authoritatively.

The seaman, disciplined to obey orders implicitly, attempted to rise. He realized that he was addressed by some one having authority; but to arise was beyond the power of his numbed limbs and exhausted body.

"We'll have to unship the tent," declared Dacres as he rejoined his comrades. "There's one of them alive, if not more; but he cannot move."

"Is there a lamp burning?" asked Dr. Hambrough.

"No; there is one but it's gone out," replied Whittinghame. "I noticed that."

Quickly the foot of the tent was freed from the wall of snow that had been built around it, and the flimsy structure thrown aside.

The man whom Dacres had roused was asleep once more.

One by one the doctor examined the five men. "They are all alive," he said; "but we are only just in time. We must get them on board as quickly as we can."

It was impossible to distinguish Cardyke from the rest of the party. The men's faces were encrusted with soot and grease, while they had allowed their beards to grow and these were clogged with the same uncongenial mixture.

"We'll have to hurry up," said Whittinghame anxiously, as an extra loud groan gave warning that the ice around them was ready to part company with the rest of the pack. "It will take two of us to assist each man to the 'Meteor'."

"That will help their blood to circulate," agreed the doctor, "but will this rotten ice stand the strain? It's pretty shaky between us and the 'Meteor,' if you'll remember."

"Then the 'Meteor' must come to us," rejoined the Captain.

In spite of the distance—nearly half a mile—the airship was within hail. In the rarefied atmosphere sound travels with the utmost facility, and instances have been recorded of men engaging in conversation at distances of two miles apart.

"Ay, ay, sir," replied Setchell, and without delay the airship's anchors were broken out and the propellers began to revolve.

Almost touching the ice the "Meteor" again brought up, this time so close that, as she swung to the light breeze, the men on the ground had to give a united heave and pass her immense bulk over their heads.

Already the alert Setchell had seen what was required and had rigged up a bos'n's chair from the entry port. In ten minutes rescuers and rescued were safely on board the airship.

Cardyke and his four men slept throughout the embarkation process; they slept during the run of the "Meteor" to Cape Columbia; they still slept when they were taken on board the "New Resolute," only awakening when they were being washed with slightly chilled water. And, strange to relate, Cardyke's first words were those of reproach at not being allowed to complete the journey by his own efforts.

He remembered resting in his tent; realized that he was back on the "New Resolute," and consequently came to the conclusion that a rescue party from the ship had taken a mean advantage by finding him and his comrades asleep and had hauled them on sledges for the rest of the way.

He was, in fact, light-headed. He could give no coherent account of what had occurred. It was Bates, the petty-officer, who was the first to relate their hazardous adventures.

Beyond the loss of two days, Cardyke's party reached the eighty-seventh parallel without mishap. Then accidents happened with alarming frequency. The portable wireless apparatus was irreparably damaged through the sledge capsizing on rough ice. Then two complete dog teams were lost in crevasses, leaving only six dogs to haul the remaining sledge.

Fortunately the weather remained exceptionally fine, and the party were able to make good progress. There still remained plenty of food, while a reserved store had been cached some days before the accident to the two sledges.

Cardyke, therefore, resolved to push on. The freshly fallen snow afforded easy travelling, for in the absence of wind there was very little "drift."

He reached the Pole. The making of certain important observations that had been entrusted to him he carried out, carefully and methodically, yet without undue loss of time; then setting their faces southward the five began their homeward journey.

It was a record of one continued struggle between grit and personal exertion on the one hand, and the relentlessness of the elements on the other. A blizzard impeded their progress; they lost their way and missed their store of spare provisions. The supplies they took with them were running short; the remaining dog had to be killed for food.

They began to realize that it was to be a race against time, unless they were met by a rescue party. Resting as little as possible, badly attacked by frostbite, and at times partially blinded by the glare of the snow, they toiled on, till hope was all but dead. And, fortunately unknown to them, a broad sea had opened out between them and their comrades at Cape Columbia.

At length they regained their proper course. It was during the time that they were making the detour that the "Meteor" must have passed them, about ten miles to the eastward. Human endurance could hold out no longer. They pitched their tent, filled their lamp with the last remaining oil, and resolved to rest for six hours—six hours when for days they had halted for two periods of two hours in every twenty-four.

It was a case of the triumph of matter over mind. Utterly done up, their intellects dimmed by their vicissitudes, the men fell asleep, and with the exception of a partial rousing in the case of the seaman Dacres had spoken to, they knew nothing till they found themselves back on board the "New Resolute."

The written results of Lieutenant Cardyke's observations were found in his possession, and so complete was the data that there was no longer any need for the Arctic Expedition ship to remain at Cape Columbia. The channel was still open, and eagerly her officers and crew prepared for the homeward voyage.

By the time Cardyke had recovered sufficiently to be told of the manner of his rescue, the "Meteor" was no longer in the Arctic. Returning by Davis Strait she reached England in thirty-four hours from the time of parting company with the "New Resolute."

The tidings of his achievement had preceded her, for even her prodigious speed could not outstrip the magical wireless. Had Captain Whittinghame felt so inclined he would have been fêted until further orders. But he had no such desire. His avowed mission was not yet accomplished. It was not in the dreary and desolate Arctic that his ambitions were centred, but upon the aggressive little Republic of Valderia. His dash for the Pole was humanity's call which could not be denied, also, it served the purpose as a means to put Reno Durango off his guard; but the publicity given to his return had undone all the good that Whittinghame had hoped for in that direction.

"We'll return to the New Forest base, Dacres," said he. "A rest after being half-frozen for the last few days will do us good. By that time the 'Maranhao' will be nearing Pernambuco, and we shall then be able to start in pursuit of our friend Señor Durango. By the by, aren't you anxious to interview your father?"

Dacres hardly knew what to reply. He was anxious to explain matters to the Colonel, but, although a full-grown man, he had a strange dread of his father's temper. It was, he knew, only putting off the evil day, for Colonel Dacres was bound to know sooner or later that his son had been requested to resign his commission. Yet, on the other hand, Dacres had a sort of presentiment that before long he would be reinstated in his former rank in his Majesty's service.

"You don't seem keen on it," remarked Whittinghame.

"No, sir, I do not," admitted Dacres. "Of course I know the governor has no legal control over me, yet somehow—I can't exactly explain—I feel in an awful funk about it."

"About what?"

"Having to tell him I've been more or less pitched out of the Service."

"That needn't worry you, old chap."

Dacres looked curiously at his chief.

"You don't know the governor," he replied. Whittinghame smiled. It was not on that account that he told Dacres not to worry. He held an official document, the contents of which he would have greatly liked to communicate to his comrade. But for the present his hands were tied.

Naturally the news of the rescue by the "Meteor" of the gallant Cardyke caused immense excitement, not only in Great Britain but throughout the civilized world. But the public curiosity was unsatisfied. The names of the individuals who undertook the voyage were not mentioned. In vain the Press appealed to the Admiralty. Never was a secret better kept, for up to the time of the "Meteor's" departure for Valderia the identity of her owner and crew remained a mystery.

# CHAPTER XVII
## ZAYPURU'S BOLD STROKE

MEANWHILE, events were moving quickly in the Republic of Valderia. The demands of the British Government for satisfaction had been rigorously pushed forward, but the prisoners had not been released, nor was there any apology tendered.

President Diego Zaypuru was biding his time. Although desirous of measuring steel with the British he was loath to act until Reno Durango was back at Naocuanha. He had been advised that the Mexican was on his way via Brazil, and that his arrival would be a matter of a few days. Durango was the President's right hand, although, did but Zaypuru know it, the "right hand" was not desperately enamoured with the task before him.

When Durango heard of the disagreement between Great Britain and Valderia, he cursed the stupidity of the Dictator of the Republic. He could clearly foresee the result: Valderia would be beaten. Willingly would he have turned back and left Zaypuru to meet with his deserts, but for the fact that he had vast interests in the Republic. To do so would mean financial ruin, and to a man of unbounded cupidity the idea was unthinkable. He decided that he must run the risk, lay his hands on as much of his wealth (and, incidentally, other peoples') as he possibly could, and make use of the airship which had been constructed from the plans stolen from Gerald Whittinghame to get clear of the sinking ship of State.

Zaypuru miscalculated the British temperament. He was firmly convinced that as long a as he delayed negotiations the British Government would be content. His plans, however, received a nasty shock when the Republic was peremptorily informed that diplomatic relations with Great Britain were broken off, and that a British fleet under the command of Rear-Admiral Maynebrace was to proceed at once to Zandovar, the port of Naocuanha, and obtain immediate satisfaction, or else the town was to be shelled.

As the situation stood Zaypuru knew that it was a race between the British Admiral and Reno Durango. If the former appeared at Zandovar before Durango reached the capital the President would have to give way.

That would result in another revolution. On the other hand, if the Mexican arrived first, Zaypuru would have sufficient confidence to resist.

Immediately upon receipt of the intelligence that a rupture had occurred, the "Meteor"—having been previously granted a letter of marque—set out for South America.

Vaughan Whittinghame also realized that there was a possibility of his having to choose one of two alternatives, unless by a lucky stroke he could carry off two projects simultaneously. His duty to his country urged him to attempt the capture of Durango and the recovery of the submarine plans. Fraternal devotion called upon him to effect the rescue of his brother before he fell a victim to the vindictive President.

It fell to Dacres to suggest a plan.

"Let's collar the Mexican, by all means, if we can," he urged. "Without him that Zaypuru fellow will be tied up in knots. Once we get Durango in our hands the President will think twice before proceeding to extreme measures with your brother."

"But you are not taking into consideration the effect of the appearance of the British fleet," objected Whittinghame.

"Including my late ship," added Dacres. "Yes, there, again, is a complication. If Zaypuru shows fight there'll be short work made of Zandovar, but I doubt whether there will be sufficient seamen and marines to undertake a march on the capital. Personally, I fancy that when the President realizes that we mean business he'll knuckle under."

"I hope he does," agreed Whittinghame; "but that won't prevent us from collaring Durango. Those submarine plans must be recovered, Dacres. As I said before, the bother won't end with Valderia, if the rascal takes it into his head to open negotiations with one of the Great Powers."

Flying at a great height and avoiding the regular steamship routes the "Meteor" arrived off the coast of Brazil one day before the time the "Maranhao" was expected.

Waiting till it was dark the airship passed inland and before morning broke she was hovering over the desolate country in the neighbourhood of Salto Augusto, a town in the province of Matto Grosso and approximately sixteen hundred miles west of Pernambuco.

It had never been Whittinghame's intention to effect Durango's capture on Brazilian territory. Wireless information from his brother's trustworthy agent at Naocuanha had been received to the effect that the airship built according to the plans stolen from Gerald Whittinghame was to leave Valderia for Salto Augusto, and there to take Durango on board.

Here, then, was the "Meteor's" opportunity. She was to lie in wait for her rival and imitator, to which the name "Libertad" had been given. When it could be safely assumed that Durango had joined the Valderian airship the "Meteor" was to stand in pursuit until both craft were out of neutral territory. Then Whittinghame could and would act.

For five days the "Meteor" waited and watched, floating practically motionless at an altitude of fifteen thousand feet, at which height, unless deliberately sought for, she would escape observation. During that time no information came from Naocuanha announcing the departure of the "Libertad"; but other news, quite as momentous, reached him by the aid of wireless from the Valderian capital.

In less than a week events had moved rapidly. As soon as it was definitely known that Admiral Maynebrace's squadron was actually on its way to Zandovar, the fighting nature of the Valderians showed itself. They were not without a considerable reserve or cunning; for, realizing the impossibility of their one Super-Dreadnought making a stand against the predominant ships of the "Royal Sovereign" class, they promptly sold the battleship to Peru.

Peru had for years past sought to purchase a Super-Dreadnought, with the idea of forming a fleet superior to that of Chili. She was only too glad of the chance to buy the Valderian battleship at a remarkably low price.

The destroyers and submarines upon which President Zaypuru relied proved to be a broken reed. The Valderian crews—never seamen by choice or instinct—refused to put to sea when they were ordered to make a surprise attack upon the British fleet. The destroyers, manned by skeleton crews, were thereupon sent to Callao, there to be interned till the hostilities ended; while the submarines were kept in the harbour of Zandovar in the hope that they might be able to inflict damage upon the ships under Admiral Maynebrace's command.

On the morning of the 21st of July, corresponding to the second day of the "Meteor's" vigil at Salto Augusto, the British fleet came in sight of Zandovar. The battleships were in two columns in "line ahead" formation, led respectively by the "Repulse" and "Royal Oak." Overhead flew the six seaplanes attached to the squadron, their duty being to watch for the presence of hostile submarines, whose movements could be easily discerned in the clear waters of the Pacific.

At first the British tars were under the impression that the Valderians would not fight, but when a shell from one of the batteries whizzed past one of the seaplanes the delight of the crews of the warships showed itself in three hearty cheers. The signal to open fire was hoisted on the flagship, and without further ado the eight battleships began the bombardment.

Grimly workmanlike looked the floating monsters. Stripped for the fray, the top-hamper sent down, boats and combustible gear dropped overboard, they showed no dash of colour except the White Ensigns, of which each ship displayed three flown in positions where they would not effect the training of guns. Everything else that was visible on these modern leviathans was painted a dull grey; and in a very short time from the opening of the bombardment that grey was merged into a shapeless blurr by the haze from the cordite.

The noise was deafening. Punctuating the loud detonations of the fourteen-inch guns could be heard the sharp bark of the quick-firers, the scream of the hurtling projectiles, and not unfrequently the appalling crash as the Valderian shells struck the steel plating of the British warships.

For a quarter of an hour the batteries replied vigorously. Generally speaking the aim of the Valderian gunners was erratic, but one unlucky hit brought the aftermast of the "Renown" crashing down on the deck, completely putting out of action the guns on the two after turrets. The flagship had her bridge shot away and the foremost funnel demolished early in the action, while the "Royal Oak" was considerably damaged by a twelve-inch projectile that, finding its way into one of the nine-inch-gun casemates on the starboard side, disabled every man of the gun's crew.

At the end of half an hour the Valderian fire was very feeble. The earthworks of the forts were practically levelled. Wherever one of the huge shells struck the ground it burst and tore a deep pit, into which, as often as not, the nearmost gun and its mountings promptly tumbled. Many of the projectiles, flying high, dropped into the town and did enormous damage. The submarines, lying in the inner harbour, were quickly sunk by gun-fire; and within an hour of firing the first shot the resistance on the part of the garrison of Zandovar ceased.

Admiral Maynebrace promptly gave the order to cease fire, and before the haze had cleared away, the seaplanes dashed forward to investigate. Soon they returned with the information that the batteries were completely knocked out of action and that a stream of fugitives were observed making towards Naocuanha by road and rail.

As soon as the boats of the fleet were brought alongside their respective ships preparations were made to land a force of seamen and marines and occupy the town. It was a needless task, for any communication between the Republic and the victors could be received with equal facility on board the flagship; but Admiral Maynebrace, with the idea of making a display, resolved to land and hoist the British colours over the ruined forts.

One of the principal fortifications—Belgrano—stood on lofty ground in the rear of the town, but it had not escaped the hail of projectiles. Owing to its elevation it could be seen from the capital and on that account Maynebrace determined to take possession of it and hold it with a strong force in the event of an attack on the part of the Valderian army before Naocuanha.

The advance guard, composed of Royal Marine Light Infantry, traversed the narrow deserted streets without seeing a sign of any living Valderians. By the time they reached Belgrano the main body of the invaders reached the plaza, or open square in the centre of the town. Pickets were posted to command the various approaches, and due precautions having been taken, the Admiral and his staff proceeded to the fort of Belgrano.

Amid ringing cheers the Union Jack was hoisted over the captured mound that a short time before had been a strongly fortified position. Light field guns and maxims were brought up and trained to command the road to Naocuanha, and the force of occupation prepared to receive either an attack or—what was more likely—a proposal for an armistice. About an hour before sunset Admiral Maynebrace made his way towards the harbour, intending to return to the flagship. He was accompanied by his secretary and flag-lieutenant, and escorted by a guard of marines.

The Admiral was in high spirits. Throughout the whole of his career he had never smelt powder in real earnest until this eventful day. He was close upon the age limit, and now he had survived the action and had the honourable distinction of having won glory for the King and country before being relegated to the limbo of retirement.

His pleasing reveries were suddenly interrupted by hearing a furious commotion. He was dimly conscious of hearing the marine officer give a hurried order to his men to face about, while from one of the narrow streets issued a number of horsemen. They were not members of the regular Valderian army, but rough-riders from the grass country of the middle plateau, men who had practically lived in the saddle from childhood.

Before the marines could fire a shot the avalanche of men and horses were upon them, through them, and off out of sight between the massive stone buildings. And with them were carried the Admiral and his staff, prisoners in the hands of the enemy.

In vain the marines fired their rifles in the air to warn the outposts. The latter, imagining that an attack was impending from without, stood to their arms, while dashing along with loose rein and unspared spur rode the daring horsemen with their captives, never slacking pace until they drew up outside the plaza of Naocuanha.

It was certainly a daring and well-executed plan on the part of the President. With these important hostages he realized that the outlook from his point of view had considerably improved. The British force in possession of Zandovar was too small to advance upon the capital, and weeks would elapse before reinforcements could be sent from England. During that interval he might be able to make satisfactory terms.

Under the circumstances Zaypuru felt it safe to allow the airship "Libertad" to leave the country and pick up his adviser, Reno Durango.

# CHAPTER XVIII
# THE DISASTER TO THE "LIBERTAD"

"HERE'S a pretty how d'ye do!" remarked Whittinghame when the news of Zaypuru's daring stroke was received by the "Meteor." "That alters the state of affairs, I'm thinking. What would you do, Dacres? Wait till the 'Libertad' I arrives, or make a dash across the Sierras into Valderian territory and attempt the rescue of the prisoners?"

"Wait for Durango—that would be the best course, I think. I don't suppose Admiral Maynebrace will come to any harm. But I was forgetting your brother."

"I wasn't," said the Captain of the "Meteor." "We must find out where the Admiral and his staff are imprisoned. If they are shut up in the Cavarale—that's the name of the prison on the outskirts of Naocuanha—Gerald will have company. Then, again, will Durango return to Valderia now that the submarines are destroyed? The phase of the situation seems to point to the possibility of the Mexican deserting the sinking ship and trying his luck with the plans elsewhere."

"But he has large pecuniary interests in Naocuanha."

"True. After all, I think we might hang on a little while longer. I have no reason to doubt my agent's report that the 'Libertad' is ordered to proceed to Salto Augusto; unless the report is a false one issued to put us off the scent. Durango might have followed his original plan and proceeded by rail."

"In that case we have been nicely had," said Dacres.

"We'll remain here twenty-four hours longer," decided Whittinghame; "then, if the 'Libertad' does not put in an appearance, we'll make a night descent upon Naocuanha."

While the officers of the "Meteor" were at lunch Callaghan brought in a message received by wireless that the "Libertad" had left Naocuanha at seven that morning, bound east.

"Good!" ejaculated Whittinghame. "Left Naocuanha at seven? She has a thousand mile flight. Allowing her speed to be the same as that of the

'Meteor'—although I doubt it—she ought to reach Salto Augusto by about noon or one o'clock. They couldn't have chosen a better time as far as we are concerned, for the sun will be almost directly overhead. At five thousand feet we'll run no risk of being spotted."

At exactly fifteen minutes past twelve the watchers on the British airship saw her rival approaching. The "Libertad" was flying low—at an altitude of about five hundred feet. This proved that her speed was approximately the same as that of her opponent. In appearance she strongly resembled the "Meteor," but, of course, Whittinghame was not aware of the details of her construction and propulsive arrangements. Durango had had the secret of the ultra-hydrogen, but whether he knew how to render the gas non-inflammable was a question that could not be satisfactorily answered by the Captain of the "Meteor."

Keeping the "Libertad" under observation by means of their powerful binoculars the officers of the "Meteor" saw the Valderian craft alight at less than half a mile from the outskirts of the town. She did not remain long. Almost skimming along the ground, like a snake crawling stealthily through the grass, she turned westward.

Although the "Meteor" could not adopt offensive methods over Brazilian territory, there was now no further need of concealment. She could follow the "Libertad" relentlessly, keeping her in view until she crossed the border. Then she would act promptly and decisively.

Swooping downwards, but still maintaining a superior elevation, the "Meteor" began to chase. With her motors running "all out" she slowly yet surely overhauled her prey, till a sudden spurt on the part of the "Libertad" announced the fact that she had sighted her pursuer, and was putting on extra speed.

Mile after mile the two airships tore at a terrific rate. On board the "Meteor" the bomb-dropping gear was made ready, and the light quick-firers manned. But even had Whittinghame wished to open fire upon the enemy, the speed at which the "Meteor" was travelling put that out of the question, until the "Libertad" was overhauled sufficiently for the British craft's guns to be trained abeam. Nor could the machine guns on the promenade deck be worked. No man could stand to serve them in the howling gale that swept past the rapidly moving vessel.

On the other hand Durango could make use of the two after guns on the "Libertad" without risk. To open the bow-ports of the "Meteor" meant serious damage both to the structure of the hull and to her crew, unless the speed were materially reduced.

The Captain of the "Libertad" cared not one jot for international rights now that he was on his way back to Valderia. He opened fire upon the "Meteor," two shells fitted with time-fuses screeching past the huge flimsy target and bursting three hundred yards astern.

"This won't do," remarked Whittinghame calmly. "We cannot afford to be potted without chance of replying."

He turned and gave a brief order. The elevating planes and an addition of ultra-hydrogen resulted in the "Meteor" quickly bouncing up another two thousand feet. Her Captain's plan was to gain an important advantage in altitude and continue to overhaul the "Libertad." He would thus have what corresponded to the weather-gauge in old-time frigate actions.

In the excitement of the chase the hours sped quickly—so quickly that Whittinghame uttered an exclamation of surprise when Dacres announced that the frontier was passed and that the "Meteor" was above Valderian territory.

"Are you quite sure?" he asked.

"Of course, sir, I couldn't obtain an absolutely correct reading on account of the motion and the slight refraction of the glass scuttles," replied Dacres. "But I am quite convinced that, allowing a margin of safety, we are between twenty and thirty miles over the dividing-line."

"There are the Sierras," announced Setchell, pointing to a row of snow-topped peaks. "If the 'Libertad' doesn't begin to ascend, she'll have a stiff climb."

"We have her right enough," said Whittinghame, rubbing his hands gleefully. "We have her. Before she can ascend sufficiently to clear those peaks we'll have overhauled her."

"Unless she finds a pass between the mountains," added Dr. Hambrough, who, in his shirt-sleeves, was going through the contents of an ambulance-chest.

Nearer and nearer drew the formidable chain of peaks. Both airships were continually ascending, but it was quite apparent to the crew of the "Meteor" that unless the "Libertad" rose at a fairly steep angle she would never clear the summit. Even if she attempted it her speed must be greatly retarded, during which time the "Meteor" would have overlapped her antagonist.

Suddenly the Valderian airship ported her helm, slowing down as she did so. Whittinghame instantly ordered the "Meteor's" motors to be stopped.

"She means to show fight!" he exclaimed.

Once again Durango had gained the better position by skilful manoeuvring. Owing to the great difference in height the "Meteor's" bombs stood little chance of hitting the target, immense though it was. She was provided with only two quick-firing guns that could be trained immediately beneath her; while the six weapons on vertical mountains on the "Libertad's" upper platform could be brought into play.

"The cunning sweep!" ejaculated Whittinghame.

Round swung the "Meteor," then, plunging steeply, she made off at full speed at right angles to her former course, until she was barely two hundred feet above the height of her antagonist.

The craft were now seven thousand yards apart. Each, when viewed from the other, resembled a thin dark line against the deep blue sky.

It was a long range, but Whittinghame decided to try his luck. The five broadside quick-firers spoke simultaneously. No reply came from the "Libertad," which now set off as fast as she could towards the mountains.

Evidently Durango was adopting Fabian tactics. Whittinghame muttered angrily. He had been out-witted by their manoeuvres and had lost the advantage of altitude which he had hitherto possessed.

Ten minutes later the "Libertad" vanished from sight behind a precipitous bluff in the mountains. Evidently the pilot of the Valderian airship knew of a means of escape. He had taken her into one of the deep gorges that penetrate these stupendous walls of rock.

Well it was that the Captain of the "Meteor" had not ordered the upper deck guns to be manned. There was, in consequence, no delay while the promenade-deck was being cleared.

At half-speed the "Meteor" again stood in pursuit of her rival.

A hundred miles an hour is a dangerous pace to navigate an airship between mountainous walls, but Whittinghame was not to be denied. What the "Libertad" could do, he would do—and more. Even then, he argued that if the pursued maintained her utmost rate of speed she would be practically out of sight before the "Meteor" emerged from the narrow valley. At all costs the "Libertad" must be brought to bay ere she reached Naocuanha.

Whittinghame now realized that, with true British contempt of foreigners, he had underrated the capabilities of his rival. He resolved, with bulldog tenacity, to carry on, heedless of risks.

On the other hand Reno Durango never thought for one moment that the "Meteor" would follow the "Libertad" through the mountain pass. He fully expected that his rival would laboriously climb to a height sufficient to enable him to cross the snow-clad range. By that time the "Libertad" would be under the cover of the guns of Naocuanha.

Acting under this supposition the Mexican ordered speed to be reduced during the passage of the gorge, and at a bare fifty miles an hour the "Libertad" entered the gloomy defile. On either hand the cliffs towered almost vertically to a height of two thousand feet; above this the mountainside rose with less declivity until it reached far above the snow-line. The pass itself averaged two hundred yards in width, and, although winding, its curves were gradual enough to allow the thousand odd feet of airship to be manoeuvred with comparative ease.

"Steady on your helm, Callaghan," cautioned Whittinghame as the "Meteor" swung round the projecting bluff.

With every nerve on the alert the crew of the pursuing craft stood at their posts, those for'ard half-expecting to see their rival brought up to bar their way, those aft, unable to use their powers of vision, trusting implicitly in the energy and skill of their young commander.

Ahead lay the narrow gorge, desolate, forbidding and withal majestic. There were no signs of the "Libertad."

Bend after bend was negotiated in safety. In four minutes the "Meteor" traversed the pass, then, to the surprise of her officers, they found the "Libertad" waiting broadside on, at a distance of less than half a mile.

Nor was the dramatic appearance of the "Meteor" as she suddenly emerged from between the lofty mountain range any the less surprising to Durango and his crew. So intent were they in watching the peaks of the Sierras that for the moment they could scarce believe their eyes.

That the "Libertad" meant to fight was evident from the fact that she had slackened speed and had hoisted Valderian colours from an ensign staff at the after end of her upper deck.

Before the "Meteor's" guns could open fire a fusillade of musketry and a broadside from the guns on the upper deck of the hostile airship woke the silence of the valley. The British craft reeled, then, several of her ballonettes pierced through and through, she began to drop vertically through space.

As Whittinghame sprang to the emergency lever for charging the reserve sub-sections to the full capacity, a shout from his companions attracted his attention. Thrusting down the metal rod he turned to follow the direction of Dacres' outstretched arm.

The "Libertad" was turning turtle.

Slowly, but with increasing speed she rolled over to port, till the whole extent of her upper deck sloped at an angle of sixty degrees. Her guns broke from their mountings and went crashing through the light metal stanchions into the depths. Men, frantically struggling to keep a foothold or clinging to the railings, slipped off her aluminium deck to a swift yet awful death in the vast abyss below.

Still falling she turned on her longitudinal axis till she described a complete semi-circle. All the while her propellers were driving her ahead. The horizontal planes, that in her normal position would tend to make her ascend, now acted in a totally opposite direction. She was descending rapidly under her own power rather than the force of gravity towards the earth.

Spellbound and too enthralled to notice the injuries to their own craft the crew of the "Meteor" watched the scene of disaster, till, with a crash, accompanied by the hiss of the escaping ultra-hydrogen, the bows of the "Libertad" plunged into a thick clump of mountain pine-trees. For a few seconds the wreckage hung in an oblique position, then, the framework slowly collapsing, the Valderian airship finished her brief career upon the unsympathetic soil of her native land.

"Good heavens!" ejaculated the doctor, breaking the tense silence. Strong nerved though he was and used to the scientific horrors of the operating room, the appalling tragedy made him feel giddy and sick.

Whittinghame moved to the telephone.

"Stand by to anchor," he ordered coolly. Then turning to his companions: "There is no time to be lost; we must repair damages and investigate the wreck. Since there is no sign of fire, we may be able to recover the plans intact."

# CHAPTER XIX
## INVESTIGATING THE WRECK

ALREADY, owing to the introduction of additional ultra-hydrogen, the earthward descent of the "Meteor" had been arrested. The damage done by the broadside from the ill-fated "Libertad" was serious enough. A large quantity of gas which could be ill spared had been lost, nine ballonettes having been pierced. Most damage had been done to No. 4 section, the officers' cabins being reduced to a state of chaos. Fortunately there were only four of the crew stationed in that part of the ship, and with one exception they had come off unscathed. The exception was Williamson, the quartermaster of Dacres' watch, who had received a deep flesh wound in the left shoulder.

To the south of the wood upon which the airship had fallen was an expanse of fairly level ground, barely sufficient to accommodate the whole length of the "Meteor." In her disabled condition her Captain would not risk bringing her down in one piece. The only alternative was to separate her between Nos. 2 and 3 sections, since Nos. 3 and 5 were necessary to support the riddled No. 4.

With considerable misgivings the order was given to release the cam-action bolts. The foremost part of the "Meteor" being practically intact, gave no trouble; but before the remainder of the ship could be brought to the ground even more ultra-hydrogen had to be made use of.

When, at length, the two portions were safely anchored fore and aft all hands set to work to make good the damage. Every ballonette that still contained gas was emptied, the ultra-hydrogen being forced into spare emergency cylinders. By the time this task was accomplished in the short tropical twilight, the work had to be abandoned till the next day.

Had the Valderian capital been informed of this double calamity, the capture of the "Meteor" and her crew could have been easily undertaken by a comparatively small body of troops, for the British airship was quite as incapable of motion as was her totally wrecked rival.

"What caused the 'Libertad' to turn turtle?" asked Setchell during dinner. "We didn't fire a shot at her during the last part of the chase."

"I think it can be explained," replied Whittinghame. "Those fellows had too much top-hamper. They carried six quick-firers on the upper or promenade deck. Added to that there were several of the crew armed with rifles. The broadside did more harm to them than it did to us, although, goodness knows, we've been badly knocked about. The recoil of the broadside was the finishing touch, so to speak. She was already bordering on a state of unstable equilibrium, and over she went."

"Will our repairs take long?" asked Dacres.

"I think not. The material of which the ballonettes is made is very amenable to treatment. We shall have to force air into each of the ballonettes to find out which are gas-tight and which are not. Those which require only slight repairs we will patch. The others must wait until we return to our base. Fortunately there was an ample reserve of buoyancy."

"And the reserve of ultra-hydrogen?" asked Dr. Hambrough.

"That is a more serious question, doctor. We have enough and barely enough to impart sufficient lifting power to the 'Meteor.' Perhaps I must sacrifice No. 4 section. It contains our cabins, gentlemen, but judging by the state they are in I do not think you will be put to greater inconvenience than the present condition promises. However, we shall be in a position to decide that point tomorrow. One thing is pretty certain: had the gas been of an explosive nature not one of us would be here to tell the tale."

"And the wireless room?" asked Setchell.

"Still intact, so you will be able to communicate with your relations and friends in England and let them know that you are still in the land of the living," replied the Captain. "Now, gentlemen," he continued, "I suggest that those who are not on duty should retire. Mr. Setchell will be in charge of the armed patrol until midnight, and then, doctor, you will kindly change the guard and relieve Mr. Setchell. To-morrow, I promise you, will be a strenuous day for all hands."

The night passed without interruption. With the first sign of dawn the officers were out and about. At his chief's request Dacres accompanied him to the wreck of the luckless "Libertad," four of the crew armed with rifles going with them in case of danger from either man or beast.

In a few minutes the debris was sighted. Owing to the velocity of the "Libertad's" descent many of the young pine-trees had either snapped off or bent, and thus the fore part of the airship was resting on the ground.

The motors from the forward compartment were lying nearly a hundred yards from the rest of the wreckage. Aluminium plates, twisted and ripped out of almost all recognition, fractured girders, pieces of oiled silk from the interior of the ballonettes, and a miscellaneous assortment of other material gave silent evidence of the completeness of the disaster.

The after-part, having subsided more slowly, since the "Libertad" struck the ground obliquely, was in a more recognisable condition, except that the motors had broken from the bearings.

"Pretty mess!" ejaculated Whittinghame.

"There seems little chance of recovering the plans," remarked Dacres. "After all, it won't matter so very much if we don't. They are doubtless lost in that heap of wreckage."

"It would be more satisfactory to know definitely," added Whittinghame. "Do you fancy a climb? If so, we'll investigate the after-sections of the wreck."

Dacres willingly assented, and soon both men were climbing along the twisted framework, cautiously testing each piece of metal ere they trusted their weight to it.

The Captain of the "Meteor" laughed at their careful precautions.

"It's a strange thing," he remarked, "how seriously we, who are used to altitudes running into thousands of feet, regard a possible fall of twenty or thirty."

"Yet there is a good reason," added his companion. "Were we to fall out of the 'Meteor' and drop a few thousand feet through space the consequences would be a matter of complete indifference to us. On the other hand, we might slip off this girder on to the ground and live for years afterward, no doubt, crippled for life. I've known a blue jacket go aloft in a strong wind to clear the pennant—a man's life at stake for the sake of a few yards of bunting—and to do it without turning a hair. Ashore that same man would think twice before alighting on a greasy road from a tramcar in motion."

Beyond a state of disorder caused by movable articles being thrown out of place by the concussion the cabins were practically intact. Rapidly Whittinghame made his way from one to the other until he reached one that had the appearance of belonging to the "Libertad's" Captain.

In one corner was a pedestal desk, its top "stove-in" by coming into contact with the bulkhead. Charts, maps, and documents littered the floor, in company with a clock, barometer, articles of clothing and books. From a peg hung a light coat, its pocket bulging considerably.

"We'll put etiquette on one side," said Whittinghame, "and see what is in this gentleman's pockets."

There was a revolver with about fifty loose cartridges in one pocket. Jerking open the weapon Whittinghame broke it across his knee and threw the pieces into the tree-tops. In the corresponding pocket was a leather case stuffed with papers. Amongst them was the counterfoil of a steamship ticket from Southampton to Pernambuco, a Brazilian railway time-table and almost a dozen envelopes bearing the stamps of four different European countries besides those of Valderia.

Without examining their contents Whittinghame thrust the envelopes into his pocket and resumed his search. In the breast-pocket of the coat were two South American newspapers dated the day previous and, what was especially useful, a large scale plan of the city of Naocuanha.

"This is Durango's cabin," he observed.

"Without a doubt," assented Dacres; "but we've had no luck with the plans."

"He may have stowed them away in one of these drawers. There's no immediate hurry. We'll have a look round the rest of the wreck, and remove the contents of the desk later on."

Although the impact had been violent several of the ballonettes still retained gas. Whittinghame was about to release their contents when Dacres interposed.

"Better be careful," he said. "There must be still a considerable amount of buoyancy in that end of the ship, since she's supported only by a few slender trees. If we release the ultra-hydrogen we may be involved in a supplementary disaster, and have that forty-foot fall we were discussing."

"Right," replied the Captain laconically. "Do you know, there's something remarkable about this wreckage?"

"In what way?"

"We've examined every part of the two after-sections, and we haven't seen any of the bodies of the crew. They couldn't have all been on deck. Those below were not pitched overboard when she turned right over; where, then, are they?"

"I saw twenty men, at least, drop off her when she turned turtle. There are four bodies at least under the fore-part."

"Then, assuming her crew to be at least as numerically as strong as that of the 'Meteor,' where are the rest? The fact that some of the ballonettes are still charged points to the suggestion that the shock to the after-part was not sufficient to kill a man. Therefore there are survivors. That being so, where are they?"

"I noticed something like a muster-book in one of the cabins," said Dacres. "I'll get hold of it and see if it is."

So saying he made his way to the place where he had noticed the book in question. As he passed along the alley-way a door swung to.

Dacres stopped and listened intently. He could have sworn that he heard footsteps on the upper deck.

Giving the alarm to his companion Dacres dashed up the metal ladder leading to the promenade deck, pushed back the hinged flap, and, crawling on his hands and knees, gained the stanchion rails on the lee side of the steeply shelving platform. He could see or hear nothing of a suspicious nature.

"What's wrong?" asked Whittinghame, thrusting his head and shoulders through the hatchway.

"Thought I heard some one moving," replied his comrade. "Below there!" he shouted, hailing the men who had accompanied their officers to the scene of the wreck.

"Ay, ay, sir," replied Callaghan.

"Have you seen anyone about?"

"No, sir."

"Have any of you been climbing on the wreckage?"

"No, sir; we've been standing here ever since you went on board."

"Must have been mistaken, then," said Dacres to his Captain. "I saw a door swing to, and I felt sure that I heard footsteps on the deck."

"You must have been. With the airship lying at this angle the door must have swung accidentally. We may have left it just ajar, and a tremor of the hull set it in motion."

With that Dacres crawled back to the hatchway. It was a tricky business, for the smooth metal plates afforded a very insecure foothold.

"Here's the book, sir," he said. "It does contain the names of the crew—thirty-nine, by Jove! And Durango's tally is not amongst them. That's forty, at least, for there may have been others on board whose names are not on the list."

"H'm! Well, we'll throw overboard the papers we found in Durango's cabin and our men can take them back to the 'Meteor.' After that we'll make a careful examination of the wreckage of the fore-part and see if we can identify any of the victims. Tell Callaghan to stand by as we throw the gear over-board."

As the two officers re-entered Durango's cabin they "brought up all standing," and looked at each other in amazement. They had left the coat hanging on its peg. It now lay on the floor, with the lining of the pockets turned inside out, while the loose ammunition had been thrown about and had rolled into a corner to leeward.

"That rascal has been on board!" exclaimed Whittinghame.

# CHAPTER XX
# A HAZARDOUS PROPOSAL

"YES, we've had a narrow squeak," continued the Captain. "It's easy to reconstruct the case. Durango was either concealed in the woods or else hiding on board. More than likely he was stowed away somewhere on the airship, otherwise Callaghan and the other men ought to have spotted him."

"But they didn't see him leave," objected Dacres.

"Quite true. Conversely they didn't see him come on board; but that is a side issue. One thing is certain; he was aware of our presence. He must have been stalking us. Directly we left the cabin he crept in, knowing that there was a revolver and ammunition in his pocket. With these in his possession it would have been an easy matter for him to shoot the pair of us, as we were quite in ignorance of his being here; but fortunately, as far as we are concerned, I smashed the revolver and threw the pieces over the side."

"With this possibility in your mind?"

Whittinghame shook his head.

"Don't credit me with too much, my friend. I saw the look on your face when I deliberately destroyed a particularly neat little weapon. Had it been of the same calibre as ours I would have kept it. As it wasn't, I put it out of the way of others who might make use of it against our interests. Anyhow, Durango was foiled on that count. He then remembers that he had documents of importance in those coat-pockets, so he hurriedly turns them inside out. In the midst of the search he hears you coming along the alleyway, and being without a weapon and afraid to tackle you on equal terms, makes a hurried retreat. The door slams, and your suspicions are aroused."

"Perhaps he's still on board?" suggested Dacres.

"You heard him on deck."

"But there are other hatchways he could make use of besides going over the side."

"There are; we'll investigate. I'll tell Callaghan to send up half a dozen armed men, and then we'll search every nook and cranny."

The reinforcements were quick in responding to the call. First of all the woods in the immediate vicinity of the after-part of the "Libertad" were searched; men were posted to prevent anyone leaving the wreck without being seen, while the rest joined the two officers in exploring the still intact practical portion of the airship.

For an hour the search was kept up, but without result. Satisfied at length that none of the original crew remained on board, Whittinghame gave orders for the whole of the documents to be removed.

This done the fore-part was examined. Under the wreckage were found the bodies of eight men, all terribly mangled, but sufficiently recognizable for the searchers to decide that Reno Durango was not amongst them.

The cunning rogue, instead of fighting his ship from the navigation room for'ard, had delegated that duty to a subordinate, and had taken up his position in the after-part which, when the disaster occurred, had escaped the destruction meted out to the rest of the ill-fated "Libertad."

Upon returning to the crippled "Meteor" Whittinghame, assisted by Dr. Hambrough and Dacres, proceeded to examine the documents found in Durango's cabin. From the contents of the letters it was soon made evident that the rascal had already entered into negotiations with several of the Great Powers for the disposal of the plans of the British submarines.

The original specifications and constructional drawings of the airship—those that had been appropriated by the Valderian authorities when Gerald Whittinghame had been arrested—were found intact.

"That's good," ejaculated Whittinghame. "It was more than I dared hope. I expected to find tracings of the original plans, but these rascals have evidently thought it unnecessary to make duplicates. If they haven't—and judging by the state of these drawings I don't think they have—they will never be able to make another imitation of the 'Meteor.'"

"What do you propose to do with the wreck?" asked the doctor.

"We'll wait until the repairs to the 'Meteor' are complete and then, I think, we'll set fire to the trees around the 'Libertad.' I would do so earlier, but we must try, if possible, to prevent the alarm reaching Naocuanha."

"But surely Durango will make a dash for the capital?"

"I think not. The Valderians do not look favourably upon those leaders who have come to grief. He will, for a dead certainty, leave Zaypuru in the lurch, and try his luck elsewhere—unless we prevent him."

"And the submarine plans?" asked Dacres.

"I have not forgotten that point," replied Whittinghame; "since they are not here nor in the wreck of the 'Libertad' it can be reasonably surmised that Durango has them in his possession—unless he left them with a trustworthy agent in Pernambuco. From the documents we found on board we know that he had not got past the preliminary negotiations. My immediate plans are as follows, gentlemen; if you have any suggestions or objections to make I shall be pleased to hear them:—

"In the first place we must make the 'Meteor' fit to resume her flight. Then, on the principle of striking while the iron's hot, we must attempt the rescue of the British prisoners at Naocuanha. Whether we succeed or not we can then devote our attention to the capture of Señor Reno Durango. Under the most favourable conditions it will take him six weeks to reach the nearest railway station. He has to recross the Sierras and make a long journey across the Voyocama Desert. By that time we shall have either succeeded or failed in our enterprise in Valderia. By making inquiries of any of the few Indians who exist in the Voyocama Desert we shall be able to get upon Durango's trail and run him to earth."

"Perfectly straightforward, sir," observed Setchell.

"Unless anything should go wrong," added Whittinghame guardedly. "Now, having settled these points, suppose we make an examination of our own craft?"

It did not require much inspection from the Captain to decide that No. 4 section was useless for further service. It had borne the brunt of the "Libertad's" fire. Only one ballonette retained its supply of ultra-hydrogen. The others, pierced through and through, resembled gigantic colanders, being completely riddled by the small calibre shell. Since the "Libertad's" magazine was situated in the corresponding section her crew had come to the conclusion that the same state of affairs existed in the "Meteor," and had hoped by directing most of their fire upon No. 4 section to destroy utterly their antagonist by exploding her ammunition-room.

In the other sections the damage was comparatively slight. Wherever a ballonette was pierced the high velocity of the projectiles had made a clean circular hole. All that was required to be done—for the ultra-hydrogen had already been exhausted from the intact ballonettes and stored in the high-pressure cylinders—was to patch the silken inner envelopes, rivet aluminium plates on the outer plating and test each gas compartment by forcing air into it. Should an escape still exist the hissing of the compressed air would be a sure indication of the precise position of the leak.

Officers and men worked with desperate haste, yet without sacrificing efficiency. In order to guard against a surprise attack sentries were posted at some distance from the stranded "Meteor," while several of her quick-firing guns were unshipped and remounted in positions commanding the approach from the Valderian capital.

Nevertheless, had Durango and his surviving comrades been men of pluck and determination, they might have entirely prevented the work of repairing the "Meteor." Under cover of darkness it would have been a comparatively easy matter to fire the dry grass, and the destruction of the British airship would have been a foregone conclusion. But the Mexican was a man to run no great risk. As soon as he had secured certain property from his wrecked cabin he had resolutely set out towards the Brazilian frontier.

Being a born gambler he realized that as far as Naocuanha and Valderia were concerned his luck was out. He still had the means of recouping his losses, but he was too wily to tempt fate in the country that had already proved so disastrous to his projects. Whittinghame was perfectly correct in his surmise. The Mexican was already on his way to pastures which, if not new, could provide abundant sustenance for his cupidity and cunning.

The day passed without any signs of Valderian activity. The news of the disaster had not reached Naocuanha, and as the mountain pass was an unfrequented one there was little risk of detection from passing travellers.

At daybreak on the following morning work was renewed. The condemned section, stripped of everything of value that had escaped the hail of hostile shot, had been removed from the adjoining divisions. Most of the leaks had been stopped, and Whittinghame had good reasons for hoping that the air test could be applied that afternoon.

Just before noon one of the outposts signalled that three armed men were approaching, but whether they were alone or merely the advance guard of a force of Valderian troops he could not determine.

Whittinghame, Dacres and Setchell were quickly on the spot, where, sheltered behind a ridge of rocks, they could command the approach of the three strangers.

Bringing their glasses to bear the officers saw that the party consisted of an elderly man and two who might be anything between eighteen and twenty-five, even when taking into account the effect of the climate. Each had a rifle slung across his back and a short native knife, somewhat resembling the Mexican machete, in a sheath on the right hip.

They had naturally seen the several separated portions of the "Meteor" as well as the after-part of the wreck of the "Libertad," and had left the beaten track with the evident intention of making a closer inspection.

"Not much strategy shown there," observed Dacres. "They make no attempt to conceal themselves. Who and what are they, I wonder?"

"We'll soon find out," replied Whittinghame, and beckoning to six of the crew he ordered them to make a detour in order to cut off the strangers' retreat.

Nearer and nearer came the three men, chatting unrestrainedly and gesticulating excitedly. Whittinghame, who spoke Spanish with tolerable fluency, strained his ears to catch the drift of their conversation.

"Frenchmen, by Jove!" ejaculated Dacres.

"I think not," whispered his chief. "Now!"

Simultaneously the officers and several of the "Meteor's" crew sprang to their feet, while at the signal those in ambush stepped into the path which the strangers had traversed.

In spite of the odds against them the three men were not wanting in courage, although deficient in strategy.

They stopped, unslung their rifles, and having given their opponents ample opportunity to shoot them down had the Englishmen felt so inclined, they flopped down on the rocky path and took what cover they could behind the small boulders.

"*Amigos!*" shouted Whittinghame.

"*Si, señor,*" replied the elder man, and without any hesitation he jumped up, spoke a few words to his companions, and then strode towards the spot where Whittinghame stood.

"*Americanos?*" he asked interrogatively.

Whittinghame shook his head.

"*Inglese,*" he replied.

"*Bien,*" rejoined the stranger, removing his hat and making a profound bow. "I am ver' pleased to speak with you, monsieur."

"You are a Frenchman, then?"

"Assuredly. I am called Antoine de la Fosse, I am an engineer of electricity. Gaston, Henri!" he shouted in his native tongue; "come here and make the acquaintance of these English airmen."

De la Fosse required but little "pumping." He seemed bursting with anxiety to explain his presence to Whittinghame and the rest of the officers.

He lived at Adiovonta, a small town about thirty miles from Naocuanha and nearly forty from the scene of the combat between the rival airships. He was on his way to San Carlos, where he had to inspect the electric-lighting apparatus of a newly opened copper-mine. Accompanied by his two sons and twenty Indian porters he was within ten miles of the mountain pass when he heard the dull detonations of the "Libertad's" guns. At first he did not know what to make of it, for he was in ignorance of the fact that hostilities had broken out between Great Britain and Valderia.

During his journey upon the succeeding day he made good use of a pair of binoculars, and at length spotted what appeared to be the wreckage of half a dozen airships. Leaving his men on the beaten track he set out with his two sons to investigate the scene of the disaster.

"So there is war between Great Britain and Valderia, eh? And the port of Zandovar is taken? Then I think I will not go to Naocuanha just *à l'instant*."

"Were you bound for the capital, then?" asked Dacres.

"As soon as I finish the work at San Carlos. I have to see the installation of the electric light at several of the buildings public—the Cathedral and the Cavarale, for example, but I think it will wait."

Whittinghame was too good a diplomat to come straight to the point and ask for direct information concerning the Cavarale—the prison where his brother and the British officers were confined. But the chance was too good to be thrown aside. He would put the question indirectly at a more opportune moment.

"Come and have lunch with us," he said courteously. "We cannot, unfortunately, offer you of the wines of *la belle France*, but our stores are by no means exhausted. After we have lunched we will show you the airships, or rather ours and the remains of the Valderian one."

"The Valderian one?" replied de la Fosse incredulously. "I did not know that Valderia possessed an airship. *Mais*, perhaps it is well not to show too much interest in a country that is not ones own."

During the meal Whittinghame, who attended to his guests' wants with the utmost politeness, related the salient facts of the dispute between the two countries and the events leading up to the chase of Señor Reno Durango.

"*Nom de Chien!*" ejaculated de la Fosse excitedly, bringing his hand down violently upon the edge of his plate, and sending the contents into his lap. "Reno Durango! Is it possible?"

"A friend of yours, monsieur?" asked Whittinghame.

"He is no friend to me," retorted the indignant Frenchman. "I remember well his master, the pirate Karl von Harburg, who captured 'La Touraine' and stole fifty thousand francs from me. Again, Señor Durango—*que le diable l'importe*—did his best to kill me at Zandovar a little more than a year ago. *Peste!* I have no love for Señor Durango. *Voyons,* let me rejoice over the debris of his airship."

Accordingly Whittinghame, Dacres, and the doctor accompanied the Frenchman and his two sons to the scene of the disaster. De la Fosse, with a Frenchman's typical sagacity, took the greatest interest in all he saw, and asked innumerable questions, while his two sons joined vivaciously in the conversation.

Suddenly a sharp report, unlike that of a rifle, came from the direction of the "Meteor." The three officers exchanged glances.

"Something gone this time!" exclaimed Whittinghame.

Something had gone. One of the ballonettes in No. 3 section had burst under the pressure of the compressed air introduced for the purpose of testing its non-porosity. The explosion resulted in the partial wreckage of the wireless room. Until the damage could be made good the "Meteor" was practically cut off from intercourse with the outside world. Before the days of wireless, isolation counted for little, but once having enlisted the aid of the Italian wizard, Marconi, the exigencies of civilization could ill bear being deprived of this means of communication.

"Anyone hurt?" asked Whittinghame anxiously, as he and his companions arrived on the scene of the accident.

"No one, sir," replied Callaghan saluting.

"That's a blessing," said the Captain fervently. "One man down is one too many; we don't want any more casualties to our small crew. Now let us see the extent of the damage to the wireless room."

"*Ciel!* It is of little consequence to one who knows," replied de la Fosse, after a brief yet comprehensive examination. "I know not how you call this— —"

"The magnetic detector, sir," volunteered Callaghan.

"Ah! the magnetic detector: it is out of—how you call it?—tune, *ne c'est pas?* The air-gap around the edge of this plate is destroyed. In two days the damage is made good."

"To anyone who understands the business," added Whittinghame.

"*Oui, monsieur.* Very well, then: I do you good turn. I will stop. Gaston will take my men to San José. Then in a few days I follow."

"It's awfully good of you, monsieur," said the Captain gratefully.

"*Pouf!*" ejaculated the Frenchman, throwing out his hands in a deprecatory gesture. "It is nothing. I will help you set it right."

This latest accident, coming on top of the previous misfortunes to the "Meteor," meant that the airship would not be ready to resume her flight for at least a week; and during a week history might be made in Valderia without Whittinghame and his companions being aware of what was going on.

Dacres got on excellent terms with Antoine de la Fosse and his son Henri, and before the end of the week he felt emboldened to tackle the Frenchmen on the subject of the Cavarale Prison.

"You seem very anxious to know all about the prison, *mon ami*," remarked the elder de la Fosse. "One would think that you would like to pay it a visit."

"That I should," replied Dacres. "Not as a prisoner, monsieur, but just to find my way about. You remember Mr. Whittinghame told you we were making an attempt to rescue some English prisoners there."

"And I showed you the plan of the Cavarale," said de la Fosse. "A plan like that to a man with ordinary intelligence is worth a hundred thousand books of direction."

"Quite true," assented Dacres. "But I have a strong desire to see what the prison is like. To put the matter bluntly, could you get me a pass to enter the Cavarale?"

The Frenchman did not reply for a few moments. "See you here," he exclaimed. "I would help you, for I like not the President Zaypuru. But it is too difficult. If they catch you, then you are shot as a spy, and I am arrested for assisting an Englishman to spy. You understand?"

"I quite see your point, monsieur," said Dacres. "You would be betraying the country which you have made your temporary home."

"You do not see the point, Monsieur Dacres," corrected the Frenchman. "It is not a question of betray: it is revenge. I have no cause to like the present government, for when Zaypuru made the insurrection his soldiers looted my house. I was then living close to Naocuanha. It is a long story and I will not now tell it you. But if I could I would help you."

He paused and puffed vigorously at his cigar. Dacres watched his face eagerly. De la Fosse was pondering the question over in his mind. Dacres let him think undisturbed. He realized that he had stirred the Frenchman's passions. He was brooding under a heavy grievance. De la Fosse, like many other Europeans, had good cause to hate President Zaypuru and all his works.

"I have a plan," exclaimed de la Fosse suddenly. "I tell you. Suppose I send Henri to inspect the Cavarale? It must be examined before I can start work with the electric light installation."

"Well?"

"Then Henri must have an assistant, *bien entendu*? Suppose you go as assistant to my son? I give your name on the pass as Monsieur— —"

"As Monsieur le Plaisant," added Dacres, a thought flashing across his mind.

"You, then, know a Monsieur le Plaisant?" asked the Frenchman.

"Yes, I believe I do," replied Dacres grimly, with a lively recollection of his prank on the midshipmen on H.M.S "Repulse."

"*Bien!* Then I will inform Henri. Only, monsieur, if you are detected you will be shot."

"That I quite understand," replied Dacres coolly.

"If you are detected," continued de la Fosse, "I know that you are an English gentleman and will absolve Henri from blame."

"Of course," agreed Dacres. "I promise on my honour that if anything goes wrong—I don't think it will, by the by—I will make out that I deliberately deceived your son. He, of course, must be told to repudiate me, should the Valderians spot me."

"You are a good impersonator, Monsieur Dacres?"

"Fairly," replied Dacres modestly. "I bluffed a flagship's officers once, only— —"

He pulled himself up. It was not desirable, on the eve of a similar episode, to proclaim the failure of the former attempt.

"Very well," agreed de la Fosse. "I will put the name of Monsieur le Plaisant on the pass, and Henri will show you the road to Naocuanha."

# CHAPTER XXI
# WITHIN THE CAVARALE PRISON

"LOOK here, Dacres, I won't have you running this risk," said Whittinghame when his subordinate unfolded his plan for investigating the place of captivity of Admiral Maynebrace and his compatriots in misfortune.

"There'll be no risk," replied Dacres. "That is, if I act with a reasonable amount of caution. Besides, I want to have another little game with old Maynebrace—bless his grey hair!"

Whittinghame shrugged his shoulders deprecatingly. "How long do you reckon this mad freak of yours will take?" he asked.

"If we leave here at daybreak to-morrow we ought to be back at the end of the fifth day. It's only half a day's journey to La Paz railway station, so de la Fosse informs me. We'll have to hire a couple of Indians to carry our professional gear and clothing, so as to give more colour to the scheme. Henri could take some of his father's men, only they might start talking about the stranded airships and give rise to suspicions."

"Honestly I don't like your scheme, Dacres, but since you think it's feasible and its results will be beneficial to our proposed operations I suppose I mustn't raise any more objections."

Henri de la Fosse entered into the project with the greatest eagerness. He, too, had cause to hate the present Valderian government like poison.

Had it not been for Zaypuru and Durango, the Frenchman and his two sons would have been able to attain their desires and return to their native country long ago. The revolution had practically ruined de la Fosse. His accumulated earnings had been fraudulently appropriated. He was almost without sufficient means to pay his passage back to Marseilles. He had, therefore, been obliged to remain in Valderia, working desperately at his profession in the hope of being able, to some extent, to retrieve his lost fortune.

When Whittinghame requested Antoine de la Fosse to name a sum for repairing the wireless gear the little Frenchman waxed indignant. He would take nothing, he replied proudly. It was a pleasurable task to be able to assist the Englishmen in their effort against Zaypuru and Durango.

Whittinghame was equally indignant. Finally the matter was compromised. Should Dacres' adventure prove a success, and should the "Meteor" contrive to rescue the prisoners from the Cavarale, de la Fosse was to put forward a claim on the British Government, and Whittinghame would back it up for all he was worth.

Antoine de la Fosse realized that he was making a great sacrifice in allowing his son to go to Naocuanha. Had it not been for the fact that he himself was the only one capable of effecting the delicate repairs to the wireless gear he would have insisted on being Dacres' companion. But having Dacres' assurance that in the event of detection the Englishman would accept all responsibility his doubts were set aside.

"Are you disguising yourself?" asked Whittinghame, for his comrade was turning out the contents of a small portmanteau in which the extraordinary "get up" he had worn on board the flagship was conspicuous.

"No," replied Dacres. "At least, not with false moustaches or whiskers. It would be too risky: the things might come adrift while I was fooling about pretending to take measurements."

"But we must take certain possibilities into the question," continued Whittinghame. "Suppose, for instance, Durango has, in spite of our surmises to the contrary, returned to Naocuanha?"

"Hardly likely," replied Dacres. "Had he done so we should have had a crowd of Valderian soldiers buzzing about before this."

The eventful morning came round. Antoine de la Fosse was to go with Dacres and Henri as far as the place where the mules had been left in charge of an Indian servant.

"By the by," remarked Whittinghame casually. "You haven't forgotten a rule. You must have one if you have to take measurements, you know."

"I'll get one," said Dacres, and presently he returned with a two-foot rule in his hand.

"If it weren't a very serious matter, Dacres, I'd simply roar with laughter," declared the Captain of the "Meteor." "I asked you simply to see what you'd do, and you've simply given the whole show away. Imagine a supposed Frenchman taking measurements in a country where the metric system is in force and using a British two-foot rule."

Dacres flushed under his tanned features.

"By Jove! I must be more careful."

"You must, not only on your account but for the sake of your companion. It's a good thing de la Fosse didn't see what you were up to."

Amid the hearty good wishes and farewells of the "Meteor's" officers and men Dacres and Henri, attired in sombreros, loose grey shirts, buckskin trousers, and native shoes fitted with formidable-looking spurs, set out on their hazardous enterprise.

Soon Dacres found himself in the high-peaked saddle of a mule. Although fairly docile as mules go, this animal required a considerable amount of skill on the part of the rider. Like most sailors Dacres rode awkwardly, hanging on more by good luck than good management, the performance causing the high-spirited Henri no end of amusement, especially when the inapt rider was slung out into the dust no less than three times during the first half hour.

"Pardon me, monsieur, I cannot help it," said young de la Fosse apologetically, although tears of laughter were trickling down his face.

"Neither can I," replied Dacres as he picked himself up and essayed to clamber into the awkward saddle.

"But if you ride thus into La Paz the Valderians will have suspicions," resumed Henri doubtfully. "In Valderia everyone rides superbly."

"I'll manage the brute all right long before we get to La Paz," declared Dacres stoutly. "Gee up, you rascal!"

Evidently the Valderian mule strongly objected to being urged on in English, for his hind-quarters suddenly reared. Dacres found himself rising in the air. Clearing the pommel by a few inches he alighted on the animal's crupper, whence he cannoned off into a particularly prickly clump of cacti.

Leaping from his saddle Henri handed the reins to his companion, then devoting his attention to the refractory mule he made it trot round and round in a small circle until the youth was almost ready to drop with sheer giddiness. This treatment also proved most subduing to the mule, for from that time Dacres had no further trouble.

The road to La Paz was with few exceptions mostly down hill. In places it wound round forbidding spurs of the mountains, where a false step would send animal and rider into the almost fathomless depths below.

So narrow was the track that Dacres wondered what would happen if they met persons coming in the opposite direction.

"That is easily managed," replied Henri when his companion expressed his doubts. "We would dismount. The other travellers would do likewise.

We speak with them; they speak with us. There is no hurry in these parts. Then the mules going that way would crouch down, and the mules coming this way would step over them. It is so simple when one knows how."

"Thanks, I would rather not have any," remarked Dacres, and later on he reiterated his thanks when he found himself once more in open country.

Feeling so stiff that he could scarcely dismount Dacres arrived at La Paz. The mules were handed over to the care of a most villainous-looking innkeeper, and their baggage given to four miserable-looking Indians, who for a few centavos could be engaged to act as servants.

While waiting for the train to start—it would be a fortunate event if it left the station within an hour of the supposed time—Henri, who spoke Spanish excellently, made several judicious inquiries of the men who were loafing about—for leaning against the adobe walls and smoking huge cigars seemed the total occupation of the visible inhabitants of La Paz.

When at length the train started on its journey to the capital, young de la Fosse had an opportunity of communicating to his companion the news he had gathered from the loungers at the station.

If it were true the situation looked very grave. There were reports that a battle had been fought outside the town of Zandovar between the gallant Valderians and the invaders. The British had been compelled to retreat to their ships, leaving over five hundred men prisoners in the hands of the victors. More, two English battleships had been sunk by mines, and the rest had stood out to sea.

Dacres simply roared. The rumours were so utterly unlikely.

"It may be true," said Henri gravely. "The best generalled armies make the mistake at times. The Italians at Adowah, the Russians in Manchuria, and the English in South Africa, *par exemple*."

"Then, if it is true we'll find the Cavarale chock-a-block with British prisoners," said Dacres. "So we'll wait and see."

When, after a slow and irksome journey, the train entered Naocuanha station, Dacres and his companion were pounced upon and questioned by half a dozen gaudily-uniformed officials. Their pass had to be examined, signed and countersigned by men who could hardly write their names, their baggage being searched, and even the contents of their pockets scrutinized. Dacres realized that had he attempted to don artificial hair and whiskers as a disguise he would have been detected before he left the platform.

At length the ordeal was passed, and escorted by four soldiers the two "electrical experts" made their way to an hotel.

The city of Naocuanha was under martial law. There were troops—for the most part ill-clad, ill-armed, and badly disciplined—everywhere. Most of the shops were shut, and had their windows boarded up. In several places barricades had been thrown across the streets and machine guns placed in position. The steam-cars and public vehicles had either been kept in their sheds or pressed into military service. Everywhere notices were posted up, warning the civil population to be in their houses by sunset under pain of fine and imprisonment.

"This doesn't look like a British reverse," thought Dacres. "The whole crowd of them are in a mortal funk. That's quite evident."

Acting on his companion's advice Dacres feigned a bad headache on their arrival at the hotel and promptly went to bed. Until Henri felt fairly certain that none of the guests—who, fortunately, were few in number—understood French it was advisable for the pseudo-electrician to keep to himself.

All night long bugles were blaring and drums beating. The garrison of Naocuanha were evidently expecting an attack from the British forces in possession of Zandovar. Consequently Dacres spent a restless night, while the swarms of mosquitos that found their way in through the rents in the mosquito curtains of his bed added to his discomfort.

Next morning, after Henri had paid a compulsory visit to the commandante's office, the two men, with their Indian servants, set out for the Cavarale.

The prison stood about two miles from the city. It occupied an isolated position, being on a broad grassy plain. The building was of rectangular formation with squat square towers at the four corners. It was surrounded at a distance of twenty feet from the main walls by a mud and rubble wall surmounted by a *chevaux de frise*.

In the centre of this outer enclosure on the city side was a gateway with an adobe hut close by; but this entrance was apparently neglected, for the gate stood wide open, and no one seemed to be on guard.

In the intervening space ran a dry ditch crossed by a broad wooden bridge leading to the inner gateway.

This was a more imposing affair, the stone archway being surmounted by the arms of the republic. The door was of very massive wood and pierced by a wicket. On either side were loopholes so that the approach could be commanded by rifle fire if necessary; while above each of the four towers grinned the barrels of an old type of machine gun of the Nordenfeldt pattern.

Pacing up and down the parapet or else lolling in the shade of the towers were several sentries, each with the inevitable cigar or cigarette in his mouth. They eyed the approaching strangers with apparent unconcern, making no attempt to challenge them.

Directly Henri pulled the bell the wicket was opened and a serjeant gruffly demanded to know the business of the two strangers.

In reply young de la Fosse pulled out the pass and presented it. The fellow took the document, pretended to read it while holding it upside down, and calling to a soldier who happened to be standing close by, bade him hand the pass to the serjeant of the guard.

Apparently, this non-commissioned officer could make no more of it than did his subordinate; but, throwing aside his cigar, he leisurely strolled off to the quarters of the commandante of the prison.

Half an hour later the Frenchman and the pseudo compatriot were permitted to enter. An empty store was allotted for the reception of their belongings, and the Indians were told to remain there until wanted.

"You remain also," said Henri in a low voice to Dacres. "I have to see the commandante."

Presently Henri returned with a bundle of papers, showing the general plan of the prison on a large scale, and the various parts that it was proposed to fit with electric lighting apparatus.

To show undue energy would arouse suspicion, so the two electricians spent quite an hour in ostentatiously examining the documents before proceeding with the actual work of "measuring up."

Then, having offered a cigarette to the soldier told off to attend on them, Henri and Dacres made their way to the *patio* or courtyard in the centre of the quadrangle.

While busy with the tape Dacres kept his eyes wide open. Evidently three sides of the building were intended for the prisoners' quarters, for they were lighted by small square windows heavily barred and at a height of twenty feet from the ground. The remaining side was in the occupation of the troops who formed the joint rôle of garrison and jailers, while in one corner of the *patio* and farthest remote from the entrance was a stone building in which the commandante of the prison lived. It was two-storyed, with a flat roof, from which a light gangway communicated with the flats of the quarters surrounding the quadrangle. A covered way also led from the commandante's residence to the guard room.

"The commandante says that he is busy to-day and does not wish to be disturbed by having men to measure the rooms of his house," said Henri, "so that will be much better for us. We can go sooner to the quarters of the prisoners."

"Very good," assented Dacres.

They conversed in English, since Dacres was a precious bad French scholar. There was no need to do otherwise since de la Fosse, by a simple, seemingly aimless question to the soldier who accompanied them, found out that he understood no language but his own.

Having finished their ostentatious work in the *patio*, Henri tapped the plan he held in his hand and pointed significantly towards the prison-buildings.

The soldier shrugged his shoulders indifferently, then slouched towards the door. In response to a knock the door was opened by a fierce-looking mulatto who, apparently satisfied that the two foreigners were properly escorted, passed them in without further ado.

The prison was two-storyed. The cells on the ground floor were not lighted from without, and were constructed for the reception of common criminals. Recently these occupants had been transferred *en bloc* to the civil prison in Naocuanha, and consequently they were now unoccupied. The political and foreign prisoners were distributed in cells on the upper story, to the number of nearly a hundred. Of these nine were Englishmen, including the two who were arrested before the outbreak of hostilities, and whose detention formed one of the principal causes of the rupture between Great Britain and the republic of Valderia. In addition to the nine were partisans of the late President San Bonetta who, having escaped the extreme measures adopted by the ferocious Diego Zaypuru, were still in rigorous confinement and in constant fear of being summoned to execution.

Fearing to cause suspicions by asking where the British prisoners were lodged, Dacres and his companion had to take each cell in order, measuring the distance from the centre of the corridor, and the height of the position of the proposed lamp. To hurry over the task would raise doubts in the officials' minds as to the *bona fides* of the avowed electricians. Thus the short working-day ended without Dacres having an opportunity of entering into communication with any of his former brother-officers.

On the following day the prospect looked brighter, since there was no needless delay in the *patio*. Don Alonzo da Costa, the commandante, was still indisposed to allow the electricians to enter his quarters, so, thankfully, Dacres and his companion resumed their tedious tour of the cells.

At length the jailer unlocked the door of a cell situated in the north-east angle of the building, and the two engineers solemnly filed into the room.

It was slightly larger than the others, but sparely furnished, the latter consisting of a plain deal table and chair, and an iron cot-frame, on the foot of which were two rolled blankets and a thin straw mattress.

As the men entered a stentorian voice exclaimed,

"Bless my soul, Dacres, what on earth are you doing here?"

The speaker was his late chief, Rear-Admiral Maynebrace.

# CHAPTER XXII
# DACRES REMINDS THE ADMIRAL

"STEADY, sir," remonstrated Dacres, addressing the Admiral and at the same time turning his head away as if consulting with his colleague. "This won't do; you'll spoil the whole show."

"Surely, Mr. Dacres, you haven't signed on with these——"

Admiral Maynebrace's remarks were cut short by the soldier bringing the butt of his rifle down upon the stone floor with a resounding clang and causing the astonished old officer to skip more agilely than he had done for years past.

"That's excellent," exclaimed Henri addressing the sentry in Spanish. "Keep the rascally prisoner in his place. We do not want to be hindered in our work."

"Sit down, sir, and pray be calm," continued Dacres, still talking as if he were referring to the task of measuring the walls. "Don't pay any outward attention and listen. (Twenty-five centimetres from that cornice, Henri: have you got that down?) We hope to bring the airship 'Meteor' to your rescue in a few days, sir, so be prepared. Turn in all standing, if you can, for we may have to hurry you up. (Do you think that will be far enough from the wall for the position of the switch, Henri? Good!) I can't expect you to answer any questions, sir. It isn't pleasant to be prodded on the toes by the butt-end of a rifle. Yes, sir, I am once more impersonating a Frenchman. Let us hope with more success than on the last occasion. Then I was literally slung out of the Service; now, by a similar means, I hope to get you slung out of here. (You think so, Henri? Suppose we carry the wiring down in this direction?)"

Dacres paused in his monologue, partly to allay any signs of curiosity on the part of the soldier and partly to enjoy his little joke with his one time superior officer. It wasn't every day in the week that an ex-sub-lieutenant could talk like a Dutch uncle to an admiral on the Active List. The idea of heaping coals of fire on Maynebrace's head commended itself to the pseudo-Frenchman, and he made good use of the opportunity.

"I am indeed sorry that you cannot express in words your gratitude for what we are doing for you, sir," he continued. "I know the feeling under which one labours when a man has to listen to a sermon without being able to put his spoke in the wheel (unwind the tape a little, please, Henri. *Merci, bien*). However, we will not dwell on that point. We hope at about six bells in the middle watch on the first convenient night to pay a surprise visit to the Cavarale. We may have to use explosives, so, sir, pray do not be unduly alarmed. (That is right, Henri, six metres will be quite sufficient.)"

Dacres methodically paced the cell, motioning the Valderian sentry to stand aside so as not to impede his work. The fellow, impressed by the zeal of the "electrician," stepped back without a murmur or gesture of remonstrance.

"If in the meantime you can get into communication with the rest of your staff, sir," continued Dacres, "perhaps you will mention what I have told you in case we have to pack up before our professional work is completed. That being so, Messieurs Henri de la Fosse and Jean le Plaisant—you may have heard that name before—must bid you their adieux."

Admiral Maynebrace stood his unaccustomed gruelling like a man. He knew quite well what Dacres was driving at. He was generous enough to admit that his former subordinate was to a certain extent justified in "pulling his leg." Moreover, he admired the cool audacity of the ex-naval officer in risking his life by entering the Cavarale prison.

"Hang it all!" he soliloquized. "I was much too hard on the young rascal. We all make mistakes. It was a mistake on my part that landed me in this hole. The Service lost a promising officer when Dacres sent in his papers. If ever I get clear of Naocuanha I'll do my very best to make things right for him."

With this praiseworthy resolution Rear-Admiral Maynebrace sank back in his chair to endure the dreadful monotony of his cell, for the only diversion he had was to make a systematic onslaught upon the swarm of insects that pestered him with their lively attentions.

While the Valderian soldier was securing the door of the Admiral's cell Dacres took particular notice of the lock. It was not morticed into the woodwork but simply screwed on from the outside. A fairly heavy hammer and a cold chisel would, he reflected, soon make short work of the lock on the door of No. 19, for that was the official designation of Rear-Admiral Maynebrace's substitute for the cabin of H.M.S. "Repulse."

The next cell was empty, but prudence compelled the two "electrical engineers" to spend a few minutes in taking bogus measurements. The adjoining one was occupied by a bearded man whom Dacres rightly surmised to be Gerald Whittinghame. There was a strong facial and bodily resemblance between him and the Captain of the "Meteor."

Still pursuing his quasi-professional tactics Dacres explained who and what his visitors really were, and at the same time cautioning the prisoner to act with discretion and not to speak a word in reply. Acting implicitly on these instructions Gerald Whittinghame assumed a despondent air, burying his hand on his arm as if completely indifferent to the presence of the three men.

But, presently, in the lull in his monologue Dacres' quick ear detected a systematic tapping made by the prisoner's fingers upon the deal table. He was replying in Morse.

"Carry on, I understand," said Dacres who, rule in hand, was fumbling on his knees in one corner of the cell, while Henri was taking down the measurements in his notebook.

"Tell Vaughan to attempt rescue before Friday," rapped out the message. "Zaypuru is coming here. Wants me to be a traitor to my country, or——"

The message broke off abruptly. Of the ominous nature of the incompleted part there could be no doubt.

"I say, Henri," said Dacres. "There's precious little time to be lost. I vote we make some excuse to leave Naocuanha to-night. Cut and run for it, if necessary."

"We will try," agreed young de la Fosse. "I understand."

"We'll do our best," said Dacres for Gerald Whittinghame's information. "So stand by, say, on Thursday night, if it can possibly be managed."

When the second day's work was accomplished the two "electricians" left the Cavarale, and followed by their Indian servants set their faces towards Naocuanha.

"We must clear out," said Dacres decisively.

"How?" asked Henri. "To go before we have finished there will arouse suspicions. We shall be seen when we enter the train."

"There are more ways than one of boarding a train."

"But the peons—the Indian servants?"

Dacres whistled.

"We mustn't leave them in the lurch, by Jove!" he said. "If it comes to leaving our hotel unpaid I think the exigencies of the business will be sufficient excuse; but I don't relish the idea of those fellows left to the mercies of Zaypuru and company."

"It is not that," replied de la Fosse. "They would come to no harm. They would as easily serve one master as another; but they would betray my father."

"If that is the only objection I don't see that that matters in the slightest," observed Dacres. "After this it will not be safe for your father or any of your family to remain in Valderia while Zaypuru is in power. Whittinghame will see you all safely through and send you back to France with a guarantee of sufficient money to keep you in comfort for the rest of your days."

"Very good: I am content," replied the young Frenchman simply.

"Then send the Indians on to the town," continued Dacres. "We'll take a stroll. I've a wish to see what the approaches to Naocuanha are like on the eastern side."

"Not in that direction," expostulated his companion. "It is towards Fort Volador, and if we go towards it we shall probably be arrested as spies."

"Very well, we'll bear away to the right," said Dacres reassuringly. "It doesn't so very much matter."

Henri dismissed the Indians and proceeded with the Englishman in the direction the latter had indicated. Young de la Fosse did not at all relish the new phase of the adventure. To run the risk of being captured he was willing to enter the Cavarale, but outside the prison a bid for freedom seemed fraught with more peril than he had bargained for.

Less than half a mile from the road to the prison ran the Naocuanha and La Paz railway, the course diverging slightly from that of the highway. Although the country around the capital was generally level at this spot, there was a slight valley, through which the Rio del Sol made its way to join the waters of the Pacific.

The railway, consisting of a single track, crossed the river by means of a steel girder bridge, while on the Naocuanha side of the valley was a siding.

As Dacres and his companions approached the bridge a goods train rumbled out of the city, panted heavily up the slight incline, and came to a stand-still on the siding. There were two locomotives attached to the train, one at either end, but upon pulling up there, no attempt was made to detach one of the engines.

"Look here," said Dacres. "We'll nick that rear-engine."

"What do you mean?" asked Henri dubiously. "What do you mean by nick?"

"Take possession of it. We have our revolvers. We'll terrify the driver and the fireman and make them disconnect the engine and push off towards La Paz."

"But the train from La Paz will be on its way," objected de la Fosse.

"I know; but we can wait till that goes by and then have a shot at it. We'll do it all right, never fear."

There was something so utterly confident in Dacres' tone that the young Frenchman's objections vanished.

"Very good," he replied. "I am ready."

As the two adventurers drew nearer the nature of the goods train became apparent. The twenty odd trucks were loaded with blasting powder, and were escorted by a dozen armed men.

It occurred to Dacres that it was rather an unusual thing to be taking explosives away from the seat of hostilities, until he realized that in anticipation of a siege of the capital Zaypuru thought it would be wiser and safer to send the blasting powder out of the city. It was a case of straws showing which way the wind blew. The president was beginning to fear for the safety of Naocuanha.

Henri's face lengthened when he saw the armed party, but having once signified his intention of going through the business, the plucky little Frenchman was not one to back out.

The display of force was more than Dacres bargained for, but knowing the temperament of the Valderians he felt convinced that on the sudden approach of two determined men the dozen irregulars would in all probability bolt like frightened hares.

However, he felt mightily relieved when the escort clambered down from the train and made their way down to the brink of the river, where, stripping off their raw hide shoes and canvas gaiters they paddled about in the water.

"Don't hurry, My festive friends!" exclaimed Dacres. "Take your time, and you'll do us a favour."

It was certainly a daring move on Dacres' part, for the plain was almost without cover, and the two men were in full view of anyone on Fort Volador or Fort Banquo who happened to be using a telescope or binoculars.

Nor was it advisable to attempt to take cover. The only feasible plan was to saunter towards the train and make a sudden rush at the last twenty yards.

Presently a dull rumble announced the approach of the La Paz and Naocuanha "express."

Dacres was half afraid that the escort hearing the noise of the on-coming train would hasten back to their charge, but fortunately the South American habit of procrastination was as deeply rooted in these Valderian irregulars as it could possibly be. An hour or two made very little difference to them: "to-morrow" was their creed.

With a rattle and a roar the train crossed the bridge, passed the siding and began to slow down as it approached the terminus of Naocuanha.

The time for action had arrived.

"Take it easily," cautioned Dacres. "Keep your hands away from your pockets till we make a dash for it."

Calmly lighting cigarettes the Englishman and his companion ambled towards the engine at the rear of the goods train. The driver was leaning out of his hooded cab, with the inevitable cigar in his mouth. The fireman had descended and was leisurely awaiting the approach of the two strangers.

His apathy quickly changed to an attitude of consternation as he found himself looking down the muzzle of Henri's revolver. His knees shook and almost automatically he raised both arms to their fullest extent over his head.

With a quick, deft motion de la Fosse plucked the revolver from the fireman's holster and threw it far into the thick grass, and, still keeping the man well covered, sternly ordered him to uncouple the engine.

Meanwhile, the driver made an attempt to draw a pistol, but Dacres was too quick for him. There was an ominous glitter in the Englishman's eye that told the Valderian engineer the uselessness of offering resistance. The next moment Dacres swung himself into the cab and clapped the muzzle of his weapon behind the ear of the terrified man.

Hidden by the brink of the declivity the escort was in total ignorance of what was going on. Their first intimation that something was wrong was a warning whistle from the foremost locomotive as the captured engine began to back away from the rest of the train.

"I hope to goodness that the other chap doesn't leave the siding," muttered Dacres, "or our retreat will be cut off."

Fortunately the driver of the first engine contented himself with giving the alarm. Had he backed on to the main line the Englishman's fears would have been realized.

In thirty seconds the captured engine ran over the points. Hearing the noise the pointswoman—a half-caste—came out of the hut and looked suspiciously at the crowded cab of the engine.

A sharp order from Henri was sufficient. The driver, thoroughly cowed, shouted to the woman to shift the points, and with the coupled wheels racing furiously the engine gathered speed in the direction of La Paz.

The race for freedom had begun.

# CHAPTER XXIII
# LOCOMOTIVE VERSUS AEROPLANE

DACRES had overestimated the advantage caused by the escort being barefooted. The men, unslinging their rifles, scaled the sun-dried bank with considerable agility and prepared to pour a volley into the fugitive locomotive. One thing only deterred them: they feared the presence of the dangerous contents of the trucks.

Still gathering speed the engine dashed across the bridge, greeted by an irregular and futile volley from the Valderian soldiers. Every shot either flew high above the cab or went wide.

The oscillation of the engine now began to be greatly in evidence. The speed soon mounted up to fifty miles an hour, practically a record for the La Paz railway. Dacres, still holding his revolver in readiness, was glad to lean back against a pile of coal and grasp a rail with his left hand; while his companion, standing behind the trembling fireman, kept looking anxiously through the square window in front of the cab.

The line, badly laid and maintained, caused the engine to swerve and jolt till at almost every instant it seemed as if it would leave the metals. Without a load the pace was exceedingly dangerous, till at Dacres' suggestion Henri gave orders for speed to be materially reduced.

Mile after mile sped by. Although the driver assured his captors that no other train was on the line between them and La Paz, Dacres had his doubts. He knew that the telegraph would soon be working, and utterly regardless of the lives of the engineer and driver, the railway authorities at La Paz would not hesitate to send a number of empty trucks down the long, gradual incline, or possibly tear up and portion off the track and derail the captured engine.

"Stop her!" ordered Dacres, an inspiration flashing across his mind, and his companion communicated the order to the driver, who seemed only too glad to obey.

With a heavy grinding of brakes the engine was brought to a standstill. The two Valderians, wondering what was going to happen, cowered in front of their resolute kidnappers.

During the run Dacres' sharp eyes had caught sight of a magazine-rifle of an American pattern stowed away inside the cab. Evidently the lot of an engineer on the republic of Valderia government railways was not a happy one, since one he had to be provided with a rifle to defend the train from robbers and "express agents."

Seizing the weapon Dacres jerked back the bolt. A loaded cartridge falling out and another appearing ready to be thrust into the breech, told him that the magazine was charged.

"Keep an eye on both men for half a minute," he cautioned, then resting the barrel of the rifle on a ledge of the cab he took deliberate aim at one of the two insulators of the nearest telegraph post.

Simultaneously with the sharp crack of the rifle the insulator flew into pieces, while the copper wire dropped to the ground, cut completely through.

With a hideous yell of fright the engineer, imagining that his comrade had been deliberately shot from behind, leapt from the cab.

"Don't fire," shouted Dacres, as Henri was about to blaze away with his revolver. "Mark time on the fireman."

So saying Dacres jumped from the engine and started in pursuit of the fugitive. Ere the latter had covered fifty yards the Englishman overhauled him. The moment the Valderian felt himself gripped by the shoulder he stopped short, whipped out a formidable-looking knife which he had hitherto kept concealed, and made a savage lunge at his pursuer.

Dacres felt the keen blade pass between the right arm and his ribs. Adroitly springing backwards he raised his revolver and fired—not at the half-frantic engineer but at the glittering blade.

The knife was wrenched from the Valderian's grasp. He fell on his knees, begging for mercy. "Get up, you silly idiot," roared Dacres. "We are not going to hurt you. Get back to the engine."

Although the fellow knew not a word of English, the gestures that Dacres used were sufficiently emphatic to be understood. Like a lamb he allowed himself to be taken back towards the post he had but recently deserted.

Henri was alone on the engine. The fireman, profiting by the diversion caused by Dacres' revolver shot, had made a bolt for liberty. Forbearing to fire on the fugitive, the Frenchman watched the fellow running for dear life through the long grass of the plain that stretched on either hand as far as the eye could see.

"Can't be helped," said Dacres cheerfully. "We'll have to do our own stoking—putting the coals on the furnace, you know. Tell that engineer he's in no danger so long as he sticks to his post and obeys orders. After all, it doesn't very much matter. In fact, it's a good job, since we've only one man to keep in order. Now for the remaining telegraph wire. Tell the fellow to turn round and see what I am going to do, in case he gets another jumpy fit."

With the second shot the wire was severed. Telegraph communication between Naocuanha and La Paz was, for the time being, totally interrupted.

"Hope we're not too late," muttered Dacres.

"They may have wired through already. If they have there's ten precious minutes thrown away. Tell the fellow to start her up again, Henri."

As the engine gathered speed Dacres glanced back. The single track was visible for nearly four miles. There were no signs of pursuit from that direction.

Ejecting the cartridge from the magazine of the rifle, the Englishman found that there were still eleven rounds. Having made this reassuring discovery he reloaded, set the weapon carefully in a corner, and devoted his attention to keeping a sharp look-out.

The engine had now gained the foot of the forty-five mile incline up to La Paz. Along this section the danger of being derailed by a loaded truck was not only possible but probable, provided the authorities at La Paz had already been warned. So long as the rail ran in a fairly straight direction there would be ample time to slow down and jump off before the impact occurred; but the fugitives knew that before long the railway would make several sharp and awkward turns.

Soon it became evident that more coal was required. Ordering the engineer to step back and face aft, Dacres plied the shovel while Henri still kept the prisoner covered.

As the vile Lota coal was shovelled into the furnace, clouds of black smoke poured from the squat inverted triangle-shaped funnel, and eddying downwards momentarily obscured the out-look.

The amateur fireman was in the act of throwing on another shovelful when Henri shouted into his ear and with his disengaged arm pointed obliquely in the direction of Naocuanha.

A rift in the pungent cloud of smoke revealed a very unpleasant sight. Overhauling the fugitives, hand over fist, were two large biplanes.

The engineer saw them also, and a wave of ashy grey passed over his sallow olive features.

"Madre!" he gasped. "They will blow us all up."

He realized that the danger was greatest from his compatriots. Without the least compunction the Valderian airmen would sacrifice the luckless engineer if by so doing they would involve the fugitives in the destruction of the engine.

"Tell that fellow to get back upon the foot-plate," ordered Dacres, at the same time picking up the rifle. "Keep a bright look out ahead, Henri. We'll stop their little game."

The young Frenchman was now entirely carried away by the excitement of the wild ride. What little fear he had at the commencement of the adventure had completely left him. Although he lacked the cool, calculating manner of his Anglo-Saxon companion, and manifested all the vivacity of the Gaul, he was not deficient in courage.

There could be no doubt as to the intentions of the two aeroplanes. Flying low—less than three hundred feet from the ground—they followed the line of rails. In front and slightly the pilot in each was a light automatic gun. The airman-gunner, however, was busy not with this weapon but with a number of cylindrical objects that Dacres recognized as bombs. The idea of the airman was to overtake the fugitive engine and drop a charge of high explosive on or immediately in front of it. This manoeuvre must be frustrated at all costs.

Setting the sliding bar of the back-sight to a hundred yards, the Englishman waited. He realized that he was at a disadvantage owing to the jarring and swinging of the engine, but the targets were fairly large ones and moving at less than ten miles an hour more than the object of their pursuit.

Soon the whirr of the aerial propeller of the leading biplane was audible above the rush of the wind and the rattle of the locomotive. The bomb-thrower poised one of his missiles.

"Idiot!" muttered Dacres. "He'd make a better show of it with that automatic gun—well, here goes."

Gently pressing the trigger, the Englishman let fly. The bullet passed close enough to the pilot to make him duck, but without cutting any of the wire stays and struts it zipped through the upper plane and whistled away into space.

"Lower, Basil, my boy," quoth Dacres reprovingly.

The pilot, realizing the danger to which he was exposed, tilted the elevating planes.

As the biplane darted upwards the Englishman's rifle spoke again. The brilliant sunshine seemed out-classed by the vivid flash that followed. Fragments of the aeroplane flew in all directions, falling with widely varying velocities to the ground, while only a trailing cloud of smoke marked the position of the unfortunate Valderian biplane a second before it was blown out of existence.

Struck by the furious eddy that followed the detonation the second aeroplane rocked violently. The gunner grasped one of the struts as if expecting the frail craft to plunge headlong to the ground. It lurched through the still falling debris of its disintegrated consort, then, gradually recovering its equilibrium it followed grimly in the wake of the fleeing locomotive.

"There's pluck for you," said Dacres under his breath. "I should have thought it was enough to knock the stuffing out of those fellows. Ah! they're going to tickle us up with that gun."

Three shots from Dacres' rifle in quick succession had no apparent effect. The biplane, soaring upwards, was momentarily presenting a smaller target against the dazzling light of the afternoon sky.

"*Phit, phit, phit!*" The automatic gun began spitting out bullets. Most of the shot went wide. One perforated the funnel, another ricochetted from the huge bell that takes the place of a steam whistle on American locomotives; the rest kicked up the dust.

Crack went the Englishmen's rifle: this time a bad miss.

"*Phit, phit, phit!*" The Valderian bullets were finding billets now. One, penetrating the boiler plate, let loose a fierce blast of hissing steam; another, piercing the roof of the cab, struck a pressure gauge, sending fragments of glass in all directions. The speed of the locomotive began to decrease appreciably.

This was more than the driver could stand. He threw himself flat upon the foot-plate, holding his hands to his ears as if to shut out the din of the unique engagement.

"Take cover!" shouted Dacres to his comrade. "Don't worry about the engine: she's stopping, worse luck."

The comparatively rapid diminution of speed on the part of the locomotive resulted in the aeroplane overshooting the limit at which it could use the automatic gun. The respite from the missiles was welcome until Dacres noticed the observer making ready to drop a bomb.

Three cartridges only remained in the Englishman's rifle; after that he would have to trust to his revolver. Beyond a range of fifty yards that weapon was practically useless for deliberate aiming.

Once again Dacres raised his repeater. He lingered over the sights till the biplane was almost overhead, then pressed the trigger.

"Missed, by Jove!" he ejaculated disgustedly. "Try it with your revolver, Henri."

Before Dacres could reload the Frenchman emptied four of the chambers of his revolver. The Valderian aeroplane, swinging like a wounded bird, began to fall towards the earth. The left aileron, bending upwards, threw the tottering fabric more and more on one side. The pilot, still grasping the wheel, was wedged against the padded rim of the chassis. His companion, hurled from his seat, fell to the ground with a dull thud thirty seconds before the biplane crashed upon the track.

Then with a detonation that shook earth and sky the six dynamite bombs exploded, blowing the wrecked aircraft to atoms and leaving a hole six feet in depth where the railway lines had been.

Almost at that identical moment the locomotive came to a standstill a hundred yards from the scene of the disaster. Fortunate it was that Dacres and his companion were sheltered from the blast of the explosives by the riddled hood of the cab, for stones and fragments of metal flew all around them.

Well-nigh deafened and with their senses dulled by the awfulness of the termination of the encounter the two men rose to their feet. The engineer was still lying face downwards upon the foot-plate.

"Now what's to be done?" asked Dacres, more of himself than with the idea of asking Henri's opinion. "Here we are stranded fifty miles from the 'Meteor' and with that rotten town of La Paz between us and our friends."

"We must walk," said the Frenchman. "See, there is our guide: the peaks of the Sierras. But this poltroon?" and he pointed to the motionless Valderian.

"Let him stop," replied Dacres. "He'll buck up when he finds he's alone. It will be all the better for us if he doesn't see in which direction we go."

Removing the breech-action from the rifle, Dacres began to make preparations for the long tramp. A bottle half-full of wine, a couple of small cakes made of Indian corn, and a piece of sun-dried meat comprised their stock of provisions after a careful search of the lockers of the cab had been made.

Presently Henri astonished his companion by shouting *"Prenez garde!"* and pointing through the forward window, which was partly obscured by the steam that was still escaping from the boiler.

Whipping out his revolver in anticipation of another attack, Dacres looked in the direction indicated.

Travelling swiftly down the long incline was a number of trucks. In another two or three minutes they would be crashing into the stationary engine.

# CHAPTER XXIV
# A BRUSH WITH THE INDIANS

"JUMP for it!" exclaimed Dacres.

Henri hesitated, then, prodding the engineer with his foot, gave additional warning of the threatened danger.

The fellow moved not a muscle. Thinking he had fainted through sheer fright, the Englishman grasped him under the arms and dropped him out on the ground. As he fell the Valderian rolled over on his face. He was stone dead: a bullet from the second aeroplane had pierced his heart.

Looking over his shoulder Dacres ran, following his fleeter-footed companion.

"Lie down when I give the word," he exclaimed breathlessly. "Now—lie down."

Both men threw themselves flat upon the ground at eighty yards from the railroad.

The noise of the impact was deafening. The splintering of wood, the clang of iron, and the hiss of the water upon the scattered contents of the furnace were outvoiced by the thud of the debris, which, hurled far and wide by the concussion, fell in showers about the prostrate survivors from the stolen locomotive.

Dacres rose to his feet. It was a bad enough smash, but he had expected it to be worse, for the trucks looked suspiciously similar to those left on the siding near Naocuanha. He felt convinced that had the authorities at La Paz the means at their disposal they would not have hesitated to dump a heap of dynamite cartridges into the trucks to make a complete business of "wiping out" the two fugitives.

He realized that their position was far from enviable. The mere fact of the attempt on the part of the Valderians at La Paz was sufficient to prove that Dacre's act of cutting the wires had failed to attain its desired object.

The two comrades had a dangerous journey before them. Ill-equipped, ill-provisioned, and in an open country where the Republican irregulars were practically certain to be in evidence, many perils would beset them ere they rejoined the "Meteor."

On the other hand, there was a chance that when the Valderian troops arrived at the scene of the disaster they might come to the conclusion that the two fugitives were either killed in the collision and buried under the debris, or else that they were blown to atoms in one of the two explosions caused by the head-long fall of the biplanes. Taking this for granted, the Valderians might abandon the pursuit.

Again, Dacres and his companion had dealt the Republic a heavy blow. In addition to the loss of the two aeroplanes the railway track between Naocuanha and La Paz had been torn up in two places, the damage being beyond all chance of a speedy repair. In the event of the Valderians having to abandon the capital and fall back upon La Paz, their retreat would be seriously impeded.

Having shared their scanty load of provisions the two comrades set out on their long and necessarily circuitous route towards the Sierras. Fortunately the grass was dry and left little or no indication of their tracks. In places the plain was composed of mud, still moist from the recent rains. In crossing these patches Henri suggested that they should walk backwards, so that should the faint trail be followed through the grass the trackers would come to the conclusion that they had hit upon the route of two men walking towards the railway instead of from it. To heighten the deception Dacres and his companion removed their boots when crossing the plastic mud. Their trail then resembled that of two Indians of the plains, who invariably go barefooted, although they mostly ride on horseback.

Before nightfall they had put twelve miles between them and the place where they had made their compulsory landing from the locomotive.

"It is time to halt for the night," declared de la Fosse, pointing to the sun, now about to dip beyond the horizon.

"Tired?" asked Dacres laconically.

"No, only we cannot see our way after dark."

"Is that all?" asked the Englishman. "If so we may as well carry on and sleep during the day. I can shape a course by the stars."

With the fall of night the temperature dropped rapidly. The travellers could well have done with the poncho or South American cloak, for in spite of their steady progress the keen air of the uplands cut them like a knife. They were already footsore; the long, tough grass impeded them; they were unable to see the ruts in the hard ground; nevertheless, they toiled on, Dacres setting the direction by means of the relative position of the Southern Cross.

"What is that glare in the sky?" asked Henri, stopping and pointing behind him. Away to the west and close to the horizon a blur of pale light flickered incessantly.

"Search light," replied Dacres.

"Where, then?"

"From the British fleet. On a clear night like this we can see the glare nearly a hundred miles away. Well, suppose we rest for half an hour and have some food?"

To this proposal Henri willingly assented. He was more done up than he would admit, but had gamely struggled to overcome fatigue and an almost irresistible desire for sleep.

Sitting back to back, as a mutual protection from the cold, the two men ate and drank in silence. They dare not smoke, knowing that the flicker of a match or the glow of a cigarette might indicate their presence.

"Time," announced Dacres in a low voice.

It required a great effort for them to regain their feet. The cold had numbed their weary limbs, and the Englishman was forced to come to the unpleasant conclusion that the halt had done them more harm than good.

On and on they trudged till the dawn. The Sierras, their snow-clad peaks crimsoned by the rising sun long before the orb of day appeared above the horizon, seemed as far off as they had on the previous night.

"You sleep for a few hours," suggested Dacres after another scanty and unappetising repast. "I'll keep watch."

The young Frenchman protested, but in vain. His companion was obdurate. With a quaint gesture of despair Henri stretched himself upon the grass and was soon fast asleep, utterly worn out with his long period of wakefulness.

Although Dacres was heavy-eyed he stoutly resisted the inclination to slumber. Very easily he could have shut his eyes and dozed while he was standing. More than once his head fell upon his chest to the accompaniment of a painful jerk of the back of his neck. Then with a sudden start he would open his eyes and survey the seemingly boundless expanse of waving grass in every direction, save where the distant mountains reared themselves in solitary grandeur. For two hours he kept the tedious vigil, the rapidly increasing heat of the sun adding to his discomfort.

"What's that?" he muttered, as a number of small moving objects at a distance of at least two miles caught his attention.

He rubbed his eyes, thinking possibly that his sense of vision was playing him a trick. No, he was not mistaken. There was movement—the movement of horses and possibly horsemen.

Without attempting to awaken his comrade Dacres dropped on his knees and watched. His sleepiness had temporarily vanished. He was now in full possession of his mental and bodily faculties.

"Horsemen, by Jove!" he muttered. "Indians probably. I'll keep well out of sight and perhaps they will pass by at a safe distance."

The riders were approaching rapidly: not from the direction Dacres and his companion had come, but from the south-east. If they maintained their present course they would pass about two hundred yards from the place where the travellers lay concealed.

Presently one of the riders reined up. His example was followed by the rest of the group. They sat on their horses like living statues, awaiting their leader's orders.

The Englishman was right in his surmise. They were Indians of the plains, more than half savages, born horsemen and crafty fighters. Most of them were naked save for a piece of hide round their waists and descending nearly to their knees. They were all armed with long knives, while, in addition, some carried spears of about ten feet in length and others had bolas coiled up ready to throw at any moment.

They evidently were suspicious. It seemed incredible that even their sharp eyes could detect the presence of the two men crouched in the long grass, but Dacres came to the uncomfortable conclusion that the Indians were about to advance towards the spot where he and his companion lay hidden.

Dacres grasped the sleeping Frenchman gently and firmly by the hand. The pressure caused him to open his eyes and to become wide awake without a spasmodic start that would have inevitably betrayed them.

"Indians!" he whispered.

Henri rolled over, then quietly raising his head peered between two tall tufts of grass. Without replying he deliberately drew his revolver.

Presently the horsemen—there were eleven of of them—broke into two parties and galloped towards the two Europeans, yet sufficiently apart to pass within fifty yards on either side.

Still wondering how the Indians were aware of their hiding-place, and hoping against hope that such was not the case, the two comrades still crouched in the grass; but in a very short time their doubts were at an end, for having formed a complete cordon the horsemen began to gallop round and round and at the same time gradually closing in upon their quarry.

"Do not let them get close enough to throw their bolas," cautioned Henri, "or we shall be entangled and as helpless as rats in a trap."

"Back to back, then," said Dacres. "Don't fire unless it is absolutely necessary."

The Indians had received warning in the night from one of their number who had come across the strange trail. Knowing that the two men were without horses—a rare occurrence on the plains—they came to the right conclusion that the strangers were in difficulties. Thus, they decided, it would be an easy matter to kill them, rob their bodies and bury them. The disappearance of two white men in a country where murder is a common, everyday occurrence, would raise little or no comment on the part of the lax authorities of the Valderian Republic.

Up sprang the two comrades, and steadying their revolvers in the crook of the left arm, each aimed at the Indian nearest to him. The crowd, without slackening speed, increased the distance between them and their intended victims, shouting the while in a jargon of which Henri, who could understand the language of his father's servants, failed to grasp the meaning.

After a while the Indians, who failed to understand why the two men refrained from opening fire, began to contract their circular formation. They could only come to the conclusion that the strangers' ammunition was exhausted, and that they were merely pointing empty weapons in the hope that the horsemen would beat a retreat.

Nevertheless, the attackers took ample precautions. Still keeping their horses at a hot pace, they threw themselves sideways out of the saddle, holding on only by one foot thrown across the backs of their steeds. Thus, practically sheltered by their horses' bodies, the Indians presented no great target to the white men's weapons.

Dacres understood their tactics. The constant whirling of the living circle tended to daze the senses of the two men in the centre. The Indians, having come within easy throwing distance, would hurl their bolas, then rush in and complete their murderous work with their keen knives.

"Fire!" exclaimed Dacres.

Two shots rang out as one. The Englishman's bullet brought down a horse, throwing its rider headlong and causing the animal immediately behind to stumble. As the Indian behind the second horse fell clear another shot from Dacres settled his little account.

Henri's shot was equally fortunate. Apparently it hit one of the Indians in the thigh, for he dropped and lay still. The horse instantly stopped, its fore legs thrust straight in front of it. Although untouched it remained by its master.

This totally unexpected welcome was more than the cowardly Indians could stand. With wild shrieks they rode off at full gallop, leaving two of their number and three steeds on the scene of action.

"We will take that horse!" exclaimed Henri, pointing to the one that remained by the body of its rider.

So saying he advanced cautiously so as not to affright the animal. Dacres, having recharged the empty chambers of his revolver, watched the proceedings. He did not feel at all capable of tackling a partly savage animal.

The Indian to whom it belonged still lay on the grass, his body huddled up and the long hide rope that served as a bridle and tether combined grasped in his hand.

"Look out!" shouted Dacres.

The warning came a trifle too late. With a spring resembling that of a jaguar the Indian threw himself upon the unsuspecting Frenchman, who had replaced his revolver in his holster.

In vain Henri leapt backwards and raised his left arm to ward off the stroke of the Indian's keen knife. The blade glittered in the sunlight. Even as it fell Dacres raised his revolver and fired. Although the distance between him and the Indian was a good twenty yards the Englishman's aim was true. Shot through the head the fellow dropped, writhed convulsively for a few seconds and then lay quiet—as dead as the proverbial door-nail.

"Hold up, old man!" exclaimed Dacres encouragingly, but to his great consternation he saw his companion reel. Before he could get to him the young Frenchman was lying on the ground close to the body of his treacherous assailant.

A rapidly darkening stain on Henri's shirt left no doubt as to the locality of the wound. Deftly cutting away the cloth Dacres found that the knife, partially parried by de la Fosse's left arm, had missed his heart, but had made a fairly deep gash between the third and fourth ribs; while in addition there was a clean cut on his forearm about four inches from the elbow.

Being without medical bandages and knowing that their scanty supply of water was none too pure, Dacres was puzzled as to what was to be done. Finally he tore the cleanest portions of his own shirt into long strips and bound the wounds tightly, after allowing sufficient time for the flow of blood to wash away any impurities that might have been communicated by the Indian's knife.

"Here's a pretty mess," muttered Dacres. "This is a fine way to look after Henri, after my promise to his father. Stranded miles from anywhere, in a hostile country, and with a wounded man to look after. A nice out look, by Jove! but it might be worse."

# CHAPTER XXV
# THE CAPTURE OF THE CAVARALE

HALF an hour later Henri opened his eyes. He looked about him for nearly a minute, then bravely attempted to rise.

Dacres heard him muttering in French but could not distinguish the words.

"The horse," he murmured, pointing with his uninjured hand to the animal that was still standing quietly browsing by its dead master.

"All right," said Dacres soothingly. "I'll see about that later on. Drink some of this water."

The young Frenchman gratefully accepted the proffered bottle, but steadfastly refused to drink more than a very small quantity.

"I feel much better now," he said. "Am I hurt very much? The rogue was too quick for me."

"It's not dangerous," answered Dacres. Neither was it. Nevertheless, should complications ensue owing to the lack of proper medical attention the result might easily prove to be fatal but for the present all that could be done was to cheer his wounded comrade and persuade him to attempt to continue his toilsome journey.

"How goes it?" asked Dacres, having assisted Henri to his feet.

"I feel so: my head goes round and round, but I shall be all right soon. Try to catch the horse," he persisted.

"Suppose I must tackle the brute, if it's only to humour Henri," thought Dacres, then, with considerable misgiving, he approached the animal.

Greatly to his agreeable surprise he found that the horse allowed itself to be quietly led away from its former master. The change of ownership did not seem to matter so long as the animal had a human being to assert his authority.

The knowledge that the food supply was running short, prompted Dacres to examine the bodies of the slain Indians in the hope of finding something in their possession that would sustain him and his companion; but he was disappointed.

"Are you fit to make a start?" he asked.

"Yes," replied Henri.

"Then I'll lift you on to the horse's back."

"But you?" objected de la Fosse. "We can both ride."

"Thanks, I won't risk it," said Dacres emphatically. "If I fell off I might drag you with me. I'm game for another forty miles, I think; so let me give you a heave up."

Walking by the animal's side the Englishman set a steady pace, his face still towards the seemingly elusive Sierras. The heat was now terrific, and although Henri bore himself bravely, he suffered agonies.

Shortly after noon the travellers came across a small stream. This was indeed good fortune. The water-bottle was refilled, the horse watered, and additional wet bandages placed over Henri's wounds; while Dacres stripped and revelled in the comparatively cool stream.

"I think I know where we are," said de la Fosse. "This river flows through San Carlos and La Paz. We ought to be within ten kilometres of the road my father and I were following when we saw the two airships."

"In that case we ought to reach the 'Meteor' before to-night," said Dacres reassuringly, but in his mind he had grave doubts. The terrors of the mountain pass loomed largely in his imagination. Burdened by a wounded comrade the passage would be hazardous in the extreme.

Buoyed up with hope Henri was impatient to resume the journey, and Dacres, willing to humour him, complied. But the young Frenchman's physical strength was not equal to his mental powers, for within an hour of leaving the river he suddenly fell forward in a dead faint.

Dacres caught him before he fell to the ground, then, lowering him gently, he rested his comrade's head on a mound, at the same time sheltering the luckless man from the fierce rays of the sun.

To the Englishman's dismay the horse, hitherto quiet, reared, then galloped off at full speed. The reason for the stampede was not difficult to see; at less than a mile off were the Indians, reinforced till they numbered thrice the original band.

Dacres was one of those men who see and enlarge upon perils a long way ahead. Perhaps it was natural caution. But the sudden appearance of the swarm of natives simply roused the British bull-dog spirit within him. He was metaphorically about to fight with his back against the wall, although actually there was nothing to protect him from a rear attack.

Carefully he drew Henri's revolver from his holster, opened the breech and assured himself that the six chambers were loaded. Then, placing the remainder of the cartridges on the ground within easy reach, he knelt with a revolver in each hand, ready to open fire.

Again the attackers prepared to execute their enveloping tactics. They were now within two hundred yards.

"Come on, you brutes!" shouted Dacres furiously. "Come on, and have a jolly good thrashing."

The possibility of being wiped out never entered his mind. He was now a fighter who "saw red."

A yell burst from the horsemen; then, simultaneously, the whole crowd broke into a gallop, the hoofs of the horses making a terrific din upon the hard ground.

Suddenly, just as the attack was about to split into two sections, one of the men reined in his horse, almost pulling it on its haunches. He pointed towards the sky, with fear and astonishment written plainly on his dark brown features.

The next moment the Indians had turned tail and were riding for dear life.

Dacres looked over his shoulder, half expecting to have fallen out of the frying-pan into the fire, and that the cause of the panic was the approach of a body of Valderian roughriders.

But to his astonishment and delight he beheld the "Meteor" flying at full speed and momentarily looming up larger and larger.

Dacres sprang to his feet and emptied both revolvers at his retreating foes. They were already out of range, but the shots served to attract the attention of the airship in case Whittinghame had not yet sighted his absent comrade.

Five minutes later the "Meteor"—still gigantic in spite of the fact that she had been shortened by two hundred feet—alighted upon the grassy plain The instant the rope-ladder was dropped men hastened to the assistance of Dacres and his stricken friend, foremost amongst them being Whittinghame and Antoine de la Fosse.

"My son—is he dead?" asked the elder Frenchman, who was almost beside himself with anxiety.

"No; he's fainted," replied Dacres. "He'll be all right directly Hambrough takes him in hand."

Quickly the crew of the "Meteor" rigged up a rigid stretcher, and upon this, lashed on to prevent him from slipping, Henri de la Fosse was taken on board the airship. As soon as the rest of the officers and men were embarked the Dreadnought of the Air rose to a height of ten thousand feet.

"Well?" asked Whittinghame with his characteristic brevity when asking a question.

"It's all right up to the present, sir," said Dacres. "Your brother is safe and so is Admiral Maynebrace. I've seen them both. It is essential that we should attempt their rescue at three o'clock Friday morning."

In spite of his efforts to suppress it, Dacres gave a prodigious yawn.

"Excuse me," he continued, "but I've had no sleep for nearly forty hours and precious little food."

"Then, make a good meal," said Whittinghame, "and have a sound sleep. There's plenty of time before the day and hour you mention. When you've told your story we'll lay our plans—no, not now. I refuse to hear another word till you have eaten and slept."

The appearance of the "Meteor" in the very nick of time was not a coincidence. As soon as Antoine de la Fosse had set the wireless apparatus in order a message came through from Whittinghame's secret agent at Naocuanha to the effect that two Europeans, posing as electrical engineers, had escaped from the city by taking forcible possession of a locomotive. Directly Whittinghame heard this he ordered the final work of assembling the four remaining sections of the "Meteor" to be carried out with the utmost celerity; but before the ballonettes could be recharged, another "wireless" was received announcing that the locomotive had been derailed after having been the means of destroying two of the Valderian air-fleet. It was supposed that the fugitives had escaped since there were no traces of their bodies under the wreckage.

"They've outwitted the rascals, de la Fosse," exclaimed the Captain when he received the news. "Trust Dacres to wriggle out of a tight corner. He'll see that your son comes through this business, too. Now, where do you think they'll make for?"

"Not to the south side of the line, monsieur le capitaine; Henrie has too much sense to go to our home. He will doubtless lead Monsieur Dacres across the plain to the south."

"Very well; we'll make a search," decided Whittinghame.

Thus the "Meteor," the damage having been made good as far as possible, set out on her voyage of investigation. Keeping at a great altitude she passed within ten miles of La Paz and shaped a course parallel to the railway till almost abreast of the place where the engine was derailed. Then, by a pure chance, the crew "spotted" the bodies of the Indians and their horses who had fallen in the first encounter.

Descending they made a careful search, and Dacres' trail as he led the captured horse was picked up across an expanse of bare ground. The general direction was followed by the "Meteor" till the alert look-out saw the Indians about to charge down upon the Englishman and his unconscious comrade.

For the next twenty-four hours the "Meteor" remained at a height of ten thousand feet, drifting with the light air current towards the Sierras. Whittinghame did not mean to anticipate the time arranged by his brother for the arrival of the airship at the Cavarale. For one thing he wished Dacres to be as fit as possible after his arduous experiences. He also was influenced by the fact that quietude was essential to Henri de la Fosse, if he were to be saved from an attack of fever following his wounds.

Whittinghame would have landed the patient and his father but for the fact that, in consequence of the affair at the Cavarale it would not be safe for the Frenchman to risk a meeting with any of the Valderian troops. As for Gaston he was miles away from the seat of war, and would not be in any danger, at least, for some considerable time. Ere that Whittinghame proposed to embark him and take the reunited family on board the "Meteor" when she started on her homeward voyage.

As soon as the sun set the "Meteor," still keeping at a great height, started on her run to the outskirts of Naocuanha. There was plenty of time, since the actual attempt to rescue the prisoners was not to commence till one in the morning.

Fortunately the night was dark. The stars were obscured; the searchlights of the capital were directed solely towards the seaport of Zandovar, for the garrison was in hourly dread of a surprise attack on the part of the British seamen and marines.

Shortly after midnight the "Meteor" arrived above the city of Naocuanha—unseen and unsuspected. The capital was at her mercy. Had Whittinghame wished he could have dropped powerful charges of explosives upon the buildings, but the idea of taking a mean advantage did not commend itself to his chivalrous instincts.

At 12.30 Dacres with Callaghan and ten of the crew entered No. 5 compartment. They were fully armed, while in addition a supply of short cords and two sponges saturated with chloroform were provided.

"All ready?" asked Whittinghame.

"Ay, ay, sir."

A metallic clang echoed through the after-section. The bolt action had been unlocked and No. 5 compartment was no longer joined to the remaining three divisions.

Slowly the ultra-hydrogen was pumped out of several of the ballonettes, and gently the independent division sank towards the earth.

Stationed at an open flap in the floor, Dacres "conned" the descending part of the airship under his command. Once or twice it was necessary to start the motors to bring the two hundred odd feet of gas-bag immediately over the rectangular courtyard of the Cavarale.

By the aid of his night-glasses Dacres could distinguish the outlines of the prison with tolerable ease. Nevertheless, every moment of the descent was one of suspense.

At any instant the huge overhead bulk might be seen by an alert sentry. In that case a bomb was to be thrown into the soldiers' quarters, and profiting by the confusion the airship was to descend as fast as possible and let loose her armed crew upon the terrified garrison; but only in case of extreme necessity were explosives to be used.

Only five hundred feet more. Perfect silence reigned below, while the only sound that came from No. 5 section was the laboured breathing of the twelve men as they strove with their pent-up feelings.

"Sentry!" whispered Callaghan pointing to a motionless figure on the wall nearest to the city.

Dacres nodded. He would not trust himself to speak.

Four hundred feet.

Suddenly a light flashed from one of the towers, and a number of men, one of them carrying a lantern, emerged and marched along the broad flat roof. "Rounds, by Jove!" gasped Dacres, then springing to the emergency switch controlling the supply of ultra-hydrogen and the ballonettes, he thrust it down.

The hiss of compressed air that followed seemed to the crew loud enough to arouse the whole garrison. Simultaneously the downward movement was checked and the section leapt quickly to a height of a thousand feet.

"Keep her there," ordered Dacres, then, glass in hand, he returned to his post of observation. Thank heavens the visiting rounds had neither heard nor seen the danger that threatened them. The crew could catch the sibilant challenge of the sentry as the soldiers approached his post. Having satisfied themselves that all was well, the rounds passed on to the next sentry, and so on till they had completed a tour of the walls. Then, descending to the courtyard by a flight of steps, the party crossed the *patio* and disappeared within the guard-room.

"We'll wait another half-hour," said Dacres. "Perhaps by that time the sentries will not be on the alert."

"Very good, sir," replied Callaghan. "I've tumbled across South American soldiers before now, and, between you and me, sir, they ain't up to much."

"Cap'n coming alongside, sir," reported one of the crew as coolly as if announcing the approach of the captain's gig towards a man-of-war.

Silently the major part of the "Meteor" glided within fifty feet of No. 5 section.

"What are you waiting for?" demanded Whittinghame.

"We saw the rounds were out, sir," replied Dacres.

"Oh, all right. I thought perhaps that something had gone wrong with the exhaust pumps."

"Oh, no; they are working most splendidly," announced Dacres. "We've decided to wait till the sentries quiet down after being visited by the rounds."

"Do you think you could do better by descending about a mile from the prison and scaling the walls?" asked the Captain.

"The difficulty would be to get the rescued prisoners to the airship, sir; I think we had better stick to our original plans."

"Very good," was Whittinghame's only comment.

Slowly the minutes sped, till Dacres, shutting the case of his watch with an emphatic snap, gave the order to descend.

Far below the glimmer of a match told its own tale. One of the sentries was lighting a cigarette.

"Look out," whispered Callaghan. "Blest if the four of 'em aren't altogether. That's a bit of all right."

The quarter-master spoke truly. Three of the Valderian soldiers had deserted their posts and had joined the one stationed on the west wall—that nearest to the city.

"Silly asses!" ejaculated Dacres "they are playing into our hands."

The four men were apparently having a friendly argument. More cigarettes were produced and lighted. Then after a short interval the sentries entered one of the towers and shut the door leading on to the roof. A gleam on the stonework told the aerial watchers that the unsuspecting soldiers had lit a lantern.

Two hundred—one hundred and fifty feet.

No. 5 section was now barely twenty feet above the walls and immediately over the courtyard. Her fabric, dimly illuminated by the distant searchlights, could not have escaped the notice of the sentries had they been at their posts.

Dacres now felt tolerably certain of success. Even had the sentries emerged from their unauthorized place of shelter the sudden transition from artificial light to the darkness of the night would have prevented them from seeing anything for at least half a minute.

With a slight tremor the detached portion of the "Meteor" alighted fairly equidistant from the encircling wall. Quickly Dacres and eight men descended and anchored the craft by means of ropes secured to the railings surrounding the *patio*.

Silently the adventurers followed their leader up the outside flight of stone steps on to the roof. Twenty yards farther on was the tower in which the faithless sentries were skulking.

Dacres looked through the narrow space formed by the door being ajar. The four Valderians were standing around an upturned barrel on which stood a candle. The men were deep in a game of faro, peering through the smoky atmosphere with eyes intent only upon the cards which were being thrown upon the impromptu table.

Signing to his men to approach, Dacres held up his revolver.

"Now," he exclaimed.

Pushing open the door he entered, following by his men.

For a moment the Valderians could not credit their senses. They stared stupidly down the muzzles of half a dozen revolvers. The cards dropped from their nerveless fingers, their winnings clattered on the floor. At the same time the candle toppled over and went out, leaving the room illuminated only by a lantern set in one corner.

Then one of the soldiers raised both hands above his head. His companions followed his example with surprising celerity. Without uttering a sound they tamely surrendered.

"Secure them," ordered Dacres.

In a trice the four trustworthy sentries were gagged and bound hand and foot. The knots were tied as only seamen know how: there was little fear of the prisoners being able to slip their bonds; while to prevent them from moving to each other's assistance each Valderian's rifle was lashed to his legs by cords above the knees and round the ankles. The captives were as helpless as logs of wood, and incapable of uttering a sound.

"Now for the guard-room," whispered Dacres.

This building, situated in one corner of the courtyard, could be gained either by descending the steps leading to the roof of the buildings abutting on the outer wall, or else by a covered way communicating with the quarters occupied by the rest of the troops.

The first was the only practicable way for the British airship's men to tackle the guard; but the great danger now was that should any of the soldiers on duty escape into the living-rooms by means of the covered gallery all chances of a complete surprise would be lost.

The guard-room was roughly furnished. There was a long table on which stood several empty wine glasses. Round the walls were wooden forms on which two men were sitting. Half a dozen more, including the serjeant, were lying on the floor, wrapped in blankets. In a rack close to the door were the rifles of the soldiers on duty.

Without hesitation Dacres and his men rushed as quietly as they could into the guard-room and planted themselves between the arms-rack and the surprised Valderians.

One of the latter, more daring than his comrades, made a dash for the farther door communicating with the men's quarters. Before he could open it Callaghan struck him on the temple with his clenched fist. The fellow dropped like a felled ox, the Irishman catching him ere his body flopped noisily upon the floor.

This slight commotion was sufficient to arouse the sleeping soldiers.

"Surrender or we shoot!" ordered Callaghan in the execrable Spanish he had picked up during a three years' commission in Gibraltar dockyard.

Without hesitation the men threw up their arms.

"Now what's to be done with this lot, sir?" asked the Irishman. "We can't waste time lashing 'em up."

Dacres saw that the windows were small and heavily barred, and that the locks on the door were strong.

"Remove the bolts of those rifles," he ordered. "Now, Callaghan, tell these men that if they attempt to escape or utter a sound we'll make it hot for them."

This the Irishman did, uttering threats that he had learned from the Scorps of the Rock which, judging by the speaker's ferocious gestures, struck terror into the hearts of the cowardly Valderians. They vowed compliance with such vehemence that they had to be told to keep silence lest the noise should alarm the rest of the garrison of the prison. Locking both doors and taking possession of the keys, Dacres led his men towards the barrack-quarters where the remainder of the rank and file—thirty all told—were asleep.

Now it was that Dacres' knowledge of the plan of the buildings was put to good account. He knew that underneath was a large storeroom, to which the only means of access was by a trap-door in the corridor outside the barrack-room. Once the soldiers could be forced into this semi-dungeon they would be incapable of doing any mischief.

The room was in darkness. A delay ensued till one of the "Meteor's" men took down a lantern that was hanging in the covered way.

"Two at a time," whispered Dacres, pointing to the triple line of sleeping men who were stretched in various attitudes on straw palliasses on the floor.

The first two sleepers were rudely awakened to find their arms and legs pinioned and a horny hand over their mouths. Incapable of resistance they were carried to the top of the ladder leading to the cellar, then fiercely threatened by the huge Irishman they were compelled to descend into utter darkness.

Twenty Valderians were served this way, when one fellow managed to give vent to a terrific yell, at the same time gripping with his powerful teeth the hand that strove to stifle his cry of alarm.

Instantly the remaining soldiers were awake, but being unarmed, they saw the uselessness of resistance. Without further trouble they were made to join their comrades in the underground cellar.

Without loss of life on either side, the Cavarale was in possession of the crew of the "Meteor."

# CHAPTER XXVI
# UNABLE TO RISE

"CUT the telephone wires, Callaghan," ordered Dacres.

"Beg pardon, sir," expostulated that worthy.

"Well?"

"Might I make so bold as to suggest, sir?"

"Carry on, then," replied Dacres, who from previous experience knew that the Irishman's suggestions were well worth taking into consideration.

"Suppose those chaps at Naocuanha telephone to the prison and get no reply, they'll find out that there's something up. I think, sir, it would be best to let the wire alone, and station a chap there to answer all inquiries and complaints, in a manner o' speaking."

"Quite so; but who will be able to do so?" objected his superior officer. "You're the only man amongst us who has any knowledge of Spanish, and with all due respect to your capabilities, Callaghan, I think they would spot your brogue."

"Yes, sir; but how about the Valderian chaps imprisoned here—the fellows old Zaypuru's got his knife into? They'd do the business with the greatest of pleasure."

"Good idea," assented Dacres. "But before we release the prisoners we must secure the commandante. Meanwhile, Callaghan, you might post two men at the door of the orderly-room in case there's a call, or if there are any of the garrison who have escaped our notice."

Silently the quarters occupied by Commandante Don Alonzo da Costa were surrounded. Then, having severed the telephone wire communicating with the orderly-room, Dacres knocked at the door.

After considerable delay the door was opened by a military servant, who was promptly knocked down and secured.

Don Alonzo was a widower and lived alone in the official residence except for the company of two servants. Owing to his refusal to let the pseudo-"electricians" enter his quarters, Dacres was not well acquainted with the interior. Three empty rooms were examined before the raiders came to the one in which the commandante was fast asleep. The door was locked.

Dacres knocked. A voice replied in Spanish demanding to know what was amiss?

Not trusting himself to reply the Englishman knocked again. He could hear the occupant getting out of bed. Then the jalousies across one of the windows were opened and a pistol shot rang out.

Don Alonzo, finding himself summoned in an unorthodox manner, had suspected that something was amiss. Going to the window he saw the section of the airship in the courtyard. Partly with the idea of giving the alarm and partly with the idea of damaging the ballonettes he fired almost point blank at the huge target.

"Lie down, men," ordered Dacres, then clapping his revolver to the door he blew away the stout lock. Before he could push open the shattered woodwork five shots in rapid succession whistled along the corridor. Had Dacres or any of his companions been standing they would have been in the direct line of fire.

The commandante had emptied his revolver. Before he could reload he was pounced upon, disarmed, and secured.

Meanwhile, the noise of the firing had reached the ears of the prisoners. The British ones, having been warned of what was taking place, maintained silence, but the Valderian political prisoners, thinking that either a mutiny or a counter revolution had broken out, shouted, cheered, and kicked up a terrific din.

Leaving a man to keep guard over the governor Dacres led the rest of his command to the prisoners' quarters. The captives had been left for the night, the authorities taking it for granted that there would be no use for any military warders. Since the keys could not be found, and Don Alonzo stubbornly refused to answer any questions put to him by Callaghan, the doors of the cells had to be broken open.

"Knock off this lock for me," ordered Dacres, pointing to the one on the door of No. 19—that tenanted by his former Admiral.

A telling blow with a sledge-hammer wielded by a former armourer's mate of the Royal Navy, sent the metal-work clattering on the stone floor of the corridor.

"Come aboard, sir!" said Dacres, saluting. Rear-Admiral Maynebrace did a thing he had never done before. He grasped the hand of his former subordinate and wrung it heartily. He tried to speak, but his emotion prevented him from uttering a single word.

"Smith," said Dacres, addressing one of his men. "Escort Admiral Maynebrace to No. 5 section. Place him safely on board and return. Now, lads," he continued, "we'll have the British prisoners out before we release the Valderian ones. We can't take them with us; they must shift for themselves. One moment: open this door."

The cell Dacres had indicated was tenanted by a Valderian general who had been a partisan of the ill-fated President San Bonetta.

Upon the situation being explained to him by Callaghan the Valderian readily agreed to take command of the rest of his fellow-prisoners. Going from cell to cell and addressing the inmates through the grille, he quickly obtained some semblance of order. The shouts and cheers died down, and the luckless Valderians, who for months past had been in hourly dread of death, assented to obey whatever orders their rescuers might give.

"Thanks, Mr. Dacres," said Gerald Whittinghame, when he was let out of his place of confinement. "I hardly know how to express my gratitude. President Zaypuru will, I hope, be disappointed in the morning."

"I trust it won't be the only disappointment," rejoined Dacres. "But there is little time to be lost. If you will go on board the section of the 'Meteor' will be with you presently."

Meanwhile, two more Valderians had been released and ordered to remain by the telephone in the orderly-room. Should any message come through they were to give a reassuring reply, and lead the authorities at the capital to believe that all was in order at the Cavarale. They were then told that as soon as the section of the airship rose clear of the prison, they were to open the doors of the remaining cells and take whatever steps they thought best for their own safety.

As soon as the nine Englishmen were released the order was given to return to the airship. As soon as the crew were on board, the two cables were slipped and additional ultra-hydrogen pumped into the ballonettes.

No. 5 section refused to rise.

"That's that rascal of a commandante," declared Dacres. "Up aloft, there, and report damage."

Armed with an electric torch one of the crew ascended the aluminium ladder between the double rows of ballonettes and gained a longitudinal gangway from whence it was possible to examine each individual gas subdivision. It was not long before he returned.

"Four badly holed, sir. All of them on the starboard side."

"Which ones?"

"B2, 3, 4, and 5, sir. They are quite flabby."

"Very good. Close the valves of the supply pipes to these ballonettes and charge the others to their fullest capacity."

Promptly this order was carried out. No. 5 section no longer stuck stubbornly to the ground: she was lively, with a tendency to list to starboard; but still the upward force of the ultra-hydrogen was insufficient to raise her.

Just then a vicious blast of wind whistled over the walls of the Cavarale, causing the airship to rock violently. The night, hitherto calm, was rapidly becoming stormy.

Ordering the crew to fall in, Dacres addressed them.

"My lads," he said, "we're in a bit of a hole. Owing to the damage done to some of the ballonnettes No. 5 section is incapable of lifting the additional weight. Some of us must remain. We may be rescued by the 'Meteor'—we may not. Owing to the rising wind, the odds are against us."

He paused. Taking advantage of the lull several of the men stated their willingness to remain.

"What's this, Dacres?" asked the Admiral. "You clear out and leave us. You've done all that is humanly possible, and if you fall into the hands of Zaypuru it will go hard with you. He won't dare to go to extreme measures with us."

"I don't know so much about that, sir," replied Dacres. "In any case, please let me remind you that I am in charge of these operations.

"Now, lads, I mean to stop. When we are discovered the forts will no doubt try to shell us to pieces, unless"—then raising his voice he added—"unless we contrive to capture President Zaypuru and hold him as a hostage. Now, my lads, who will remain with me?"

# CHAPTER XXVII
# PREPARING FOR THE PRESIDENT'S VISIT

"NOT all of you," remonstrated Dacres, although well pleased at the devotion of the men under his immediate orders. "Seven will be sufficient. That will lighten No. 5 section enough to give it proper buoyancy. Callaghan, you will take charge of the section until it is rejoined to the rest of the airship. Explain matters to Captain Whittinghame and say that we will sit tight so long as we can. Ask him to take the 'Meteor' out of sight of Naocuanha till ten this morning. If then it is advisable for him to return, a blue and white flag will be hoisted from the flagstaff of the Cavarale."

"One moment, Dacres," interposed Gerald Whittinghame. "I am ready to abide by your decision, but couldn't I render some assistance by remaining with you? My knowledge of Spanish, for instance? If you are to lure Zaypuru into the Cavarale you'll have to be very wary."

"I quite agree," replied Dacres, "but at the same time I think you ought to rejoin your brother."

"It's not a question of ties of relationship," objected Gerald. "It's a question of duty. That idea of yours, Dacres—if it comes off—will be a means of bringing the war to an end. With Zaypuru in our hands the resistance of the Valderian troops will crumble like a pack of cards."

"Very well, then," agreed Dacres. "We shall be very glad of your assistance. We'll discuss the plans later."

"I say, Dacres," persisted the Admiral's flag-lieutenant, "I mean to stay——"

"I'll put you under close arrest if you don't obey orders," retorted Dacres with well-assumed severity.

"Landing-party, fall in!" he ordered.

The seven men quickly descended and fell in upon the courtyard. Dacres bade the released prisoners farewell, gave a few necessary orders to the trustworthy Callaghan, and followed Gerald Whittinghame down the ladder.

"All clear!" he shouted.

Once more the ultra-hydrogen was forced into the reserve ballonettes. Carried sideways by the wind No. 5 section rose, cleared the wall by less than six feet, and shot upwards at a rapid pace till lost to sight in the darkness. Her movements, however, had been followed by the anxious Captain of the "Meteor," and without delay he started to get in touch with the tail portion of the Dreadnought of the Air.

By the time the "Meteor" coupled on her No. 5 section the airship had drifted twelve miles to leeward of Naocuanha.

"That hare-brained rascal!" exclaimed Vaughan Whittinghame, when he received the Irishman's report. "I suppose he'll scrape through all right — he generally does. In any case, it's a piece of sterling work; self-sacrifice of the highest order."

"Can you land us at Zandovar?" asked Rear-Admiral Maynebrace.

"Sorry," replied Whittinghame. "Not by night. I've no fancy to be plugged by the shells of your squadron or mistaken for a hostile aircraft. After ten o'clock to-morrow I may — if I haven't to avenge Dacres and my brother." Acting under Gerald Whittinghame's instructions General Galento — for that was the name of the Valderian who had been entrusted to maintain order amongst the released prisoners — ordered his compatriots to assemble in the *patio*.

This they did, to the number of eighty. As far as Valderians went these men looked capable of giving a good account of themselves. They were all actuated by feelings of revenge towards their former captors and especially President Zaypuru. Had they got out of hand the lives of the soldiers who had formed the garrison of the Cavarale would not have been worth a moment's purchase. Without delay Gerald Whittinghame addressed them. His almost perfect knowledge of Spanish, the fluency of his words and his commanding delivery all told upon his listeners.

"Friends of the late President San Bonetta," he exclaimed. "The time is at hand when you will be able to completely turn the tables on your oppressors. To do so you must implicitly obey the orders of the Commandante Dacres here, whose mouthpiece I am. The Cavarale is entirely in our possession. Don Alonzo da Costa is a prisoner, together with every man of the garrison. At nine o'clock this morning the villainous Zaypuru will pay us a visit."

Shouts of execration burst from the lips of his listeners. Cries of "Death to the President!" "Down with Zaypuru!" were heard on all sides. At length Gerald silenced them by raising his right hand.

"Zaypuru must be captured," he continued. "It can be done. How, I will explain; but before so doing I must have your promise that if he fall into our hands he will be treated in a manner worthy of civilized people."

"We will have him shot," muttered a Valderian, and several voices backed him up.

"Very well," rejoined Whittinghame. "If that is what you are resolved to do you had better go outside the prison and do it. Remember that your only chance of safety lies in remaining here. Without, you will be seen and pursued by Zaypuru's horsemen. Detachments of his troops are at La Paz, so that your retreat in that direction is cut off. Rather than allow a prisoner in our hands to be barbarously murdered the Commandante Dacres will release and arm the soldiers who are now in his power. Think it over quickly, and let me know your decision."

The partisans of the late president saw that the Englishmen held the whip-hand. Great as was the hatred of the former for Zaypuru, the fear of what might happen should the aid of Dacres and his companions be withdrawn was greater.

"We agree," they announced. "We swear it."

"It is well," continued Gerald. "Now for our plans. When your English friends surprised the garrison many of the soldiers were in their beds. They were sent into one of the cellars under the barracks, their clothes and accoutrements remain. Thirty of you will, therefore, put on these men's uniforms, and by forming a guard of honour and placing sentries on the walls will completely deceive the President Zaypuru. General Galento will oblige us by arraying himself in the uniform of the Commandante Alonzo da Costa and acting the part of our late custodian-in-chief, until Zaypuru is safely landed in the trap."

"And what then, señor?" asked one of the Valderians.

"Be content with that, señor," replied Gerald. "With Zaypuru in our power the rest will be easy. Your lives and liberties will be assured. Now, remember, success depends upon your discretion and implicit obedience of Señor Dacres' orders. We have yet five hours before us: hasten and make ready."

Away trooped the Valderians, filled with hope and resolution, to don the uniforms of their former captors, while General Galento, accompanied by two of the crew of the "Meteor," made his way to the commandante's quarters to deck himself out, without asking the owner's permission, in the gorgeous regimentals of the luckless Don Alonzo da Costa.

At sunrise the new garrison was under arms. The men, having breakfasted, were ready for any duty that Dacres called upon them to perform.

There were no signs of the "Meteor." Acting upon Dacres' request to his chief the airship had put a safe distance between herself and the capital. The wind had fallen, the sky was cloudless and unbroken. Had the "Meteor" remained she would have inevitably been sighted by the garrison of Naocuanha and Zaypuru's suspicions would have been aroused.

Just before eight a telephone message was received at the Cavarale stating that the president would arrive half an hour earlier than he had previously arranged.

His object in visiting Gerald Whittinghame was a crafty one. He knew the value of the captive Englishman's technical skill; he totally underestimated his sense of honour. Reno Durango having, from some cause for the present unknown, failed him, Zaypuru bethought himself of Gerald Whittinghame.

His plan was to offer the Englishman his liberty and a huge sum of money if he would take charge of the aerial defences of the city of Naocuanha. He remembered that under President San Bonetta's regime Gerald Whittinghame had brought out an aerial torpedo—a monoplane carrying a heavy charge of guncotton—which could be electrically controlled by an operator on the ground. The device passed the severe tests imposed upon it with the greatest ease. Then came the revolution that caused San Bonetta to lose his life and Gerald Whittinghame his liberty. The knowledge, unlike that which resulted in the construction of the "Libertad," remained with the inventors, and hitherto threats and promises alike had failed to extort the priceless secret.

"Troops on the move, sir," announced one of "Meteor's" crew who had been posted to supplement the Valderian sentries on the wall of the Cavarale.

Dacres and Gerald ascended as quickly as possible, then taking cover behind the breastwork, used their binoculars through one of the embrasures. "That's Zaypuru's bodyguard right enough," said Vaughan's brother. "He doesn't go far without that escort."

"Quite enough to set up a fairly good fight if they've any pluck," remarked Dacres. "I don't think we ought to let the whole party into the courtyard."

"Yet I don't see how we can prevent them without arousing suspicion."

"I do," said Dacres. "You've forgotten the bridge across the dry moat. We'll fix a detonator, sufficient to bring the whole concern down without doing very much harm to the President's bodyguard. We'll have to hurry, for there's precious little time."

"But we haven't a battery," objected Gerald.

"No, but we have plenty of rifles. Smith, bring a couple of sticks of guncotton from the magazine."

Putting on a coat and *képi* belonging to one of the former garrison Dacres issued from the gateway, descended into the moat and lashed the explosive to one of the props of the wooden bridge. To the one nearest to it he fixed a loaded rifle, taking care to lock the safety bolt while he made fast a thin but strong wire to the trigger. This wire he led back to one of the narrow loopholes by the side of the gate, giving one of his men instructions to release the trigger the moment he heard the bugle give the "Alarm."

Rapidly the president and his escort approached the Cavarale. They were all splendidly mounted, while many of them were distinguishable as generals by their gorgeous uniforms. Like most revolutionary armies of the South and Central American republics staff officers were numerically out of all proportion to the size of the army.

Half a dozen troopers armed with carbines led the procession. Immediately behind them, and supported by two generals, rode the president.

Zaypuru was a little man, with iron-grey hair and moustachios. He rode very erect with his arms thrown well back, but Dacres noticed that one shoulder was slightly higher than the other. His features were sharp and pointed, his eyes close-set, while his eye-brows, slanting upwards from the bridge of his nose, gave him a saturnine expression in keeping with his character.

An arrant coward at heart he, like most men of tyrannical nature, took a delight in inflicting pain upon those who, having thwarted him, had fallen into his power. Blindly he regarded himself as being essential to the welfare of Valderia, and counting on the support of the men he had gathered around him, he was as insensible to danger as the proverbial ostrich hiding its head in the sand. It was only by relying upon others that he had any confidence in his official capacity. Reno Durango's disaffection had hit him hard. Had it not been for his successful coup in capturing Admiral Maynebrace and his staff, he would have fled from Naocuanha and sought an asylum in one of the neighbouring republics when the "Libertad" failed to return. Puffed up with success he was riding hot-shod towards ruin.

Behind the president rode a lieutenant bearing the national flag of Valderia with an eagle emblazoned in silver upon the centre horizontal stripe. This was the presidential standard of the head of the republic.

The cavalcade concluded with about forty officers and men in nearly equal numbers.

As Zaypuru and his retinue approached the outer wall General Galento ordered the general salute to be sounded. The great gate of the inner wall was thrown open and a guard of honour, composed of twenty men in the borrowed uniforms of the imprisoned garrison, presented arms.

Greatly to Dacres' delight the president gave orders for the bulk of his escort to wait beyond the dry moat. Attended only by ten of his staff Zaypuru trotted his steed across the wooden bridge, stiffly acknowledged the compliment paid by the guard, and cantered into the *patio*.

Dacres, still out of sight of the president, raised his hand. A sharp detonation was followed by the crash of shattered woodwork, as the bridge collapsed into the dry moat. Simultaneously the guard closed the gateway.

President Diego Zaypuru was trapped.

# CHAPTER XXVIII
# A PRISONER OF WAR

THE noise of the explosion and the clang of the gate caused Zaypuru to rein in his horse and give a hasty glance over his shoulder. Then, still unsuspicious, he advanced towards the officer he took to be the commandante, Alonzo da Costa, till shouts of "Treason" from his men outside the gates gave warning that something was amiss.

With a snarl of rage Zaypuru drew his horse almost on its haunches and tugging violently at the reins caused the animal to swerve. In so doing it came into violent contact with the animal ridden by one of his staff. Both chargers reared, and had their riders been anything but expert horsemen they would have been dismounted. Forcing his way between his attendants Zaypuru made for the gate, to find his progress barred by a line of glistening bayonets.

"Surrender, Zaypuru!" shouted General Galento in stentorian tones. "We will spare your life."

Two members of the president's staff alone showed any determined resistance. Drawing their revolvers and using their sharp rowelled spurs unmercifully they rode straight towards the impersonator of Don Alonzo da Costa.

Before they had covered half that distance an irregular volley of musketry burst from the men supporting General Galento. The two horses, riddled with bullets, dropped to the ground, rolled completely over and then lay feebly kicking in their death agonies. Their riders, fortunately thrown clear, were too dazed to offer further resistance to the men, who left the ranks and seized them.

"Surrender, Zaypuru!" repeated Galento.

"Is my life guaranteed?" asked the president, who was trembling like a leaf.

"You will not die a violent death at our hands," replied the general urbanely.

"You mean to murder me," howled the wretched man.

"I would have you shot by a platoon with the greatest pleasure, I assure you," remarked Galento with well-assumed indifference. "Unfortunately, as far as my inclination is concerned, I have given a promise to the English commandante of the Cavarale."

"They are referring to you, Dacres," said Gerald Whittinghame, who, unseen by the president and his followers, had followed the whole of the conversation. "There is no further need for concealment. That rascal Zaypuru will surrender to you."

Although Zaypuru had not hesitated to treat his British captives with indignity, he had a certain amount of respect for the word of an Englishman. Directly Dacres crossed over to where Galento was standing, the President got down from his horse, and unbuckling his sword, tendered it to the Englishman.

Just then a rattle of musketry was heard without. Those of the President's escort who had been left on the remote side of the dry ditch had taken cover behind the outer wall and were firing at the Valderians who held the roof of the prison. The latter briskly replied, and the exchange of shots was rapidly maintained.

"Where are you, Whittinghame?" shouted Dacres. "Tell some of these men to take the prisoner to the Commandante's quarters. I'll have to direct operations against those fellows who are kicking up a dust outside."

Directly Gerald Whittinghame appeared on the scene Zaypuru's terrors returned. The sight of the man whom he had treated with uncalled for severity filled him with the most abject fright. He fell on his knees, and, upraising his clasped hands, implored his former captive to have pity.

"Get up, and don't make a fool of yourself," exclaimed Gerald sternly. "You won't be hurt unless you give trouble."

"I never meant to do you an injury, señor," persisted Zaypuru; "it was my adviser Durango who urged it."

"The less you say about it the better," interrupted Whittinghame. "I want to hear no excuses. Party!" he ordered, addressing a file of men. "Escort the prisoner to the Commandante's quarters."

Trembling like a leaf the President was taken away and lodged in the same room as his henchman, Alonzo da Costa, while the rest of his men who had followed him into the *patio* surrendered at discretion.

Meanwhile, Dacres was directing the fire of the defenders. Although the aim of the Valderians on both sides was erratic, several of the bullets whistled unpleasantly close. The President's escort, fearing to retire, since in their retreat they would be fully exposed to the fire of the garrison, stuck tenaciously to the cover afforded by the outer wall, hoping that additional troops would be sent from Naocuanha to their support.

"Man that machine gun," ordered Dacres to those of the crew of the "Meteor" who had remained with him.

The ammunition was soon forthcoming, and a hail of small projectiles directed upon the adobe wall. This was more than the enemy could swallow, and a white flag soon appeared above the crumbling outer wall.

Keeping the defenders well under control, Gerald Whittinghame shouted to the President's men that they were at liberty to retire to the capital. For some moments there was no indication of this offer being accepted. At length, one or two plucked up courage to make a dash towards Naocuanha, and finding that they were not fired upon the rest of the escort promptly took to their heels, amid the jeers of the released prisoners.

Dacres looked at his watch. It was ten minutes past nine.

"Nearly an hour to wait," he remarked as Gerald Whittinghame came up. "If Zaypuru hadn't been so inconsiderate as to arrive an hour earlier he might have saved us some trouble."

"What do you mean?" asked Gerald.

"Unless I am very much mistaken Fort Volador will be opening fire on us."

"With Zaypuru in our hands?"

"That won't count with them, I fancy," said Dacres, as he bent the blue and white flag to the halliards in readiness for hoisting at the approach of the "Meteor."

Just then General Galento hurried up.

"Señor Whittinghame," said he, "a message has just been sent by telephone from Fort Volador. The men belonging to Zaypuru's escort whom you allowed to go without hindrance have reported the situation. The Commandante of the fort has called upon us to surrender at discretion, otherwise he will bombard the Cavarale."

"Then let him," replied Whittinghame. "That is, if he wants to murder his President. As a matter of fact I don't believe there are guns mounted on Fort Volador that are capable of doing much damage. All the heavy ordnance have been taken to the Zandovar side of the city."

"Then how shall I answer, señor?"

"Tell him to go to Jericho," replied Whittinghame, shrugging his shoulders.

"That's the way to talk to these gentry," remarked Dacres when Gerald told him of the conversation. "Treat the matter lightly and it will give our Valderian allies confidence. Ha! There's the first shot."

With a peculiar, throbbing screech a twelve-pounder shell flew handsomely over the Cavarale, bursting quite eight hundred yards beyond the building.

"Bad shot!" ejaculated Dacres coolly. "All the same I think we will withdraw our men from the wall. Order them to lie down as far apart as possible. I'll be with you in a moment."

Deliberately hoisting the blue and white flag Dacres took a final survey of the horizon. Seeing no sign of the Dreadnought of the Air he descended to the *patio*.

Another shell screeched overhead, missing the parapet of the furthermost wall by a bare five feet. Fort Volador's gunners were getting the correct range, yet the rate of firing was painfully slow.

The third shot struck that part of the prison in which the British officers had been incarcerated. With a crash that shook the place the missile burst, blowing a gap in the outer and inner walls large enough for a horse and cart to pass.

"Señor," exclaimed a Valderian breathlessly, "Zaypuru has asked me to be allowed to speak with the Commandante of Fort Volador. He says he will order the battery to cease fire."

"It will be useless," replied Whittinghame.

"It is surely worth trying," urged General Galento, who was beginning to show signs of "jumpiness."

"Very good," assented Gerald. "You might accompany Zaypuru to the orderly-room, General, and repeat to me what he says."

Catching up his long sword, Galento, still resplendent in his borrowed plumes, ran across the *patio*, his movements hastened by a shell that struck the ground within ten yards of him—happily without bursting.

He found Zaypuru ashen with fear. Both Valderians, their enmity vanishing before a common danger, hurried to the orderly-room.

With trembling fingers the President lifted the receiver, and held it to his ear.

"Is that Commandante Vilano?" he asked. "It is I, Diego Zaypuru, your President. My life is in danger from the fire of the fort. I order you to desist immediately."

He waited to listen to a jeering reply.

"I order you. I beg of you," he continued.

Galento, equally agitated, anxiously watched the face of his former persecutor.

With a gesture of despair the President threw the receiver against the wall, where it struck with disastrous results to the instrument; then burying his face in his hands he burst into tears.

"Is there no place where I can hide in safety?" he whined. In his utter selfishness he gave no thought to the members of his staff, who were in an equally hazardous predicament.

Ten minutes later Gerald Whittinghame, finding that General Galento had not returned, took two of the "Meteor's" men to look for him. The orderly-room was empty.

A muffled groan from the adjoining barrack-room attracted his attention.

Lying side by side on the bare floor and covered by a heap of straw mattresses were the President of Valderia and General Galento.

"White-livered rascals; fear, like adversity, makes strange bedfellows," he exclaimed contemptuously.

By this time the shells from Fort Volador were coming quicker and with better aim. Already the front of the Cavarale facing Naocuanha was little better than a heap of ruins, but the debris formed such an effective breastwork that Dacres ordered the garrison to take shelter behind it. The two angle-towers had disappeared, tearing away heaps of brick and stone and leaving a mound twenty feet in height. Their destruction had resulted in the removal of the recognized signal to the "Meteor" that all was well.

Even Dacres began to be anxious, although he kept his doubts to himself. The fact of being under fire without being able to return an effective shot told heavily upon the Valderian members of the garrison. He began to consider the possibilities of a retirement.

"Getting pretty hot," he said to Gerald Whittinghame.

"Yes; three men down with that last shell," replied Vaughan's brother, flicking some dust from his coat. "That makes sixteen, I believe."

"Any of the 'Meteor's' men?"

"No, thank heavens! unless one or two of them have received slight hurts. They are splendid fellows. How goes the time? My watch was stolen before I was brought here as a prisoner."

"Nine minutes to ten," replied Dacres.

"Hurrah, there she is!" shouted one of the "Meteor's" men at that moment.

Flying high and at her greatest speed the huge airship was approaching from the direction of the Sierras.

Heedless of the risk he ran, one of the British defenders of the Cavarale dashed across the heap of brickwork and recovered the blue and white flag. The bunting was torn, the staff severed, but the daring fellow waved the remains of the flag above his head.

"Come down, Jones; they've seen us!" ordered Dacres.

Two minutes later the "Meteor" passed immediately overhead and at an elevation of ten thousand feet. She made no attempt to descend.

"By Jove! I have it!" ejaculated Gerald Whittinghame. "She's going to settle with Fort Volador."

The garrison of the Valderian fort saw the danger. Their fire upon the Cavarale ceased. An attempt was made to train the quick-firers upon the airship, but the weapons were not on suitable mountings.

Panic seized the artillerymen. Abandoning the fort they fled pell-mell towards Naocuanha.

The "Meteor's" motors stopped. Rapidly she lost way, bringing up immediately above the doomed fort.

Through his binoculars Dacres observed a small black object drop from the airship. Sixty-five seconds later, having fallen vertically through a distance of nearly three thousand five hundred yards, the bomb struck the ground.

The aim was superb. Alighting fairly in the centre of the deserted fort it exploded. A burst of lurid flame was followed by a dense cloud of yellow smoke, mingled with fragments of earth, stones and bricks. The missile of destruction, powerful enough in itself to knock the defences of the fort out of action, had caused the main magazine to explode. When the smoke dispersed sufficiently for the observers on the ruins of the Cavarale to see what had taken place, Fort Volador was no more.

Apparently content with this act of vengeance the "Meteor," gliding vertically downwards, flew slowly over the four-square mass of rubble that marked the position of the state prison of the Republic of Valderia.

"All right, below there?" came a hail from the "Meteor."

"All right, sir," replied Dacres. "We've close on fifty Valderians we found in the cells. We must stand by them."

"Quite right," replied Vaughan Whittinghame. "What have you done with the Commandante and the rest of the garrison?"

"Safe in the underground cellars, sir."

"You might detain the Commandante as a hostage."

"We've a better hostage than the Commandante."

"Who, then?"

"President Zaypuru is a prisoner of war."

# CHAPTER XXIX
# WORK FOR THE SEAPLANES

"SEND him on board, by all means," said the Captain of the "Meteor," after the rousing cheer from her crew that greeted the announcement had died away. "We'll lower a rope and whip him on board in a jiffey. You might then hold your position for ten hours more. I don't suppose the Valderians will risk another assault during that interval. We are about to take Admiral Maynebrace and his staff back to his flagship. Zaypuru will go too. He will be a strong argument in favour of the Valderians asking for terms."

"I doubt it, sir," replied Dacres grimly. "Those fellows in Fort Volador ignored his request to cease firing."

"We'll see," rejoined Vaughan Whittinghame.

"Hulloa, there, Gerald, old boy! How goes it?"

This was the Captain of the "Meteor's" greeting to his brother, who for months past had been in danger of being put to death by an unscrupulous Dictator.

"See you later," was Gerald's equally unconcerned reply, although at heart the brothers were longing to shake each other by the hand. "We'll rout out old Zaypuru. He's buried himself under a regular mountain of bedding."

Still in paroxysms of terror the President of Valderia was removed from his place of concealment, while General Galento, in almost an equal state of fear, was allowed to remain in his uncomfortable position.

At the sight of the "Meteor," anchored barely fifty feet above the shattered walls of the Cavarale, with a rope dangling from one of the entry ports, Zaypuru fell on his knees, begging for mercy. The noosed rope had a terrible significance.

"We do not ill-treat our prisoners of war, señor," said Gerald Whittinghame. "Circumstances necessitate your removal from this dangerous locality to a safer sphere."

But before the President could be ignominiously seated in the bight of the rope a warning shout came from Setchell, who was on duty in the after-section.

"Look out, sir!" he hailed; "there are half a dozen aeroplanes bearing down upon us."

"Cast off, there!" ordered Vaughan Whittinghame calmly.

The "Meteor" soared skywards, although not so swiftly as was her wont. The heavy drain upon her store of ultra-hydrogen was beginning to make itself felt.

Dacres watched her receding bulk with envious eyes. He would have given much to have formed one of the band of aerial warriors; but duty compelled him to remain, an eager spectator of the forthcoming encounter, on the position he had held so doggedly against the guns of Fort Volador. Setchell had made a mistake in stating the number of the hostile aircraft to be half a dozen. There were five of the latest type of Valderian aeroplanes, each capable of rendering a good account of itself, had they been properly handled.

Hoping to take advantage of the great airship being close to the ground, the airmen left Naocuanha, and, flying fairly low, made a wide detour so as to approach from a direction whence danger was least expected.

Seeing the "Meteor" rise, they too tilted their elevating planes, and in a semi-circular formation rushed at top speed upon this surprised foe.

Suddenly the airship's propellers began to run at full speed. She did not belie her name as she shot forward, firing from her after-guns as she did so.

The aeroplanes replying with their comparatively feeble automatic guns, were completely outdistanced, till the "Meteor," slowing down, lured them on.

Before the Valderian mosquitoes could approach within range the airship was off again, till she was almost out of sight of the watchers on the Cavarale. Dacres understood her tactics. Vaughan Whittinghame wanted to entice the biplanes away from the vicinity of the Cavarale, whose garrison would otherwise be at the mercy of the aviators. On the other hand, he dared not risk an attack at an effective range, owing to the fact that, in addition to Rear-Admiral Maynebrace and his staff, the "Meteor" carried Antoine de la Fosse and his son, and also the two men from the British merchant vessel whose arrest by Zaypuru had been the commencement of the dispute.

Presently the "Meteor" was observed to be returning towards Naocuanha, the five aeroplanes hanging on in pursuit. When within a mile of the Cavarale she rose to an additional height of two thousand feet. The biplanes, fearing to be annihilated by an aerial bomb, swerved right and left. Doubling like a hare the airship proved conclusively that her turning powers were, in spite of her length and bulk, superior to those of the Valderian aircraft, but owing to her speed and the smallness of the swiftly-moving targets, she made no palpable hits with her two stern-chasers.

So intent were the garrison of the Cavarale in watching this aerial steeplechase that it was not until a loud droning almost above their heads told them that other aircraft were approaching.

"Take cover as best you may!" ordered Gerald to the Valderian allies.

"Steady on, old man," suddenly exclaimed Dacres. "I think—yes, I am certain—they are British seaplanes."

"I suppose you know," admitted Whittinghame. "But how will they know we are not the enemy? Personally, I've a strong objection to being blown sky-high by a British seaplane."

"We must risk it. I'll hail. Perhaps they might hear, although the noise of the propeller—Hulloa! They're swerving."

Paying no attention to the remains of the Cavarale with its occupants who wore the Valderian uniform, the air-squadron tore to the rescue of their Admiral.

The Captain of the "Meteor" had informed the flagship of the situation by wireless, and Captain Staggers, who, by virtue of his seniority, had hoisted the Commodore's Broad Pennant on board the "Royal Oak" during Rear-Admiral Maynebrace's enforced absence, had dispatched six of the seaplanes attached to the fleet to tackle the enemy's air-fleet.

Giving the high-angle firing-guns of the defences of Naocuanha a wide berth, the seaplanes made short work of the distance between Zandovar and the scene of the manoeuvres of the "Meteor" and her attackers.

Now, for the first time in the history of the world, was to be a pitched battle between aircraft heavier than the medium in which they soared. It was to be a fight to the finish: there could be no question of surrendering or of giving quarter.

Yet the British Flying Squadron was not one to take an undue advantage. The aeroplanes, intent upon the "Meteor," were unaware of the approach of their new foes; but the officers in command of the seaplanes waited till they were certain that their presence was observed by the Valderian airmen.

To escape by flight was impossible. The Valderian airmen, realizing that their only chance lay in vanquishing their opponents, turned and headed straight for the seaplanes. On both sides the automatic guns were sending out small but powerful shells as fast as the delicate and intricate mechanism could admit, yet ninety-nine per cent of the missiles failed to find a billet.

One of the British aircraft was the first to receive a knock-out blow. Hit fairly on the swiftly revolving cylinders it seemed to stop dead. Then, plunging vertically, it fell at a comparatively low rate of speed and with ever-widening circles through space till its descent was checked by crashing violently upon the ground.

Ten seconds later a Valderian biplane was literally pulverized by a shell that exploded in her petrol tank. Two more were quickly put out of action, while the fourth, seeing the hopelessness of the situation, vainly attempted a vol-plane.

With two of her antagonists like avenging angels following her steep downward glide, the biplane dropped to within a hundred feet of the ground without any apparent injury. Then, suddenly tilting beyond the angle of stability, she fell vertically. Under the joint action of gravity and the traction of her propeller her rate at the moment of impact could not have been far short of two hundred miles an hour.

It took all the skill at their pilots' command to save the two seaplanes from a similar fate. So intent had they been in the headlong pursuit that they temporarily lost all sense of caution.

The first seaplane succeeded in rising, but the second was not so fortunate. The sudden downward pressure on the planes as the frail craft changed her direction resulted in the carrying away of one of the tension wires. The right-hand plane collapsed like a limp rag, and the seaplane, tilting sideways, fell to the earth, her pilot getting off lightly with a few bruises, while almost by a miracle the observer escaped injury.

Only one Valderian biplane now remained. Her pilot, whether from sheer daring or whether he was incapable of realizing what he was about, headed straight for the nearest of his antagonists.

The British pilot, equally fascinated by the sight of the huge mechanical bird bearing straight towards him, held on his course. The slightest alteration to the elevating planes would have resulted in the seaplane flying either above or under her opponent; but inexplicably the naval pilot made no effort to avoid the collision.

With a crash that was plainly heard by the spell-bound crew of the "Meteor," both aeroplanes met, eight thousand feet above the ground.

The spectators saw both motors, thrown clear of the tangle of struts and canvas, drop almost side by side, followed by the mangled bodies of three of the victims. Then, slowly, the lighter debris began to fall, until, some of the spilt petrol catching fire, the wreckage blazing furiously like a funeral pyre, streamed earthwards, leaving behind it a trail of smoke resembling a gigantic memorial column to the slain.

# CHAPTER XXX
# THE FALL OF NAOCUANHA

"HEAVY firing, sir," remarked Commander Bourne to his superior officer.

"You're right," assented Captain and Acting Commodore Staggers. "It's about time we had a wireless report."

"Nothing has come through yet, sir," said Bourne.

Surrounded by a group of officers Captain Staggers stood upon the battlements of Fort Belgrano, on the landward side of the town of Zandovar. Away to the eastward, and only just discernible in the heated atmosphere, was the city of Naocuanha. Beyond the capital there was nothing to be seen, save at sunset when the peaks of the far-distant Sierras showed rosy-pink against the gloom of approaching night.

"The seaplanes ought to be returning," remarked Captain Staggers for the sixth time in half an hour. He was unable to conceal an anxiety for the naval aircraft that, two hours previously, had proceeded to the assistance of the handicapped "Meteor."

Drawn up just outside the fort was every available man who could be landed from the fleet: one thousand seamen and five hundred Marines, with the usual quota of light quick-firers and maxims. Why the men were there under arms none of them knew; they could only conjecture. Once again there was work to be done and they meant to do it right well, to wipe off the slur upon British prestige caused by the capture of Admiral Maynebrace and his staff.

"Speak to the 'Royal Oak,' Mr. Eccles, and ask if there's any news," continued the Captain.

Away doubled the lieutenant to the signalling station, only to return within five minutes with the disconcerting report that the battleship had not been able to "pick up" the "Meteor" by wireless.

"Seaplanes returning, sir!" announced the Commander, whose attention had been drawn to the fact by a petty officer.

"How many?" demanded the Captain abruptly, his anxiety causing him to drop his customary courtesy.

"Only three, sir."

"Only three? Good heavens! Only three."

Captain Staggers set his jaw firmly. Was he to hear of another reverse? Where was the "Meteor"—the Dreadnought of the Air? Had she fallen a victim to the fire of the batteries of Naocuanha?

Flying with mathematical precision the three seaplanes alighted practically simultaneously upon a level expanse of ground on the landward side of Fort Belgrano. Under ordinary circumstances etiquette would demand that the subordinate should approach the senior officer, but casting observances to the winds Captain Staggers, holding his scabbard to prevent his sword from impeding his progress, ran towards the returned airmen.

"Five of the Valderian biplanes destroyed, sir." reported the senior lieutenant of the air squadron. "All that opposed us. G1 and G3 of ours are done for. G4 is badly damaged, but her crew are safe."

"And the 'Meteor'?" asked the Captain anxiously.

"Is standing by to the east of Naocuanha, sir. I understand that there are some British subjects, assisted by a part of the airship's crew and some of the late President's adherents, holding the Cavarale. Captain Whittinghame suggests that if an attack be made as soon as possible, while the Valderian troops are still demoralized by the destruction of their aircraft, we may be able to capture the capital without great loss."

"And where is Admiral Maynebrace?"

"I do not know, sir. Captain Whittinghame gave me no information on that point, so I concluded that he is with the party holding the Cavarale."

"Gentlemen," said Captain Staggers, turning to his officers who accompanied him, "I propose to make a reconnaissance in force immediately, and, if practicable, to deliver an assault upon Fort San Josef. If our efforts in that direction are successful, we shall hold the key of the position."

In spite of their protests the officers and crews of the seaplanes were ordered to stand by. Their places were taken by others who were fresh to undergo the trying ordeal, and the hard-worked aircraft having been given a rapid overhaul, they set off on their task of searching the intervening country in case the Valderians should offer resistance to the advance of the Naval brigade.

In sections of fours the British force set out on its seven mile march to Naocuanha, the advance covered by the seaplanes and well flanked by strong parties of Marines. The railroad had been torn up, and the rolling-stock destroyed before the evacuation of Zandovar by the Valderians, but the wide and fairly well-kept road rendered the advance practicable and speedy.

"'Meteor' heading due north, sir," exclaimed Commander Bourne, as the huge bulk of the airship, looking little larger than a needle, was observed to be making off at full speed in the direction the Commander had stated.

"What's the matter with her, I wonder?" asked Captain Staggers. "I thought she was to operate on the east side of Naocuanha? By sheering off she leaves the Valderian troops free to devote the whole of their attention to us."

"I don't know, sir," replied Bourne, "Perhaps——"

His surmise was never expressed in words, for even as he spoke, the "Meteor," having put a safe distance between her and the batteries of the capital, swung round and made for the town of Zandovar.

"Pass the word for the men to halt," ordered the captain, who was regarding the approaching mammoth with ill-disguised wonderment and admiration, for in spite of the fact that two hundred odd feet had been taken from her original length, she still appeared the embodiment of size, power and speed.

The seamen and Marines grounded arms and watched the Dreadnought of the Air with the deepest interest. She had spotted the advancing force, and starboarding her helm was making in the direction of the column.

Her propellers stopped; she lost way, then, slowly sinking, alighted on level ground at less than a hundred and fifty yards from the place where Captain Staggers and his staff were standing.

There was no wind, consequently there was no need to anchor. The "Meteor," now possessing a dead weight of ten or twelve tons, sat firmly upon Valderian soil.

"Captain Whittinghame, I presume?" asked the Commodore as he approached within convenient talking distance of the airship.

"The same," answered Vaughan. "I am in a hurry, sir; I have left several of my men in an exposed position at the Cavarale, so I must quickly return. The city of Naocuanha ought to be taken with but little trouble. Meanwhile, sir, I shall be glad if you will receive some of my passengers—Rear-Admiral Maynebrace, his staff and others."

Captain Staggers literally gasped. The fact that his superior had been rescued by the "Meteor" was quite unexpected news, for he had misinterpreted Whittinghame's appeal for the seaplanes to be sent to the airship's aid. Before he could recover from his astonishment the rope ladder was dropped from the entry-port and the Admiral's burly form was seen to be slowly descending the swaying means of communication with terra-firma.

A spontaneous cheer burst from the throats of the men as they saw their Admiral returned to them. In spite of the slight disappointment that they were not able to wipe off the slur and retrieve their commanding officer, the seamen and marines were more than willing to recognize the excellent work accomplished by the Dreadnought of the Air.

"Will you continue the advance, sir?" asked Captain Staggers, after the Admiral and his staff, the two Frenchmen, and the two men of the trader had descended.

"Certainly," replied Admiral Maynebrace. "There's nothing like striking while the iron's hot. That airship wiped out Fort Volador by a single charge of explosive. And there's news, Staggers, but I'll tell you later. Look, the 'Meteor' is ascending."

With the least possible delay the airship returned to continue her self-imposed task of threatening the city on the eastern side; while the naval brigade resumed its march.

Having received from Captain Staggers the plan of operations and duly approved his subordinate's dispositions for the attack, Rear-Admiral Maynebrace started a breezy narrative of his captivity in the Cavarale.

"And one day I was surprised to see an Englishman enter my cell. That man was Dacres."

"Dacres?" echoed Captain Staggers, completely taken aback. "Dacres in the Valderian service?" For, although the name of Captain Vaughan

Whittinghame had been communicated to the officers of the squadron operating off the Valderian coast, the Admiralty had given no information to the effect that ex-Sub-lieutenant Dacres formed one of the "Meteor's" complement.

"Yes, Dacres," declared Admiral Maynebrace. But not in the Valderian service—far from it. The youngster managed to get hold of an appointment under Captain Whittinghame. At considerable risk he managed to communicate with me. Later on the airship landed a handful of her crew under Dacres' command in the Cavarale in the dead of night. They overpowered the garrison, rescued the British officers and sent them off in the 'Meteor'."

"Capital!" ejaculated the Captain.

"More than that—it shows Dacres' devotion—the 'Meteor' being unable to take us all, he volunteered to remain in the captured prison with his men, and by a cool piece of work he made a prisoner of— —"

"The commandante of the Cavarale?" hazarded Captain Staggers.

"Yes, and President Zaypuru as well," added Admiral Maynebrace enthusiastically. "Staggers, I made a great mistake when I told young Dacres to send in his papers. We must have him back."

"We must, sir," said the Captain of the "Royal Oak" wholeheartedly. "That is, if he's agreeable. Dacres always appeared to me to be rather independent."

"Wish to goodness he hadn't played that practical joke on my midshipmen," growled Admiral Maynebrace.

Further conversation was for the time being out of the question, for the brigade was now almost within range of the batteries of Naocuanha.

A strange silence seemed to hang over the capital. There were no signs of movement. Through the field-glasses of the British officers Naocuanha appeared to be a city of the dead. There was not the slightest indication of an attempt about to be made by the superiorly numerical Valderian troops to dispute the advance.

"Wish those beggars would start firing," muttered the Admiral. "A silence like that seems suggestive of an ambuscade. Any report from the seaplanes?"

"G2 and G6 both report no signs of the batteries being manned, sir," announced Lieutenant Eccles.

"Then continue the advance in open order. Maxims in the centre, and quick-firers to cover the advance on either flank. What a rotten country, Staggers! Not a particle of cover."

Silently the attackers extended, then with six feet separating one man from another, the bluejackets and marines approached the frowning walls of Fort San Josef.

Suddenly a succession of short reports burst from seaplane G5. She had opened fire upon some object, still invisible to the attackers on the remote side of the fort.

For quite half a minute there was no reply from the Valderian position; then right and left came the sharp crackle of musketry punctuated by the bark of quick-firers.

Taking a prone position on the grass the British seamen and marines opened a steady fire upon their unseen foes, while the covering guns sent shell after shell into Fort San Josef, over which floated the flag of the republic.

"What's that?" asked Admiral Maynebrace as a report received from G6 was handed to him. "Fort San Josef evacuated? Tell the quick-firers to search the ground to the right and left and not waste time and ammunition on an empty building. By Jove! what's the matter with G5?"

He might well ask that question, for the seaplane was descending with alarming rapidity and apparently right upon the Valderian position. The attackers, seeing her glide earthwards, promptly directed their fire elsewhere, but the devoted G5 was plunging through the zone of fire of the enemy.

"She's disabled, sir," exclaimed Captain Staggers. "Look, there she goes."

The seaplane disappeared behind Fort San Josef. Her two consorts, disdainful of the fate which had overtaken her, still flew serenely over the Valderian lines, occasionally dropping bombs, but more frequently reporting the effect of the fire of the British field-guns.

"What's that?" demanded Captain Staggers, grasping his superior officer's arm in his eagerness. "Look, sir, at the fort."

Standing upon the ramparts and showing clearly against the skyline was a man in naval uniform. Rapidly he uncleated the halliards of the flagstaff and hauled down the Valderian flag. Then, even as he waved his white-covered cap in triumph, he suddenly pitched forward on his face and rolled inertly down the steep face of the earthworks.

"It's Vine, the pilot of G5, sir," said Bourne.

Enraged by the lieutenant's fall the attackers implored the officers to be allowed to storm the position. The men were like hounds in leash, eager to vent their fury upon their foes.

But Admiral Maynebrace hesitated. The significance of Fort San Josef offering no active resistance was ominous.

Up dashed a sub-lieutenant.

"G2 reports safe to advance, sir," he said.

"Fort San Josef is mined, but G5 destroyed the firing station and has cut the wires."

The Admiral hesitated no longer. Along the line the officers' whistles sounded the advance. Up from the cover afforded by the grass sprang hundreds of figures in khaki and blue. A regular clatter followed the order to fix bayonets, and at the double the gallant men raced towards their goal.

In spite of the covering fire from the British guns the Valderian troops to the right and left of the deserted fort maintained a hot fusillade. Enfiladed by the converging volleys the British suffered severely, the ground being dotted with dead and dying. Yet, undaunted, the stormers passed on, threw themselves into the dry ditch, and clambered up the steep ramp beyond. The more active of the attackers assisted those who experienced difficulty in negotiating the slippery slope. Marines and bluejackets, without any apparent semblance of order, vied with each other in the race to gain possession of the coveted position, till a ringing British cheer announced to the Admiral and his staff that Fort San Josef was in the occupation of his gallant men.

While the Union Jack was hoisted over the captured position, the bluejackets rushed to the guns to turn them upon the Valderian troops who had so severely galled the advance; but to their disappointment and rage they discovered that the breech-blocks had previously been removed.

In spite of the danger from the hostile bullets that were singing over the earthworks a signalman stood erect and semaphored for the guns to be brought up.

Two brawny bluejackets, each staggering under the weight of a Maxim, successfully crossed the danger-zone, while four man-hauled quick-firers were ordered to the fort.

At the double the guns were dragged across the open plain. Several of the men at the drag-ropes fell, but, undaunted, their comrades maintained the hot pace. The dry-ditch they made light of. In twenty seconds each gun was unlimbered and dismantled. The lighter parts, passed from hand to hand, were taken up the ramp; the heavier gear, hauled by willing hands, quickly followed.

To the tap, tap, tap of the Maxims was added the sharp bark of the quick-firers, and, swept by the hail of projectiles, the Valderian troops bolted precipitately. Outside the city they could not go, for hovering overhead was the "Meteor," and the fate of Fort Volador was still fresh in the minds of the beaten side.

At exactly three o'clock—one hour and twenty minutes from the opening of the assault—the city of Naocuanha surrendered at discretion.

# CHAPTER XXXI
## A SURPRISE FOR DACRES

"SAY, Dacres, old man, here's something that will interest you," remarked Vaughan Whittinghame, handing his comrade and able assistant a letter that had just been delivered by a marine orderly.

Dacres took the missive. The familiar heading on the envelope, "On His Majesty's Service," recalled the days not long since when he was one of the officers of the ship whence the letter came.

Drawing out the enclosure Dacres, with considerable difficulty, deciphered the crabbed handwriting of Rear-Admiral Maynebrace. That officer had written requesting the pleasure of the company of Captain Whittinghame and Mr. Basil Dacres on board the flagship at three p.m.

"Well?" asked Whittinghame in his usual manner. "Going?"

"I hardly know what to say, sir. I suppose you will accept the invitation?"

"Yes. If it were a mere formal affair I would decline, but I have reason to believe that the Admiral wishes to consult us with reference to the submarine plans. It's not a matter of etiquette exactly, but an affair of national importance, so I think you'd better decide to go with me."

The "Meteor" was lying afloat in Zandovar Harbour. Beyond the low-lying spit of sand that narrowed the entrance to less than three hundred yards could be seen the British warships lying in the open roadstead.

Two days had elapsed since the fall of Naocuanha. A provisional government had been set up in Valderia, and Señor Juan Desiro, a distant relative of the late President San Bonetta, had been nominated as acting president. The terms imposed by the British Admiral had been accepted, and the Valderians regarded the inevitable changes with comparative equanimity. The garrison of La Paz had taken the oath of allegiance to the new ruler, and with amazing rapidity the republic settled down to make the best of a hard bargain.

Ex-President Diego Zaypuru, after being officially deposed, was glad to avail himself of an offer by the British Admiral to be given a passage to a far-distant land, where, with the bulk of the riches he had amassed, he would be able to live in comparative peace and plenty.

Antoine de la Fosse, with his two sons, also shook the dust of Valderia from his feet. Henri had made rapid progress towards recovery. His wounds were healing satisfactorily, and as no signs of fever were detected, the British medical officers expressed an opinion that he could with safety undertake a sea voyage.

So the de la Fosse family, well rewarded for the parts they had played so well in the capture of the Cavarale, had been given a generous grant and a free passage to Cherbourg, and had left early that morning by a Peruvian mailboat en route for Panama.

Already a wireless message from the British Admiralty had been sent through the Admiral expressing thanks and due appreciation to the gallant captain of the "Meteor," and Rear-Admiral Maynebrace had communicated the news in person. Now, following his official visits to the Dreadnought of the Air, came an invitation for Captain Whittinghame and Dacres to repair on board the flagship.

At half-past two the Admiral's motor-barge was observed to be entering the inner harbour. In the sternsheets was a flag-lieutenant resplendent in full-dress uniform, his duty being to escort the Admiral's guests to the "Repulse."

As soon as the boat came alongside the "Meteor," Captain Whittinghame and Dacres, in their neat and serviceable uniforms, went over the side and took their places in the waiting craft.

The visit was understood to be a purely unofficial one, but the British bluejackets, always eager to recognize a brave act, were not to be denied. As the barge approached the flagship the shrill trills of the bos'n's whistle rang out. In a moment the upper decks and superstructure of the warship were black with humanity, and the waters of Zandovar Bay echoed and re-echoed to three deep, hearty cheers that only Britons can do full justice to.

Dexterously the barge was brought alongside the "Repulse's" accommodation ladder. Whittinghame stepped out of the barge, and, followed by his companion, ascended to the quarter-deck. As Dacres mounted the steps he could not help recalling the previous time he visited the flagship. Then it was with heavy heart and the well-founded presentiment that there was trouble in store for him. Now he was the guest of the very man who had "broken him."

Then to Dacres' surprise the "pipe side" was sounded by the bos'n's mate, and a serjeants' guard drawn up on the quarter-deck presented arms.

These marks of respect were, according to the King's Regulations, to be given to captains of H.M. ships in uniform. Why, then, had the regulation been officially ignored?

After being received by the Commander and the officers of the watch, Whittinghame and Dacres were shown below to the Admiral's cabin.

Rear-Admiral Maynebrace was not alone. The other occupant of the cabin was Dacres' old chief, Captain Staggers.

"Sit down, my dear Whittinghame, and you, too, Dacres," exclaimed the Admiral genially, as he drew a green curtain over the cabin door in order to balk any curiosity that the marine sentry without might develop. "We may as well proceed at once to business. I believe, Captain Whittinghame, that on the eve of your departure from England you were given honorary rank of captain in His Majesty's fleet?"

"I believe that was so," he replied.

This was indeed news to Dacres, but it was only one of a series of surprises.

"My Lords also stipulated, should events justify all that was claimed for your wonderful aircraft, that they would be entitled to buy the 'Meteor' into the Royal Navy?"

Again Whittinghame nodded assent.

"It is almost needless to say," continued Admiral Maynebrace, "that their expectations have been fully realized. The amount agreed upon has been deposited at your bankers, Captain Whittinghame. Moreover, I am empowered to offer you a full commission as commanding officer of H.M. Airship 'Meteor.'"

"I am afraid Their Lordships are a bit premature," said Whittinghame. "If I remember aright the terms of the proposal were that the 'Meteor' was to be purchased on her return from a successful mission."

"But surely you consider the part you played in the Valderian business a successful piece of work?"

"I suppose so," admitted the captain of the "Meteor."

"Then why hesitate?"

"Because I have not yet completed the work on which I am engaged. The 'Meteor' came to Valderia for three objects. Firstly, to co-operate with the British fleet and destroy the 'Libertad.' That has been done. Secondly, to liberate my brother from Zaypuru's power. That, also, is an accomplished fact. Thirdly—and from a national point of view, the most important object—the recovery of the stolen plans of the submarines. In that respect my work is still unfinished."

"I trust you will be equally successful, Captain Whittinghame. When do you propose to resume your quest?"

"Almost at once. Allowing for the slow method of travelling across the Voyocama Desert, Durango ought to be on the verge of it in two days' time. I propose to take the 'Meteor' to Salto Augusto to-morrow and watch developments."

"But that is Brazilian territory," objected Admiral Maynebrace.

"Quite so," admitted Whittinghame, "but Durango is an outlaw. Three days ago I received intimation that the British Ambassador at Rio was successful in obtaining permission from the Brazilian Government for his arrest. Directly Durango sets foot in Salto Augusto he will be detained by the authorities, extradited, and placed on board the 'Meteor' to be brought back to England."

"I hope it comes off," said the Admiral.

"So do I, sir, especially if we find the submarine plans in Durango's possession."

"To get back to the subject of the purchase of the 'Meteor,' Captain Whittinghame. I presume you are still willing to sell her to the government as soon as Durango is made a prisoner?"

"Certainly," replied Whittinghame rather stiffly. "I never go back on my word. But there is one point I should like to raise—how will my officers and men be affected by the change of ownership?"

"That is just what I was about to mention," said Rear-Admiral Maynebrace, glancing at Dacres. "I have here a copy of the Admiralty wireless message. The proposal is, should you be willing to accept the proffered commission, Captain Whittinghame, that your crew should be transferred en bloc to Admiralty service, provided that they are agreeable. I presume Mr. Dacres has informed you of the circumstances under which he left the Navy? I thought so. Well, Mr. Dacres, apart from the great personal service which you rendered me, your conduct during these operations has been praiseworthy. I regret most deeply that I took the drastic step I did when you played a somewhat unwise joke upon the midshipmen of the flagship. Had you expressed regret, Mr. Dacres, I might have overlooked it, or let you off with a severe reprimand."

"But I wasn't asked to express regret, sir."

"You had the opportunity," remarked the Admiral drily. "However, I have tendered my apologies in front of Captain Staggers and Captain Whittinghame, and I trust that you will accept them."

"I do, sir."

"I propose sending a further report to the Admiralty on the subject," continued the Admiral, "and asking whether they will give orders for your name to be restored to the Navy List. I trust that will be agreeable to you, Mr. Dacres?"

"One minute, sir," interrupted Whittinghame. "I am about to impart a piece of information of which Dacres has hitherto been in ignorance. His name was never removed from the Navy List."

"What!" ejaculated the Admiral and Dacres simultaneously.

"Fact," exclaimed Whittinghame. "I brought the case before the notice of Admiral Sir Hardy Staplers on the eve of our dash for the North Pole. Sir Hardy transmitted my request to the Admiralty, and I was informed that Mr. Dacres' resignation was to be annulled, and he was to retain his rank while serving in the 'Meteor.' Thus, before the removal of Dacres' name from the Navy List was notified, his commission was restored. Owing to my fear that I might lose the services of a very able assistant I suggested to Sir Hardy that Dacres should for the time being be kept in ignorance of what had transpired, and to this he agreed."

Dacres tried to speak but failed. There was a strange sensation in his throat. He felt tempted to dance for sheer joy even in the sanctity of the Admiral's cabin. He was still entitled to wear the uniform of the Royal Navy.

"Allow me to congratulate you, Mr. Dacres," said the Admiral, rising and extending his hand.

"And me, also," added Captain Staggers. "I wish for some reasons that you were reappointed to the 'Royal Oak.'"

"I had a good time under you, sir," was the sub's non-committal form of reply.

"There is yet another point," continued Whittinghame. He was enjoying himself. His face beamed with satisfaction. To heap pleasurable surprises on others was one of his chief delights. "According to the terms offered by My Lords, of which you have just informed me, my officers and men were to be transferred to the Royal Navy, provided they were willing to serve."

"That is so," agreed the Admiral, tapping a folded document on the table.

"Without reduction of rank?"

"Certainly; that is expressly stated."

"Then, take for example the case of Dacres. He is my chief officer, a rank, I take it, that corresponds to first lieutenant in the Navy."

"It's rather rapid promotion," remarked the Admiral. "Scores of men have waited years to obtain that rank. But, by Jove, Dacres! you jolly well deserve it. I am afraid, though, yours is a special case. I shall have to raise the point."

"If Mr. Dacres is not promoted to that rank I'm afraid I shall have something to say very strongly on the subject, sir," declared Whittinghame. "Perhaps I had better delay the acceptance of my commission pending definite information as to Mr. Dacres' status."

"I do not doubt that it will be all right," said the Admiral.

"I prefer to wait, however," added Whittinghame firmly.

"Very well," asserted the Admiral, "we'll leave it at that. I don't suppose for an instant that there will be any objections raised by the Admiralty, but, you see, I haven't authority to act in the case. For the present, then, Mr. Dacres is still a sub-lieutenant in His Majesty's Navy."

# CHAPTER XXXII
# A SUBMARINE ENCOUNTER

"THERE is one thing I didn't mention to the Admiral," remarked Whittinghame on his way back to the airship. "It has been worrying me somewhat. The 'Meteor's' supply of ultra-hydrogen is running low."

"I thought so too, sir," said Dacres. "We've had quite a series of accidents."

"And we cannot risk another mishap with equanimity," added Whittinghame. "Even under the best conditions we must be back in England before the next fortnight; otherwise we must remain here until we get a fresh supply from home. If, in the event of—Hulloa! The 'Meteor' seems to be lower in the water than when we left her."

Whittinghame's surmise was quite correct. The airship was floating with a pronounced list to starboard and slightly down by the stern.

"Anything wrong?" he demanded briskly as he ascended the swaying ladder and gained the interior of the "Meteor."

"Yes, sir," answered Setchell. "There's a leak in No. 5 compartment. We have located it, and exhausted the ultra-hydrogen from the three sub-divisions affected."

"It's lucky that the gas wasn't wasted," remarked the Captain. "The ballonette sub-divisions are flooded, I presume?"

"Yes, sir, a fairly large hole, I should think. We tried compressed air, but could not expel the water."

"Shall we lift her and ascertain the extent of the damage?" asked the sub.

Whittinghame shook his head.

"It's my belief that some rascally agent of Durango has been at work," he said. "If we rise we shall create suspicion in his mind, and frighten him away. Now we know we can take steps to protect ourselves accordingly. I'll ask the flagship to lend us a couple of divers. Fortunately the damage is easily repaired provided we save the ultra-hydrogen."

"I'll go down, sir," volunteered Dacres, "and Callaghan will accompany me."

"I'll be delighted to accept your offer," said Whittinghame gratefully. "I'd go myself only I've had no experience in submarine work of any description. Mr. Setchell, will you please signal the 'Repulse' and ask the loan of two Restronguet diving-suits?"

Callaghan expressed his willingness to accompany the sub. The Irishman had been a first-class seaman-diver in the Royal Navy, and, although unaccustomed to the modern diving-dress, could be relied upon to do his work thoroughly.

Without delay a motor pinnace from the flagship came alongside, bringing the required apparatus. The Restronguet diving-dress, the invention of the late owner of the famous submarine, "Aphrodite," had been generally adopted by the Royal Navy.

The dress was entirely self-contained, the chemically-charged air-supply being carried in metal cylinders attached to the diver, while airtubes and life-lines were no longer required.

The sub was well acquainted with the Restronguet diving-dress, and it required only a brief explanation to acquaint Callaghan with its simple peculiarities.

"Another sub-division flooded, sir," announced Setchell.

"The rascal, or rascals, must be still at work, by Jove!" ejaculated Whittinghame. "Have your knives ready in case there's any resistance."

"We have something better than that, sir," said Dacres, holding up an instrument resembling a tuning-fork. "These are issued with the diving-suits in case the divers are attacked by sharks or human beings."

"What is it?" asked Whittinghame curiously.

"Be careful, sir," cautioned the sub as his chief stretched out his hand to take hold of the weapon. "It is electrically charged, and will temporarily paralyse any living thing it touches with these two barbs. My friend Commander Hythe had a dose of it once. He said he will never forget it. It simply knocked all the stuffing out of him."

"A good substitute for the 'cat,' then," commented Whittinghame. "Now, all ready?"

The metal headpieces were placed over the wearer's heads and clamped on to the collar-plates. The two men, deprived of the outside air, were now dependent solely upon the supply contained in the portable reservoirs.

Dacres led the way. Shuffling awkwardly to the entry port he made his way slowly down the ladder till the water reached to his shoulders. Then releasing his hold he sank gently to the bed of the Zandovar Harbour.

Fortunately there were no tidal currents. The bottom was composed of fine gravel and sand, and practically destitute of marine growth. The depth being less than thirty feet, the brilliant sunshine penetrated the clear water with very little loss of intensity.

The sub waited till the Irishman joined him, then pointed significantly towards the after end of the floating airship, whose rounded hull could be traced through almost its entire length.

Callaghan raised his hand to signify assent, and slowly the two divers made their way aft.

Suddenly Dacres came to a dead stop. His quick eye detected a foreign movement. In the deep shadow cast by the lower horizontal plane a man in a diving-dress was at work. An air-tube and life-line showed that the villainous diver was equipped with an old-fashioned apparatus, but the question was, how far was he working from his air-supply? Was he alone?

Cautiously Dacres and his companion approached, but before they could get within striking-distance the bubble caused by the escaping air from the valves in the helmets gave the alarm. The fellow, dropping a large drill with which he had been studiously employed, slid off the flange on which he had been seated and gained the bed of the harbour.

Evidently his chief aim was flight, for he made his way off as fast as he could, his life-line and airtube trailing in an ever-increasing bight upon the sand. His cumbersome diving-dress so impeded his efforts that he was no match for his pursuers. Once he turned, and seeing that flight was impossible, he drew a huge knife with his left hand, while in his right he grasped a formidable-looking axe.

All prospect of taking the marauder by surprise being at an end, Dacres realized that both he and his companion were at a disadvantage. The only vulnerable portions of their antagonist to which the electric fork could be applied were his bare hands. To get in a knock-out blow would entail a great risk on the part of the attackers, for the fellow evidently meant to make good use of his weapons.

The sub did not fear the axe so much as he did the knife. Owing to the density of the water the force and velocity of the blow of the former would be considerably diminished, but a thrust of a sharp steel knife, meeting with very little resistance, was not to be regarded lightly.

Dacres stopped, and grasping the other's life-line cut it with his knife. He could, of course, have easily settled the submarine encounter by severing the rascal's airtube, but this he was loth to do. On the other hand how could the fellow be secured? If he surrendered, he could not be taken ashore, especially if there were, as was quite likely, a crowd of accomplices. The only solution, according to the sub's idea, was to compel the man to surrender, take him to the surface, and there disconnect his airtube.

Again the sub bent down, this time laying hold of the flexible armoured hose. He raised his knife threateningly, and indicated that his antagonist should either surrender or be deprived of his supply of air.

The fellow's reply was more than Dacres had bargained for. Either he mistook the invitation to give in, or else he meant to die gamely. Raising his axe he floundered towards the place where the sub stood grasping the airtube.

Dacres dropped the pipe like a piece of red-hot coal, and promptly retreated. Brave as he was he did not like the look of that long, keen knife glistening in the pale green light.

As the stranger advanced Callaghan made his way behind him, and poising his electric fork awaited an opportunity to seize the fellow by the arm and prick him on the back of his hand.

Again the mysterious diver halted and, turning alternately to his right and left, contemplated the two points of attack. By this time the sandy bed of the sea had been considerably disturbed, and the water was rapidly becoming mingled with a muddy deposit that greatly curtailed the range of vision.

It was now a complete deadlock. Neither of the unknown's antagonists could bring themselves to start the attack at close quarters, while the stranger would not surrender.

Awaiting his opportunity the Irishman stealthily gained possession of the airtube, and, grasping it in his powerful hands, attempted to curtail the supply of air. The attempt was a failure, for he was quite unable to compress the stout wire coil running around the rubber hose. He fancied he could see a grim smile of contempt upon the features of his foe. Suddenly Callaghan changed his tactics. Still holding on to the airtube he began to retreat towards the "Meteor." The unknown diver had, perforce, to follow, and since his speed was less than that of the men equipped with the Restronguet apparatus, he could not hope to overtake the Irishman. Dacres saw the latter's plan, and he, too, made for the side of the partially-submerged airship.

It seemed as if nothing could prevent the stranger from being ignominiously hauled to the surface alongside the "Meteor's" wire ladder, until he caught sight of one arm and a fluke of an old anchor that was almost buried in the sand. Round the projecting ironwork he took a turn with the flexible pipe, and the united efforts of his two foes were unable to make him budge another step.

The only solution as far as Dacres could suggest was to return to the surface and get hold of a length of rope wire. By this means the unknown diver could be capsized, made a prisoner and be taken to the airship. The only objection was that some time must necessarily elapse before the wire could be obtained, and in the interval the stranger would make good his escape.

While he was pondering over the problem Dacres saw a huge object heading straight towards him with tremendous speed. The next instant his antagonist was thrown forward, his legs working convulsively in spite of the leaden weights on his boots, while his weapons dropped from his outstretched arms. Then came a terrific blast as the air under considerable pressure burst from the man's diving-dress, while all around the water was tinged with blood. An enormous swordfish, its bulk intensified by the magnifying effect of the water, had charged the unfortunate diver from behind and had impaled him on the long, sharp, horny spike that projected from its head.

Shaking the lifeless body like a terrier does a rat the swordfish strove to disengage its formidable weapon. Dacres knew that either he or his comrade would be the next object of attack, since the ferocious swordfish is never satisfied with one victim. Discretion urged him to make a speedy retreat while there was still an opportunity, but his sense of devotion to his companion soon put that idea out of his head.

Holding his electric fork well in front of him, the sub steeled his nerves and approached his latest foe, which was still striving to withdraw its "sword" from its victim's body.

But Dacres was forestalled. Callaghan, being more in the wake of the fiercely-struggling fish, made his way through the blood-stained water and drove his electric weapon deeply into the leather-like skin. Giving one tremendous jerk that sent the Irishman on his back the swordfish became as rigid as if it were a frozen carcass of mutton in a ship's refrigerator.

As quickly as possible Callaghan regained his feet. His Hibernian blood was up. Securing the knife that had fallen from the grasp of the slain diver he plunged the blade deeply—not once but many times—into the carcass of the swordfish.

At length, satisfied with his efforts, Callaghan desisted, and pointed towards the "Meteor." Although encased in the metal helmet the sub shook his head. The Irishman saw the gesture. Dacres meant to follow the length of airtube, through which the air was still being pumped by the dead man's assistants, who were in ignorance of what had occurred, although the manometer told them that something was amiss.

# CHAPTER XXXIII
# NEWS OF DURANGO

FOR nearly two hundred feet the two divers trudged over the sandy bed, till the airtube rising obliquely towards the surface told them that they were near the end of their quest.

Overhead was a rectangular floating body measuring roughly twenty feet by ten. Dacres had found out enough to identify the craft as a kind of floating store. He remembered having seen it moored in the harbour, but previously there had been nothing to arouse his suspicions.

He touched the Irishman's hand, and pointed towards the now invisible "Meteor." The two men tramped slowly back in the direction of the airship till they came in sight of the corpse of the unfortunate diver and the body of the dead swordfish.

Again Dacres came to a halt. The idea of taking the body of the victim on board flashed across his mind. Perhaps the man might be identified. Taking possession of the dead man's axe he commenced to hew laboriously at the horny substance in the head of the swordfish. It was a lengthy task, but at length the stubborn bone was severed.

"Man, I thought you were done for," exclaimed Vaughan Whittinghame, as soon as Dacres' head-dress was removed. "What has happened?"

The Captain and the crew of the "Meteor" had good cause to think that something terrible had overtaken their comrades, for the water all around was tinged with blood and agitated by the air-bubbles that were still being thrown up through the severed tube.

"We're all right," said the sub. "We caught the fellow fairly in the act of boring holes in the under sheathing."

"You killed him?"

The sub shook his head.

"No," he replied. "There will be direct evidence in a few moments. Callaghan is still busy down there. Will you have a weighted line lowered, sir?"

While two members of the crew were divesting Dacres of his borrowed diving-suit a rope was lowered over the side, and the rest of the crew eagerly watched the course of events. Presently the Irishman's helmet appeared above the surface, then his shoulders and arms. Holding on to the ladder with one hand he motioned with the other for the men to haul away.

Up came the corpse of the unknown diver transfixed by the pointed weapon of the swordfish.

"It might have been one of us, sir," said Dacres.

"Get the man on board and let's see who he is," ordered the captain.

"That's where he descended," announced the sub, pointing to the galvanized shed on the raft. "If we are fairly sharp we ought to nab the whole crowd before they become alarmed."

"Good!" ejaculated Captain Whittinghame. "Mr. Setchell, will you please send a message to the flagship and request that an armed boat's crew be sent as soon as possible."

In double quick time a cutter was observed to leave the "Repulse." The men, instinctively realizing that the matter was urgent, bent to their oars with a will.

"There's been an attempt made to scuttle the 'Meteor,'" exclaimed Whittinghame to the lieutenant in charge of the boat. "The fellows are operating from yonder house-boat or raft."

"They're still there, I suppose?" asked the officer.

"We haven't seen them leave. Can you board and investigate?"

"Certainly," was the reply, and ordering his men to give way the lieutenant instructed the coxswain to pull straight for the raft.

Eagerly the crew of the airship watched the departing cutter. As she ran alongside the floating store the oars were boated, and the seamen, armed with rifles and bayonets, clambered on to the platform surrounding the iron shed.

The lieutenant knocked once without receiving any reply. He knocked again. This time he was greeted by a revolver shot, the bullet passing completely through the door and missing the officer's body by a hand's breadth.

Another and another shot came in quick succession, but at the first sign of resistance the lieutenant and his men had thrown themselves flat upon the platform.

"Give it to them hot, men," shouted the officer.

Seven Lee-Enfields spoke almost simultaneously The bullets, passing completely through the frail galvanized iron sheeting, whistled high above the British ships lying half a mile away in the open roadstead. From within the hut came groans and shrieks for mercy, while from a small window was thrust a white handkerchief fastened to the staff of a boathook.

One of the seamen, putting his shoulder to the frail door, quickly burst it open. In rushed the bluejackets, presently to emerge with four uninjured but badly scared men and two slightly-wounded ones as the result of their prompt action.

"Do you know any of these gentlemen, sir?" asked the lieutenant unconcernedly as the cutter returned to the "Meteor."

"I do," declared Gerald Whittinghame. "They are some of Durango's gang. Three of them, at least, were members of the crew of the 'Libertad.'"

"Never!" ejaculated his brother incredulously. "We left the 'Libertad' a total wreck. The survivors were known to have made for the Brazilian frontier."

"All the same, I'm certain I'm right," persisted Gerald. "Ask the lieutenant to send the men on board and we will question them."

To this proposal the "Repulse's" officer raised no objection. The six Valderians were made to enter the airship. The two wounded ones were handed over to Dr. Hambrough's care, while the others were told to stand against one of the bulkheads, with an armed man between each to prevent any further act of violence.

The prisoners maintained a sullen silence when questioned by Gerald Whittinghame. Promises to be treated with leniency and threats if they refused to divulge their employer's whereabouts alike were useless.

The Valderians apparently realized that being in the power of the British their lives were safe. Had they thought otherwise fear would have compelled them to speak to save themselves from summary execution.

"I'll take the whole jolly lot back to the flagship, sir," said the lieutenant. "No doubt the Admiral will send them ashore with the request that the new president of Valderia will deal with them as he thinks fit."

"One moment," replied Vaughan Whittinghame. "Suppose we see if we can identify the fellow in the diver's suit. It might even be Durango himself."

The body of the dead diver had been removed from where it had been lying close to the entry port, and had been placed in a compartment out of the sight of the captives as they were being brought on board.

When the head-dress was removed Gerald Whittinghame tapped his brother on the shoulder.

"Now are you convinced?" he asked.

"I don't know the man," replied the Captain.

"But I do. That is Sebastian Lopez, the fellow who took command of the 'Libertad' when she left Naocuanha to pick up Reno Durango at Salto Augusto. I don't mind staking any amount that Durango has doubled on his tracks and is somewhere in Valderian territory."

"Hardly likely with those submarine plans in his possession," demurred Captain Whittinghame. "He knows that Valderia is no go as far as he is concerned. He'll be making his way as fast as he can to Europe, to raise money on the plans."

"When it's a choice between cupidity and revenge there's no telling what the Mexican will do," declared Gerald. "My opinion is that he is somewhere about, and has bribed these men to cripple the 'Meteor.' I admit they went a clumsy way about it, for they could easily have fixed an electrically-fired mine under the aircraft and blown her to atoms. Look here; the best thing we can do is to separate the prisoners and try to get them to open their mouths."

"Good idea!" asserted the lieutenant of the "Repulse." "If you threaten to hand them over to President Desiro I should think they'll listen to reason pretty smartly."

"Very well, then," assented the Captain. "So long as you have no objection I haven't; they are your prisoners, you know."

The first Valderian to be questioned maintained an obstinate silence. At the threat of being sent ashore to be dealt with by the new president he merely shrugged his shoulders.

"Take him away," ordered Vaughan Whittinghame impatiently. "They show far greater solicitude for their rascally leader than Durango would show towards them."

"Before you have the next prisoner brought in we'll arrange a little dramatic episode," said the flagship's lieutenant. "I'll order my men to fire a volley."

"By all means," assented Whittinghame. "I quite follow you."

Having given his boat's crew orders for each man to break out a bullet from a cartridge and load with the blank, the lieutenant told the men to fire.

The sharp crack of musketry resounded from one end of the airship to the other.

When the second prisoner was ushered in he was pale and trembling. He was now fully convinced that the faith he had in the Englishman's reluctance to take life was a mistake, for in his mind he felt certain that the volley he had just heard meant the summary execution of his predecessor.

"Pay attention," exclaimed Gerald Whittinghame sternly. He had been deputed to act as cross-examiner-in-chief, and his intimate knowledge of Spanish stood him in good stead. "Pay attention: you have been caught in the act of committing an outrage on the property of a friendly nation; for it is useless to attempt to excuse yourself on the grounds that you were unaware of the settlement of the differences between Great Britain and Valderia. We mean to take extreme measures with you, unless— —"

Vaughan's brother paused in order that his words should carry weight, while the incompleted sentence indicated that even yet the prisoner might expect clemency.

"Unless you tell us all you know of the whereabouts of Señor Reno Durango. Do not attempt to deceive us. Already we know a great deal, so if you tell us anything that we know to be false you will have good cause to wish you had held your tongue."

"Señor, I speak the truth," replied the Valderian. "I have been made to do what I have done. I swear it— —"

"We do not ask you about your part of the affair," interrupted Gerald. "What we want to know, and what we insist on finding out, relates to Durango."

"Señor, he is not in Zandovar."

"That I know," said Whittinghame. It was a sheer piece of bluff, for up to the present he had had a suspicion that the Mexican might have returned.

"Nor is he in Naocuanha."

"We do not wish to know where he is not, but where he is."

"Señor, I know not."

Gerald Whittinghame pulled out his watch.

"You are lying," he thundered. "I give you thirty seconds. At the end of that time if you do not tell the truth— —" and he pointed significantly towards the door.

The silence was so intense that the ticking of the watch could be distinctly heard. The prisoner's face was working spasmodically.

"Twenty-eight, twenty-nine — —" counted Gerald.

Before he could say the word "thirty" the Valderian leapt upon him like a tiger. The watch was hurled across the cabin, while ere Whittinghame and his companions quite realized what was taking place the prisoner was clawing Gerald's face like a wild cat.

Two or three of the "Meteor's" crew threw themselves upon the violent prisoner and secured him.

"Shoot me!" he shouted defiantly. "Shoot me, you English cowards! I will not tell."

"Take him below," ordered Gerald. "He is a jolly sight braver than most of his countrymen. You will not be shot," he added, addressing the Valderian.

"By Jove! if they are all like that fellow we shan't learn very much," remarked Vaughan to his brother, after the man had been led away to join the first prisoner. "Either Durango has put black fear into their hearts, or else they regard him as a hero worthy of any sacrifice."

"We'll try the effect of another volley, sir," suggested the lieutenant from the "Repulse." "Number Three may be made of different stuff."

The third prisoner certainly was. With the report of the rifles ringing in his ears he was ushered into the cabin. He, too, thought he was to be sent to execution, and in the hope of saving his life he most readily agreed to tell all he knew concerning his chief.

Durango, two days after the destruction of the "Libertad," had made off for Salto Augusto, accompanied by two men who had served under von Harburg, while the other survivors, under his orders, went to Naocuanha. Apparently, the Mexican thought better of attempting the hazardous journey on foot across the Voyocama Desert; for on the eve of the fall of the Valderian capital he arrived at Naocuanha. Without attempting to inform President Zaypuru of his presence, the Mexican called together his remaining partisans and ordered them to destroy or at least seriously cripple the airship as she lay in the inner harbour.

His idea was not merely to revenge himself upon his rival, but to prevent Whittinghame from pursuing him. He had left Zandovar that morning for Nazca, a small seaport in Peru. "For what reason is Durango going to Nazca?" demanded Gerald Whittinghame.

"Señor, I do not know. I can only guess, for the Señor Durango rarely told us of his plans. I know that at Nazca dwells an inventor who has constructed a boat that can fly through the air. Some months ago this inventor wrote to President Zaypuru and offered to sell him the craft, but Durango advised the president to have nothing to do with it. Perhaps, now, Durango will buy it. *Quien sabe?*"

"How long will it take Durango to reach Nazca?"

"He has but to ride to Tuiche: there he will find an aeroplane," replied the prisoner.

"That will do; remove him," ordered Gerald, then turning to his brother he added, "we must be off almost at once, if we are to catch the villain. How long will it take for the 'Meteor' to be ready for flight?"

"Twenty minutes," replied Vaughan calmly.

# CHAPTER XXXIV
# THE CHASE

"TWENTY minutes," repeated Gerald blankly. "Why, she's half a dozen ballonettes useless."

"Quite so," assented the captain. "Fortunately they are all in the lowermost tier. We can make use of the emergency compartments. Now, Dacres, will you see about making ready to slip the moorings?"

Quickly the "Repulse's" lieutenant and his men boarded their cutter, taking with them the Valderian prisoners. Since Whittinghame was not under the orders of Rear-Admiral Maynebrace he did not have to request "permission to part company"; but he paid the Admiral the compliment, sending the message by the lieutenant.

Within a few minutes of that officer's return to the flagship the "Repulse" signalled, "Wish you success."

The "Meteor" rose slowly to a height of three hundred feet. Even then the whole of the ultra-hydrogen at Whittinghame's disposal had to be brought into play. The airship possessed sufficient gas barely to counteract the attraction of gravity. To increase the altitude she would have to depend solely upon her elevating planes unless some of the stores could be ruthlessly sacrificed, for there was no ballast available.

At quarter speed the "Meteor" passed immediately over the flagship's masts, dipped her ensign, then circling, bore away northward for the Peruvian coast.

"It's getting serious," declared Captain Whittinghame to Dacres. "The supply of ultra-hydrogen is less than I thought. We'll stick to it and attempt to run Durango's new craft down. After that the best thing we can do is to make for Jamaica, and wait there until we get a fresh consignment of ultra-hydrogen from home."

"There's a leakage somewhere," said the sub.

"Yes, unfortunately. Still, it is not to be wondered at, after what the 'Meteor' has gone through. No doubt our hurried repairs after the scrap with the 'Libertad' were not carried out so carefully as we could have wished."

"And the motors, sir?"

"Thank goodness they are good for another twenty thousand miles, if necessary. One couldn't hope for a more economical fuel than cordite."

"I suppose we could, if necessary, rest on the surface of the sea and carry on under power?"

"We could, provided the water were sufficiently calm. All the same, Dacres, I don't want to have to do it. The air is my sphere, my lad. Ha! we're approaching Nazca, I can see. Keep a good look out in case we spot this flying boat arrangement. I'm rather curious to see what it is like."

"But if Durango hasn't started yet and spots the 'Meteor' approaching? He'll give us the slip."

"He cannot go far without being noticed in a strange country," replied Vaughan Whittinghame cheerfully. "We have an extradition treaty with Peru, you know."

"He may disguise himself."

"More than likely; but to what end? Had he made for a large city like Lima or even Callao he might escape notice. But in a little place like Nazca, why, he's playing into our hands."

Both men remained silent for a few moments, then Dacres blurted out:—

"It is awfully good of you, sir, to make it all right at the Admiralty for me."

"Nonsense!" protested Captain Whittinghame. "I knew you'd be pleased. One can generally take it for granted that when a young fellow cuts off his nose to spite his face he's genuinely sorry for it, even though he won't admit it. Now, honestly, weren't you jolly sick about having to leave the 'Royal Oak'?"

"I'm very glad I joined the 'Meteor,' sir."

"That's no answer to my question, Dacres."

"Well, then, I don't mind having to leave the 'Royal Oak,' but I'm awfully pleased to find that I am still an officer of the Royal Navy."

"Then, I wasn't far out in my estimation, Dacres. All's well that ends well, you know."

"It hasn't ended yet," rejoined the sub, pointing to the land, which was now only a mile off. "Now for Durango."

Captain Whittinghame telegraphed for the propellers to be stopped. Slowly the "Meteor" descended, alighting on the south side of the town of Nazca.

Practically all the inhabitants, preceded by the alcalde, came out to see the unwonted sight of a huge airship flying the British colours, the mayor tendering the hospitality of Nazca to the visitors during their stay.

"We do not remain long, señor alcalde," replied Gerald Whittinghame. "We are in pursuit of an outlaw, one Reno Durango, who has fled from Valderia. We heard, on good authority, that he came hither."

"All strangers arriving at Nazca are known to us, señor," said the portly alcalde. "No one of that name has set foot in our town."

Gerald Whittinghame showed no sign of disappointment at the information. It was as he had expected.

"I believe, señor," he remarked, "that you have an inventor who has built a kind of boat that is capable of flying?"

"Ah, yes," replied the alcalde. "Then you, too, are anxious to purchase the boat? I fear you are too late, for an English milord has just taken her away."

"I think I know the gentleman," said Gerald. "Would you mind describing him to me?"

The mayor's description left no doubt as to the identity of the supposed English "milord." Durango had forestalled them.

"Ask the alcalde if the inventor of the boat is present," suggested Vaughan, after his brother had explained the conversation.

"Here he is, Señor Jaurez is his name," announced the mayor, indicating an alert little Peruvian, who was paying more attention to the visible details of the "Meteor" than to the conversation between the chief magistrate of Nazca and the officers of the airship.

Señor Jaurez elbowed his way through the crowd. His face was beaming in anticipation of booking another order.

"What is the radius of action of your flying-boat, señor?" asked Gerald, prompted by his brother.

"A hundred leagues, señors; that is without replenishing the petrol-tanks. I could, of course, construct another boat with twice or even thrice the capacity. Perhaps your worships would like to pay a visit to my hacienda?"

"We regret, señor," replied Whittinghame, not to be outdone in courtesy, "that such a course is at present impossible. Might we ask what is the speed of your flying boat?"

The Peruvian explained that under favourable conditions a rate equivalent to eighty-five miles per hour was possible.

"We'll overtake his craft in three hours, then," said Vaughan to his brother. "Now, let us bid farewell to Nazca."

The "Meteor" resumed her quest. Durango's destination was unknown. He had gone in a northerly direction, and since it was very unlikely that he would take overland a craft designed to alight upon the sea, it was reasonable to conclude that he would attempt a landing in Equador or Columbia, seeing that, now his identity was established, he dare not seek refuge in Peruvian territory.

Flying at her greatest speed the "Meteor" skirted the coast line. Every little harbour and creek capable of affording refuge to the winged boat—which by reason of its two forty-feet planes was very conspicuous—were carefully swept by the aid of binoculars. At Truxillo the airship brought up to hail a Peruvian man-of-war lying in the harbour. The officer of the watch replied that a hydro-aeroplane had passed overhead less than an hour previously, bound north. The motors, he added, were apparently giving trouble.

"Good! We're gaining rapidly!" ejaculated Captain Whittinghame. "I hope to goodness we pick the fellow up before dark, or he may give us the slip—but only for a time. As long as the 'Meteor' is capable of keeping the air I will continue the pursuit."

Two hours later the "Meteor" was above the small town of Mancora. Ahead lay the broad expanse of the deep indentation of the Gulf of Guayaquil—practically the only large break in the coastline on the Pacific coast between Corcovado Gulf in Southern Chile and the Bay of Panama. The question was: had Durango crossed it, or had he skirted the shore? By adopting either course he would quickly reach Equadorean territory, where he would be able to land without fear of arrest.

"We will make inquiries; it will save time," declared Whittinghame, as he telegraphed for the propellers to be stopped.

Descending to within fifty feet of the plaza the "Meteor" hung motionless in the air. Gerald Whittinghame promptly hailed the throng of spectators. A hundred voices shouted in reply, while a hundred hands pointed in a northerly direction; but not a word was intelligible to the crew.

Whittinghame tried again, only to be greeted by a chorus that conveyed no information to the anxious members of the "Meteor's" crew.

"Evidently he's gone straight across the gulf," declared Vaughan. "We'll carry on. We are only wasting precious time."

"One moment," protested his brother. "Here, take hold of this rope and let me down. I'll soon find out."

Four of the crew paid out the rope, and Gerald, turning like a joint on a meat-jack, was lowered to earth. Instantly he was surrounded by a mob of ever curious townsfolk all pointing, shouting, and pushing each other with the utmost vehemence. The airship, drifting slowly in the faint breeze, carried Gerald along the ground, and the crowd moved too.

"Hurry up!" shouted Vaughan. "You'll be jammed up against the wall of that building in half a minute."

"Haul away, then," bawled his brother in reply, at the same time throwing his arms round one of the most loquacious of his attentive audience.

The man struggled, but unavailingly. His companions, too astounded to come to his aid, watched him being taken up in the iron grip of the Englishman. Then, realizing that should he break away there would be an ever-increasing drop that would end fatally to him, the Peruvian changed his tactics and clung with desperation to his captor.

"We will not hurt you, señor," said Gerald reassuringly, as the two men were hauled into safety within the "Meteor." "We merely want information, and then we will land you in safety. Here is a five dollar piece for you."

"What information do you want, señor?" asked the Peruvian, after testing the coin betwixt his teeth. The gold reassured him. Had his life or liberty been in danger he would not have been treated in this lavish fashion.

"The boat that flies, señor?" he repeated. "*Madre!* of course I have seen her. Did not all of us say so?"

"But we could not understand: you were all shouting together. Now, where did you see that flying-boat?"

"Señor, she came down just outside the town not an hour ago. There were three men in her. Two were Valderians. Their master was not. He bought petrol: four cans of it. He poured the petrol into a metal flask in the boat and went on his way, over yonder," and the Peruvian pointed due north.

With the utmost celerity the fellow was lowered to his native soil, and again the "Meteor" darted ahead. Every man was now keenly on the alert. All depended upon Durango's craft being sighted before the sun dipped behind the waters of the Pacific. Only forty minutes' of daylight remained.

"Land right ahead, sir," reported one of the crew.

"That's St. Helena Point, then," declared Captain Whittinghame. "We've done a hundred miles in an hour and ten minutes. Nothing much wrong with the motors as far as we are concerned."

The next instant he devoutedly wished he hadn't spoken in this strain, for with a terrific crash one of the blades of the foremost port propeller became detached from the boss. Sheering through the aluminium cylinder protecting the double propellers, it ripped the metal to such an extent that a long strip of wreckage caught the remaining blade, snapping it off close to the base. The motor raced furiously until Parsons, knowing that something was amiss, promptly cut off the detonator.

"That's done it!" ejaculated Vaughan Whittinghame disgustedly. "That is the result of boasting."

"Repairable?" asked Dr. Hambrough.

"Yes, but not now. We can't afford to bring up for repairs. How's the steering, quartermaster?"

"Rather hard on her helm, sir," replied that worthy. "She wants to come round to port, sir."

"I thought so," rejoined the Captain. "That's caused by the unequal drive of the starboard engines. We must carry on and risk the consequences."

He glanced at the speed indicator. The "Meteor" was still travelling through the air at one hundred and twenty miles an hour.

"We're gaining thirty at least on that villain," continued Vaughan. For the time being he appeared to give slight attention to the damage done to his beloved airship. His whole thoughts were centred upon the pursuit of Durango.

Only ten more minutes to sunset.

"Get the two bow searchlights connected up," ordered the Captain. "See that new carbons are used. It will be like chasing a mouse by candlelight, but we— —"

"There she is, sir!" interrupted Callaghan excitedly.

"Where?" asked Whittinghame, rushing to one of the scuttles on the port bow, and following the direction of the Irishman's outstretched arm. "You're right, Callaghan. Hurrah! We've overtaken her."

Such indeed was the case. Evidently Durango had gone a couple of points out of his course in the dash across the mouth of the Gulf of Guayaquil. Consequently, although the crew of the "Meteor" were unaware of it until a few moments previously, the airship had drawn level with her quarry, but on a divergent course; while—another point in her favour—she was between the flying-boat and the shores of Equador.

"Starboard your helm, quartermaster," ordered the Captain.

Round swung the "Meteor" till her bows pointed straight for the object of her pursuit. Durango and his two companions, ignorant of the fact that they were being followed, were possibly contemplating a welcome rest on neutral ground, when one of the Valderians caught sight of their arch-enemy bearing down upon them hand over fist.

The crew of the "Meteor" saw the Mexican literally push the helmsman aside and grip the steering-wheel. The aerial boat turned almost as rapidly as a racing yacht, and made, not for the coast, but due west towards the wide Pacific.

Down plunged the sun—a red orb in a ruddy sky. Night was about to fall upon the scene of the desperate race between the airship and her prey.

# CHAPTER XXXV
# THE THUNDERSTORM

"WHERE's he making for?" asked the doctor.

Vaughan Whittinghame paid no apparent heed to the question. His eyes seemed riveted upon the small dark object against the crimson glow of the brief tropical sunset.

It was Dacres who answered Hambrough's query.

"I believe he's making a dash for the Galapagos Islands," he replied. "It's a matter of six hundred and fifty odd miles."

"If the fellow had any sense he would keep on doubling," said Gerald. "Quick as we are that craft can turn like a top. It would be like a hare dodging a hound."

"Don't send him any telepathic messages, Mr. Whittinghame," said the doctor. "The sooner we nab him the better. I am beginning to see what a London theatre looks like again."

"Now, if you were a kinematograph operator you'd make your fortune, doctor," remarked Setchell.

The Captain half turned his head. One glance was enough. The inconsequent conversation annoyed him. The rest of the officers promptly subsided.

"Switch on, there," he ordered curtly.

The two powerful beams shot out into the now fast gathering gloom. Both were focussed upon the fugitive. The flying-boat looked as if made of silver, floating motionless in the air, for the "Meteor's" speed had been reduced till the relative rates of the two craft were practically the same.

Had Captain Whittinghame wished he could have ordered the bow-gun to be manned, and the result would be a foregone conclusion. Owing to engine trouble Durango's craft was capable of travelling only at the comparatively slow rate of sixty miles an hour. At that speed the ordnance of the "Meteor" could be brought into action. But the captain of the airship, apart from his desire to recover the stolen plans, was averse to taking life unless absolutely necessary. He would pursue the Mexican until the latter, through sheer exhaustion or inability on the part of his craft to keep running, would be compelled to surrender.

Onwards and onwards tore the two craft, the huge airship in pursuit of the midget aerial boat. Durango made no attempt to double. It was his only chance, and for some unknown reason he failed to avail himself of his loophole of escape.

The two Whittinghames, Dacres, and the doctor remained in the lower fore observation room, their eyes fixed upon the apparently stationary object upon which the two searchlights played relentlessly. Not a word was spoken. The rapt attention of the watchers was centred upon their prey.

Presently Durango relinquished the steering-wheel, his place being taken by one of his Valderian companions. Stooping he drew a small leather bag from one of the lockers, opened it and produced a bundle of papers.

For a few moments he paused irresolutely, alternately looking at the tied-up parcel of documents and at the relentless Dreadnought of the Air. Then, standing up and steadying himself against the furious blast that whirled past the boat, he poised the packet.

A muttered ejaculation burst from Vaughan Whittinghame's lips. This, then, was to be the fate of the precious submarine plans, for such the documents undoubtedly were.

The Mexican was on the point of letting the packet fall when the second Valderian touched him on the shoulder and said something. Durango shook his head. Again the Valderian spoke, seemingly in remonstrance. Just then a vivid flash of lightning threw the boundless expanse of sea into strong relief.

A tropical storm was brewing. Although there was practically no wind and the sea was as smooth as glass it was quite evident that the "Meteor" and her prey were heading towards the storm-centre. A glance at the barometer showed Dacres that, allowing for the difference in altitude when the instrument was last set, the mercury had dropped nearly three-quarters of an inch in two hours.

Suddenly the helmsman of the flying-boat put the vertical rudder hard over. Round spun the craft like a top, tilting to a dangerous angle as she did so. The unexpected movement took Durango by surprise, and unable to retain his balance he sprawled ignominiously upon the floor-boards. The precious plans slipped from his grasp.

As the fugitive boat swerved from her former course the quartermaster, running the port searchlight of the "Meteor," promptly swung the giant beam in the hope of following the elusive craft. The effort was in vain. The object of the chase darted out of the path of brilliant light and was instantly swallowed up in the darkness.

"After searchlights, there!" ordered Captain Whittinghame on the telephone. "Switch on and try to pick up the flying boat."

At the same time the "Meteor's" vertical rudders were put hard over, while the remaining propellers on the port side were set astern to assist in the more rapid manoeuvring of the airship.

Four searchlights swept the air in all directions. Yet although it seemed impossible that any object floating in space within the limits of the beams could escape detection there were no signs of the craft containing Durango and his two companions.

"Perhaps, sir, she crumpled her planes when she turned," suggested Dacres.

"Quite possible," assented Captain Whittinghame. "In that case she has a drop of nearly eight thousand feet before she hits the surface of the sea."

"Then, it will be useless to expect to recover the plans," said Dr. Hambrough.

"It does not matter so long as we know they are destroyed," replied Vaughan Whittinghame. "The Admiralty have others: the danger was that there was a possibility of this set getting into the hands of a foreign power. Provided——"

His remarks were cut short by a vivid flash of lightning that seemed to envelop completely the now practically stationary airship. Almost simultaneously came an ear-splitting detonation. The whole fabric of the Dreadnought of the Air seemed to quiver.

Dacres, Hambrough, and Gerald Whittinghame looked at each other. They fully expected to find the "Meteor" rent amidships, falling with an ever-increasing rapidity into the sea.

The Captain was the only man who seemed to ignore the sublime and appalling atmospheric conditions.

"Keep a look-out!" he exclaimed; "you're missing our only chance."

Flash succeeded flash with the utmost frequency. The "Meteor" was evidently between two huge stores of electricity, for the clouds were not releasing their super-charges to earth. The airship's best chance of safety was to descend to within a few hundred feet of the sea.

Three ballonettes only were required to be emptied to allow the "Meteor" to drop rapidly, until the air, growing denser as she descended, her vertical course would be automatically retarded and eventually stopped.

The seaward plunge was awe-inspiring. The airship was passing through a bank of clouds so dense that even the powerful searchlights were as useless as candle lamps in a heavy London fog. Yet at about every ten seconds the veil of pitch dark vapour was pierced by flashes of lightning that left the crew blinking like owls suddenly transported from the depths of a lightless cave to the dazzling brilliance of the noonday sun.

Four thousand feet. The "Meteor" was still enveloped in clouds, but to add to the terrors of the situation fierce whirlwinds were assailing her on all sides. In spite of her non-rigidity the unprecedented strain to which she was subjected threatened to break her asunder amidships.

The Dreadnought of the Air was now utterly out of control. At one moment her bows were pointing upwards at an angle of forty-five degrees and to the horizontal. At another she was plunging obliquely with her nose downwards. She rolled like a barrel, and strained and writhed like a human being in torment.

Elevating planes and vertical rudders were alike useless. The only chance of escape was to drop vertically.

Staggering to the engine-room indicators the Captain ordered the motors to be switched off Now the motion was slightly less erratic. Hailstones the size of pigeons' eggs were falling upon her aluminium deck—not with the metallic clang that characterizes their fall on the land, but with comparative lightness, for the airship was still within a few hundred feet of the cloud in which the frozen rain-drops were generated.

Two thousand feet. The "Meteor" was now regaining her normal stability. Her seaward descent was momentarily becoming slower. She had emerged from the rain-cloud, and although the lightning still played, the danger seemed to have passed.

Something had to be done to save the airship from violently alighting upon the water. Her present rate of retardation was insufficient.

"Telegraph for half speed ahead," ordered Captain Whittinghame. "Trim the forward elevating planes there, doctor."

Back came the startling information from both the fore and after motor-rooms: the ignition had failed.

"Short circuit somewhere," muttered the Captain. "I'm not surprised. Recharge those three ballonettes, Dacres."

A thousand feet. With a succession of sharp hisses the ultra-hydrogen escaped from the cylinder in which it had been stored under pressure and re-entered the ballonettes. The crew could feel the sudden check to the downward plunge, but in spite of the additional gas the "Meteor" was still falling.

The four searchlights were still running: two practically parallel beams showing ahead and two astern. In the after motor-room—whence were actuated the still intact propellers—Parsons was hard at work trying to locate the source of the mischief. Could these motors be started in time the attraction due to gravity would yet be overcome.

Suddenly Gerald Whittinghame gave a shout and pointed towards the starboard observation scuttle. Dacres was just in time to see an object falling—falling with extraordinary irregularity. It was Durango's flying-boat. She was describing a succession of "loops," while her motors were still running.

In the path of the starboard searchlights' rays she appeared to check her downward course; then lurching ahead made straight for the bows of the "Meteor." Just as it seemed as if a collision were imminent the wrecked craft dipped and passed into Cimmerian darkness.

"He's done for, by Jove!"

"What's that?" asked Captain Whittinghame, who had heard his brother's exclamation but had failed to see the reason for it.

"Durango—smashed up," reported Dacres.

Vaughan Whittinghame made no audible remark. H e realized that the "Meteor" herself was in peril. In the face of impending disaster one is apt to banish thoughts of vengeance.

Two hundred feet. Dacres glanced at his watch and looked inquiringly at his chief.

"Well?" asked the Captain laconically.

"We're hardly falling, sir," said the sub. "Our downward course is being greatly retarded——"

"You're right, by Jove!" exclaimed Whittinghame. "All the same, I wish Parsons could get those motors to start."

His hopes were not to be realized for the present. With a barely perceptible jar the airship alighted on the surface of the Pacific. Her searchlights played upon an unruffled expanse of calm water. The storm had been confined to the upper strata of the atmosphere.

"Heave out the sea-anchor in case it comes on to blow," ordered Vaughan Whittinghame. "We're safe for the present. Mr. Dacres, will you please go on deck and obtain a stellar observation? It will be dawn in half an hour; but I would like to ascertain our position in case we drive ashore before daybreak."

The sub hurried to carry out his orders. It was a relief, after being cooped up in the confined atmosphere of the observation room of the heaving and pitching "Meteor," to breathe in the fresh night air.

The searchlights had now been switched off. The airship was floating motionless in a phosphorescent sea. Having taken the observation Dacres was about to go below and work out his position when a peculiar swirl in the water about a hundred yards to starboard attracted his attention.

"Surely that's not a reef?" he asked himself. "I wish I had my night-glasses."

Then came a quick succession of splashes. "Sharks—that's what it is. Or perhaps a swarm of threshers attacking a whale. A lively commotion! I'll go below and get my binoculars."

"Anything in sight?" asked Captain Whittinghame, noticing Dacres' haste.

"Something splashing, sir; I'm just going to get my binoculars."

The two men made their way to the upper deck. The sub pointed in the direction he had noticed the commotion, but all was now quiet. A careful examination of the spot by the powerful night-glasses revealed no sign of anything to account for the swirl of the water.

"Hark! What's that?" demanded Whittinghame.

"I heard nothing," replied Dacres.

"Could have sworn I heard a man's voice. Perhaps my senses are playing me a trick."

"It may be the breeze, sir," suggested the sub, as a catspaw ruffled the surface of the placid water.

"Of course. All the same, I'll have the searchlight trained on the place."

For quite ten minutes the beams swung slowly to and fro, but nothing could be seen beyond the ripples on the sea.

"There's a vessel approaching, sir," announced Dacres, who had been sweeping the horizon with his glasses. "I can just pick up her red and green lights. She's quite five miles off, I should think."

"She must have spotted our searchlight, and is altering her course to investigate. Pass the word for the searchlight to be switched off, Dacres. I don't think we need assistance, unless I'm very much mistaken about Parson's capabilities."

"There's quite a decent breeze, sir," commented Dacres as he prepared to descend the companion ladder. "We must be making a fair drift."

"Not with that sea-anchor out," said Whittinghame.

"I don't know about that, sir; you see, we're floating light. I'll work out our position, for I shouldn't be surprised if we are drifting down upon the Galapagos."

Captain Whittinghame remained on deck. He was pondering over the fate of his rival, Reno Durango, and wondering whether he could safely assert that the last of the tasks he had set out to perform had been satisfactorily accomplished. He had witnesses ready to affirm on oath that they had seen the Mexican's flying-boat being hurled to destruction. Could it unquestionably be taken for granted that the stolen plans of Submarine "M I" were no longer in existence to prove a menace to the admittedly superior construction and organization of the British submarine service?

The rapid approach of the coming day disturbed Vaughan Whittinghame's reveries.

The vessel whose navigation light Dacres had picked up had altered her course and was steaming quite two miles to windward of the practically helpless airship.

By the aid of his glasses the captain could see that she was a tramp of about eight hundred tons, and in ballast, for she rose high out of the water, while the tips of her propeller blades could be seen amid the smother of foam under her rudder-post. There was nothing about her to enable Whittinghame to determine her nationality. Her single funnel was painted a dull black without any colouring bands.

Even as he looked the tramp starboarded her helm. The dawn had likewise revealed to her sleepy watch on deck the presence of the disabled airship. She was on the point of steaming down in the hope of earning a salvage job.

"No use, my friend," quoth Vaughan.

The next moment he burst into a hearty laugh, for the tramp began to circle as if to resume her former course. The acceptance of his muttered advice to a vessel a mile and a half away tickled his sense of humour.

"Hulloa! What is the move now, I wonder?" he exclaimed. He might well evince curiosity, for instead of holding on to her former course, which was practically due north, the tramp was slowly turning due east. Even as he watched, Whittinghame could see that the cascade of foam under her rudder had vanished. She had stopped her engines.

Apparently the vessel was still carrying too much way, for again her propellers churned up the froth, this time for less than half a minute. Men were hanging over her port side and lowering ropes.

"Good heavens!" ejaculated Whittinghame aghast.

# CHAPTER XXXVI
# THE ABANDONED FLYING-BOAT

WHITTINGHAME could now see the reason for the manoeuvre. One of the derricks of the stumpy foremast was swung outboard. Her donkey-engine began to work, and from the sea, with the water pouring out of her, was hoisted the waterlogged flying-boat.

The plane on her port-side had completely vanished, and only a few fragments of her starboard one remained. Standing amidships and steadying themselves by the spars of the lifting tackle were three men—Reno Durango and his Valderian crew.

When the crippled craft was half-way up the side of the tramp the donkey-engine stopped. The captain of the vessel, leaning over the bridge rail, shouted to the three castaways. Durango replied, vigorously shaking his head and gesticulating wildly in the direction of the "Meteor."

Apparently his protests were unavailing, for he grasped a rope trailing from the tramp's rail and clambered on board. His companions followed suit.

The argument proceeded. Evidently the master of the cargo vessel wished to steam towards the airship, and to this suggestion Durango demurred strongly. After a while the wrecked flying-boat was lowered into the water again, and the lifting tackle cast off, the Mexican pointing towards the abandoned craft and talking volubly.

With a shrug of his shoulders the skipper walked to the centre of the bridge and telegraphed to the engine-room. The tramp's propeller began to revolve, and the lumbering vessel gathered way.

For some moments Durango stood as if in despair, then leaning over the bridge-rail shook his fist at the disabled airship.

Through his binoculars Captain Whittinghame saw his expression clearly. The rogue, despite his own troubles and obvious disappointment, was gloating over his rival's misfortunes.

Without saying a word to his comrades in the observation room, Vaughan Whittinghame went below and made his way to the after engine-room, where Parsons was found lying on his back with portions of the partly-stripped motor all around him.

"How long, now?" asked the Captain.

"A couple of hours, maybe, sir," replied the engineer.

"Can you manage in an hour? The after-motors will be sufficient."

"I'll try my best, sir," replied Parsons, unwilling to commit himself.

"Very good; carry on," rejoined his superior, and without another word he left the engineer to do his level best towards restoring the motors to a state of efficiency.

"We are sixty-four miles east a quarter north of the Galapagos, sir," announced Dacres.

"Thank you," replied Vaughan. "Just one minute, Mr. Dacres; will you please come on deck with me?"

The sub followed his chief. Whittinghame said nothing more until the two officers were out of earshot and on the deck of the water-borne airship.

"There's the vessel whose lights you picked up an hour ago, Dacres."

"Yes, sir; has she communicated?"

"She apparently meant to, but changed her mind. Do you see something floating about two and a half miles dead to windward of us?"

The sub brought his telescope to bear in the direction indicated. It took him some time to locate the object, as it was almost in the reflected glare of the early morning sun.

"I have it, sir," he said.

"What do you make of it?"

"Cannot say, sir. Wreckage of some sort."

"It is," added Whittinghame. "More, it is the wreck of the flying-boat, and that rascal Durango has eluded us again."

"Surely he didn't survive the fall?"

"He did. I saw him boarding yonder tramp. Now, this is what I want you to do: take a compass bearing of the wreckage, and observe the direction and rate of our drift. In an hour Parsons hopes to have the after-propellers working. We will then forge ahead and investigate Durango's flying-boat. Do not say a word to any of the others until after breakfast. I know them: they would throw aside any idea of food until we are fit to get under way;

and, with all due respect to their zeal, I am no believer in a man working on an empty stomach."

In exactly forty-nine minutes from the time that the Captain left the motor-room, Parsons had the engines ready for work. The fault, once discovered, was easy to remedy.

"Gentlemen," began the Captain after the morning meal was over, "I have unpleasant news to announce; but I can rely upon your co-operation sufficiently to know that you will face it with your characteristic determination. Reno Durango is not only alive, but he is on board the vessel we saw approaching us just before dawn. Fortunately we are no longer in a totally crippled state. Although the supply of ultra-hydrogen is insufficient to lift the bulk of the 'Meteor' our after-motors are once more in working order. I propose, therefore, to bring the 'Meteor' up to the wreck of the flying-boat and investigate. We will then take a drastic step. We will pump all the remaining ultra-hydrogen in Nos. 2 and compartments into Nos. 1 and 5; abandon and scuttle the first two compartments I have mentioned, and resume the pursuit in a 'Meteor' that will be only two-fifths of the size of the one that left England only a few weeks ago. I mean to chase that rascal as long as there is sufficient buoyancy to keep us in the air and as long as an ounce of cordite remains to actuate the motors."

"Hear, hear!" exclaimed the doctor, as if he were at a medical students' smoking concert. The others present contented themselves by inclining their heads, but resolution was plainly visible on their bronzed features.

The "Meteor" was navigated from the upper deck, her course set according to Dacres' observations. Meanwhile, owing to the now steady breeze the airship had drifted nearly five miles from the scene of the disaster.

"There she is, sir," shouted the look-out man, "a point on the starboard bow."

Travelling at a modest ten knots the waterborne craft made straight for the flying-boat that was lying practically awash in the slight swell. Owing to her immense bulk and to the fact that she had little or no grip upon the water the airship was almost unmanageable. To run to leeward of the wreck was to court disaster, for the thin aluminium plates were especially liable to be stove in should they come in contact with the water-logged craft.

"I'll swim to her, sir," said Dacres. "If we bring the 'Meteor' bows on to the wreckage I can easily take a light line to her and make her fast. She will serve as a good sea-anchor while we make investigations."

"How about sharks?" objected Whittinghame.

"Must risk that, sir. A couple of men with rifles will scare them off."

"Very good; I'll see that they are the best shots we have on board. I shouldn't like to see you plugged, Dacres—especially by one of our own men."

Dacres smiled, then proceeded to strip. Waiting till the "Meteor" was dead to leeward of the remains of the flying-boat, and moving ahead only enough to counteract the drift caused by the wind, the sub lowered himself over the bows. Round his waist was made fast one end of a length of mackerel-line, which though strong was not heavy enough to impede his progress.

"Pay out!" he shouted, at the same time slipping into the sea. The water was agreeably warm and remarkably buoyant. Dacres swam with ease, fifty strokes being sufficient to enable him to gain the wreck.

As he scrambled over the gunwale the boat dipped stern-foremost, but on sitting on one of the thwarts with the water up to his chin she quickly resumed a horizontal position.

Dacres' first act upon getting on board was to haul in the light line, to which was attached a stout grass rope. The latter he made fast to a bollard in the bows of the craft, which enabled the "Meteor" to ride comfortably to her practically submerged "mooring."

Considering the weight of her motors it seemed wonderful that the flying-boat kept awash, till the sub discovered that fore and aft were air-tight lockers. Indeed, the hull of the boat seemed but little damaged. Evidently as she was executing a loop she struck the water with very little speed in a vertical direction. It was certainly strange that Durango and his companion had not been hurled clear of her as she fell, and the only conclusion Dacres could come to was that the men when they felt their craft falling must have thrown themselves under the waterways and held on tightly during her erratic downward plunge.

"Much amiss?" shouted Captain Whittinghame.

"Very little, I believe, sir," replied Dacres. "She may be slightly strained."

"Is she fitted with slings?"

"Yes, sir."

"Then, stand by; we'll haul you to windward and abreast of No. 3 section."

Evidently, thought Dacres, the skipper had some scheme in his mind's eye. Whittinghame had. It would be possible to stow the boat aboard the airship, for in her curtailed displacement there would be sufficient ultra-hydrogen to lift the slightly added weight. Should occasion serve the hull of the flying-boat, if repaired, would make a handy tender.

In response to an order several of the crew brought up stout fir spars from below. These they lashed to the deck, allowing their slightly tapered ends to project seven feet clear of the extreme beam of the airship. To these, stout purchase blocks and tackle were secured, the falls manned, and the lower blocks lowered to the water's edge.

It was now an easy matter to cant the airship sufficiently for the water-logged craft to be brought immediately under the improvised davits. Deftly the sub adjusted the hooks of the lower blocks and gave the word to haul away.

Under the heavy strain the "Meteor" took a list to starboard, and by the time the gunwales of the boat were a foot out of water the airship's decks were at an angle of fifteen degrees.

"She won't stand it, sir," expostulated Setchell, "unless we station at least twenty men on the port side."

"I don't mean her to," replied Vaughan Whittinghame. "Couple up a length of hose to the auxiliary pump. We'll soon throw the water clear of her. One blessing, it shows the boat's topsides are fairly tight. I was rather afraid of it, when I remember seeing the water pour from her as the tramp's derrick heaved away at her; but I suppose it was that she was not slung accurately. Any signs of the water leaking out of her, Mr. Dacres?"

"None, sir," replied the sub, who had now emerged from his liquid surroundings, and was perched upon the turtle back deck.

"Very good. We're sending down a hose."

Ten minutes later the pump sucked dry. Relieved of the weight of water the salvaged boat's keel was a foot clear of the surface, while the "Meteor" had practically recovered from her awkward list. The lightly constructed hull and the motor together weighed less than two-and-a-half hundredweight, so that on being hauled up level with the upper deck it was a comparatively easy matter to get the craft inboard and secure her on that part of the platform over No. 5 section.

Two of the crew, skilled shipwrights, at once proceeded to overhaul the planks, while Parsons and his assistant attended to the motor, which, owing to its comparatively short period of submergence, was hardly affected by the salt water.

It did not take Dacres long to resume his clothing and report himself ready to carry on with his duty, for there was much to be done and very little time in which to do it.

All the stores and gear that were absolutely essential were removed from those compartments that were to be abandoned, and carefully stored in the remaining divisions. The ultra-hydrogen was then exhausted and recharged into the ballonettes of the fore and aft sections. In an hour from the time of salving the flying-boat the "Meteor" was ready to shed her now superfluous 'midship divisions.

Meanwhile, Dacres and Gerald Whittinghame had carefully examined the interior of the hull of Durango's craft, but no trace of the submarine plans were forthcoming. Nor had Captain Whittinghame seen them in the Mexican's possession as he boarded the tramp steamer. During the chase Durango had been seen holding the precious documents ready to drop them into space, but none of the men in the "Meteor's" observationroom could state definitely what happened to them after the Mexican had been thrown upon the floor-boards of the boat.

"I wish I knew that they were actually destroyed," said Vaughan when the result of the search was reported to him. "Circumstantial evidence is always most unsatisfactory. However, Durango cannot get away from the ship until she touches port, and long before that I hope to be able to have a few words with him. All ready, there, Mr. Setchell?"

"Ay, ay, sir."

"All clear aft, there?"

"Ay, ay, sir," replied Dr. Hambrough, who looked more like a South American stevedore than a member of an honourable profession, for he had neither spared himself nor his clothing in assisting to clear the condemned divisions of the airship.

Giving a final glance around to satisfy himself that all was in order, Captain Whittinghame touched the switch operating the cam-action bolts. Instantly the "Meteor" split into four separate divisions. The two central ones, stripped of heavy gear and with their ballonettes devoid of gas, rolled over and over on the surface of the sea, for very little water had as yet entered the scuttles, which had been left open.

The bow and stern sections shot upwards to a height of nearly a thousand feet. The bow division, being unable to be manoeuvred under motor-power, had to float aimlessly until the after section, skilfully steered under Dacres' direction, was brought end on and quickly secured.

The "Meteor," although now but four hundred and forty feet in length, was again fit to resume her pursuit of the arch-rogue, Reno Durango.

Vaughan Whittinghame showed no immediate desire to take up the chase. Gripping the stanchion rails he lent over the stern, his eyes fixed upon the two cylindrical objects far beneath him: the abandoned sections of his beloved airship. He watched them as they slowly filled. They were no longer lively, but wallowed sluggishly in the slight swell. They sank slowly: quite three-quarters of an hour elapsed ere one section slipped quietly beneath the waves. Its downward course was clearly visible long after it had sunk beneath the surface of the Pacific. Five minutes later No. 3 section plunged to its ocean bed—a sacrifice to the force of circumstances.

Whittinghame turned abruptly. His eyes looked suspiciously moist, but without a tremor in his voice he gave the order "Clear upper deck."

# CHAPTER XXXVII
# THE GALAPAGOS FISHERMEN

IN spite of the drastic reduction in length, and the fact that the motors in the bow section were still disabled, the "Meteor" was able to maintain a respectable speed of ninety miles an hour. Owing to her comparatively small midship-section she offered less resistance to the wind than do the standard types of British dirigibles.

Apart from the restriction in crew and store space the only disadvantage of the reduced "Meteor" was the fact that she yawed considerably. Formerly she was "drawn" by the for'ard propellers and "pushed" by the after ones, but now the tractors were out of action the whole of the driving effort was aft. Consequently the motion was rather erratic, the greatest inconvenience being experienced by those of the crew stationed in the bow division.

"You there, Callaghan?" asked the Captain at the telephone communicating with the new wireless room; for previous to abandoning the two midship compartments the wireless operator had transferred his delicate apparatus to a cabin immediately abaft the for'ard motor-room on the starboard side.

"Ay, ay, sir," replied the Irishman.

"Call up the 'Repulse,' will you, and ask the Admiral if he can conveniently detach a light cruiser. Tell him we are still in pursuit of Durango, who is on board a tramp, nationality unknown. Our present position is 1° 45′ 20″ N. lat., and 86° 2′ 10″ W. long., approximate."

"That ought to settle the business," continued Vaughan Whittinghame, turning to his comrades in the observation room. "I hardly like the responsibility of compelling a strange vessel to heave-to: it might lead to awkward international complications; besides, it would be a difficult matter for us to board her, even if her skipper offered no objections."

"Let's hope the Admiral will be willing to detach a cruiser," added the doctor. "There is no reason why he should not, as far as I can see, since things have quieted down in Valderia. It reminds me— —"

Dr. Hambrough's reminiscences were interrupted by the wireless man entering the observation room.

"What's amiss now, Callaghan?" asked the Captain, who could read bad news on the Irishman's face.

"Something wrong, sir," replied the operator. "I can't call up the flagship, nor any other ship or station, if it comes to that. I was very particular, sir, when I transferred the gear— —"

"When was it last used?" asked Vaughan.

"At seven o'clock last Tuesday, sir."

"That was before the storm. I shouldn't wonder if the same electrical disturbance that crippled our motors has not played the wireless a nasty trick. Any way, Callaghan, see what you can do, Unfortunately, we have not Monsieur de la Fosse with us."

The Irishman backed out of the cabin.

"Must make the best of a bad job," continued the Captain without visible signs of annoyance at the latest misfortune. "At any rate, we shall have to use discretion when we tackle the business with the tramp. What course do you suggest, Mr. Dacres?"

"I think we ought to wait until we overhaul the vessel, sir; then, when he have discovered her nationality, we can act accordingly. It's a seventy-five per cent chance that she's either a British or a Yankee."

"But, surely, if she were," demurred Setchell, "that rascal wouldn't have the cheek to be taken on board?"

"You must remember Durango is as full of resource as a Christmas turkey is full of stuffing," replied Dacres. "He's had the cheek to pose as an Englishman—an Englishman, mind you!—more than once. It's pretty certain, if the tramp sails under a red ensign, that Durango has bluffed her 'old man.' Bluffing, as a fine art, is a valuable asset."

The "Meteor" was now heading N.E. by N., at less than five hundred feet above the sea. She was passing over a number of small sailing craft that reminded the sub of a scene off the Dogger.

"They are principally engaged in carrying turtles from the Galapagos to Panama," remarked Gerald. "Recently there's been a big demand for turtles, and the industry has revived. It's strange that most of the export trade should be carried on in craft like those; yet one rarely hears of any of them coming to grief."

"I hope that Durango hasn't been put on board one of them!" suggested the irresponsible Setchell.

"Don't say that," expostulated Dacres.

"Mr. Setchell has named a possibility," added Captain Whittinghame. "The thought never occurred to me. If, when we overhaul the tramp, we are satisfied that Durango is not on board we can return and make investigations amongst the turtle fleet. It will be a week or more before they fetch Panama."

By this time a stiff south-easterly breeze had sprung up, so that the drift of the airship was considerable. In less than an hour it had developed into half a gale.

"That's the worst of this part of the globe," remarked Dacres. "In the Doldrums it is either a flat calm or blowing hard enough to carry away one's sticks. There are no half measures."

"Sail in sight, sir," announced one of the look-out men. "Dead ahead."

"It's one of those Galapagos boats," declared Captain Whittinghame, after making a careful scrutiny through his binoculars. "Poor brute! she's tried to steal a march on the rest of the fleet and has run into this gale of wind."

"She's got it well on her starboard quarter, though," said Setchell. "She's almost running free."

"The worst direction for a craft of that build," added Gerald. "Look, there goes her canvas, ripped to ribbons."

The turtle boat—she was barely thirty feet overall and entirely open—was now at the mercy of the waves. Wallowing sluggishly in the trough of the huge crested seas she was in momentary danger of being swamped.

Captain Whittinghame was not long in making up his mind. He quickly weighed the difficulties: the "Meteor" unable to manoeuvre so easily as before; the practically crippled motors; the urgency of the quest, all flashed through his brain. On the other hand, human life was in danger.

As quickly as possible the "Meteor" was brought head to wind and about half a mile to leeward of the dismasted craft. With the propellers running ahead just sufficiently for him to counteract the force of the wind the airship rolled and pitched like a barrel.

"Clear away a coil of three-inch manila," ordered Vaughan Whittinghame. "Stand by to veer out a buoy."

Several of the crew of the "Meteor" hastened to carry out their captain's orders and, in spite of the howling wind, they succeeded in getting the necessary gear on the upper deck.

The men in the turtle boat, seeing that help was at hand, were waving their arms frantically.

"Pity those fellows didn't make use of their energy in cutting away that raffle and riding to it," remarked Dacres. "What will happen when we forge ahead with that craft in tow, sir?"

"We'll lie steadier than we are at present," replied the captain. "All the same, we'll approach her stern-foremost. It will give the propellers a better chance."

Round swung the "Meteor," dropping half a mile to leeward during the operation, but as soon as she made towards the crippled boat the new conditions suited her admirably. Instead of rolling she settled down to a steady undulating motion.

"Pay out the rope," ordered Captain Whittinghame.

The airship was now only two hundred feet above the raging sea. As soon as the whole coil, one hundred and thirteen fathoms in length, was paid out and allowed to trail in the water, she forged ahead immediately over the disabled craft.

Dexterously one of the crew of the latter caught the trailing rope and made it fast round the stump of the foremast. Just then a tremendous broken sea was observed to be bearing down upon the already sluggish vessel.

The three men who formed the crew saw it coming. The master attempted to put the helm down, but the craft had not yet gathered way. A shout of terror, barely audible above the roar of the wind and water, arose from the men; the two who were for'ard deftly fastened themselves to the slack of the rope trailing from the "Meteor." The helmsman, seeing what they were about, promptly abandoned the tiller, ran to the bows, and cast off the tow-rope. Even as he did so the huge wave surged down upon the doomed craft and swept completely over her. She sank like a stone.

"Take a couple of turns round the capstan," shouted Dacres, who saw what had occurred; then thrusting the starting lever hard down he bade one of the crew stand by while he himself went to the guard-rail to direct operations.

Fortunately the master of the lost craft was a man of powerful physique and held on to the rope like grim death. His two companions, being lashed on, were in no actual danger, but could the master retain his hold sufficiently long to enable him to be hauled into safety?

Whittinghame had now ordered the motors to be switched off, and the "Meteor," scudding before the gale, no longer dragged the three men against the hard wind. Foot by foot the three-inch manila came home. It had to be stopped while the first of the rescued men was assisted over the bulging side of the airship, and again when the second was hauled into safety.

Dacres, keenly on the alert, saw that the master's strength was ebbing. Quickly bending a stout rope round his waist and calling to three of the crew to take a turn, he leapt over the guard-rail, slid down the convex slope and grasped the wellnigh exhausted master by his wrists.

Forty seconds later the sub and the man he had risked his life to save were standing almost breathless upon the upper deck of the airship.

"Take them below," ordered Dacres, "coil away this rope and make all snug, then clear upper deck."

Directly this was done the "Meteor" forged ahead and quickly settled down to her former pace.

As soon as the rescued men had been supplied with food and drink General Whittinghame asked them whether any steamer had passed them.

To this the master replied that one had, about four hours previously. His description of her left no doubt but that she was the craft which had picked up Durango and his companions from the waterlogged flying-boat.

"Do you know her name?" asked his questioner.

"No, señor, I do not. Do you, Enrico?"

The man addressed shook his head. Neither could his companion give a satisfactory answer. He remembered that it began with Q, and that the name of the port she belonged to was Boston.

"Good!" ejaculated Captain Whittinghame when, his brother had interpreted the information. "She's a Yankee. I don't suppose we shall have much trouble now. Four hours ago, eh? Allowing her eight knots at the very outside with this sea running we ought to overhaul her in less than half an hour. Tell those fellows not to worry. We will pay them well for the information and put them ashore at Panama, or else the first vessel we speak that will serve their purpose."

Vaughan had not over-estimated the time taken to overhaul the Boston tramp. Eighteen minutes after resuming the chase the look-out reported a column of smoke rising above the horizon. Four minutes later the sought-for vessel was plainly visible.

On her short rounded counter appeared the words "Quickstep, of Boston, Mass."

Being high in ballast she was rolling furiously. Cascades of water were pouring from her scuppers. Spray was flying in sheets over her bows and dashing against the wheel-house on the bridge, for owing to a sudden change of wind she was plugging almost dead into the teeth of the gale.

"It is impossible to communicate with her with this sea running," remarked Captain Whittinghame. "All we can do is to slow down and wait until the gale moderates."

As he spoke an oilskinned figure was observed to stagger out of the wheel-house and make his way to the starboard side of the bridge. Casting off the halliards leading to a block on a shroud between the two stumpy masts he hoisted a signal.

Owing to the direction of the wind it was for the time being impossible to read the flags, and it was not until the 'Meteor' forged ahead and was almost abeam of the tramp that Dacres could interpret the message.

"I—F—that's something to do with communicate," he announced. "Where's the code-book?"

"Here you are," replied Setchell rapidly turning over the pages.

"'I—F: I cannot stop to have any communication.' Like his impudence!"

"Or Durango's," added Whittinghame. "We cannot acknowledge, so we will mark time on the 'Quickstep.' How's the glass, Mr. Dacres?"

"Steady, sir, with a slight tendency to rise. This gale will soon blow itself out."

"Then the sooner the better," declared the Captain.

The rest of the day passed in tedious inaction Night fell, and the bow searchlights of the airship played incessantly upon the tramp. Day dawned and found, as Dacres had predicted, that the gale had expended itself, and although the seas still ran high, the angry waves were rapidly subsiding.

It was now safe for the "Meteor" to approach within hand-signalling distance. The officers and crew of the "Quickstep" were all on deck, curiously regarding the airship, but there were no signs of Durango and the two Valderians.

"What airship is that?" came from the tramp.

"The 'Meteor.'"

"We doubt it."

"But we are; if you'll heave-to and send a boat we will prove it."

"What do you want?"

"You have three men on board, rescued from a water-logged boat."

"What of it?"

"One is the outlaw, Durango."

"I guess not."

"You guess wrongly, then. Durango and two Valderians."

"Sure? He said he was a Britisher."

"We'll soon prove it if you send a boat."

"I will. We'll heave-to."

Captain Whittinghame slapped his brother on the back.

"At last!" he exclaimed.

# CHAPTER XXXVIII
# CORNERED

BEFORE the "Meteor" could alight and throw out her huge sea-anchor the "Quickstep" had hove-to and was lowering a boat. Into the latter tumbled four lean-jawed men and a hatchet-faced youngster of about nineteen years of age.

There was no doubt about it: those New Englanders knew how to manage a boat in a seaway. Dexterously the falls were cast off, and bending to their oars the rowers made the whaler shoot over the long, heaving waves.

Before they had made twenty strokes the report of a pistol shot came from the tramp. Without a moment's hesitation her skipper jumped from the bridge without troubling to make use of the ladder, and bolted aft, followed by half a dozen of the deck hands.

It was not long before he was back on deck with a revolver in his hand. At his command one of the men signalled to the "Meteor."

"Sorry! You're right. Laid the skunk by the heels."

As soon as the "Quickstep's" boat came alongside the airship the lad in charge swarmed up the rope ladder and gained the deck.

"Guess you're the boss of this hyer packet?" he exclaimed. "I'm Silas P. Cotton, second mate of the S.S. 'Quickstep.' Shake."

Vaughan Whittinghame smiled and accepted the invitation. He extended his hand and shook the proffered tarry paw of the self-possessed young Boston man.

"That skunk Durango has been throwing dust into the old man's eyes," continued Silas P. Cotton. "So the boss has sent me to square things up. I reckon we've heard of the wonderful 'Meteor,' but we didn't calculate on her being so short in length."

"Neither did we," agreed Whittinghame. "Come to my cabin and let us hear about your three passengers. What will you have to drink?"

"Guess rum's my pizen, boss."

A jar of Navy rum that had been sent on board the "Meteor" by the fleet paymaster of one of the ships of Admiral Maynebrace's squadron was produced and uncorked. Filling half a tumbler with the dark spirit the second mate tossed it down at one gulp.

"Now, bizness, boss. This hyer Durango swore that he was a Britisher, and that the airship was one of those blarmed Valderian craft that wanted to lay him by the heels. Our skipper bit the bullet. Sez he: 'There ain't no British airship of that size off this hyer coast; I'll reckon we'll have no truck with that one. I don't want no greasers on my hooker.' So he ordered the helm to be put up, leaving you lying on the water as you are doing now. Durango—Mister Turner of London, he said he was—had heaps of dollars and offered to square up handsome-like if the 'old man' would land him at Guayaquil. The boss said the best he could do was to put him ashore at Panama. With that the skunk seemed right down sick, for he went below to the berth we'd given him, and wouldn't stir."

"Do you happen to know if he had any papers on him?"

"Rolls of paper dollars," replied the second mate. "That's all, I guess. What do you say to coming aboard and seeing how the old man has fixed him up?"

"With pleasure," said Whittinghame. "I hope you won't mind if two of my officers accompany me?"

"Guess they'll get a wet shirt apiece if they ain't particularly slick in getting aboard," replied Silas P. Cotton with a grin.

"Come along, Gerald; and you, too, Mr. Dacres," said the Captain. "We may as well——"

"Message just been signalled from the 'Quickstep,' sir," reported Callaghan. "Captain Gotham asks you to come aboard and bring pistols with you."

"Then, all the fun is not yet over," exclaimed Vaughan Whittinghame. "Take arms, gentlemen. Durango evidently means to give as much trouble as possible."

As the boat ran alongside the "Quickstep" another shot rang out from below. Thinking that there was no time to be lost Vaughan Whittinghame seized hold of the man-ropes and, ably supported by his comrades and the whaler's crew, gained the deck.

To his surprise Whittinghame found Captain Gotham, with his hands thrust deeply into his pockets, leaning against the after guard-rail of the bridge. A huge cigar was jammed tightly betwixt his teeth, and his peaked cap raked at an alarming angle.

"G'day, gentlemen," he exclaimed without attempting to remove his cigar. "Guess you've come to take that wild critter off my hands? Great snakes! If I had a-known he was a low-down Mexican greaser I'd thought twice before he set foot on this hooker."

"Where is he?" asked Whittinghame.

"In the mate's cabin. He's locked himself in, you bet. Thorssenn tried to boost open the door, but the sarpint let fly some. Thorssenn's got more than he can chew, I reckon."

"Was he hit?"

"Clean through the shoulder, boss. Say, how are you going about it?"

Going below and making their way along the narrow alley-way the two Whittinghames and Dacres approached the place where Durango had taken refuge. The hard-visaged Yankee skipper and Silas P. Cotton, not to be outdone in the business of securing the renegade, also joined the attacking party.

Through the cabin door two small jagged holes marked the tracks of Durango's shots. One bullet was embedded in the panelling on the opposite side of the alley-way; the other the unfortunate first mate was nursing in his shoulder.

"The game's up, Durango," said Captain Whittinghame sternly. "You cannot escape, so surrender."

The Mexican's reply was to send another shot through the door, the bullet whizzing between Vaughan and the sub.

The attackers promptly backed out of the danger zone.

"Say, why not let rip at him altogether?" asked Captain Gotham, raising his heavy Colt revolver.

"We want him alive," replied Vaughan Whittinghame. "I cannot explain now, but he's worth more alive than dead."

"Then aim low and cripple the skunk," rejoined the skipper bluntly. "If we've got to wait till he's starved out I reckon we'll be in the latitude of Cape Hatteras before he bails up. Say, what's your programme?"

"Have you a piece of boiler-plate handy?"

"You bet," drawled the Yankee, blowing out a cloud of smoke through his nose, for the cigar was still tightly held between his teeth. "Cut away, sonny, and tell Andrews to send up a piece of biler plate as much as one man can hold—git."

With remarkable agility Silas P. Cotton, who had been addressed as "sonny," made off to carry out the old man's orders. Presently he returned, staggering under the weight of a slightly curved three-sixteenths plate.

Using this as a shield Whittinghame, Dacres, and the master of the "Quickstep" exerted their whole weight and strength against the comparatively frail door. It creaked, but refused to give. The Mexican had barricaded it with the first mate's furniture and bedding.

Durango let fly another shot. The ping of the lead against the boiler-plate told its own tale. He fired again, this time low down. The bullet cut a groove in the Yankee's sea-boots and caused that worthy to let fly a string of oaths.

"Guess I'm master of my own ship!" he shouted. "Who tells Captain Gotham not to use his shooting arms? Here goes."

He raised his revolver and sent six shots in rapid succession through the door. Then he listened, only to skip and dodge behind the iron plate as another bullet cut the peak of his cap.

"Have you any sulphur on board, captain?" asked Dacres, as the American was about to reload.

"Sulphur? Wal, I guess I have some."

"Then we'll smoke him out," continued the sub. "All we want is a brazier and some short lengths of copper pipe and a pair of bellows."

"Bully for you!" exclaimed Captain Gotham enthusiastically. "Git, sonny, and tell Andrews to lay out with the gear."

Off hurried the second mate, to return accompanied by the engineer, a man as lantern-jawed as the rest of the officers of the "Quickstep." With him came a deckhand, who, under Cotton's orders, had stove in a barrel of sulphur.

Soon the yellow rock-like substance was burning. Its pungent fumes caused water to run from the eyes of the operators. More than once during their preparations they had to beat a hurried retreat and gasp for breath in the open air.

At length two pipes were inserted through the shot-holes in the door; the bellows were filled with reeking fumes and discharged through the pipes.

Durango began to cough. The men without could hear him fumbling with the things he had used to barricade the door, with the intention of plugging the pipes and preventing the invasion of the sulphur fumes. Again the attackers hurled themselves against the woodwork. The Mexican realized that he had either to abandon the barricade or submit to be smoked out.

Sheltered behind the boiler-plate Dacres vigorously plied the bellows. After five minutes a strange silence prevailed. Gerald Whittinghame, risking the chance of being shot, peeped through one of the bullet-holes in the upper part of the woodwork.

The interior of the cabin was full of yellow vapour. He could discern the Mexican. Durango had his face jammed up against the open scuttle.

"Tarnation thunder!" ejaculated Captain Gotham. "I fair forgot that scuttle. Keep the pot bilen', boss."

With this injunction the master of the "Quickstep" made his way to the poop deck and peered over the rail. He could see the tip of Durango's nose projecting beyond the rim of the scuttle, while clouds of sulphur fumes wafted past the Mexican's head and eddied along the ship's side.

"Lower that fender—look alive, there!" ordered Captain Gotham.

Two men dragging a huge globular rope fender lowered it over the side and adjusted it so that it blocked the Mexican's sole means of obtaining fresh air. He immediately pushed the obstruction aside with his knife.

The Yankee skipper was not to be baulked. A long handspike was procured; one end was wedged between the lower part of a convenient davit and the vessel's side; a tackle was clapped on to the other end and bowsed taut, thus jamming the fender hard against the scuttle.

The end was now in sight. Durango was gasping for breath.

"Will you surrender?" demanded Captain Whittinghame.

There was no answer.

The attacking party waited a few moments longer. There was a dull thud upon the cabin floor. Still suspecting that this was a ruse on the part of the trapped man they waited another minute, then the door was burst open.

The rush of sulphurous air almost capsized them. Dacres, tying a handkerchief over his mouth and nose, crawled in. His hands encountered the Mexican's resistless form. With a heave he dragged him into the alleyway. Other hands relieved him of his burden and carried Durango on deck.

"Dead?" asked Gerald Whittinghame.

"Snakes don't die easy," grunted Captain Gotham. "Take him away, boss, and welcome to him."

The unconscious form of Durango was lowered out into the "Quickstep's" whaler. The British officers shook hands with the Yankee skipper as they prepared to go over the side.

"One moment, boss," said the latter. "Guess you know I've got those two Valderians aboard?"

"Yes," assented Vaughan. "Can you give five men a passage to Panama? I'll see that you are not out of pocket by it."

"Five?" queried Captain Gotham.

"Yes, these two Valderians and three men of a Galapagos boat we picked up just now. Will fifty dollars be sufficient?"

"Guess that'll fix 'em up, cap. Send the others along."

Twenty minutes later the airship and the tramp parted company, the "Quickstep" to flounder along at a sedate eight knots, while the "Meteor," with Durango in safe keeping, was speeding aloft at ninety miles an hour, homeward bound at last.

# CHAPTER XXXIX
# DACRES' PROMOTION

WHEN Reno Durango recovered from the stupifying effects of the sulphur he found himself in a cabin destitute of furniture and securely locked and barred. He knew by the peculiar undulating motion that he was on board an airship. Then the truth flashed across his mind: he was in the hands of his rivals.

Rage and despair filled his heart. At one moment he thought of dashing his head against the metal bulkhead of the cabin; at another he contemplated putting an end to his existence and evading well-merited punishment by strangling himself. But his nerve failed him. Never backward in delighting to cause pain to the unfortunate wretches who had fallen into his hands at various times, he shrank from inflicting the slightest injury upon himself.

His frenzied thoughts were interrupted by the entry of Captain Whittinghame, Dacres, and Dr. Hambrough.

The Englishmen had not come to gloat over their captive; the doctor was there in his official capacity of surgeon of the "Meteor," while the others were there in case the Mexican should become violent.

"Well, my man, how do you feel now?" asked the doctor in a matter-of-fact tone, as if he were addressing a hospital patient.

Durango's reply was to roll his yellow eyes and thrust out his leathery under lip. He wanted to curse his captors, but blind rage held him speechless.

Deftly Dr. Hambrough took hold of his wrist. The Mexican, snarling like a wild beast, shook him off.

"I cannot do anything more for the patient at present," said the doctor suavely, and the three men turned to leave the prisoner to his own devices.

Just as Whittinghame, who was the last to leave, was backing out of the door—for he gave Durango no chance of making a sudden dash—the Mexican found his tongue.

"Curse you, Whittinghame!" he shouted with a torrent of oaths. "If I had thrown those plans overboard instead of stowing them in under the boat's fore-deck, I'd have the laugh of you yet."

Vaughan Whittinghame made no reply, but pushing Dacres across the threshold he closed and relocked the door.

"By Jove!" he exclaimed delightedly. "Durango's let the cat out of the bag. He imagines that we have already found the plans."

"Let's hope it won't be long before we do," rejoined the sub, and the three men hastened to search the hull of the flying-boat.

The "Meteor's" speed was materially reduced to enable the searchers to go on deck, where the boat was made fast to four strong ring-bolts.

Leaping over her coamings Dacres dived under the fore-deck. The place had already been cleared out, but on each side a skirting had been fastened to the ribs to within a foot of the deck-beams.

The sub thrust his hand into one of the spaces thus formed. He could feel nothing. The second gave no better result, but in the third his fingers came in contact with some moist paper.

Carefully withdrawing his band the sub found that he had recovered a bundle of documents tied with red tape. Although damp they were little the worse for their adventures in sea and air.

"Hurrah!" shouted Dacres. "We've discovered the object of our search, sir. Here are the submarine plans."

The great Naval Review at Spithead was over. On board H.M.S. "Foudroyant," the flagship of the Commander-in-Chief, Sir Hardy Staplers, a grand dinner was being held. The flag-officers and captains of the various divisions and ships, the principal military officers of the garrison of Portsmouth, and the heads of the Dockyard establishments were present.

After the customary loyal toast had been proposed and duly honoured, Sir Hardy rose to reply to the toast of The Navy.

The Commander-in-Chief was by no means a fluent speaker, but when he "warmed up" to his subject he lost all sense of time. His speech was practically a résumé of the vast strides that the British Navy had made during his lengthy career. At last he spoke of the Flying Wing:—

"Gentlemen, I need say but little more (the majority of his listeners heaved an inward sigh of relief). We now know of the sterling work performed by the subsidized airship 'Meteor.' When the time comes for that noble craft to be taken over by H.M. Government—and I venture to assert that the day is not far distant—our Flying Wing will have a unit that is second to none.

"It is a matter of regret that the 'Meteor' was not present at the memorable display at Spithead to-day. As all of you are no doubt aware the latest dispatches from Zandovar stated that the airship left in pursuit of the outlaw, Durango. A week has elapsed and no further news of her has been forthcoming. Personally, I do not think we need labour under any misapprehension as to her safety; but at the same time the silence—especially in this age of wireless—is somewhat inexplicable. An airship that could with safety undertake at short notice a successful dash to the North Pole (hear, hear!) can be relied upon to take care of herself. Therefore, I feel confident in expressing my opinion that before many hours have elapsed news will be received from the Senior Officers at Zandovar announcing the return of the Dreadnought of the Air from yet another successful mission.

"One more point I should like to mention, and that is the great changes in the near future in in engineering. I refer to the cordite motors as carried in the 'Meteor.' It is, of course, too early to predict with certainty that cordite will be the fuel used on our great battleships in place of oil, but to a great extent the era of the coal and oil-fed furnace is doomed."

Now, it so happened that amongst the guests was Engineer-Captain Camshaft, an engineering officer of the old school, who swore by triple-expansion engines, took ungraciously to turbine machinery, and scoffed at internal combustion engines. He was particularly scathing in his opinion of cordite as fuel for propulsion, and had offered to bet any of his brother-officers that the "Meteor" would never return to England under her own power. Perhaps he had had more champagne than was good for him; at anyrate, at this point of Sir Hardy's speech, he exclaimed in a "stage aside," "Question."

A deadly silence prevailed in the crowded ward-room. The protest was plainly audible, yet save for Camshaft's immediate neighbour, no one knew who had had the temerity to contradict the Commander-in-Chief.

"Did I hear some one say 'Question'?" asked Sir Hardy with his customary urbanity.

The culprit recognized that he had overstepped the bounds. It meant that his future career was in jeopardy, especially as it was freely mooted that Sir Hardy Staplers was shortly to be made First Sea Lord of the Admiralty.

Fortunately the engineer-captain was a man of resource in such matters.

"Beg pardon, Sir Hardy," he exclaimed thickly, "I said unquestionably—unquestionably."

A badly suppressed titter ran round the table. The situation was saved.

"Yes, of course," agreed the Commander-in-Chief blandly. "Now I quite understand; you said 'unquestionably', Captain Camshaft."

Before Sir Hardy could resume the thread of his lengthy discourse a voice on deck was heard hailing "Boat ahoy!"

Loud and clear came the reply that electrified every member of that convivial dinner-party:—

"Meteor!"

The Commander-in-Chief's speech was never finished. Following Sir Hardy's example the officers and their guests rushed upon the quarter-deck and crowded to the starboard guard-rails.

They were just in time to see a motor-boat of unusual design run alongside the accommodation-ladder. The glare of the electric lamps fell upon the bronzed features of Captain Vaughan Whittinghame and Sub-lieutenant Basil Dacres.

"How in the name of wonder!" exclaimed the astonished Commander-in-Chief.

"We've brought two-fifths of the original 'Meteor' back, sir," reported Whittinghame. "She's lying off the Warner Lightship. Our wireless is out of gear, or we would have reported our progress. Durango is a prisoner on board; and here, sir, are the plans of the 'M' class of submarines."

Shortly before lunch-time on the following morning Basil Dacres—specially promoted by virtue of an Order-in-Council to the rank of commander (Flying Squadron, Naval Wing) of His Majesty's Fleet—arrived at his father's country residence, Cranbury House.

"Governor in, Sparkes?" he asked as the footman opened the door and stared with amazement at the "young master." Years of training had steeled Sparkes to most shocks, but this time he was completely taken aback.

"Yes, Mr. Basil, Colonel Dacres has just come in. He's been out rabbit-shooting, sir."

"Then don't tell him who I am," cautioned Dacres. "Take in this card and say that someone wishes to see him."

Sparkes took the pasteboard and vanished. Half way up the stairs he paused to look at the card.

"Mr. Basil's up to some of his pranks, I'll be bound," he said to himself. "Hope to goodness the master doesn't jaw me for it."

"Gentleman to see you, sir," he announced.

because the 'Meteor' brought me home; fourthly and lastly, I am really a commander in His Majesty's Fleet, my appointment being dated at the Admiralty yesterday."

"'Meteor?'" repeated the colonel. "You were on the 'Meteor'? I knew nothing of this."

"Naturally, sir. Our mission was a confidential one. Even Rear-Admiral Maynebrace was in ignorance of who formed her crew until we pulled him out of the Cavarale."

"Were you the officer who was reported to have distinguished himself in rescuing the Admiral, then?" asked Colonel Dacres amazedly.

"Yes, sir; but the newspaper reports may have been exaggerated. They often are," declared Dacres modestly. "But the fact remains that I am specially promoted, for which I have to thank Captain Whittinghame, who has been made Commandant of the Airship Section; the 'Meteor' is to undergo a hasty refit and reconstruction—we left three-fifths of her in different places, you know—and after that—well, we must hope for something fairly exciting to turn up. For the present I have three weeks' leave."

"Leave!" echoed the colonel. "Won't you have to give evidence at the trial of Durango?"

"Yes, I suppose so," replied the young commander. "He is to be indicted on a list of charges as long as my arm. However, I am not at all keen on that part of the business. Hunting him down was exciting enough, but now the rascal is laid by the heels I wish I could regard the incident as closed. After a turn at active service in the air a fellow doesn't want to descend to the stuffy atmosphere of the Law Courts. I want to be up and doing, in a double sense, pater; I feel as keen as mustard."

"Basil, my boy, I'm afraid I've misjudged you."

"I don't think so, pater; I believe that once or twice you've blamed me for practical jokes I didn't play, but that's a mere detail. The mater's teapot, for example."

"I don't mean in that way," continued the colonel. "I thought that you might let your chances slip through your fingers, but, by Jove! you're a true Dacres after all."

"Thank you, pater," said the young commander simply.

Colonel Dacres took the card and read,

"Commander Basil Dacres, R.N."

"Commander Basil Dacres, R.N.," he repeated. "Wonder who the deuce he is? Some distant relation, I suppose, after something or the other. Sparkes, where's the Navy List?"

"You lent it to Admiral Padbury the morning before last, sir," replied the footman smartly.

"So I did, Sparkes, so I did. Never mind. I'll see this gentleman. Where is he, Sparkes?"

"In the green room, sir."

"What sort of a man is he?"

The footman coughed to clear his throat, and nearly broke a blood-vessel in striving to suppress a grin.

"Cannot say as how I took particular stock of him, sir; but he's a smartish-looking gentleman, sir."

"Then he must belong to our branch of the family," thought the colonel complacently. "But dash it all, what does he want to come just before tiffin for?"

Colonel Dacres waited to put a few finishing touches, then hastened downstairs to conceal, under a guise of cordiality, any traces of his annoyance at being disturbed before lunch.

To his unbounded astonishment he found himself confronted by his son, whom he supposed to be still on board H.M.S. "Royal Oak" off Zandovar. He could only come to one conclusion—a hastily formed one—on the situation: Basil had been in trouble, and had turned up, in spite of his parent's fiat, like a bad halfpenny.

"What's the meaning of this, sir?" he demanded, holding up the card. "Are there no limits to your senseless pranks? I had hoped when that Valderian business took place that you might have proved yourself worthy of the name of Dacres. Instead of that you turn up with a handle to your name to which you have no right. Explain yourself, sir."

"It's all right, dad," said the youthful commander coolly.

"But it isn't all right. I— —"

"Steady on, pater! You've asked me a lot of questions; give me a chance to reply. In the first place there is a limit to my pranks, and I don't mean to exceed it. Secondly, I was in the Valderian affair; thirdly, I came home